JULIE KAGAWA

# SHADOW of the FOX

YOUNG ADULT
HQ

HQ
An imprint of HarperCollins*Publishers* Ltd
1 London Bridge Street
London SE1 9GF

This paperback edition 2018

1
First published in Great Britain by
HQ, an imprint of HarperCollins*Publishers* Ltd 2018



Julie Kagawa asserts the moral right to be identified as the author of this work.
A catalogue record for this book is available from the British Library.

ISBN: 978-1-84845-739-3

MIX
Paper from responsible sources
FSC® C007454

This book is produced from independently certified FSC™ paper to ensure responsible forest management.

For more information visit: www.harpercollins.co.uk/green

Printed and bound by CPI Group (UK) Ltd, Croydon CR0 4YY

To Misa. Thank you for everything, sensei.

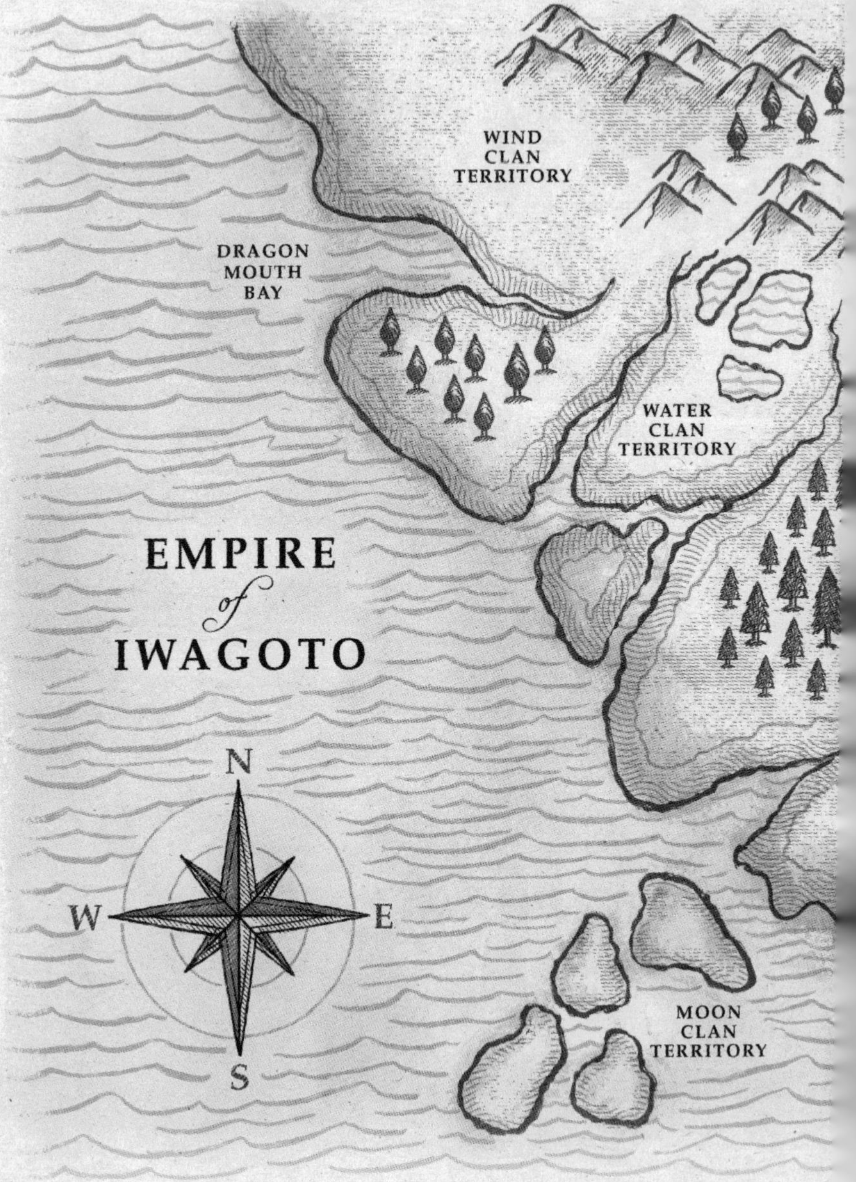
WIND
CLAN
TERRITORY
DRAGON
MOUTH
BAY
WATER
CLAN
TERRITORY
EMPIRE
of
IWAGOTO
N
W
E
S
MOON
CLAN
TERRITORY

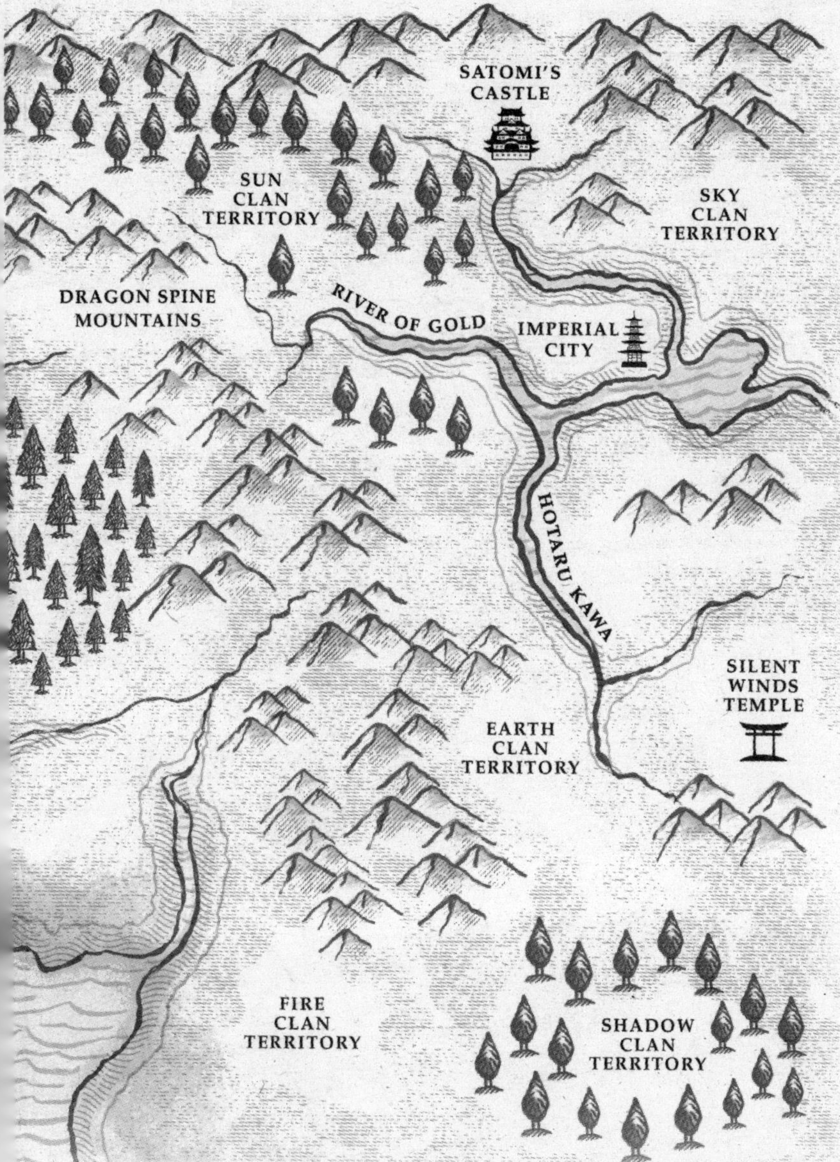
SATOMI'S CASTLE
SUN CLAN TERRITORY
SKY CLAN TERRITORY
DRAGON SPINE MOUNTAINS
RIVER OF GOLD
IMPERIAL CITY
HOTARU KAWA
SILENT WINDS TEMPLE
EARTH CLAN TERRITORY
FIRE CLAN TERRITORY
SHADOW CLAN TERRITORY

# PART 1

# 1

## Beginnings and Endings

*I*t was raining the day Suki came to the Palace of the Sun, and it was raining the night that she died.

"You're the new maid, are you?" a woman with a narrow, bony face demanded, looking her up and down. Suki shivered, feeling cold rainwater sliding down her back, dripping from her hair to spatter the fine wood floor. The head housekeeper sniffed. "Well, you're no beauty, that's for sure. But, no matter—Lady Satomi's last maid was pretty as a butterfly, with half the wit." She leaned closer, narrowing her eyes. "Tell me, girl. They said you were running your father's shop before you came here. Do you have an intelligent head on your shoulders? Or is it as full of air as the last girl's?"

Suki chewed her lip and looked at the floor. She *had* been helping to run her father's shop within the city for the better part of a year. The only child of a celebrated flute maker, she was often responsible for dealing with the customers when her father was at work, too engrossed in his task to eat or talk to anyone until his latest piece was done. Suki could read and do numbers as well as any boy, but being a girl, she was not allowed to inherit her father's business or learn his craft. Mura Akihito was still strong, but he was getting old, his once nimble fingers stiffening with age and hard use. Rather than marry Suki off, her father had used his meager influence to get her a job in the Imperial Palace, so she would be well taken care of when he passed away. Suki missed home, and she desperately wondered if her father was all right without her, but she knew this was what he wanted. "I don't know, ma'am," she whispered.

"Hmph. Well, we'll see soon enough. But I would think of something better to say to Lady Satomi. Otherwise your stay will be even shorter than your predecessor's. Now," she continued, "clean yourself up, then go to the kitchen and fetch Lady Satomi's tea. The cook will tell you where to take it."

A few minutes later, Suki walked down the veranda, carrying a full tea tray and trying to remember the directions she'd been given. The emperor's Palace of the Sun was a miniature city in itself; the main palace, where the emperor and his family lived, loomed over everything, but a labyrinth of walls, structures and fortifications lay between the keep and the inner wall, all designed to protect the emperor and confuse an invading army. Nobles, courtiers and samurai paraded to and fro down the walkways, dressed in robes of brilliant color and design: white silk with delicate sakura petals, or a vivid red with golden chrysanthemum blooms. None of the nobles she passed spared her a second glance.

Only the most influential families resided this close to the emperor; the closer you lived to the main keep of the palace, the more important you were.

Suki wandered down the maze of verandas, the knots in her stomach growing tighter as she searched in vain for the right quarters. Everything looked the same. Gray-roofed buildings with bamboo and paper walls, and wooden verandas between them so the nobles wouldn't sully their clothes in the dirt and dew. Blue-tiled turrets towered over her in regal splendor, and dozens of different songbirds trilled from the branches of the perfectly groomed trees, but the tightness in Suki's chest and the churning of her insides made it impossible to appreciate any of it.

A high, clear note cut through the air, rising above the rooftops, making her freeze in her tracks. It wasn't a bird, though a thrush perched in a nearby bush warbled loudly in reply. It was a sound Suki knew instantly, had memorized each and every note. How many times had she heard it, drifting up from her father's workshop? The sweet, haunting melody of a flute.

Mesmerized, she followed the sound, momentarily forgetting her duties and that her new mistress would almost certainly be very annoyed that her tea was so late. The song drew her forward, a keening, mournful melody, like saying goodbye or watching autumn fade. Suki could tell that whoever was playing the instrument was skilled indeed; so much emotion lay between the notes of the song, it was as if she was hearing someone's soul.

So hypnotized was she by the sound of the flute, she forgot to look where she was going. Rounding a corner, Suki squeaked in dismay as a young noble in sky blue robes blocked her path, a bamboo flute held to his lips. The teapot rattled and the cups shook perilously as she swerved to avoid him, desperately trying not to spill the contents. The sound of the flute ceased as the noble, much to her amazement, turned and put out a hand to steady the tray before it toppled to the veranda.

"Careful there." His voice was high and clear. "Don't want to drop anything—that would be an awful mess. Are you all right?"

Suki stared at him. He was the most handsome man she had ever seen. *No, not handsome*, she decided. *Beautiful.* His broad shoulders filled the robe he wore, but his features were graceful and delicate, like a willow tree in the spring. Instead of a samurai's topknot, his hair was long and straight, falling well past his shoulders, and was pure white, the color of mountain snow. Even more amazing, he was smiling at her—not the cold, amused smirk of most nobles and samurai, but a real smile that reached the mirthful crescents of his eyes.

"Please excuse me," the man said, releasing the tray and taking a quick step back. His expression was calm, not irritated at all. "That was my fault, planting myself in the middle of the walk, not thinking anyone could be rushing around the corner with a tea tray. I hope I did not inconvenience you, miss…?"

Suki opened her mouth twice before anything came out. "Please forgive me, lord." Her voice was a whisper. Nobles did not speak like this to peasants; even she knew that. "I am Suki, and I am only a maid. Please don't trouble yourself with the likes of me."

The noble chuckled. "It is no trouble, Suki-san," he said. "I often forget where I am when I am playing." He raised the flute, making her heart leap. "Please do not think any more of it. You may return to your duties."

He stepped aside for her to pass, but Suki didn't move, unable to tear her gaze from the instrument in his slender hand. It was made of polished wood, dark and rich and straighter than an arrow, with a distinctive band of gold around one end. She knew she shouldn't speak to the noble, that he could order her flogged, imprisoned, even executed if he wished it, but words escaped her all the same. "You play magnificently, my lord," she whispered. "Forgive me. I know it is not my place to say anything, but my father would be proud."

He cocked his head, a flicker of surprise crossing his beautiful face. "Your father?" he asked, as understanding dawned in his eyes. "You are Mura Akihito's daughter?"

*"Hai."*

He smiled and gave her the barest of nods. "The song is only as beautiful as the instrument," he told her. "When you see your father again, tell him that I am honored to possess such a masterpiece."

Suki's throat closed up, and her eyes grew hot and blurry. The noble politely turned away, feigning interest in a cherry blossom tree, giving her time to compose herself. "Ah, but perhaps you are lost?" he inquired after a moment, examining a chrysalis on one of the slender branches. Turning back, his slender brows rose, but Suki caught no derision in his stance or voice, only amusement, as one might have when speaking to a wandering cat. "The emperor's palace can be dazzling indeed to the uninitiated. Whose quarters are you assigned to, Suki-san? Perhaps I can point you in the right direction."

"L-Lady Satomi, my lord," Suki stammered, truly

stunned by his kindness. She knew she should bow, but she was terrified she would spill the tea. “Please forgive me, I have come to the palace only today, and everything is very confusing.”

A slight frown crossed the noble’s face, making Suki’s heart nearly stop in her chest, thinking she had offended him. “I see,” he murmured, mostly to himself. “Yet another maid, Satomi-san? How many does the emperor’s concubine need?”

Before Suki could wonder what that meant, he shook himself and smiled once more. “Well, fortune favors you, Suki-san. Lady Satomi’s residence isn’t far.” He raised a billowy sleeve, pointing an elegant finger down the walkway. “Go left around this building, then walk straight to the very end. It will be the last doorway on the right.”

“Daisuke-san!” A woman’s voice echoed down the veranda before Suki could even whisper her thanks, and the man turned his beautiful face away. Moments later, a trio of noblewomen in elegant green-and-gold robes sashayed around the building and gave him mock frowns as they hurried forward.

“There you are, Daisuke-san,” one of them huffed. “Where have you been? We are going to be late for Hanoe-san’s poetry recital. Oh,” she said, catching sight of Suki. “What is this? Daisuke-san, don’t tell me you were here all this time, talking to a maid.”

“And why not?” Daisuke’s tone was wry. “A maid’s conversation can be as interesting as any noblewoman’s.”

The three women giggled as if that were the funniest thing they had ever heard. Suki didn’t see what was so amusing. “Oh, Taiyo Daisuke, you say the most wicked things,” one of them chided from behind a white fan painted with cherry blossoms. "Come, now. We really must go. You," she said, directing her gaze to Suki, "get back to your duties. Why are you just standing there gaping? Shoo!"

As quickly as she could without spilling the tea, Suki hurried away. But her heart still pounded, and for some reason she couldn't catch her breath. *Taiyo.* Taiyo was the name of the imperial family. Daisuke-sama was of the Sun Clan, one of the most powerful families in Iwagoto, the blood of the emperor himself. The funny feeling in her stomach intensified, and her thoughts became a swarm of moths, fluttering around the dazzling memory of his smile and the melody from her father's flute.

Somehow, she found her way to the correct door, at the very end of the veranda, looking over the magnificent gardens of the palace. The shoji panel was open, and Suki could smell the smoky hint of burning incense wafting from the darkened interior. Creeping inside the room, she peered around for her new mistress but saw no one. Despite the nobles' unified preference for simplicity, this apartment was lavishly cluttered. Ornamental screens turned the room into a small maze, and tatami mats lined the entire floor, thick and soft beneath her feet. Paper was everywhere; origami sheets of every style and texture lay in piles around the apartment. Folded paper birds peered at her from atop every flat surface, dominating the room. Suki brushed a flock of origami cranes from the table so that she could set the tea down.

"Mai-chan?" A gossamer voice drifted out of the adjoining room, and the sound of silk rustled over the floor. "Is that you? Where have you been? I was getting worried that you—oh."

A woman appeared in the doorway, and for a moment,

they stared at one another, Suki's mouth hanging open in amazement.

If Taiyo Daisuke was the most handsome man she had ever met, this was the most elegantly beautiful woman in the whole palace. Her billowing robes were red with silver, gold and green butterflies swarming the front. Shimmering black hair was beautifully styled atop her head, pierced with red-and-gold chopsticks and ivory combs. Dark eyes in a flawless porcelain face regarded Suki curiously.

"Hello," the woman said, and Suki quickly closed her mouth. "May I inquire as to who you are?"

"I… I'm Suki," the girl stammered. "I'm your new maid."

"I see." The woman's lips curved in a faint smile. Suki was sure that if her teeth showed, they would light up the room. "Come here, if you would, little Suki-chan. Please don't step on anything."

Suki obeyed, placing her feet carefully to avoid squashing any paper creatures, and stood before Lady Satomi.

The woman struck her across the face with her open palm.

Pain exploded behind her eye, and she collapsed to the floor, too stunned to even gasp. Blinking back tears, she put her hand to her cheek and gazed blankly up at Lady Satomi, who loomed over her, smiling.

"Do you know why I did that, little Suki-chan?" she asked, and now she did show her teeth. They reminded Suki of a grinning skull.

"N-no, my lady," she murmured, as her numb cheek started to burn.

"Because I called for Mai-chan, not you," the lady replied in a relentlessly cheerful voice. "You might be a stupid country girl, Suki-chan, but that does not excuse your complete ignorance. You must come only when called, is that understood?"

"Yes, my lady."

"Smile, Suki-chan," Satomi suggested. "If you smile, perhaps I can forget you have the accent of a sweaty country barbarian and the face of an ox. It will be dreadfully difficult not to loathe you on sight, but I will do my best. Isn't that generous of me, Suki-chan?"

Suki, not knowing what to say to this, kept her mouth shut and thought of Daisuke-sama.

"Isn't that generous of me, Suki-chan?" Satomi repeated, an edge to her voice now.

Suki swallowed hard. "*Hai*, Lady Satomi."

Satomi sighed. "You've smashed my creations." She pouted, and Suki glanced down at the origami creatures that had been crushed by her body. The lady sniffed and turned away. "I shall be very angry if you do not replace them. There is a quaint little shop in the Wind district that sells the most delicate lavender sheets. If you run, you should catch them before they close."

Suki gazed through an open screen at the storm clouds roiling above the palace. Thunder rumbled as silver-blue strands chased each other through the sky. "Yes, Lady Satomi."

The passing days made Suki long for her father's shop, for the quiet comfort of sweeping, stitching torn clothing and cooking meals three times a day. For the comforting smell of sawdust and wood shavings, and for the customers who barely gave her a second glance, concerned only with her father and his work. She'd thought it would be easy enough to be the maid to a great lady, to help her dress and run her errands and see to the mundane little tasks that were beneath the notice of the nobility. Perhaps that was how it should have been—certainly, the other maids did not seem to share her plight. Indeed, they seemed to go out of their way to avoid her, as if associating with Lady Satomi's maid would attract the ire of her mistress. Suki couldn't blame them.

Lady Satomi was a nightmare, a beautiful nightmare of silk, makeup and heady perfume. Nothing Suki did suited the woman. No matter how she scrubbed or cleaned, the laundry never met with Satomi's satisfaction. The tea Suki brewed was too weak, too strong, too sweet, always too something. No amount of cleaning sufficed within Lady Satomi's chambers—there was always a speck of dirt to be found, a tatami mat out of place, an origami creature in the wrong spot. And each failure brought a little smile from the lady and a shockingly powerful slap.

No one cared, of course. The other maids looked away from her bruises, and the guards did not look at her at all. Suki did not dare complain; not only was Lady Satomi a great and powerful lady, she was the favored concubine of the emperor himself. To speak poorly of her would be insulting Taiyo no Genjiro, the great Son of Heaven, and would result in a flogging, public humiliation, or worse.

The only thing that saved Suki from complete despair was the thought of running into Daisuke-sama again. He was a great noble, of course, far above her station, and would not care about the troubles of a lowly maid. But even catching a glimpse of him would be enough. She looked for him on the verandas and the paths to and from Lady Satomi's chambers, but the beautiful noble was nowhere to be seen. Later, she learned through servant gossip that Taiyo Daisuke had left the Palace of the Sun not long after she arrived, heading off on one of his mysterious pilgrimages across the country. Perhaps, Suki thought, she would catch a glimpse of him when he returned. Perhaps she would hear her father's flute again, and follow it until she found him on the verandas, his long white hair flowing behind him.

A ringing slap drew her from her daydream, knocking her to the floor. "Oh dear. You are such a *clumsy* girl." Lady Satomi stood over her, resplendent in her stunning silk robes. "Get up, Suki-chan. I have a task for you."

In her arms, the lady carried a coil of fine silken cord, bloodred in color. As Suki staggered to her feet, the rope was thrust into her arms. "You are such a feebleminded little thing, aren't you? I despair of ever making a good maid out of you. But surely even you can take care of this one small task. Take this rope to the storehouse in the eastern gardens, the one past the lake. Surely you can do that much? And *do* stop crying, girl. What will people think of me, if my maid goes around weeping everywhere?"

Suki awoke to darkness with a throbbing in her skull. Her vision swam, and there was a weird coppery taste in the back of her throat. Overhead, thunder growled, and a sharp, ozone-scented wind blew into her face. The floor beneath her felt cold, and hard, stony edges were pressing uncomfortably into her stomach and cheek. Blinking, she tried pushing herself upright, but her arms would not respond. A moment later, she realized they were tied behind her back.

Ice flooded her veins. She rolled to her side and attempted to stand, but her knees and ankles were bound as well—with the same rope she'd brought to the storehouse, she realized—and a rag was stuffed into her mouth, tied with a strip of cloth. With a muffled shriek, she thrashed wildly, writhing on the stones. Pain shot up her arms as she scraped along the ground, cutting her skin on rock edges and leaving bits of flesh behind, but the ropes held firm. Panting, exhausted, she slumped against the stones in defeat, then raised her head to gaze at her surroundings.

She lay in the center of a courtyard, but not the pristine, elegant courtyard of the Sun Palace, with its swept white stones and trimmed bushes. This one was dark, rocky, ruined. The castle it was attached to was also dark and abandoned, looming over her like some great sullen beast, tattered banners flapping against the walls. Dead leaves and broken stones were scattered throughout the courtyard, and a samurai's helmet, empty and rusting, lay a few feet from her. In the flickering light overhead, she could see the glint of eyes atop the walls—dozens of crows, watching her with their feathers spiked out against the wind.

"Hello, Suki-chan," said an eerily cheerful voice somewhere behind her. "Did you finally wake up?"

Suki craned her head back. Lady Satomi stood a few paces away, her hair unbound and tossed by the wind, the sleeves of her red-and-black kimono fluttering like sails. Her eyes were hard, and her lips were curled in a tiny smile. Gasping, Suki flopped to a sitting position, wanting to cry for help, to ask what was happening. Was this some terrible punishment for disappointing her mistress, for not cleaning, fetching, or serving to her standards? She tried pleading with her eyes, hot tears leaking down her cheeks, but the woman only wrinkled her nose.

"Such a lazy girl, and so fragile. I cannot abide your constant weeping." Lady Satomi sniffed and moved a few feet away, not looking at her anymore. "Well, be happy, Suki-chan. For today your misery will come to an end. Though it will mean I must acquire yet another maid—what *is* it with all these serving girls running away like mice? Ungrateful wretches. No sense of responsibility at all." She gave a long-suffering sigh, then looked at the clouds as lightning flickered and the wind picked up. "Where is that oni?" she muttered. "After all the trouble I went through for suitable compensation, I shall be very cross if he does not arrive before the storm."

*Oni?* Suki must've been hearing things. Oni were great and terrible demons that came from Jigoku, the realm of evil. There were countless stories of brave samurai slaying oni, sometimes armies of oni, but they were myths and legends. Oni were the creatures parents threatened wayward children with—*don't wander too close to the woods or an oni might get you. Listen to your elders, or an oni will reach up from beneath the floorboards and drag you down to Jigoku.* Scary warnings for children and monstrous foes for legendary samurai, but not creatures that walked Ningen-kai, the mortal realm.

There was a blinding flash, a boom of thunder, and a great horned creature appeared at the edge of the courtyard.

Suki screamed. The gag muffled it, but she kept screaming until she was out of breath, gasping and choking into the cloth. She tried to flee and fell hard against the stones, striking her chin on the rock, but she barely felt the pain. Lady Satomi's lips moved as she gave her a withering look, probably chastising her shrillness, but Suki's mind couldn't register anything but the huge demon, for it could only be a thing of nightmares, prowling forward into the torchlight. The monster that shouldn't exist.

It was massive, standing a good fifteen feet overhead, and just as terrible and fearsome as the legends described.

Its skin was a dark crimson, the color of blood, and a wild black mane tumbled down its back and shoulders. Sharp yellow tusks curled from its jaw, and its eyes glowed like hot coals as the demon lumbered forward, making the ground shake. The tiny part of Suki's brain not frozen in terror recalled that, in the stories, oni dressed in loincloths made of great striped beasts, but this demon wore plates of lacquered armor; the red shoulder pads, thigh guards and bracers of the samurai when they rode into battle. True to the myths, however, it carried a giant, iron-studded club—a tetsubo—in one hand, swinging it to a shoulder as if it weighed no more than an ink stick.

"There you are, Yaburama." Lady Satomi lifted her chin as the oni stopped in front of her. "I am aware that time in Jigoku doesn't exist, and it is said that one day is akin to eight hundred years in the mortal realm, but punctuality is a wonderful attribute, something we can all aspire to."

The oni grunted, a deep, guttural sound emerging between his fangs. "Do not lecture me, human," it rumbled, its terrible voice making the air shiver. "Calling on Jigoku takes time, especially if you wish to summon an army."

Behind the demon, spreading around him like a colony of ants, a horde of smaller monsters appeared. Standing only a few inches above the knee, their skin different shades of blue, red and green, they looked like tiny oni themselves, except for their huge flared ears and maniacal grins. They spotted Suki and began edging forward, cackling and licking their pointed teeth. She shrieked into the gag and tried wiggling away, but got no farther than a landed fish.

The oni growled a warning, deep as distant thunder, and the horde skittered back. "Is that mine?" the demon asked, glowing crimson gaze falling on Suki. "It looks tasty." He took a step toward her, and she nearly fainted on the spot.

"Patience, Yaburama." Lady Satomi held out a hand, stopping him. He narrowed his eyes and bared his teeth slightly, but the woman didn't seem disturbed. "You can have your payment in a moment," she went on. "I just want to make certain you know why you were summoned. That you know what you must do."

"How could I not," the oni replied, sounding impatient. "The Dragon is rising. The Harbinger of Change approaches. Another thousand years have passed in this realm of horrible light and sun, and the night of the wish is nearly upon us. There is only one reason a mortal would summon me into Ningen-kai at this time." A look of amused contempt crossed his brutish face. "I will get you the scroll, human. Or a piece of it, now that it has been scattered to the four winds." The burning red gaze slid back to Suki, and he smiled slowly, showing fangs. "I will do so, after I collect my payment."

"Good." Lady Satomi stepped back, as the first drops of rain began to fall. "I am counting on you, Yaburama. I am sure there are others who are scrambling to find all the pieces of the Dragon scroll. You know what to do if you meet them. Well..." She opened a pink parasol and swung it over her head. "I leave it to you. Enjoy."

As sheets of water began creeping across the courtyard, Lady Satomi turned and began walking away. Suki screamed into the gag and threw herself after her mistress crying and begging, praying to the kami and anyone else who would hear. *Please*, she thought desperately. *Please, I cannot die like this. Not like this.*

Lady Satomi paused and glanced back at her with a smile.

"Oh, don't be sad, little Suki-chan," she said. "This is your proudest moment. You will be the catalyst to usher in a whole new era. This empire, the whole world, will change, because of your sacrifice today. See?" The lady tilted her head, observing her as if she were a whimpering puppy. "You've actually become useful. Surely that is enough for someone like you."

Behind Suki, the ground trembled, and a huge claw closed on her legs, curved talons sinking into her skin. She screamed and thrashed, yanking at the ropes, trying to writhe out of the demon's grip, but there was no escape. Lady Satomi sniffed, turned and continued on, her parasol bobbing through the rain, as Suki was pulled toward the oni, the minor demons shrieking and dancing around her.

*Help me. Someone, please, help me! Daisuke-sama...* Abruptly, her thoughts went to the noble, to his handsome face and gentle smile, though she knew he would not be coming. No one was coming, because no one cared about the death of a lowly servant girl. *Father*, Suki thought in numb despair, *I'm sorry. I didn't mean to leave you alone.*

Deep inside, anger flickered, momentarily snuffing the fear. It was terribly unfair, being killed by a demon before she could do anything. She was only a servant, but she had hoped to marry a good man, raise a family, leave something behind that mattered. *I'm not ready*, Suki thought in desperation. *I'm not ready to go. Please, not yet.*

Clawed fingers closed around her neck, and she was lifted up to face the oni's terrible, hungry smile. Its hot breath, smelling of smoke and rotten meat, blasted her face as the demon opened its jaws. Mercifully, the gods decided to intervene at that moment, and Suki finally fainted in terror, her consciousness leaving her body the moment before it was torn in half.

The scent of blood misted into the air, and the demons howled in glee. From Suki's mangled body, unseen by the horde and invisible to normal eyes, a small sphere of light rose slowly into the air. It hovered over the grisly scene, seeming to watch as the minor demons squabbled over scraps, Yaburama's booming roar rising into the night as he swatted them away. For a moment, it seemed torn between flying into the clouds and remaining where it was. Drifting aimlessly higher, it paused at a flash of color that gleamed through the rain, a pink parasol heading toward the doors of the castle. The sphere's blue-white glow flared into an angry red.

Zipping from the sky, the orb of light flew soundlessly over the head of the oni, dropped lower to the ground and slipped through the door to the castle just before it creaked shut, leaving the oni, the demons and the torn, murdered body of a servant girl behind.

# 2

## The Fox in the Temple

"Yumeko!"

The shout echoed over the garden, booming and furious, making me wince. I'd been sitting quietly by the pond, tossing crumbs to the fat red-and-white fish that swarmed below the surface, when the familiar sound of my name bellowed in anger rang from the direction of the temple. Quickly, I ducked behind the large stone lantern at the edge of the water, just as Denga stalked around the opposite bank, his face like a thundercloud.

"Yumeko!" the monk shouted again as I pressed into the rough, mossy stone. I could picture his normally stern, placid face turning as red as the temple pillars, the flush creeping all the way up his bald forehead. I'd seen it too many times to count. His braided ponytail and orange robes were no doubt flapping as he spun, searching the edges of the pond, scanning the bamboo patches surrounding the garden. "I know you're here somewhere!" he raged. "Putting salt in the teapot…again! Do you think Nitoru likes having tea spat right in his face?" I bit my lip to stifle the laughter and pressed against the statue, trying to be silent. "Wretched demon girl!" Denga seethed, as the sound of his footsteps turned from the pond and headed farther into the garden. "I know you're laughing your fool head off now. When I find you, you'll be sweeping the floors until the hour of the Rat!"

His voice drifted away. I peeked around the stone to watch Denga continue down the path into the bamboo, until he was lost from sight.

Blowing out a breath, I leaned against the lantern's weathered body, feeling triumphant. *Well, that was entertaining. Denga-san is always so uptight; he really needs to try out new expressions or his face will crack from the strain.* I grinned, imagining the look on poor Nitoru's face when the other monk discovered what was in his teacup. Unfortunately, Nitoru had the same sense of humor Denga did, which was none at all. *Definitely time to make myself scarce. I'll steal a book from the library and go hide under the desk. Oh, wait, but Denga already knows that spot. Bad idea.* I cringed at the thought of all the long wooden verandas that would need a thorough sweeping if I was found. *Maybe it's a good day to not be here. At least until this evening. I wonder what the monkey family in the forest is doing today?*

Excitement fluttered. A dozen or so yellow monkeys lived within the branches of an ancient cedar that rose above all other trees in the forest. On clear days, if one climbed to the very top, one could see the whole world, from the tiny farming village at the base of the mountains all the way to the distant horizon. Whenever I found myself at the top of that tree, swaying with the monkeys and the branches, I would gaze over the multicolored carpet stretching away before me and wonder if today would be the day I'd be brave enough to see what lay beyond the skyline.

I never was, and this afternoon would be no different. But at least I wouldn't be here, waiting for an angry Denga-san to shove a broom into my hands and tell me to sweep every flat surface in the temple. Including the yard.

Drawing back from the statue, I turned around…and came face-to-face with Master Isao.

I yelped, jerking back and hitting the stone lantern, which was bigger and heavier than I and obstinately refused to budge. The ancient, white-bearded monk smiled serenely under his wide-brimmed straw hat.

"Going somewhere, Yumeko-chan?"

"Um…" I stammered, rubbing the back of my head. Master Isao wasn't a large man; thin and spindly, he stood a head shorter than me when he was wearing his wooden geta clogs. But no one in the temple was more respected, and no one had such control over his ki as Master Isao. I'd seen him chop a tree in half with a flick of his hand, and punch a giant boulder into rubble. He was the undisputed master of the Silent Winds temple, able to quiet a room of strong-willed ki practitioners just by appearing. Though he never raised his voice or appeared angry; the harshest expression I'd ever seen him make was a mild frown, and that had been terrifying.

*"Ano…"* I stammered again, as his bushy eyebrows rose in patient amusement. No use in lying, Master Isao always knew everything about everything. "I was…going to visit the monkey family in the forest, Master Isao," I confessed,

figuring that was the least of my crimes. I wasn't exactly *forbidden* to leave the temple grounds, but the monks certainly didn't like it when I did. The amount of chores, training and duties they imposed on me when I was awake indicated that they tried to keep me busy whenever possible. The only free time I could get was usually stolen, like today.

Master Isao only smiled. "Ah. Monkeys. Well, I am afraid your friends will have to wait a bit, Yumeko-chan," he said, not sounding angry or surprised at all. "I must borrow your time for a moment. Please, follow me."

He turned and started around the pond, heading toward the temple. I dusted off my sleeves and fell into step behind him, down the bamboo trail dappled by sun and green shadows, past the singing stones where the breeze hummed playfully through the holes worn into the rocks, and over the red arched bridge that spanned the stream. A drab brown bird flitted to the branches of a juniper tree, puffed out its chest and filled the air with the beautiful, warbling song of a nightingale. I whistled back at him, and he gave me an indignant look before darting into the leaves.

The trees opened up, the foliage falling away, as we walked past the tiny rock garden with its meticulously raked sand, and up the steps of the temple. As we entered the dim, cool hall, I spotted Nitoru glaring at me across the room, and dared a cheeky wave, knowing he would not approach while I was with Master Isao. I'd probably be sweeping the steps until next winter, but the look on the monk's face was worth it.

Master Isao led me through several narrow hallways, passing individual rooms on either side, until he slid back a door panel and motioned me through. I stepped into a familiar room, small and neat, empty but for a large standing mirror on the opposite wall and a hanging wall scroll beside it. The scroll depicted a massive dragon soaring over a raging sea, and a tiny boat tossed by the waves beneath it.

I masked a sigh. I'd been in this room a few times before, and the ritual that followed was always the same. Knowing what Master Isao wanted, I walked lightly across the tatami mats and knelt in front of the mirror, the only one in the entire temple. Master Isao followed and settled himself beside it facing me, his hands in his lap. For a moment, he sat there, eyes serene, though it felt like his gaze passed right through me to the wall behind my head.

"What do you see?" he asked, as he always did.

I looked at the mirror. My reflection gazed back at me, a slight girl of sixteen winters, straight black hair falling, unbound, to the center of her back. She wore straw sandals, a white sash and a short crimson kimono that was tattered in places, especially the long, billowy sleeves. Her hands were grubby from kneeling at the pond talking to the fish, and dirt stained her knees and face. At first glance, she looked like a ragged but perfectly normal peasant girl, perhaps a fisherman's or farmer's waif, kneeling on the floor of the temple.

If you *didn't* happen to notice the bushy orange tail, peeking out from behind her robes. And the large, triangular, black-tipped ears poking up from the top of her skull. And the glowing golden eyes that very clearly marked her as not normal, not human at all.

"I see myself, Master Isao," I said, wondering if, this time, it was the right answer. "In my true form. Without illusion or barrier. I see a *kitsune*."

*Kitsune.* Fox. Or half kitsune, more accurately. Wild kitsune, the foxes that roamed the hidden places of Iwagoto, were masters of illusion magic and shapeshifting. While it was true that some kitsune chose to live as normal wild animals, all foxes possessed magic. Kitsune were yokai, creatures of the supernatural. One of their favorite tricks was to take human form—usually in the guise of a beautiful woman—and lure men astray. To the naked eye, I was an ordinary human girl; no tail, pointed ears or yellow eyes. Only in front of mirrors and reflective surfaces was my true nature revealed. Lacquered tables, still water, even the edge of a blade. I had to be very careful where I stood and what I was around, lest an acute observer notice the reflection on the surface did not quite match the girl in front of it.

Or so the monks warned me. They all knew what I was, and made certain to remind me of it often. *Half-blood, demon child, fox girl*: phrases that were part of my everyday life. Not that any of the monks were cruel or heartless, just practical. I was kitsune, something not quite human, and they saw no reason to pretend otherwise.

I glanced at Master Isao, wondering if he would tell me anything different this time, any hint of what he really wanted me to say. We'd played the *what do you see?* game numerous times in the past, and none of my answers—be they human, demon, fox or fish—seemed to satisfy him, because I'd always find myself right back here, staring at the kitsune in the mirror.

"How are your lessons progressing?" Master Isao went on, giving no indication that he'd heard my answer, or if it was the right one. I very seriously doubted it.

"Fine, Master Isao."

"Show me."

I hesitated, casting about for a suitable target. There weren't many to be found. The mirror, perhaps. Or the wall scroll. But I had already used both in the past, and Master Isao wouldn't be impressed with the same tricks over and over again. This, too, was a game we'd played often.

I spotted a yellow maple leaf, caught on the end of my sleeve, and grinned.

Picking it up, I twirled it between fingers and thumb, then carefully put it on my head. Kitsune magic needed an anchor, something of the natural world, to build an illusion around. There were stories of very old, very powerful kitsune who could weave illusions out of thin air, but I needed something to attach the magic to. Focal point in place, I half closed my eyes and called on my powers.

Since before I could remember, magic had come naturally to me, a gift from the yokai side of the family, I was told. Even when I was a toddler, I had shown impressive talent for it, floating little balls of kitsune-bi, the heatless, blue-white foxfire, through the halls of the temple. As I'd gotten older and my magic had grown, a few of the monks thought Master Isao should put a binding on me, sealing away my power so I wouldn't hurt anyone, or myself. Wild kitsune were notorious troublemakers. They weren't inherently malicious, but their "pranks" could range from merely annoying—stealing food or hiding small items—to truly dangerous: spooking a horse on a narrow mountain path, or leading someone deep into a marsh or forest, never to be seen again. Better that I didn't have that temptation, at least according to Denga and a few others. But the master of the Silent Winds temple had adamantly refused. Fox magic was part of a kitsune's life, he said, something as natural as sleeping or breathing. To deny it would do more harm than good.

Instead, I practiced my magic every day with a monk

called Satoshi, in the hopes that I would learn to control my fox-given talent, and not the other way around. The monks had been skeptical at first, but I knew Master Isao trusted that I would not use my powers for mischief, so I tried not to give in to temptation. Even though some days it was very hard not to disguise the cat as a teapot, or to make a closed door look open, or to turn a log invisible in front of the steps. Fox magic was nothing but illusion and trickery, Denga-san had seethed on more than one occasion, usually on the tail end of a prank. Nothing useful could ever come of it.

*That might be true*, I thought, as the heat of the fox magic rose up inside me. *But it certainly is a lot of fun.*

A ripple went through me, like my body was made of water that someone had just dropped a pebble into, and a puff of white smoke engulfed me from the ground up. As the tendrils of smoke dissipated, I opened my eyes and smiled at the image in the mirror. Master Isao stared back at me in the reflection, a perfect replica of the man sitting beside the mirror, if you didn't count the rather smug grin on his weathered face. And the white-tipped tail behind him.

The real Master Isao chuckled and shook his head. "Is this what you and Satoshi have been practicing?" he asked. "I shudder to imagine the day 'I' suggest Denga-san should go and catch a monkey."

"Ooh, do you think he would? That would be hilarious. Um, not that I would ever do something like that, of course." Reaching up, I plucked the maple leaf from my head, and the illusion frayed apart, fox magic scattering to the wind, until I was just me once more. Twirling the leaf in my fingers, I wondered how much trouble I'd be in if I *did* disguise myself as Master Isao and told Denga to go jump in the pond. Knowing the monk's fanatical devotion to his master, he would do it without question. And then he'd probably kill me.

"Sixteen years," Master Isao remarked in a soft voice. I blinked at him. That was new. Normally by this time, our conversation would be over and he'd be instructing me to return to my duties. "Sixteen years to the day that you have been with us," he went on, almost wistfully. "Since we found you outside the gate in a fish basket, with nothing but a tattered robe and a note pinned to the cloth." *Forgive me, but I must leave this child in your care*, the letter said. *Do not judge her harshly, she cannot help what she is, and the road I walk is no place for innocence. Her name is Yumeko, child of dreams. Raise her well, and may the Great Dragon guide your steps, and hers.*

I nodded politely, having heard this story dozens of times. I'd never known my father or my mother, and hadn't given either of them much thought. They weren't a part of my life, and I saw no point in worrying about things I could not change.

Though there was one very hazy memory, from when I was just a toddler, that continued to haunt my dreams. I'd been wandering the woods outside the temple that day, hiding from the monks and chasing squirrels, when I'd felt eyes on me from behind. I'd turned and seen a white fox staring at me from atop a fallen log, yellow eyes glowing in the shadows. We'd watched each other for a long moment, child and kitsune, and even though I was very young, I'd felt a kinship with this creature, a sense of longing that I didn't understand. But when I'd taken a step toward it, the fox had disappeared. I'd never glimpsed it again.

"Sixteen years," Master Isao continued, unaware of my thoughts. "And in that time, we have taught you our ways, steered you down what we hoped was the right path, trained you to seek the balance between human and kitsune. You have always known what you are—we have never hidden the truth. I have witnessed both the fox's cunning and human compassion within you. I have seen callousness and kindness in equal measure, and I know you are balanced on a very thin edge right now, one of yokai and human. Whatever you choose, whatever path you wish to take, even if you attempt to traverse them both, you must decide for yourself, soon. It is almost time."

He didn't give any explanation of what he meant. He didn't ask me if I understood. Maybe he knew that half the time I could never untangle his riddles, and the other half I really wasn't listening. But I nodded and smiled, like I knew what he was getting at, and said, "Yes, Master Isao. I understand."

He sighed and shook his head. "You have no idea what I'm babbling on about, child," he stated, making me wince. "But that is all right. It is not the reason I brought you here today." He looked away, his gaze going distant, that shadow falling over his eyes once more. "You are nearly grown, and the world outside is changing. It is time you knew our true purpose, what the Silent Winds temple truly protects."

I blinked and, in the mirror, the kitsune's ears twitched forward. "What we...protect?" I asked. "I didn't know we protected anything."

"Of course not," Master Isao agreed. "No one ever told you. It is our greatest secret. But it is one you must know. The Dragon is rising, and another age comes to an end."

"A very long time ago," Master Isao began in the lyrical tones of a master storyteller, "there was a mortal. A young lord who commanded a great army and had servants that outnumbered the grains of rice in the field. His name has been lost to legend, but it is said he was an arrogant, foolish human who wished to become an immortal kami—a god. To this end, he assembled his greatest warriors and ordered them to bring him the Fushi no Tama, a jewel that was said to grant immortality to any who possessed it. Unfortunately, the jewel of immortality resided in the forehead of the Great Dragon that lived under the sea. But the lord coveted immortality, and told his warriors to retrieve Fushi no Tama by whatever means possible.

"His retainers, a little more sensible then their master, pretended to set off on this quest at once, and so sure of their success was the lord that he adorned his rooms with gold and silver, and draped silken cloth over the roof of his house, as was befitting a god.

"Several months passed with no word, and the young lord, growing impatient, journeyed to the sacred cliffs of Ryugake, where it was said the Dragon lived beneath the waves. As it turned out, not one of his warriors had taken a boat to search for the Dragon but had fled the province at first opportunity. Angry at this news, the lord threw caution to the winds, hired a helmsman and a ship, and embarked on the quest himself.

"As soon as the unfortunate ship reached deep ocean, a fierce storm blew in and the sea turned on the lord and his crew like an enraged beast. To make matters worse, the lord was struck with a terrible sickness and lay close to death while the sea raged and howled around them. As the storm grew in ferocity, and the ship itself threatened to break apart, the helmsman cried out that surely the gods were angry with them, and that the lord should offer a prayer to pacify the Great Kami of the deep.

"The lord, finally realizing his mistake, was ashamed and horrified at what he had attempted to do. Falling to his face, he prayed no less than a thousand times, repenting of his folly to slay the Dragon, vowing that he would challenge the Ruler of the Tides no more.

"Afterward, some legends claim that the lord returned to his homeland, and that nothing happened except the crows stole the fine silk cloth from his roof to line their nests. However, one legend goes on to say that, after the lord finished his thousandth prayer, the seas boiled and a mighty Dragon rose from the ocean depths. He was thrice the length of the ship, his eyes burned like torches in the night and a shining pearl was embedded in the center of his forehead.

"The lord was very frightened, and rightly so, for the Dragon looked most displeased. He fell facedown and begged the mighty serpent to have mercy on him. The Dragon then presented the lord with a choice. He would grant the mortal one wish, anything he desired—riches, immortal life, power over death itself—or he would leave him his soul. The lord chose to keep his soul, and returned home a wiser man.

"Now, every thousand years—one year for each prayer the lord uttered—the Dragon will rise again to the mortal who summons him. If the mortal's soul is pure, if his intentions are just and his heart is honorable, the Dragon will grant him his heart's desire. However, if the soul is found wanting, the Dragon rips it from the body and takes it as forfeit for the arrogance of the mortal who sought to become a god, so long ago."

Silence fell after Master Isao finished his tale. I sat there, thinking it was an intriguing story, but what it had to do with our temple and the thing we were supposed to protect, I hadn't a clue. Master Isao watched me for a moment, then shook his head.

"You do not know why I told you that story, do you?"

"I do," I protested, and Master Isao raised his bushy eyebrows. "It's so that I can…um…well. No, I don't."

He said nothing, only waited patiently, silently insisting, as he often did, that I figure it out myself. I racked my brain, trying to understand. He mentioned a dragon, both in the story and earlier with the mirror, so it must be important. What had he said, exactly?

"The Dragon is rising," I repeated, earning a nod of approval. "And, in the story, every thousand years, it can be summoned. To grant a mortal whatever they desire." I paused, frowning slightly. "So…*why* does the Dragon grant wishes? It's a god, isn't it? Surely it has more important things to do than pop in every thousand years. Does it like granting wishes?"

"The Dragon is not a wish-granting puppet, Yumeko-chan," Master Isao said. "It is a Great Kami—the God of Tides and the Harbinger of Change. Every time it appears, for good or ill, the world shifts and goes down a different path."

"So, that must mean…is it time for the Dragon to rise again?"

"Very good, Yumeko-chan." Master Isao gave another solemn nod. "You are correct. The time of the Dragon is nearly upon us. And there are many, even now, who are searching for a way to call on it. But the Dragon will rise only if it is properly summoned, and the only way to do that is to recite the young lord's prayers, word for word. All one thousand of them."

"A thousand prayers?" I cocked my head. I had trouble remembering what day of the week it was. I couldn't imagine having to recite one thousand prayers from memory. "That sounds terribly difficult," I remarked. "I don't suppose it's the same prayer, over and over again, either. Someone should have written them down..."

*Oh.*

And the pieces clicked into place. The mystery of the temple, the sacred duty of the monks. I glanced at the hanging scroll on the wall, the Dragon and the doomed ship, realizing its significance for the first time. "That's what we protect," I guessed. "The prayer to summon the Dragon. It's...here."

"A piece of it," Master Isao said gravely. "You see, Yumeko-chan, long ago, someone used the power of the Dragon's wish for a terrible thing. Darkness and chaos ruled, and the land was very nearly torn asunder because of it. It was decided that such power should never be used again, so the prayer was split into three parts and hidden throughout Iwagoto, so such darkness could not rise a second time."

"But... I thought the Dragon only granted a wish to an honorable mortal," I said. "One 'whose heart is pure.' How could the wish be used for evil?"

"The path to Jigoku is lined with honorable intentions," Master Isao replied. "And absolute power can corrupt even the purest of hearts. Such is the folly of men. Regardless, now that you know what we protect, Yumeko-chan, we must be very careful. This is why we are so isolated, why the temple never receives visitors. With the coming of the Dragon, the balance will shift. Outside these walls, the land is in chaos. Men fight each other for power, unnatural things stir and rise, drawn by blood and violence, and the world grows dark with fear. It is our duty to ensure that the Dragon's prayer never sees the outside world, that we guard this piece of the scroll from all who would call upon its power. This is our greatest responsibility, and now, it is yours, as well. Do you understand, young one?"

A spider of frost ran up my spine, even as I nodded. "I think so, Master Isao."

"There is a shadow approaching this place, little fox." Master Isao's voice had gone soft, almost distant. He wasn't looking at me, instead gazing at the wall over my head. "It draws ever closer, and some of us may not survive. But it will not catch you, if you can find the path between and hold on to the light." Blinking, he glanced at me again, the distant expression fading as he smiled. "Ah, but I am rambling again, aren't I?" he said brightly. "And I believe you had something to do today, didn't you, Yumeko-chan? Oh… and if you want to avoid Denga and Nitoru this afternoon, I would sneak over the western wall." One eye closed in a slow wink as he rose. "I will see you tonight at dinner. Give the monkeys my regards."

He shuffled out, closing the door behind him, but for a few minutes I sat there, the story of the Dragon's wish swirling through my head, taunting and ominous. I'd had no idea that this temple guarded something so powerful, that Master Isao and the others were not simple monks, but the protectors of a great and terrible artifact. A prayer that could summon a god.

*The Dragon is rising.*

A shiver ran up my spine. Was that the reason I was here, in this room? I'd always suspected Master Isao had been testing me for something, but could never figure out what. My own future was never clear, and I'd rarely wondered about it, too preoccupied with the present and what I could do today. Deep down I'd always assumed that, when I was old enough, or brave enough, someday I would leave the Silent Winds temple. Did Master Isao expect me to become a protector of the Dragon scroll? To stay here and guard it from those who wished to summon the power of the Dragon? Forever?

I shook myself. *Stay in this temple for the rest of my life, sitting on a dusty old scroll? That can't be what he meant.* I thought back to my daily lessons with Jin, learning about the outside world and what life was like beyond the temple walls. I'd never actually seen a samurai, but I'd read all about them in books and scrolls. I knew the names of the clans, their customs and the history of Iwagoto going back three hundred years. Why bother to teach me if I was just going to stay in the temple protecting a scroll? Why would Master Isao have me learn so much about a world I would never get to see?

*He wouldn't. He's not that cruel.* Wrinkling my nose, I stood and dusted off my knees, already dismissing the notion. *I'm not strong; I'm not a guardian or a warrior or a ki master. I'm a kitsune who can make a teapot dance around like a loon. Besides, Master Isao has Denga, Jin, Satoshi and everyone else to protect the Dragon's prayer. They don't need my help.*

I stepped to the door, trying to dissolve the ominous weight in the pit of my stomach. The feeling that the world had changed. That something was out there, coming closer, and I was powerless to stop it.

*Stop it, Yumeko. Just because you know about the scroll doesn't mean something will instantly pop in, trying to steal it.* I flattened my ears, trying to convince myself that this was foolish, that the cold creeping up my spine was because

Master Isao was a brilliant storyteller. Not an omen of what was to come. *I'm being paranoid. I've never liked scary stories. Maybe some time in the forest will clear my head.*

Bolstered, I slid the door open a crack…and met a pair of stern, unamused eyes peering at me on the other side. Silently accepting the broom from Denga-san, I trudged out of the room. By the time I had swept the floors, the verandas, the steps, the pathways, the halls and every horizontal surface inside the temple and out, the story of the scroll and the Dragon's wish had long faded from my mind.

# 3

## The Warrior of Shadow

*T*he night smelled of death. Both presently and to come.

Crouched in the branches of the gnarled wisteria tree, I scanned the grounds of Lord Hinotaka's estate, taking note of every guardsman, sentry and patrol walking the perimeter. I had been here for nearly an hour, memorizing the layout of the grounds, and had timed the patrol's rotations to within a few seconds. Now, with the moon fully risen and the hour of the Ox reaching its peak, the light in the topmost window of the castle finally winked out.

A warm wind stirred the branches of my perch, tugging at my hair and scarf, and the faint scent of blood brushed my senses.

There was a flicker at the back of my mind, an impatient stirring that was not my own. Kamigoroshi, or rather, the demon trapped within Kamigoroshi, was restless tonight, sensing the violence about to be unleashed. The sword whose name meant *godslayer* had been a constant fixture in my mind as far back as I could remember, from the day I had been chosen to carry the blade. It had taken over half of my seventeen years to master the volatile weapon, and without the training and guidance of my sensei, I would have succumbed to the rage and insatiable bloodlust of the demon trapped within. It pulled at me now, urging me to draw the sword, to leap down and paint the grounds of the estate in red.

*Patience, Hakaimono,* I told the demon, and felt it subside, though barely. *You'll get your wish soon enough.*

I crept down the branch and dropped onto the outer wall, then ran along the parapets, the ragged edge of my crimson scarf floating behind me, until I reached a point where the corner of the blue-tiled castle roof swept close to the wall. Still a good fifteen feet overhead, but I took the rope and grapple from my belt, swung it twice and hurled it toward the roof above. The clawed hook clicked softly as it caught one of the fish gargoyles on the corner, and I shimmied up the rope and onto the tiles.

Just as I pulled up the rope, a single samurai came around the castle and passed below me, patrolling the inner wall. Immediately I froze, listening to the footsteps shuffle past, and breathed slowly to control myself and my emotions. There could be no fear, no doubt or anger or regret. Nothing to give Hakaimono a foothold into my mind. If I felt anything at all, if I allowed emotion to overcome me, the demon would take control, and I would lose myself to Hakaimono's rage and bloodlust. I was an empty vessel, a weapon for the Shadow Clan, and my only requirement was to complete my mission.

The samurai walked on. Unmoving, a shadow against the tiles, I watched until he circled around the castle and vanished from view. Then, stalking silently over the rooftop, I made my way toward the top of the keep.

As I crept toward an open window, voices echoed beyond the frame, making me tense. My pulse jumped, and Hakaimono pounced on that moment of weakness, urging me to cut them down, to silence them before I was seen. Ignoring the demon, I pressed against the wall as two men—samurai, judging by their marching footsteps—strolled past, talking in furtive tones.

"This is madness," one was saying. "Yoji missing, and now Kentaro disappears without a trace. It's like the very walls are swallowing us whole. And Lord Hinotaka suddenly declares the top floors off-limits?" His voice dropped to nearly a whisper. "Perhaps it's the ghost of Lady Hinotaka. There are rumors that she was poisoned—"

"Shut your fool mouth," hissed the other. "Lady Hinotaka died tragically of an illness, nothing more. Keep that dishonorable tongue behind your teeth before it gets you into real trouble."

"Say what you will," the first samurai returned, sounding defensive. "This castle feels darker every day. I, for one, am happy to be mobilizing tomorrow, even if it's a fool's mission. Why our lord requires a dozen men to fetch an ancient artifact somewhere in the Earth Clan mountains, I do not understand."

The voices faded and the castle was silent again. I slipped through the window and found myself in a long narrow hallway, the walls and floors made of dark wood. It was very dark; the only light came from the glow of the moon outside, and shadows clung to everything. I crept farther into the castle, senses alert for voices or approaching footsteps, but except for the two patrolling guards, the floor appeared deserted. No servants wandered the halls, no samurai played *go* games in their rooms or sat together drinking sake. An aura of fear hung in the air, tainting everything it touched. The demon in Kamigoroshi sensed it as well and stirred excitedly against my mind, a living shadow coiling about like a snake, eagerly anticipating what was to come.

The staircase to the last floor of the keep sat unguarded in a darkened corner of the castle, at the end of the long, narrow hallway. The aura of evil was stronger here, and tendrils of purple-black miasma trickled down the stairs, invisible to the normal human eye. The railing and wooden steps were starting to rot, and the floor around the stairs seemed blighted and weak. A white moth fluttered in from the nearby latticed window and instantly spiraled to the floor, dead.

Setting my jaw, I started up the stairs, ignoring the taint that swirled around me, trying not to breathe it in. The top floor opened up, thick wooden walls with latticed windows showing open sky. A dark mist writhed along the floor, coming from a pair of thick wooden doors against the opposite wall.

I walked to the doors and put a hand against the wood, feeling the sickness that warped it from the inside, then pushed it open.

A fog of purple-black corruption billowed out of the room and writhed into the air. Pausing on the threshold, I stared into the darkness. The walls and floor of the large, square room were covered in sheets of white webbing that hung from the ceiling and stuck to the floor. They wrapped around pillars and dangled from the rafters, tattered curtains rippling in the breeze. Here and there, clusters of bleached bones dangled from the webs, clinking together like grotesque wind chimes, and a few large, man-size cocoons were plastered to the walls, held immobile in the strands.

I stepped through the frame and heard the door creak shut behind me. The webbing on the floor stuck to my tabi boots, but not enough to slow me down. It rustled as I walked forward, vibrating the strands around me and rattling the bone chimes. I made no attempt to be silent. My target was here; there was no reason for stealth any longer.

A low chuckle drifted out of the darkness, soft and feminine, and the hairs on the back of my arms stood up. "I hear the patter of little male feet," crooned a voice, echoing all around me, though I couldn't see anything through the webs and strands. "Has Lord Hinotaka sent me another plaything? Something young and handsome, who yearns to be loved? Come to me, sweet one," it continued in a haunting whisper, as I gripped the hilt of Kamigoroshi, feeling the demon's savage anticipation. "I will love you. I will wrap my love around you, and never let you go."

The last few words echoed directly overhead, just as Hakaimono gave a warning pulse in my mind. I threw myself forward on instinct, not bothering to look up, and felt something catch my jacket sleeve as I dove away. As I rolled to my feet, I spun to face a huge and bulbous form dangling from the ceiling, eight chitinous legs curled around the spot where I had been standing a moment before.

"Sneaky little man bug."

The huge creature uncoiled its legs and dropped to the floor, clicking as it turned to face me, revealing the head and torso of a beautiful woman fused to the body of a giant spider. An elegant black-and-red kimono covered her human half but looked ridiculously small where the spider's thorax emerged from beneath it. Looming above me, the jorogumo cocked her head and smiled, tiny black fangs sliding between full red lips.

"What's this?" she breathed, as I dropped into a crouch and gripped the hilt of my sword. Hakaimono roared through my head, eager and vicious, sharpening my senses and making the air taste of blood. "A boy? Have you come into my lair, looking for me?" She tilted her head the other way. "You are not like the others, the men Hinotaka sends up to my lair, so proud but then so terrified. They flail like frightened crickets at first. But you…are not afraid. How delightful."

I didn't answer. Fear was the first thing that had been purged from my body; the most dangerous emotion of all. Fear, my sensei had taught me, was simply the body's aversion to pain and suffering. A samurai who encountered a starving bear wasn't afraid of the bear itself, but what the bear could do to him. He feared the claws that could rip his flesh, the teeth that could crush the life from his bones. I had been trained to withstand what many could not, the weakness beaten, burned, cut and stripped from my body, until only a weapon remained. I did not fear pain, nor did I fear death, because my life was not my own. A giant, man-eating spider woman was no more concerning than a starving bear. The worst she could do was kill me.

The jorogumo giggled. "Come then, little man bug," she crooned, holding out slender white arms. Her voice turned soothing, almost hypnotic. It droned through my head, coiling around my will and laying spiderwebs in my mind. "I can feel the lonely desire in your heart. Let me love you. Let me ease all the worry and grief weighing down your soul.

You can taste the sweetness of my kiss, and feel the softness of my embrace, before I send you gently into ecstasy."

The jorogumo drew closer, smiling, her face filling my vision until there was nothing left. "You have the most beautiful eyes," she purred. "Like the petals of a nightshade flower. I want to pluck them out and hang them in my parlor." She reached down, and curved black nails touched the side of my face. "Adorable little human…we should not be strangers tonight. What is your name, man bug? Tell me your name, that I might whisper it lovingly as I devour you whole."

I felt the demon within smile and heard my voice speaking to the spider woman, though they weren't my words. "You already know my name."

I drew the sword, and Kamigoroshi flared to life, bathing the room in a baleful purple glow. The jorogumo shrieked and skittered backward, her serene expression twisting with hate.

"Kamigoroshi!" she hissed, baring her fangs. Her black eyes narrowed, appraising me. "Then you are the Kage demonslayer."

Smiling coldly, I stepped forward, feeling the sword's power expand, filling my veins with fury and bloodlust. The jorogumo retreated, multiple legs clicking over the floor, her face pale in the flickering purple light of Kamigoroshi. "Why?" she demanded, long fingers curled into claws as she stared at me. "I have everything I want here. All I have taken are the men not loyal to Hinotaka, those he has declared unworthy to serve him. What are the lives of a few samurai to you, demonslayer?"

I didn't answer, continuing to stalk forward, the blade pulsing in my hand. It was not my place to question the orders of my clan, or why they wanted this yokai destroyed. Though, if I had to guess, the arrival of the jorogumo within Shadow Clan territory was reason enough to act. We, the Kage family, specialized in darkness; we knew the secrets of the shadows and the creatures that lurked within better than any other clan in the empire. I was the Kage demon-slayer; this was my job.

The jorogumo swelled with hatred and fury. "Wretched human," she spat as her jaw unhinged, curved black fangs sliding between her lips. "You will not slay me as you slaughtered Yaku Hundred Eyes, or the nezumi tribe of Hana village. I'll bite off your head and savor your blood as you slide down my throat."

She lunged, a scuttle of yellow and black across the floor, shockingly quick for her bulk, and my senses spiked, as well. I leaped aside as one of those legs stabbed down and smashed into the wood with enough force to snap a floor-board in two. Whirling, I lashed out with Kamigoroshi, cutting through another limb in a spray of black ichor, and the jorogumo shrieked in rage.

Hakaimono howled with approval in my mind, reveling in the violence, urging me to fully release its power. I kept a tight grip on my self-control, even as I dodged the jorogumo's furious reprisal, her long legs scything down at me as she charged. Backed into a corner, I whispered a quick incantation in the language of Shadow, and another Tatsumi split away from me as we darted in opposite directions.

The jorogumo hesitated, confused with the appearance of my reflection, giving us enough time to circle around her. Hissing, she whirled toward the Tatsumi on her left and slashed down with a leg. It passed through the reflection without pause and crashed into a pillar, and the mirror image dissolved into writhing darkness and vanished. Now behind the huge yokai, I raised Kamigoroshi and slashed it across the bulging abdomen.

Yellow ichor spattered, hissing to the floor, and the jorogumo's scream vibrated the webs around us. "Evil human!" she shrieked, spinning to face me, leaving a dripping trail of ooze behind her. "How dare you touch my beautiful body?" She staggered, legs scrabbling for purchase, and I lunged, aiming for the spot where human and spider fused together, intending to split them in half once and for all.

The jorogumo bared her teeth as I came at her. "Curse your eyes!" she hissed, and a spray of green liquid shot from her jaws and misted into the air. I twisted aside to avoid it, but felt a spiderweb mist settle on my face, a second before my eyes started to burn. Blinking rapidly, I staggered away, keeping Kamigoroshi raised as I scrubbed at my face with a sleeve. Through streaming tears, I saw a blur of yellow and black fill my vision, and slashed at it blindly. The sword edge bit into something large as the chitonous leg struck me like a mallet blow, smashing me aside. I felt Kamigoroshi tear from my grasp as I rolled over the floor, tangling myself in sticky webs before I hit the wall.

Dazed, still half-blind, with Hakaimono snarling in my head in frustration, I pushed myself upright and searched desperately for my sword, but my feet were abruptly yanked from beneath me. I hit the floor on my stomach and looked back to see thick strands of webbing wrapped around my legs, the ropes stretching back to the jorogumo's abdomen. The huge yokai smiled, baring black fangs, and began reeling me in like a fish.

"Come to me, tasty little man bug," she crooned, as I began the inescapable slide toward her. Flipping to my back,

I tried tearing the webs from my legs, but they were as strong as silk ropes and wouldn't budge. Desperately, I cast about for something to free my limbs, furious with myself and my mistake, imagining what Ichiro would say if I let myself get eaten by a jorogumo. I searched the floor for a sharp bone or discarded blade, but except for dust and a few finger bones trapped in webbing, there was nothing close.

"I have a special treat for you, human," the yokai continued, still reeling me across the floor. "You can be the host for my next batch of children. I will lay a hundred eggs in your stomach and keep you alive until the day they hatch and devour you from the inside." She giggled through her fangs, continuing to pull me across the floor with unnatural strength. "I wonder if my babies will be stronger than any before them," she mused, "because they feasted on the Kage demonslayer?"

I was now only a few yards from the huge yokai, close enough to see the triumph in her black eyes, the venom dripping from her smile, and my stomach recoiled in disgust. There was no other choice. Slumping to my back, I relaxed, closed my eyes and opened my mind to the demon in the sword.

It responded instantly, a bright flare in the darkness, filling me with rage. I felt the sword hilt bite into my palm as I clenched my fist and opened my eyes.

The jorogumo's face was above me, jaws gaping and curved black fangs descending toward my throat. I saw my own reflection in her gaze, eyes blazing crimson, and caught the split-second fear as she realized too late what she'd really caught. Kamigoroshi flashed, cutting across her face, and she reeled back with a scream, hands going to her eyes.

I sliced through the webs on my legs, leaped upright and

shoved the blade into the bulbous body of the yokai directly overhead, sinking it to the hilt. Before the jorogumo could move, I sprinted beneath her, continuing to carve the sword through the bulging abdomen, until I came out the other side.

Panting, I lowered Kamigoroshi, flinging yellow ichor to the ground, as the jorogumo behind me collapsed with a scream, segmented limbs clattering against the floor as she flailed. She flipped to her back, thrashing, strangled choking sounds coming from her mouth, until her legs curled over her split stomach and were finally still.

*Not enough.* Hakaimono still raged through my mind, wanting more. More blood, more killing. Its rage wasn't nearly satisfied, but it never was. Though only a small piece of my soul had been offered to the blade, the demon sank its claws in deep and struggled to maintain its grip. Taking a deep breath, I closed off my mind and my emotions, becoming a blank vessel with no weaknesses to latch on to. The demon fought me, loath to relinquish control, to return to the darkness, but I concentrated on feeling nothing, being nothing, and Hakaimono's presence finally slipped away.

"What have you done?"

The horrified voice rang out behind me. I turned, gripping my sword hilt, to face a squat, middle-aged man standing in the doorway. His blue-and-gray kimono was very fine, and he had the soft, fleshy look of a man who ate well and sat on the softest cushions. His doughy face was pale as he gazed wildly around the room.

"You killed her," he gasped, dark gaze falling on the twisted form of the dead jorogumo. "You killed her! Why? Do you realize what you've done?"

I didn't answer. Of course I realized what I'd done—

killed the yokai my clan sent me to destroy. The reasons didn't matter. I was simply a weapon. A weapon did not question the intent of those who wielded it.

"How could you," the man went on, moaning as he came forward. "That creature was the only thing that cared for me. The only living being that ever gave me love. My hateful wife only offered spite and condemnation. Even my men sneer and talk about me behind my back. This creature—" he gazed mournfully at the body on the floor "—freed me. She promised she could help me achieve my heart's desire, my greatest wish." His eyes hardened, jowly chins quivering as he set his jaw. "I would have gladly fed her appetites with a thousand men in gratitude for what she offered."

Lord Hinotaka's legs shook, and he sank to his knees, his gaze never leaving the corpse of the jorogumo behind me. "Whoever you are," he said in a trembling voice, "depart my keep before I alert the guards. I assume you were sent to slaughter the monster of Usugurai castle, and you have done your duty. Now go, and may the curse of a thousand grudge spirits follow you for the rest of your days. You've killed your mark, now leave me to my misery."

"Not yet," I said softly, and raised Kamigoroshi once more. "There is one more monster I must kill, before my mission is complete."

Hinotaka frowned, but then his eyes widened and he grabbed for the sword at his obi—too late. Kamigoroshi sliced through his neck in one smooth motion, and the man's head toppled from his shoulders, bounced once and rolled to a stop beside the corpse of the jorogumo. The headless body hit the floor with a thump and soaked the carpet of webs in liquid crimson.

I flicked blood off Kamigoroshi and took a moment to

watch the lord bleed out beside his monster. I took no pleasure in killing Hinotaka. The clan had demanded his death; I had simply been the instrument to carry it out. The lord of Usugurai castle had murdered his wife to placate the jorogumo and had sacrificed his men to her desires, but he was only a puppet. This jorogumo was a two-hundred-year-old yokai that had plagued Iwagoto for many years. She would claim a lonely part of a castle, seduce its lord with promises of love or power and then slowly consume all the men from the inside. When the time came, she would inevitably turn on the lord, paralyzing and hiding him away in her lair, before leaving the castle and vanishing into the dark. Her last victim would be found days later, hanging in the webs, his insides hollowed out and empty from the hundreds of baby spiders that had chewed their way free. For a time, the jorogumo would vanish, fading into rumor and legend, but about twenty years later she would reemerge, targeting another castle, and the cycle would begin anew.

No longer. The yokai was dead, and there would be no more humans sacrificed to her hunger. Hinotaka would be the last. How the Kage knew when and where she would emerge, and why I had been sent to kill her now, I did not know. It wasn't my place to ask questions; all that mattered was completing the mission.

Gazing down at Hinotaka's corpse, I felt a faint flicker of pity. He was just another casualty in the long line of the yokai's victims, but what would drive a man to allow such a monster into his castle, much less his affections? I didn't understand, but it didn't matter. He was dead, and his end had been much cleaner than if the jorogumo had finished what she came to do.

Sheathing my blade, I left the room, slipped out a window onto the roof of the keep and disappeared into the night.

Sheets of rain pounded the road as I approached the edge of town, about a half mile from Usugurai castle. I crept along the roof of a two-story building that served as the rendezvous point for the mission, then dropped onto an overhang and slipped through an open window.

Instinctively, I ducked and rolled away as a shuriken embedded itself in the sill, the four-pointed metal star sinking into the wood. Springing into a defensive crouch, I put a hand on my sword hilt, as a snicker echoed out of the darkness and a shadow disengaged from the corner.

"Oh, sorry, Tatsumi-kun." The female voice was an amused murmur, as Ayame came into view, grinning at me. Like myself, she was sheathed in black, wearing bracers and tabi boots, her long hair tied behind her. The hilt of a short sword poked over her shoulder, and a kusarigama—a chain with a sickle attached at the end—hung from her waist. "I thought you were a big wet rat, climbing in the window."

"Ayame." I straightened cautiously, watching as the other shinobi sauntered to the window and pried the shuriken from the wood. We had been raised together since we were young, had gone through basic shinobi training together. It was hard to remember now, but she might have been my best friend. That was before the circle of majutsushi, the mages of the Shadow Clan, had chosen me to be the new bearer of Kamigoroshi, and I had been taken away for private instruction. I hadn't seen Ayame again until years down the road, and we had both changed. Now I was the Kage demonslayer, and she was a skilled shinobi. It made sense that she would be here now, watching and protecting from the shadows. "Where is Master Ichiro?"

"Here."

The door slid open and a man came into the room, making no sound as he stepped across the threshold. He could be described as unremarkable, a short, middle-aged man with features one could easily forget. All deliberately crafted on his part. He moved with a fluid grace that belied his humble appearance, and his sharp black eyes were as keen as a hawk's.

Ayame backed away, melting into the shadows once more. I sank to my knees and bowed, keeping my gaze on the floor as the man approached, feeling his stare on the back of my neck.

"Is it done?" he asked in a low voice.

"Yes, sensei," I replied without looking up.

"Hinotaka as well?"

"All the targets have been eliminated, sensei."

"Good." I felt him nod. "The clan will be pleased. Were you injured?"

"The jorogumo spit venom in my eyes," I answered, "but it's cleared."

He grunted. "You weren't paying attention, then. I told you spiders will spit when they're feeling cornered. Did you have to call on Hakaimono?"

"Yes."

*"Bakamono."* I felt a sharp, stinging blow upside my head, rocking me forward a bit. I had been expecting it and didn't move as Ichiro made a sound of disgust. "That's the second time in as many months, Tatsumi. You're getting careless."

I placed my hands on the floor and bowed even farther,

touching my forehead to the tatami mats. "Forgive me, sensei. I'll try harder next time."

"Keep making mistakes and there won't be a next time," Ichiro growled. "Keep using the demon's power and one day, you won't be able to control it. One slipup, one death that the clan didn't call for, and they *will* kill you, Tatsumi. And then I will have no choice but to commit seppuku for my failure in teaching you control."

"Now, Ichiro-san," came a new voice, high and breathy, and the sound of hakama trousers shushed into the room. "Don't be too hard on the boy. We told him to kill a dangerous, two-hundred-year-old yokai who has been feeding on men for centuries, and the traitorous lord who was plotting against the Kage. He's done his duty, and the clan is pleased."

I lifted my head, blinking as lantern light spilled over me, illuminating the stranger who had come into the room. Tall and reed-thin, he wore a black robe with swarms of white sakura blossoms, and a white silk fan was clutched between long fingers. The faintest wisp of a goatee graced a delicate jaw, and he lifted an eyebrow as thin as a line of ink, regarding me as one would a curious insect on the floor.

"So, this is our little demonslayer, is it?" The stranger cocked his head, holding his fan before his nose. I could sense he was smirking at me behind the silk. "How very... intriguing. Well, Ichiro-san, don't be rude. Aren't you going to introduce me?"

Ichiro sighed. "Tatsumi, this is Kage Masao," he said gruffly. "He honors us with his presence, as he is the chief advisor to Lady Hanshou herself."

*Lady Hanshou?* The Kage family daimyo? A flicker of surprise went through me. Lady Hanshou was the elusive leader of the Shadow Clan, a mysterious woman shrouded in legend and rumor, rarely seen or spoken of, lest her personal spies hear and take action. She almost never left her chambers in Hakumei Castle, and very few people had ever laid eyes on what lay beyond the castle doors. It was said Hanshou was surrounded by the deadliest shinobi in the land, a group so loyal that they cut out their own tongues to make certain they never betrayed her secrets. As for Hanshou herself, the darkest rumors claimed she was immortal, but not even her own clan knew much about her, who she was, even what she looked like. Most were content to let the mystery be.

"Don't look so shocked, Tatsumi-san." Masao closed his fan with a snap and steepled his long fingers together. "Lady Hanshou has been watching your exploits, and your continuous triumphs have gotten her attention. In fact, that is why I am here. She wishes to meet you in person, young demonslayer. I am to take you to her, tonight."

"So stop gaping like a landed fish," Ichiro snapped before I could say anything, "and go get yourself cleaned up. We can't have you meeting the daimyo of the Shadow Clan looking like a drowned rat."

I bowed to the two men and obeyed, slipping out of the room and down the steps to the first floor.

*I am to meet the daimyo of Kage, the leader of the Shadow Clan.* A ripple of what might've been apprehension went through my stomach. Immediately, Hakaimono stirred, intrigued by that flicker of emotion, and I coldly crushed it, telling myself to feel nothing. Intellectually, I knew this was a great honor; few were called into Lady Hanshou's presence, fewer could claim that the daimyo of the Shadow Clan had spoken to them face-to-face. My missions were passed to me through Ichiro and the other sensei; there was no reason the leader of the Kage would assign them to me in person. I'd heard of samurai earning rewards, recognition and honor through great deeds and acts of valor, but such opportunities were not granted to one such as I. I killed demons, monsters and yokai because that was the purpose of my existence. A weapon needed no praise or recognition to do its job.

So, why would Lady Hanshou want to see me?

A servant waited for me at the foot of the stairs, and I followed him into the small bath where, per normal, I was I met by a pair of Shadow Clan healers. Dressed in ash-gray robes, they greeted me with the same clinical detachment they showed at every post-mission examination.

"Remove your weapons and clothes," one told me in a bored tone, pointing to a stool in the middle of the room, "then sit. Let's get this over with quickly."

I obeyed, disarming myself of weapons—shuriken, grappling hook and the kunai throwing knives hidden in my bracers—before setting Kamigoroshi in the corner. The servant, as well as the two healers, stayed far away from the sword as I laid it down, as if it were some terrible beast that would savage them if given a chance. I knew they regarded me in much the same way. All Kage were aware of Kamigoroshi's curse and interacted with me as little as possible to avoid prodding the demon. When I was a child, it had been terribly lonely, the way everyone recoiled like I had the plague. Now, it meant nothing to me.

After peeling off my soaked black suit, I sat on the stool while the pair examined me. One tilted my head up to look at my eyes, while the other prodded my side, eliciting a sharp twinge of pain.

"Hmm," he muttered, digging his fingers into my skin, poking and pinching. I set my jaw and didn't make a sound. "One cracked rib, and several deep bruises along his side, nothing broken."

The other pulled down my eyelid, wrenching my head toward the light. "Traces of venom in his eyes, not enough to blind, fortunately. Did the jorogumo bite you?" he asked me.

"No."

"So your innards aren't turning to soup as we speak, good to hear. And you managed to keep most of your blood on the inside this time, well done. It becomes very tiresome when you continuously show up half-dead in the middle of the night." He released my chin and turned to gesture to the servant. "We're done here. Bathe him, bandage the cuts and send him to Master Ichiro when you're finished."

The servant bowed silently as the healers left the room, then picked up the bucket sitting beside the stool and dumped it over my head. The frigid water drenched my hair and seemed to rake talons of ice over my skin, but I didn't move as the servant sluiced the dirt and grime from my body, scrubbing my wounds until the flesh around them turned pink. When I was clean, he sloshed another bucket of water over my head, bandaged the cuts and left without a word.

Standing, I gazed around and saw that another servant had left a change of clothes on the edge of the tub: a pair of hakama trousers, a dove-gray obi sash and a black haori jacket bearing a white crescent eclipsed by a dark moon—the crest of the Shadow Clan—on the back.

Ichiro and Masao waited for me in the next room, speaking quietly with a pair of sake cups between them. I didn't see Ayame, but I knew she was close. My sensei only grunted as I knelt on tatami mats and bowed low, but I could feel Kage Masao watching me with an almost predatory smile as I touched my forehead to the floor.

"There you are," Ichiro remarked as I raised my head. "Well, you look like a dog chewed on you, but at least you no longer resemble a drowned rat. Masao-san has a pair of kago waiting outside to take you across town. Are you ready?"

"Yes, sensei."

"Excellent!" Masao-san rose in a fluttering of robes and fan. "Come then, little demonslayer. We mustn't keep Hanshou-sama waiting."

He swept out of the room. I rose to follow, but Ichiro grabbed my arm as I passed him, rough fingers digging into my flesh as he leaned close.

"Listen to me, boy," he growled, as I went still in the grip of my sensei. "You are about to meet the most important person in the Kage, the leader of the Shadow Clan herself. Do *not* embarrass me. If you dishonor me in front of the lady, I assure you, the beating you took tonight will feel like a massage compared to what I will do to you. Do you understand?"

"Yes, Master Ichiro."

"Remember what we taught you. Repeat it to me, now."

"I am nothing," I said automatically. "I am a weapon in the hands of the Kage. My life exists only to be the bearer of Kamigoroshi and to obey the orders of the Shadow Clan."

"Good." He nodded and released me. "See that you remember when speaking to the lady. Now go."

Kage Masao stood on the covered veranda, gazing distastefully at the rain, a colorful parasol held over his head. A pair of kago—individual palanquins made of lacquered wood and carried by four trained bearers—waited at the bottom of the steps. I had never ridden in a kago; they were usually reserved for nobles and important individuals, not lowly assassins. But, glancing at Kage Masao and his flowing robes, I realized he had not traveled here by horse and certainly not on foot.

"What horrible weather." He sighed, bringing his fan to his face, as if the rain itself offended him. "Fitting for this backwater little town. I shall be glad to be done with it." Glancing at me, he offered a bright smile and gestured to a kago. "Well, Tatsumi-san? Shall we be off?"

The ride was fairly short, as the town wasn't large, and soon the servants were sliding back the door of the kago, revealing a large, two-story ryokan—an inn—looming at the edge of the muddy road. Inside, I followed Masao up the stairs to a room at the end of a corridor and waited in the hall while he entered. A moment later, a servant slid back the door, releasing a few wisps of gray smoke, and beckoned me inside. The room beyond was cloaked in shadow and smelled of incense and tobacco. Cautiously, I stepped through the door and as it slid shut behind me, I dropped to my knees and pressed my forehead to the tatami mats.

"Kage Tatsumi," Masao purred. "The demonslayer."

"Come forward, boy," a voice rasped, startling me with its harshness. "Come into the light. Let me see the bearer of the legendary Kamigoroshi."

Blinking away smoke, I raised my head and inched forward on my knees, squinting to see past the lamp that burned on the edge of a low table. Sake bottles lined the polished surface like ranks of warriors protecting their general, and incense hung thick in the air, smelling of smoke and sandalwood.

Peering past the haze and the bottles, I caught a glimpse

of the speaker and clenched my jaw to stop the sharp inhalation of breath. Only years of training and practice kept my features expressionless. It seemed as if Lady Hanshou's face had been flayed, beaten and left out in the sun to burn before being set back on her sunken neck. Folds of skin hung from her sticklike arms; her hands were wizened bird's claws, one of them clutching a long-handled pipe as if it was her lifeline to the living world. A few wispy white threads were still attached to her scalp, floating on the air like spider silk. One milky eye was half-shut, the other burned with such intensity that it bordered on madness.

Lady Hanshou smiled a wide, toothless grin at my silence. "Not quite what you were expecting, eh, demonslayer?" she cackled. "Keep staring, but this face isn't going to get any prettier." Immediately, I pressed my face to the tatami mats again, but Lady Hanshou let out a snort. "Oh, get up, boy," she snapped, sounding impatient. "Let me look you in the eyes. Merciful Kami, you're young," she exclaimed as I rose. "How old are you, boy? Fourteen?" Without waiting for an answer, she swatted Kage Masao's leg with the back of her hand. "Masao-san! How old is he now?"

"He is seventeen, my lady."

"Is he?" Hanshou's face took on an expression that could have passed for surprise. "He looks younger than that. Ah, but you all look like babies to me." She groped for a sake bottle, somehow managing to leave the empty ones undisturbed. Masao took the bottle and poured her a cup of the rice wine, which she downed in a single gulp, then held the cup out for more.

"You hide your disgust well." With a start, I realized she was speaking to me. Her unclouded eye rolled up to fix me with a bright, intense stare. "Better than Ichiro-san, his lurking little pupil, or even Masao-san here. I was not always like this, you know." She sniffed and blew out a cloud of smoke, which curled around me like grasping tendrils. "Once, I was so beautiful Emperor Taiyo no Gintaro himself wished to make me his bride, and pined after me when I refused."

I did not know that emperor's name. Taiyo no Genjiro was the current emperor ruling from the Golden Palace, and Taiyo no Eiichi was the emperor before him. Not knowing what to say, I remained silent. Hanshou eyed me, her voice turning sly, her lips twisted into a leer. "I could have stolen even your affection, demonslayer," she stated in a raspy voice. "Made you lust after me as the demon in your sword lusts for battle. You would not have been able to resist. What do you think of that?"

Masao cleared his throat. "My lady, time grows short," he said. "You will not be able to remain out in this weather much longer. We need to return to Hakumei Castle tonight."

Hanshou pouted. "Oh, very well," she sighed. "I suppose I shouldn't tease the boy any longer. But you're no fun at all, Masao-san." Sitting a little straighter, she stuck the pipe in her mouth and glared down her nose at me. "Kage demonslayer, I have called you here personally for a very important task. Tonight, I will send you on the mission you were born for."

She gestured, and Masao came forward to lay several sheets of paper on the table before me. I picked them up. A few were travel documents with the Kage daimyo's seal; papers that let you pass through the territories of the other clans without being detained at the checkpoints. I was surprised, but only for a moment. Technically, the land was at peace. The last emperor had forbidden open warfare, and the clans had been enjoying a rare period of calm between centuries of fighting and bloodshed. Recently however, it had flared up again, surprising no one. There was too much animosity, too many grudges and feuds and personal vendettas between the Great Clans; all it would take was a single aggressive act, an insult that could not be ignored, and the daimyos would be at each other's throats again. If I was discovered sneaking through a rival clan's territory without permission, that might be the act of aggression needed to declare war. And though I was certain I could do it without being caught, I understood Lady Hanshou's precaution.

The other paper was a scroll that, when smoothed out, displayed a map of the mountains somewhere in Earth Clan territory. A river snaked across the map, cutting through forest and plains, heading north. I thought I recognized it as the Hotaru Kawa, the river that eventually led to Kin Heigen Toshi, the great capital city in the center of Sun Clan territory. The capital, however, was not my destination. By the *X* marked at the top of the largest mountain peak, I assumed that was my target.

"The Silent Winds temple sits atop the Niwaki Mountains on the eastern edge of Tsuchi lands," Lady Hanshou said, confirming my suspicion. "You will go to the gates posing as a pilgrim, asking to spend the night. If they let you in, so much the better. If not, you will infiltrate the temple some other way. It doesn't matter how you get in, only that you find what you were sent for."

"Understood," I replied. A temple full of monks was not my normal mark; most orders were peaceful, reflective organizations that stayed neutral from the politics and fighting of the clans. But it was not my place to question my daimyo. "Who is my target?"

"This is not a killing," Lady Hanshou replied, to my immense surprise. "I am sending you to retrieve an item for me. I would rather there not be slaughter, but there could be instances where your particular talents will come in handy. I am sending you, Tatsumi, because Ichiro believes that among your fellow shinobi, you are the best, and getting to the item might prove challenging, even for one such as yourself." Her good eye narrowed, her words becoming harsh. "But it is *imperative* that you retrieve the item. I don't care what it takes, who you have to kill. Do not dare to return without it—that is an order from your daimyo." Her voice grew even harsher, becoming a raspy growl that send a chill up my back. "Kage demonslayer, know that if you fail me, the consequences will be dire. We will be watching you, and the Shadow Clan does not tolerate disobedience. Do you understand?"

"My lady, my life is bound to the Kage." I bowed low once more, reciting the words that were expected. It didn't matter if I meant them; they were true nonetheless. "And to you. I will not fail. Only tell me what I am searching for, and it will be done. What must I retrieve?"

Lady Hanshou's eye burned feverishly bright in the darkened room, and her lips curved in a faint smile. "A certain scroll I lost," she whispered, "years and years ago."

# 4

## Tanuki Tea

*I* hated lighting the candles in the main hall.

Two hundred and seventy-seven. There were two hundred and seventy-seven candles that had to be lit, individually, around the room. Every evening, before sundown, so the monks could hold their nightly meditations. I don't remember when it officially became my duty to light the candles; I suspected Denga or Nitoru had suggested the idea to Master Jin, the old monk who cared for the hall, to "teach me patience and dedication." Certainly, you had to have both for this task. The main hall was enormous, with towering pillars and dark wood floors polished to such a sheen that you could see every flickering candle flame within. At the end of the hall stood the enormous green statue of the Jade Prophet, whose teachings all monks sought to emulate. There were no windows, and the only natural light came through the massive wooden doorway at the entrance, so the chamber was constantly dark and quiet. When all the candles were lit, they created a hazy orange glow throughout the room, transforming the hall into a surreal haven of shadow and dancing lights.

But it took forever to light them all.

I sighed, lowering the candlestick to gaze mournfully around the room. So many more to go. I hadn't even reached the thirty or so candles on the altar. If only there was a way to light them all at once...

I paused, and a grin spread across my face at the idea. Actually, I *could* light them all at once. I was kitsune, after all. Kitsune-bi was fire, wasn't it? Heatless, magical fire, but much easier to manipulate than normal flames. The monks wouldn't like it, of course. Nitoru and Denga definitely would not approve, but then, they didn't approve of anything I did.

I blew out the candle in my hand, then set it on the floor. Rising, I half closed my eyes, brought my open palm before my face and called on my magic.

A ghostly, blue-white flame sputtered to life between my fingers. It flickered and danced harmlessly against my skin, casting eerie shadows over the walls and pillars, growing steadily larger until I cupped a glowing sphere of foxfire. For just a moment, I saw my shadow on the wall of the temple: a human figure with pointed ears and a bushy tail rippling behind it.

Raising my head, I flung my hand out in an arc, and kitsune-bi scattered in all directions, tiny flames that flew across the room like falling stars. Lowering my arm, I observed my handiwork smugly. The hall now glowed with blue-white foxfire, luminescent flames that hovered on the end of candlewicks. In my opinion, it was much prettier than ordinary fire, though it did give the chamber a rather eerie, ghostly feel.

But more important, all the candles were lit. And it was still a good hour until evening meditations. I was free until then. Dusting my hands, I headed for the exit.

Voices outside made me freeze. I sidled along the wall to the door and peeked through the frame. Jin was walking up the steps toward the main hall and worse, Denga was beside him.

*Oh no.* My ears flattened in alarm, and I backed swiftly away. If they caught me, I'd probably get a lecture: maybe on the value of *patience* and *dedication to one's task.* Maybe they'd forbid me from using magic again. At the very least, they'd make me start over, lighting every candle one by one, under supervision this time.

*Hiding place. I need a hiding place, quickly.*

I hurried to the far wall and, with a whispered apology, ducked behind the enormous statue of the Jade Prophet, just as a furious shout rang from the entrance.

"Foxfire!" Denga's footsteps stalked into the room, and I peeked from behind the statue to watch him. The kitsune-bi cast a flickering white glow over his outraged face as he whirled, gesturing furiously. "The demon girl lit the candles with foxfire! Of all the…" He sputtered with rage. "When I find her—"

"Now, Denga-san." Jin's voice echoed behind Denga, calm and amused. "She is just a child, after all, and a kitsune at that. She does not understand."

"No." Denga spun one more time, glaring around the hall, before he turned and marched back toward the exit. "This has gone far enough. It's become perfectly clear that she is more fox than mortal, that her yokai nature is overshadowing her humanity. Something must be done. I'll not stand for her pranks any longer."

Jin blinked, watching him depart. "What are you planning to do, Denga-san?"

"Speak to Master Isao and convince him to put a binding on her," Denga replied, making my stomach twist. His voice drifted up the steps as he left the hall. "Seal away that infernal fox magic for good. Before we wake up and find a true demon in our midst."

My heart pounded. Jin watched Denga storm off, then sighed and began blowing out the kitsune-bi flames above the candles. He extinguished them one at a time, slowly and deliberately, his entire attention focused on his task. He would be done in a few minutes, but I did not want to stay here any longer, in case Denga returned with Master Isao and made good on his promise. Trying to slip out while Jin was in the room would likely get me caught, but I had one last, supremely forbidden, trick up my sleeve.

At the statue's base, I knelt, dug my fingers between a certain board and lifted it away, revealing a narrow hole that led under the floor of the main hall. It was too small for a human, even a petite human, to fit through. But I wasn't just human. I was also kitsune.

Closing my eyes, I summoned my power once more, feeling my heart start to pound with anticipation. Most fox magic was illusion and trickery, just as Denga had said. Images laid over truth, making you see and hear things that weren't there. Flawless copies, but no more substantial than a reflection in a mirror. But there was one form that I could shapeshift into for real, though I was forbidden from using it without permission.

Today seemed a good day to break all the rules.

My body grew warm, and I experienced the abrupt sensation of shrinking rapidly, along with the familiar cloud of white smoke. When I opened my eyes, I was much closer to the floor. Sounds were sharper, shadows nearly nonexistent, and the air was alive with new smells: the musty earth, the sharp tang of metal and the hint of candle smoke still in the air. In the blurred reflection in the statue's pedestal, a pointed muzzle and golden eyes stared back at me, a bushy, white-tipped tail curled around its legs.

Master Isao did not approve of me being a fox. *You are human*, he'd told me on more than one occasion. *Yes, you are kitsune, but being Yumeko is much harder than being a fox. If you spend too much time in that body, someday you might forget what it means to be mortal.*

I wasn't quite sure what he meant by that and right now, it didn't matter. Ducking my head, I slipped easily into the hole, glided beneath the floorboards and came out beneath the veranda. After making sure no monks, and especially Master Isao, were nearby, I headed into the garden, to the old maple tree leaning against the temple walls. Fox paws were quick and nimble, and the wood was very rough; I scurried up the gnarled trunk, dropped to the other side and escaped into the cool stillness of the forest.

Later that evening, I was sitting on a flat rock beside my favorite quiet pond, dangling my bare feet in the water, as I pondered what to do next. Jewellike dragonflies zipped over the mirrorlike surface, and small whiskered fish swam lazily below my feet, eyeing my human-again toes. The sun had warmed the rock, and a breeze whispered through the bamboo grove surrounding the pond. It was a good place to forget your troubles, and I often came here when life at the temple got too dull, or when I was hiding from Denga. Normally, the water, the breeze and the fish could erase my worries in no time. But today, I couldn't forget what had been said in the temple hall.

*Seal away my magic?* Just like that? Make it so I couldn't weave illusions, change my shape, or call upon my foxfire? That seemed excessive. I'd never actually *hurt* anything with my pranks, except Denga's pride. And maybe a sliding panel or two.

I glanced at my reflection in the water. A girl with pointed ears and yellow eyes stared back, bushy tail curled behind her. *She is more fox than mortal*, Denga had raged as he'd stormed out of the hall this evening. *Her yokai nature is overshadowing her humanity.*

"That's not true," I told the kitsune staring back at me. "I'm still mostly human. At least, I think I am."

"Talking to yourself, little fox cub?"

I glanced up. A squat old woman was making her way slowly around the edge of the pond. She wore a ragged robe, a wide-brimmed straw hat and tall wooden sandals that sank into the grass as she minced along the bank. In one gnarled hand she held a bamboo pole, resting on a shoulder; the other gripped a cluster of tiny fish dangling from a string. Her eyes glimmered yellow beneath the brim of her hat as she looked up at me.

I smiled. "Good evening, Tanuki-baba," I greeted politely. "What are you doing out here?"

The old woman snorted and raised the cluster of fish. "Planting flowers, what does it look like?"

I frowned in confusion. "But...those are fish. Why would you be planting flowers, Tanuki-baba? You don't eat them."

"Exactly. Some of us actually have to work for our food, unlike some spoiled, naive half foxes I won't name." She eyed me from under her hat, raising a thin gray eyebrow. "But what are *you* doing out so late, cub? Those humans of yours don't like it when you wander off." She chuckled, showing a flash of yellow teeth. "Is Denga-san on the warpath? Did you turn the cat into a teakettle again?"

"No, not in a long time—it scratches me when I try to put a leaf on its head. But..." I shivered, clutching at my arms. The sun-warmed rock suddenly felt cold. "Denga-san was angry," I told her. "More than I've ever seen before. He said I was more yokai than human, and that Master Isao should put a binding on me. What if Master Isao listens to him? What if he really does seal off my magic? I..." I faltered, feeling my stomach twist at the thought losing my power. "I can't imagine having no magic. It would be worse than cutting off my fingers or plucking out my eyes. If that happens, what will I do?"

Tanuki-baba snorted. "Come," she said, gesturing down the trail with the end of her bamboo rod. "I'll make you some tea."

I hopped down and followed the hunched form away from the pond, onto the narrow winding path through the bamboo forest. Her pole bobbed as she walked, and the tip of a bushy brown tail peeked from beneath the hem of her robe. I pretended not to notice, just as I knew she pretended not to see *my* ears and tail. It was an unspoken rule among yokai; one did not call attention to their...yokai-ness if one did not want be haunted, harassed, or cursed with extremely bad luck. Not that I was afraid Tanuki-baba would do so. To me she had always been a grandmotherly old yokai, and the stories of the tricks she used to play on humans when she was a young tanuki were always entertaining, if sometimes scary.

We emerged from the bamboo into a deeper, darker part of the forest. Here, ancient trees grew close together, intertwining branches nearly shutting out the sun. Thin streams of light cut weakly through the leaves, dappling the forest floor, and the air had a still, almost reverent feel. Curious kodama, the tree spirits of the forest, peered at us from behind leaves or followed us down the trail, their ethereal green bodies no larger than my finger.

Tanuki-baba led me along a familiar babbling brook, over a tiny arched bridge that was being eaten by toadstools and fungi, and toward a wooden hut that had been completely swallowed by moss. Long, long ago, she'd said, it had belonged to a yamabushi, a wandering priest who sought harmony and balance within nature, who could see and communicate directly with the kami. But that mortal had moved on or died, and the hut was now hers. Part of the thatched roof had fallen in and trees and brush surrounded it; if you didn't know there was a dwelling there, you might miss it in the vegetation. The interior, as always, was a mess, with junk piled in every corner and along every wall.

"Sit," Tanuki-baba gruffed, gesturing to a low wooden table in the center of the floor, the only clear space in the room. "I'll make us some tea—assuming I can find the pot, that is."

There were two or three teapots resting in different places throughout the clutter. I didn't say anything, because my suggestions were always met with refusal. *That* teapot was cracked, or dirty, or had a family of birds living in it. No, the *right* teapot was here, somewhere, and only she could find it. I knelt at the wooden table until Tanuki-baba finally stumbled upon what she was looking for, an ancient and dinged iron pot, and yanked it out of the pile.

"Empty," she sighed, peering in the top. "That's good, I suppose. No mice this time. Means I have to fill it up, though. I'll be right back," she told me, waddling out again. "Don't touch anything."

I waited patiently, rolling little flames of kitsune-bi across the table surface, while Tanuki-baba filled the teapot, set it on the brazier and lit the coals at the bottom. She then bustled about the room, taking things from the clutter along the walls and muttering to herself. Finally, she returned to the table with the teapot, two chipped cups and a tray bearing the fish she had caught, still raw and unscaled, laid out in a row.

"Ahhh," she sighed, settling onto the threadbare pillow opposite me. After several moments of shifting around and making herself comfortable, she took off her hat and tossed it in a corner, where it blended into the clutter. Politely, I dropped my gaze, careful not to glance at the round, furry ears that poked up from the top of her gray head. "Go on and pour the tea, cub," Tanuki-baba ordered, waving a hand at the pot and cups. "At least make yourself useful."

I carefully poured a thin green liquid into the two cups, then offered one to her. She took it with a crooked smile and set it down before her.

"You don't mind if I switch forms while we eat, do you?" she asked, eyeing the tray of fish in the center of the table. "This body is more useful for tea-making, but I'd rather be comfortable in my own house."

I shook my head. "Not at all, Tanuki-baba. Please do."

She snorted, raised her head and shook herself. Dust flew everywhere, rising from her body like a cloud, swirling into the room. I sneezed, turning away from the explosion, and when I glanced back, a furry brown creature with a dark mask and a bushy tail sat where the old woman had been. I set a teacup in front of her, and she picked it up with two dark brown paws before raising it to her narrow muzzle.

"Ah, much better." She put the cup down with a clink and snatched a fish from the tray, tossing the whole thing into her jaws before crunching down with sharp yellow teeth. "Now," she continued, as I sipped my tea. It was far more bitter than I liked, but it wasn't polite to say so. "Tell me then, cub. What kind of trouble have you gotten into with those humans of yours?"

Briefly, I told her about my trick with the candles this evening, and how it had infuriated the monks, particularly Denga-san. When I got to the part about Denga wanting Master Isao to seal away my magic, Tanuki-baba gave a violent snort and nearly knocked over her teacup.

"Ridiculous," she growled, taking the last fish and biting into it with the snapping of delicate bones. "Binding a yokai's magic, hah! It is blasphemous to even suggest such a thing. I wouldn't put up with that sort of nonsense."

"What should I do, Tanuki-baba?"

"Well, I know what *I* would do in that situation," Tanuki-baba said, an evil look crossing her masked face. "But you're probably too young for such chaos. And the solution is obvious, is it not? You need to leave."

"The monks don't like that," I said. "They're always very cross when I run off like this. I'll probably get a scolding when I return tonight."

"No," Tanuki-baba growled. "You need to leave…and not go back."

"You mean…leave the temple permanently?"

"Of course." The old yokai gestured to the door of her hut. "Do you think the temple is the only place you can live? And that the monks' way of life is the only one?" Her muzzle wrinkled. "There's a whole huge world out there, cub. Full of wonder, riches, chaos and things you can't even imagine. You're wasting both your life and your talents, staying behind those temple walls, listening to humans drone on about morality. A kitsune is not meant to be caged. Don't you want to get out there and see what you're missing?"

Something inside me stirred, the yearning, intrigue and curiosity for the world beyond the walls rising to the surface again. I did want to know what was out there. I wanted to see the places Master Isao spoke of—the sprawling cities and tangled wilderness not meant for human feet. I ached to visit Kin Heigen Toshi, the great golden capital, and travel to the top of Finger of God Mountain, the highest peak in Iwagoto, which was said to touch the sky. I wanted to see samurai and merchants, nobles and peasants, geisha and bandits, and farmers and fishermen. I wanted to see it all.

And, in a tiny thought that I barely admitted even to myself, I was tired of always having my magic restricted. To practice fox magic only under supervision, or to be punished whenever I used it for pranks, jokes, or to get out of work. If I was truly free, there would be no limitations; I could use my kitsune powers however I wanted.

But to do that, I would have to leave behind the monks, the temple and the only life I'd ever known. And while the order of the Silent Winds temple was small, confining and rigid, it was also safe. I was just one kitsune, not even a full-blooded yokai. I wasn't quite ready to be that brave.

"I can't leave, Tanuki-baba," I told the hunched figure across the table. "Where would I go? How would I live?"

Tanuki-baba blinked. "What do you mean, how would you live?" she snapped. "You're *kitsune*, girl! You'd go where you want. You live however you like."

"I'm only half kitsune," I pointed out. "And I've been with the monks my whole life. I don't know how to be a fox."

"Don't know how to be a fox?" Tanuki-baba threw back her head and cackled. Flecks of spittle flew from her narrow jaws as she laughed, shaking her head. "Poor little kitsune," she mocked. "You've lived with these humans for too long, letting their mortality infect you." She chuckled, giving me a look of exasperation. "You are a *fox*. You don't have to learn how to be kitsune. You just are."

"But—"

"And don't give me any excuses about your 'human' side." Tanuki-baba curled a lip, showing sharp yellow teeth. "Even a drop of yokai blood is enough to suppress any hints of humanity, if you want it to. You just have to choose to be more kitsune than mortal."

Choose to be more kitsune? How did I do that? Was there a ritual for it? I thought back to what Denga-san had said this evening, about my yokai nature overshadowing my humanity. Was that what the monks were afraid of? Did they fear I would turn into a nogitsune, an evil wild fox that delighted in fear and chaos and preyed on humans whenever it could?

I swallowed hard. "But what if I don't want to be more kitsune?" I asked, making Tanuki-baba frown. "What if I'm happy as a human and a fox?"

She sniffed. "Then you are a fool," she stated bluntly. "And you are fighting a losing battle. It is very hard to be human, little fox. Even the humans themselves don't do a great job of it. The mortal world is full of hatred, betrayal, sadness and death. Most yokai and kami alike find that it is too much for them. Everything the humans think they value—love, honor, empathy, compassion—we yokai need nothing of those, especially when they so often lead to suffering and despair. It is far easier to abandon everything that is human and just be kitsune. The world of spirits and yokai is far less complicated than the world of men."

"I don't understand, Tanuki-baba."

"Of course not." Tanuki-baba shook her shaggy head, but did not elaborate. "You are a cub, with no sense of the world. But you will learn. If you continue to try to balance your two natures, you will. And in time, when you finally experience what the human world is truly like, you will decide that being a fox is much less difficult than being human." She glanced down at the table, nostrils twitching. "But now, our teacups are empty, and the fish is gone. That means it is time for bed."

I rose and bowed to the ancient tanuki. One did not question the habits or behaviors of yokai as old as she. "I should go home," I said, taking a step back. "The monks will probably be waiting with a lecture. Thank you for the tea and the conversation, Tanuki-baba."

"Fox cub," the old yokai called as I reached the door. I glanced back to see the squat, furry creature sitting in the squalor of her house, watching me with eyes that glowed yellow in the shadows. "You walk a thin line, little kitsune," she said, and her voice was a warning, though I didn't know from what. "The place between the spirit realm and the mortal realm is a difficult one, indeed. Remember, you can always give up your humanity if things become too hard. It is far easier for a kitsune, even a half kitsune, to abandon it than one who is fully mortal."

I still didn't know what she meant by that, so I simply nodded and left, slipping into the dim quiet of the woods.

Immediately, I knew something was wrong.

In the time I had spent in Tanuki-baba's home, night had fallen, and the forest had gone deathly still. Instead of birdsong or the rustle of small creatures scampering through the undergrowth, an ominous silence hung in the air. The forest kami had vanished like they'd never been, leaving empty, lifeless woods behind. And a new scent was creeping through the trees, raising the hairs on the back of my neck. The sharp, acrid scent of smoke.

I sprinted through the forest, retracing my steps past the hollow, the stream and the bamboo grove, until I reached the pond. The green-and-silver wall opened up, showing the night sky with a faded crescent moon overhead and a smear of crimson sinking into the west.

My heart twisted. A dark smudge was rising over the tree line, coiling and ominous, like a terrible black dragon. It snaked into the air, blotting out the stars, coming from the direction of…

"Home."

# 5

## Demons in the Bamboo

*I* was close.

Even on horseback, it had taken me several days to reach Earth Clan territory and the Niwaki Mountains where the Silent Winds temple was said to be located. The tiny farming community in the valley below the forested peaks stared at me, wide-eyed, as I rode past terraced fields and thatched huts, following the path that snaked toward the mountains. A pair of small children trailed behind my horse, palpably curious and getting steadily closer, until they were snatched away by worried-looking adults. Traveling samurai were likely rare to this part of the valley, members of the Shadow Clan even more so, and farmers naturally gave the warrior class a wide berth. For this mission, I was dressed in the part of a Kage samurai, in hakama trousers and a black haori jacket, the crest of the Shadow Clan on my back. My shinobi gear was tucked into the saddlebags of my horse in case I needed it, though a shadow warrior never revealed himself to outsiders. If I was denied entry at the gates, I would slip over the walls and infiltrate the temple as silently as a yurei ghost, but for now, I was a samurai on a warrior's pilgrimage, seeking wisdom at the shrines across Iwagoto.

A thin farmer wearing a ragged tunic and a cloth tied around his forehead bowed low as I passed, dropping his gaze to the dirt. I pulled the horse to a stop and glanced down at him, or rather, at the top of his bald head.

"Is the Silent Winds temple nearby?" I asked softly. The man didn't look up, only bobbed once at the waist, his eyes on his sandaled feet as he replied.

"*H-hai*, my lord! The temple is right up this path, at the top of the mountain."

"Thank you."

I gave the horse a nudge and continued on, leaving the farmers and the village behind. The path became a narrow, twisting trail that grew more treacherous the farther it wound through the forest. I surmised that the monks of this temple rarely received, or encouraged, visitors. Perhaps they simply wished to meditate and study in peace, far removed from the chaos of the world, or perhaps they were hiding—protecting—something.

As night fell and the shadows grew long, the trail nearly vanished, melting into the brush and thick undergrowth, as if the forest itself took offense to intruders. But I had been trained to spot the hidden and the invisible, and darkness was no hindrance for me. I continued, passing bamboo groves and huge trees strung with sacred rope, signifying they were home to the kami.

In my head, Hakaimono stirred. I pulled the horse to

a stop and sat, motionless, trying to hear past the labored breaths of the animal beneath me. Around us, the woods were silent and still, evening shadows cloaking all but a few spots of mottled red sunlight.

Very slightly, I opened myself up to the sword and felt the terror in the woods around me, the rapid heartbeats of many living things. Coming toward us? There was a rustle in the bushes ahead, and my horse froze, every muscle taut.

With an eruption of leaves and vegetation, a herd of spotted deer leaped out of the trees and bounded toward me, causing my pulse to spike and my horse to rear up with a squeal. I kept my seat as the animal tried to bolt, squeezing with my knees and pulling back the reins, managing to bring it under control. It snorted and trembled, ears pinned to its skull, as the deer sprang past us and continued into the forest. Hakaimono flared, and I shoved the demon's presence down, as well.

As the horse calmed, I breathed cautiously and caught the hint of smoke on the wind. I gazed through the canopy overhead, saw a curl of blackness rising over the treetops and kicked the horse into motion. We sped down the trail, Hakaimono pulsing eagerly in my mind, knowing violence was not far away, and death would soon follow.

The air grew hazy and sharp, smelling of burning timber, and my stomach clenched. Looking up, I saw a faint crimson glow against the sky. Small forest creatures, rabbits, squirrels and others, fled through the undergrowth, going in the opposite direction, and my horse began to balk, fighting my orders to continue. Grimly, I set my heels to its ribs and continued, knowing it wasn't the fire that was spooking it. Something was here, in the forest. And whatever it was, I couldn't allow it to hinder my mission. I had to get to the scroll.

As we reached a narrow, half-eroded flight of steps through a bamboo forest, a kama sickle flew from the bushes, spinning end over end, and struck my mount in the neck. As the horse screamed and fell, crashing to the steps, I sprang from the saddle and rolled, feeling the jarring impact through my shoulder, then came to my feet several yards away.

A flood of small grotesque creatures spilled from the bamboo forest, cackling and waving spears and crude blades. They swarmed the horse, leaping atop its back, shrieking and poking as it struggled to its feet. Panicked, the mortally wounded horse fled, bucking wildly down the path with its demonic passengers clinging to the saddle, while the rest of the horde spun on me.

*Amanjaku?* I felt a ripple of both shock and unease, even as Hakaimono flared excitedly at so many things to kill. I had dealt with them in the past, but never in these numbers. How were there so many?

I drew Kamigoroshi as the demons shrieked, baring their fangs, and attacked. One sweep split the first wave in half, severing heads and torsos, and the amanjaku howled as they were sent back to Jigoku. Leaping forward, I dodged a spear thrust at me, stabbed a demon in the eye and beheaded another as I yanked the blade out. Then I was in their midst, and it was nothing but teeth and claws and flashing blades. I gave myself over to the dance of death, Hakaimono's unrestrained glee surging through my veins.

With alarmed shrieks and howls, the remaining amanjaku scattered into the bamboo forest, their small forms fading quickly from view. Panting, I lowered Kamigoroshi and looked around, wondering where they'd come from, who had brought them here. Amanjaku were minor demons of Jigoku; they couldn't appear out of nowhere, but the blood magic needed to summon them was a dangerous power that was strictly forbidden throughout the empire. The key component to working the magic of Jigoku was, of course, blood. Sometimes it required other things: souls, organs, body parts, but mostly it called for the life force that ran through all mortal veins. The larger, more powerful the spell, the more blood was required to successfully cast it.

But, the dangerous catch was, it didn't have to come from the practitioner. Jigoku didn't care whose blood was spilled, be it man, woman or child, as long as it was human, and as long as the price was paid. Although, as befitting the realm of evil and corruption, the more you cared for the person whose blood was being spilled, the more powerful the magic that came of it. A lover, brother or child whom you betrayed would bestow far more power than a nameless stranger. This was the reason the empire forbade blood magic, why practicing the dark arts was an immediate death sentence. Even a single amanjaku required a blood sacrifice to draw it into the mortal realm; I couldn't imagine the amount an entire horde would call for.

I didn't know *who* had summoned the demons, but I could certainly guess *why.* After sheathing Kamigoroshi, I sprinted up the trail, heading for the temple and hoping I wasn't too late.

# 6

## The Flames of Despair

The temple was on fire.

I burst out of the forest, panting, staring in horror at the bright orange flames snapping against the night sky. The elegant, four-tiered pagoda roofs were ablaze, a roaring, savage inferno, the stench of smoke, ash and charred timbers scorching the air. Ripples of heat seared my skin as I approached the back wall, scrambled gracelessly to the top and dropped with a thump into the gardens.

*What did this? Who would dare?* I'd heard tales of the world beyond the temple walls, stories of warring clans and fierce, proud samurai. Tales of rival daimyo lords and their endless bickering, how they would declare war and hurl entire armies at each other over some imagined slight to their honor. But according to Master Isao, even the most savage, warmongering daimyo respected the monks, or at least, would not risk the kami's wrath by attacking a peaceful temple.

Unless they knew about the scroll.

A shriek turned my blood to ice, and I ducked behind a juniper tree. Peering around the trunk, trying not to inhale smoke and ash, I dug my nails into the bark to keep myself from gasping in terror.

A crowd of small grotesque…things were gibbering and dancing around the pond, silhouetted in the hellish light of the fires. At first, I thought they were misshapen children; they wore ratty tunics, had large, bulbous heads and stood barely past my knees. But then I saw the horns, the mouths full of pointed teeth, the tattered ears and jutting fangs. Their skin was either a mottled blue or red, and they carried crude weapons in their claws: kama sickles, spears and short knives.

My blood chilled. *Demons? Jinkei's mercy, why are demons here?* I had seen pictures of demons in the temple library, terrible red-or blue-skinned oni with horns, fangs and enormous clubs, who tormented the wicked souls sent to Jigoku. These creatures, stabbing the poor trapped carp swirling frantically around the pond, weren't as big as the monsters in the books, but I could tell they were demons nonetheless.

I clenched my fist against the trunk, feeling the bark dig into my knuckles. Why were demons here? Why were they attacking the temple? For the scroll? But I'd thought the creatures of Jigoku lived only for bloodshed and chaos; the scroll would mean nothing to demons. Unless something else, or someone else, was commanding them…

*This makes no sense. I have to find Master Isao. But first, I have to get past those demons.*

After plucking a leaf from the juniper tree, I slipped

around the trunk and placed the leaf on my head, drawing on my fox magic. For a moment, I found it horribly ironic that, just this afternoon, I'd been wishing to use my magic more often. My heart pounded, but I held the image of what I wanted in my mind, then released the magic over my body. There was a soundless explosion of smoke, and when I opened my eyes, my skin was a mottled red and my feet had hooked yellow claws on the ends of their toes.

With a deep breath, I stepped away from the tree, just as one of the demons at the pond looked up and spotted me.

It blinked for a moment, frowning, and I held my breath, hoping he saw what I wanted him to see: a fellow demon, red-skinned and hideous. I chanced a grin, baring crooked fangs, and the demon snorted, returning to its game of stabbing the carp. The once crystal clear water of the pond was now red with blood. Leaving the doomed fish to their fate, I hurried on.

The roar of the fire greeted me as I left the gardens, and clouds of swirling embers stung my skin as I passed the engulfed pagoda and ran toward the main hall, keeping to the bushes and shadows. An even bigger crowd of demons swarmed the building, waving torches and cavorting around the steps that led to the entrance. When I peeked through the leaves, my stomach gave a painful twist. A few yards away, a body lay sprawled on the stones of the courtyard, a pair of spears jutting from its chest, vacant eyes staring into nothing.

*Jin.* I clapped both hands over my mouth to keep the cry from escaping, feeling my eyes start to burn. Jin had always been kind to me, always patient and understanding, never growing irritated or raising his voice. And now he was gone. Behind the monk, I could see another pair of bodies lying in pools of blood, their faces turned away so I didn't recognize them in the shadows. But I would. As soon as I saw them clearly, I would know them.

Shaking, I lowered my arms and wrenched my gaze from the bodies. *I can't mourn them now*, I told myself, forcing back the blurriness in my eyes. *I have to keep going.* I wondered why none of the demons had gone into the building; the main entrance lay open and unguarded, since the hall had no doors to speak of. As I watched, a larger blue demon gave a raspy cry, lifted a wooden mallet above its head and rushed the door, scuttling toward the stairs. But as it reached the bottom step, there was a flash like a burst of lightning, and the demon bounced off like it had hit a stone wall, to the cackles and high-pitched laughter of the rest.

My eyes widened. *A ki barrier?* I had seen such a thing before; Master Isao had sometimes demonstrated the power of ki for the other monks, creating walls of force that could not be breached, or surrounding an object with an invisible barrier that made it impossible to touch the thing inside. But…a whole building? The amount of concentration that must require was unfathomable.

*Also, how am I supposed to get through? The barrier covers the whole building. Unless...*

My heart beat faster. Very powerful ki masters had such control over their ki that they could choose who could pass through the barrier and who could not. If Master Isao heard the demons coming and realized I wasn't at the temple, surely he would make it so I could pass through the barrier. Right?

Setting my jaw, I took a step away from the bushes, when a tremor went through the ground under my feet. Gazing back at the hall, I saw a massive horned shadow appear. My heart nearly stopped. Silhouetted against the flames, the beast walked slowly around the corner of the building, resolving itself into something huge and terrible.

*O...oni?* I stumbled backward in terror, watching as the enormous red creature lumbered toward the entrance, scattering smaller demons before it. Cold sweat trickled down my back as it came into view, fangs, horns and huge spiked club shining in the torchlight. *This* was the monster from the storybooks. Jigoku's most infamous denizens were the nightmares of legend, terrifying and near unstoppable. *Why...why is there an oni here? Why?*

But that was a stupid question. I already knew the answer: it was here for the scroll.

*Oh, why didn't I listen to Master Isao? When he told me about the scroll, and why it was so important, why didn't I listen?*

At the top of the steps, the oni paused, gazing toward the entrance of the hall, the heavy spiked tetsubo resting over one shoulder. Swinging the club in one hand, it prodded the barrier with the end of the weapon and watched the wall flicker and pulse with every poke. The smaller demons clustered around the oni's legs, waiting eagerly, their eyes glowing as red as the firelight. The oni snorted, rolled its massive shoulders and hefted its club in both hands.

It brought the tetsubo smashing down on the ki barrier, and the shock wave that pulsed out tossed the branches of the surrounding trees and sent the demon horde stumbling back. For a moment, the invisible dome shivered into view, rippling like a mirage before fading from sight again. I winced, wondering if the barrier would shatter, knowing that each blow was also an assault on the monks' concentration as they struggled to maintain their focus. The barrier held, but the oni raised the club to hit it again, and the horde cackled as they waited for it to fall.

I had to get inside, now.

*Kami protect me!* With a deep breath, I stepped from the bushes and walked as calmly as I could across the yard, praying my disguise would hold. Several demons glanced up, frowning, but most of their attention was diverted to the huge oni, who smashed its club into the barrier again. In the hellish light, the dome rippled, and I could see silver cracks creeping up the surface, making my blood run cold. It wouldn't hold much longer.

Wanting to avoid the massive oni, I slipped around the side of the building, breathing a sigh of relief as I ducked around the corner…and immediately collided with a demon sprinting the around the wall. Its blue bulbous head smacked into my stomach, driving the air from my lungs with the force of a ki punch. I reeled back and fell, gasping, and felt my hold on the illusion shatter in a puff of white smoke.

The demon, who had also been knocked back, rubbed its forehead with a claw, wincing, then glared at me. Its red eyes widened in shock as it saw, not a fellow demon, but a girl with furry ears and a tail, sitting there in the dirt. It leaped up with a howl and lunged, and I scrambled back, just managing to dodge the sword as it thunked into the spot where I had been.

Two more demons appeared from shadows: one holding a spear, the other brandishing a pair of kama sickles. They cackled as they spotted me and charged, while the blue demon continued to swipe at me with his blade. As the others closed in, I gave a snarl of frustration and hurled a ball of kitsune-bi into the blue demon's face.

It flinched back with a hiss, claws going to its eyes, as if

expecting to be burned. The blue-white flames flared bright for a moment, then faded harmlessly into nothing. But it gave me enough time to lunge past the demon, changing into a fox as I did, and dart beneath the veranda. There was a sharp tingle as I passed through the ki barrier, like a static shock along your whole body, and then the comforting darkness of the space beneath the hall closed around me. *Safe.*

My legs shook as I crawled beneath the floorboards, sliding over cold earth and pushing through webs, looking for the loose board that would lead behind the statue of the Prophet. Overhead, the booms of the oni's club shook the building, showering me with dust and causing spiders to flee in terror.

A sliver of orange light glimmered in the darkness ahead, illuminating a thin rectangle of dirt, and I hurried toward it. Squeezing between the planks, I clawed myself onto the floor of the great hall, the statue of the Jade Prophet looming overhead. I staggered away from the statue and looked around for Master Isao.

My stomach twisted. He sat before the statue of the Prophet, hands cupped in his lap, eyes closed and face serene. The rest of the monks sat around him, also in meditation, though I could see sweat pouring from their faces, their brows furrowed in concentration. Each time the oni's club hit the barrier outside, one of them would flinch, clenching his jaw or pressing his lips together. I saw Denga sitting behind Master Isao, a stream of red running from his nose as he fought to maintain the barrier. His eyebrows twitched with every blow, and his jaw was set, even as blood dripped from his chin to spatter his hands.

As I forced myself back to human form, Master Isao's eyes opened to gaze right at me. Smiling, as if this meeting was over the dinner table and I had come in late, he raised a hand and beckoned me forward.

"Ah, there you are, Yumeko-chan. I've been waiting for you."

"Master Isao!" I flung myself beside him. "What are we to do? The oni is almost through the barrier. How will we escape?"

"There is no escape," Master Isao said calmly, making my heart plummet. "Not for us. We have done our duty. But you, Yumeko-chan. You must continue it."

Horrified, I stared at him. "I don't… I don't understand, Master Isao," I whispered. "What do you mean, I must continue it? How?"

I trailed off, as the wizened monk reached into the sleeve of his robe and drew something into the light. A simple case, made of dark lacquered wood, a red silk ribbon wrapped around the cylinder. I gasped as he held it up.

"Is that…?"

"Take it, Yumeko-chan," Master Isao ordered, and held it out to me. "It must not fall into the hands of demons. You must keep it safe at all costs." Another boom rattled the beams overhead, and one of the monks behind us drew in a sharp breath. Master Isao's gaze never wavered from mine. "Take the scroll," he said again, "and leave this place. Run, and don't look back."

Frantically, I shook my head. "I can't," I whispered, as my eyes grew hot, tears welling in the corners. "I can't leave you. Where will I go? I don't know anything about the outside world. How can I keep the scroll safe?"

"Fox girl." Master Isao's voice was firm, and I blinked at him in shock. Though the other monks often used that phrase, he never called me anything related to my true nature. "Listen to me. There is something I have not told you, a piece of your past I must reveal. When you first came to us, in the fish basket with the note pinned to your blanket…" He paused, a shadow of regret passing through his eyes, so quick I might have imagined it. "I have told you most of what the letter said," Master Isao continued, "but not all. The part that you have not heard is this…"

His words echoed strangely in my head, like they were coming from a great distance away.

*Humble monks, I beg you to be patient and to not judge, for I have seen a vision of the future. In this vision, I have seen blood and flames and death, demons shrieking and rivers of bones, and the world grows dark with fear. But a single fox stands above it all, untouched, a great dragon cast in her shadow. Her name is Yumeko, child of dreams, for she is our hope against the coming darkness.*

My insides turned to ice. Master Isao smiled gently and raised the scroll once more. "So you see, Yumeko-chan," he said, "our fate was already foretold. Whoever left you at the gates of the temple knew this was coming, and that you would play a part in the tale, the fourth coming of the Dragon."

Numb, I stared at him, not really comprehending what he just told me. A thud echoed through the hall, and with a gasp, one of the monks behind us collapsed, holding his head. For the first time, a bead of sweat appeared on Master Isao's forehead and ran down his face. I shook myself out of my trance and clutched at his sleeve. "Why?" I whispered. "I'm not ready. Why does it have to be me?"

His withered hand closed over mine. "Because you are the only one who can do this. Listen carefully, Yumeko-chan." Master Isao squeezed my hand, and the strength in his fingers calmed me somewhat. "We are not alone in our mission, nor are we the only guardians. There is another temple, another order that guards a piece of the scroll. You must go to them. Warn them of what happened here. They will protect you, and the Dragon's prayer. It is their sacred duty to do so."

"Where are they?"

"I cannot tell you," Master Isao said. "I do not know, myself. It is a legendary place of myth and rumor, and its location has been lost to the ages. I know only its name—the Steel Feather temple. And that it is somewhere very far from here.

"But..." he added before I could protest in despair. "There is one who knows the location of the temple. You must travel to Kin Heigen Toshi, the capital city in the center of the Sun lands. Within the city is the Hayate shrine—go there and ask for the head priest, Master Jiro. He can tell you the location of the Steel Feather temple."

"Master..." Tears were running down my cheeks; my stomach was curling around itself in both terror and anguish. "I can't. I can't do it alone."

"You can," Master Isao said firmly, and held up the scroll once more. "You must. This is my last request. Take the scroll to the Steel Feather temple. Warn them of what transpired here, that someone wishes to bring the pieces of the Dragon scroll together once more. Do not let our deaths be in vain." Another crash sounded outside, and he closed his eyes. "Promise me, Yumeko-chan. You must protect the scroll. The fate of this land depends on it."

With shaking hands, I reached out and took the scroll, wrapping trembling fingers around the case. It was surprisingly light in my palm. "I promise," I whispered. "I swear I'll find the Steel Feather temple, warn the other monks and protect the scroll. I won't fail you."

He smiled. "Take this as well," he said, and pressed a

tanto, a short, straight dagger, into my palm. "It will come in handy, when defending yourself with words and cunning is not enough. And this." He draped a simple furoshiki—a wrapping cloth used for transporting clothes, gifts, or other possessions—around my shoulders. "To hide your burden from the rest of the world. Now, go." He nodded toward the statue. "Don't worry about us, and don't cry. We will meet again, Yumeko-chan, in the Pure Lands or in another life."

With a mighty crash that shook the entire hall, the barrier shattered. Monks gasped or cried out, hands going to their heads, and the floor trembled as the huge oni stepped into the room, a flood of demons behind him.

"Go, Yumeko-chan," Master Isao said, and his voice was icy. Stone-faced, he rose and stepped toward the hulking thing in the doorway. Feeling like a coward, I skittered half-behind the Jade Prophet, knowing I had to leave, but unable to tear my eyes away. Master Isao and the others waited calmly as the shadow of the demon grew larger, its eyes glowing like red coals against the dark.

The oni smiled as he entered the hall, ducking his massive head as he stepped into the room, looming to a terrifying height. He was so large that his horns nearly scraped the ceiling. "Monks of the Silent Winds temple," he rumbled, his terrible voice making the air shiver, "my name is Yaburama, fourth demon general of Jigoku, and I have come for the Dragon scroll." He raised his tetsubo and swung it into his palm with a meaty thump, as the small demons hissed and chortled gleefully behind him, waiting for the signal to attack. "Give me what I have come for, and perhaps I will make your deaths painless."

"Abomination!" Denga's voice rang over the snarls and cackles of the demon horde. Fearlessly, he strode forward, until he was only a few yards away from the mountain of an oni. "We will never relinquish the scroll to such evil. You are not welcome here. By the Jade Prophet, begone, and take your minions with you!"

The oni cocked his head. Abruptly, he swung his club, shockingly fast, striking Denga in the side and smashing him into a pillar. The monk hit the beam with a sickening crack and crumpled to the floor, blood streaming from his nose and mouth, eyes staring sightlessly ahead. I bit my lip to stifle a shriek, and the oni curled a lip.

"Your Jade Prophet means nothing to me," he commented, as the demons shrieked with laughter and swarmed into the room.

With cries of fury and outrage, the monks surged forward, meeting the demons in the center of the hall. They were unarmed, and their opponents wielded blades and spears as well as claws and teeth. But the monks were far from defenseless. Ki energy pulsed, turning fists into hammers and feet into weapons of destruction. A demon's skull imploded after Nitoru kicked it in the head, spraying demon blood everywhere before it writhed into crimson-black smoke and disappeared. A trio of demons swarmed Satoshi, who caught a spear thrust at him, wrenched it out of the demon's grasp and plunged it through its gaping mouth. But he didn't see the danger behind him until a second demon sank a kama sickle deep into his leg. Satoshi staggered and dropped to a knee, and the monsters piled on him, dragging him to the floor.

*Yumeko!* Master Isao's voice rang in my head, though the master of the Silent Winds temple strode right for the center of the room, ki energy crackling around him, where the terrible oni waited. *Go, now!*

I turned toward the hole in the floor and prepared to shift into fox form. But a bulbous blue head poked up between the boards, and a demon clawed itself out of the hole, followed by two friends. When they saw me, they hissed and raised their spears, and I hastily backed up.

Jinkei help me, I was trapped. I couldn't go forward with the trio blocking the hole, and I couldn't go back into the room, where the battle between monks and demons raged. The din was deafening, screams and howls mingling with flashes of ki, flying bodies and blood. As the trio of demons grinned evilly and tensed, I raised my arm, and a ball of blue-white foxfire flared to life in my palm. The blue demon glanced at the ghostly flames and sneered, making my heart sink; apparently a ball of kitsune-bi to the face wasn't going to work a second time.

With a roar, the massive bulk of the oni flew backward and crashed into the statue of the Jade Prophet, knocking her off her base. The statue teetered for a moment, giving me just enough time to scramble away, before toppling through the wall with a deafening crash of wood and stone. The three amanjaku were buried under the rubble, and a warm, smoke-scented breeze rushed into the hall from the hole it left behind.

I cringed, ducking behind one of the pillars lining the room, as the oni shook its head and looked up at Master Isao, who stood in the center of the room. The monk was breathing hard, blood running down his face from beneath his hat, both palms raised.

A deep growl came from the oni, sitting against the ruined statue. "You hit hard, for a mortal," the monster rumbled, getting to its feet. "Well done, but it will not save you. The amanjaku are tearing your brothers apart as we speak.

No one is left." He craned his neck from side to side, rolled his shoulders forward and raised his club. "It is time to end these games. Let us see if you have the ki to do that again!"

The oni lunged with a roar. As he barreled forward, raising his club high overhead, Master Isao's calm gaze flicked to me. In the moment our gazes met, he smiled.

*Go, Yumeko-chan*, whispered his voice in my head, gentle and serene. *Run.*

This time I didn't wait to see what happened, if the terrible crash from the oni's club struck home or not. I whirled and sprinted through the hole left from the fallen Prophet, scrambling over splintered beams and broken jade, whispering an apology as I stepped over a shattered green arm. Then I was outside, and the air was hot and choking. Blinded by tears, I tripped over a plank and skinned my hands when I fell, and the lacquered scroll case rolled away from me, gleaming in the firelight.

My blood chilled. Snatching it up, I half ran, half stumbled into the gardens, past the pond full of dead, floating carp, to the old maple tree leaning against the wall. After quickly tucking the scroll into the furoshiki and the tanto into my obi, I pulled myself up by the gnarled branches, wondering how the once familiar act could feel so strange and surreal. I wouldn't be doing this ever again.

At the top of the wall, I spared one final look back at my home, the temple I'd lived in all my life, and felt a lump rise to my throat. The pagoda was now a skeletal ruin engulfed by flames, and the fire had spread to the other buildings, including the main hall. I could make out only the roof over thc tops of the trees, but a stray ember on one corner had turned into a flame, which would quickly spread and consume the wooden building until there was nothing left. I didn't dare imagine what was happening inside, the lives that were lost, the monks who stood bravely against a horde of demons. Everyone I'd ever known—Jin, Satoshi, Nitoru, Denga, Master Isao and all the rest—they were gone. They'd gone willingly to their deaths, all to protect the scroll.

A tiny globe of light, pale against the smoke and darkness, rose from the roof of the burning hall. It was joined by another, and then another, until there were more than a dozen glowing orbs rising slowly into the air and leaving trails of light behind them. My throat closed up, and fresh tears streamed down my cheeks. Not one of the spheres of light hesitated or stayed near the temple; all rose steadily toward the stars. They had no regrets, no lingering sorrows or thoughts of vengeance, nothing that tied them to this world. They were free.

Deep inside my chest, a tiny, blue-white flame of anger flickered, burning away the despair, and I breathed deep to banish the tears.

"I won't fail," I promised, as the lights drifted slowly away, toward Meido or the Pure Lands, or wherever they were headed. "If…if this is truly my destiny, then I'll give it my all. Don't worry, Master Isao, everyone. I'll find the Steel Feather temple and protect the scroll, I promise."

My words had no effect on the rapidly fading lights. They continued rising into the sky until they were no larger than the stars themselves, and disappeared.

I blinked rapidly. *Safe journey, everyone. May we meet again, in this life or the next.*

A hiss in the gardens drew my attention. Looking down, I met the crimson eyes of a demon, who jerked up as he saw me, as well. As it gave a shrill cry of alarm and raised its weapon, I dropped to the ground outside the wall and sprinted into the forest.

# 7

## An Unexpected Proposal

The path had disappeared.

I hesitated in the shadows of the forest, listening, my hand curled around my sword hilt. Sometime during my dash up the mountain, the trail I'd been following had either vanished or I'd lost it somehow, for uninterrupted woods surrounded me, dark and thick. It wasn't terribly problematic; I could still hear the roar of a conflagration, and the breeze through the branches carried the scent of smoke and blood. I was going in the right direction.

I feared what I would find when I got there.

There was a rustle in the bushes ahead, and Kamigoroshi gave a warning pulse, just as something exploded from the darkness and lunged at me. My blade cleared its sheath in an instant, whipping up toward my attacker's face. It—she?—yelped and skidded to a halt, as my brain caught up to my reflexes. Hakaimono roared, goading me to continue the motion, to bathe the steel in blood. I wrenched myself from the howling bloodlust and forced my hands to stop.

The blade froze an inch from her neck. Panting, I looked across the glowing edge of the sword, into the face and wide black eyes of a girl.

She was my age, perhaps a bit younger. Small, petite, wearing a short crimson robe pattered with white swirls. Her black hair hung loose around her shoulders and down her back, and her large dark eyes, peering up at me, were round with shock.

For a moment, we stared at each other, bathed in the faint purple light of Kamigoroshi. Her face was dirty, smudged with ash and grime, and she was breathing hard, as if she had been fleeing the fire with the rest of the wildlife.

Then there was a snap in the trees behind her, and I realized why she'd been running.

"Get back," I said, and shoved her behind me, as an amanjaku leaped through the bushes with a howl, a sickle raised over its head. I smacked the curved blade aside and slashed Kamigoroshi across its face, making it shriek and reel away. More demons swarmed from the bushes, stabbing and hacking wildly as they rushed forward. They died on my sword as I carved limbs from bodies and heads from torsos, black demon blood arcing into the air. Hakaimono reveled in their deaths, but I kept myself detached from the demon's rage. I was the hand that wielded Kamigoroshi, nothing more. I felt nothing as I sent the creatures back to Jigoku.

When the last demon fell, I flicked steaming blood from my sword, sheathed Kamigoroshi despite the protests in my mind and looked around for the girl.

She peered from behind a tree trunk, watching me with

big dark eyes. Surprised, I turned to face her fully. I had half expected her to be gone, fleeing the forest while the demons were busy attacking me. I caught the glint of metal in her hand and saw the hilt of a tanto clutched in her fist. Whether it was meant for me or the demons, I wasn't certain.

"Merciful Jinkei," she whispered, sounding breathless. Her eyes shone as she gazed around, at the fading tendrils of darkness on the wind. "You…that was…" Blinking, she looked up at me, her expression caught between awe and fear. "Who are you?"

*Nothing. Nobody. A shadow on the wall, empty and unimportant.* I turned away, toward the sound of distant flames. "Run," I told the girl, not looking back. "Get out of here. Go to the village at the bottom of the mountain. You should be safe there."

"Wait!" she cried as I started forward. I paused, but did not turn back. "You can't go that way," she said, and I heard her emerge from behind the tree. "It's too dangerous. There are more demons, a whole horde of them. And there's an oni!"

*An oni.* My eyes narrowed, even as Hakaimono gave the strongest flare of excitement I had ever felt from it. I had been killing dangerous yokai for the Shadow Clan since I was thirteen, the newest in a long line of Kage demonslayers to wield Kamigoroshi, but I had never faced a real oni. From what my sensei had told me, the greatest demons of Jigoku were nothing like the monsters I'd fought before. Tough, savage and virtually unstoppable, able to regenerate wounds, broken bones, even severed limbs at an astonishing rate. They were difficult to defeat, even with Kamigoroshi. In the past, more than one demonslayer who had gone to fight an oni had not survived the battle.

Fortunately, oni encounters were rare, as summoning one from Jigoku and binding the savage demon to your will required incredible power. Unfortunately, it meant that whomever had sent an oni here, to this forest, was likely after the same thing I was. Lady Hanshou hadn't told me why she wanted this particular scroll, nor was it my place to ask. My mission was to retrieve the scroll, no matter what obstacles stood in my way.

"This oni," I asked the girl, whose gaze I could still feel on my back. "Where is it?"

"The temple," she replied, and her voice came out slightly choked. "At the top of the mountain. It killed everyone there and set the whole place on fire. Nothing is left."

My spirits sank. If the demons had attacked and destroyed the temple, then the scroll was already gone. Destroyed, or in the hands of the oni. Setting my jaw, I headed into the trees. I had to see if the scroll was still there, if I could save it. And if the oni did indeed possess the scroll, I would challenge the demon and take it back, or die trying.

*"Baka!"* Something grabbed the hem of my jacket, tugging me to a halt. I spun, barely stopping myself from drawing Kamigoroshi and slicing my assailant in half. "Didn't you hear me?" the girl asked, her dark gaze now wide with fear. "There's an army of demons and an oni that way. If you go to the temple, they'll kill you, like they did everyone else."

Her eyes watered, moisture spilling down one cheek. I suddenly understood. "You came from the temple," I stated quietly. "You saw everything."

She nodded, swiping a dirty sleeve across her face. "Everyone died," she whispered. "I barely got away. My master sacrificed himself so that I could escape. He fought the oni himself, though he knew it was going to kill him."

"What were the demons after?" I asked, watching her closely. Perhaps, if she had come from the temple, she knew about the scroll, or where it was located. "Why did they attack?" I pressed. "Did they take anything?"

For just a moment, she hesitated. Her cheeks paled and she looked up at me with those dark eyes. For some reason, my skin prickled, and I fought the urge to look away. "I don't know," she admitted. "I don't know why they came, or what they wanted. I just know my temple is gone and demons killed everyone I've ever cared for. And if you go up there now, you'll die, too." She paused again, then held out her hand as if coming to a decision. "Come with me," she said, to my surprise. "Before the demons find us. I can't… I don't want to be alone right now. We can head to the village and figure out what to do from there."

"No." I stepped back, away from her. "You can keep running. Get out of the forest. But I have business at the temple, something I must confirm."

"What?" She stared at me in disbelief, as I turned and began walking away. "You can't be serious. What is so important that you would risk your head getting crushed by an oni? Wait!"

Footsteps shuffled after mine. I turned once more and raised Kamigoroshi, making her stumble to a halt. "Don't follow me," I warned, as her gaze fell to the blade. "Go to the village. Warn them about the attack. Forget what you saw here." Sheathing the sword, I headed into the darkness, toward the temple and the battle that awaited me at the top. "What happens now isn't your concern."

"The scroll isn't there anymore."

I stopped. Slowly, I turned around. The girl stood in the same place, watching me with a wary, almost defiant expression, her jaw set. "The scroll," she repeated, so there would be no doubt. "You won't find it. It's no longer at the temple."

"Where is it?"

She hesitated. Drawing my sword, I walked toward her. Her face paled and she backed away, but hit a tree after a few steps. "I don't know," she began, and froze as I placed the edge of Kamigoroshi against her neck. "Wait, please! You don't understand."

"Where is the scroll?" I asked again, stepping close. "Tell me or I'll kill you."

"It's gone!" the girl burst out. "It's not here anymore. Master Isao…he sensed the demons coming. He knew they wanted the scroll, so he sent it away. A…a few days ago."

"Where?"

"I don't know."

I tilted the blade up so it pressed lightly under her chin, and she gasped. "I don't know!" she insisted, raising her head to escape the sword. "Master Isao didn't tell me where it's located. But… I know who does."

"Who?"

She paused, her dark eyes flicking to mine over the blade. Again, I felt that odd flutter beneath my skin, reacting to her presence. "How do I know you won't kill me if I tell you?"

"I give you my word," I told her. "On my honor, if you tell me what I want, I won't kill you."

Carefully, she shook her head. "I need more than that, samurai," she said, making me frown. A warrior's vow was absolute, his honor preventing any hint of betrayal, and it was an insult to imply otherwise. To a samurai who broke his promise, the shame would be so great that seppuku—ritually killing himself—was the only answer.

Of course, I was shinobi, a shadow warrior, and followed

a different code than the samurai. We operated in darkness, performing tasks that would make an honorable samurai cringe in horror and revulsion. But the girl didn't know that.

She continued to watch me, her head and back pressed to the trunk, chin raised to escape the lethal blade against her throat. I kept a tight hold on the sword, both in my hand and in my mind, for Hakaimono was goading me to kill this insubordinate peasant nobody. "You can kill me now," she said, "but then you'll never find what you're looking for." I narrowed my eyes, and she shivered under my gaze, seeming to lose courage, before taking a deep breath and staring at me again. "I have…a proposal for you," she announced. "So please listen before you decide to cut off my head. The demons will come after me. Once they figure out the scroll isn't here, they'll hunt me down. Right now, the scroll is on its way to another temple, a hidden temple, far away. I need to get to that temple, to warn the monks of the demon attack. I promised my mentor I would."

"But you don't know where it is," I pointed out.

"N-no," she admitted. "I don't. But Master Isao told me the name of the person who does. A priest who lives in Kin Heigen Toshi. He knows the location of the hidden temple, and can tell me where to go. But I don't think I can get there alone. I can't fight a horde of demons by myself." She appraised me, and I realized where this was going. "But…*you* kill demons, quite well, it seems. If you…come with me, protect me on the journey, then…" She trailed off, but the implication hung in the air between us, impossible to miss.

*Then she'll take me to the scroll.*

I considered. The clan wouldn't be pleased. As the Kage demonslayer and the bearer of Kamigoroshi, I wasn't supposed to have prolonged contact with anyone outside of the

Shadow Clan. The reasons for this were twofold. The Kage were a family of secrets. Our shinobi were the best in the land and possessed talents unknown to the rest of the world. We were close to the shadows, and the kami-touched among us reflected that, speaking the language of darkness and the unknown. The Shadow Clan held their secrets close and would happily kill any outsider who discovered too much. A peasant girl traveling with the Kage demonslayer would raise concerns.

But the other more pressing reason was me. I was highly discouraged from interacting with outsiders because of the danger I represented, the risk that I could lose myself to the demon in the sword. Emotion was especially dangerous, because Hakaimono used it as a gateway into the soul. Rage, fear, uncertainty; the stronger the feeling, the closer the demon came to overwhelming its host. I'd been warned, numerous times, that if Hakaimono fully took control, there was no going back. I would become a monster, and they would have no choice but to kill me.

But I was on a mission for the daimyo of the Shadow Clan, Lady Hanshou herself. I'd been sworn to retrieve the scroll and was expected to obey, even if it cost me my life and the lives of those around me. Failure was not an option.

"So," the girl ventured. "Do we have an agreement?"

# 8

## Two Souls for the Road

The stranger was silent, considering. We stood very close, and I could see every detail of his face—the high cheekbones, the full lips, the scar down his forehead and across the bridge of his nose. But his eyes… They were a luminous purple, the deep, brilliant shade of an iris flower, and yet, gazing into them caused a chill to spread across my neck and creep down my back. They were blank, revealing no emotion; showing no compassion, empathy or understanding. No hint of a soul beneath. I had never been truly afraid of another person until now; despite even Denga-san's threats, rages and numerous punishments, I'd known in my heart that the monks of the Silent Winds temple would never hurt me. But this boy… He might be young, with the face of an angel, but there was no mistaking the truth in his eyes. He was a killer.

And yet, this soulless killer might be my best chance to reach the Steel Feather temple alive. The thought made my heart pound wildly, but after watching him slaughter the amanjaku, seeing how easily he cut them down, an idea had formed in my mind—a wild, risky, probably very dangerous idea. The demons would be hunting me once they figured out the scroll was gone. The oni could be hunting me, and much as I wanted to avenge Master Isao and the others, I was no match for that abomination.

I trembled, feeling a huge painful knot in the pit of my stomach. It didn't seem real, that they were gone. That only this afternoon, I was lighting the candles of the main hall and wishing I was somewhere else. I had never been beyond the forest. I didn't know where to go, or how to talk to people. My whole life, I'd spoken only to monks, kami and the odd yokai in the woods. I had to take the scroll to the Steel Feather temple; I'd promised Master Isao I would, but I wasn't sure how to get there, or what I would do if I ran into demons.

But…*this* human could kill demons. Quite easily, in fact. He might be as dangerous as the monsters themselves. If he were protecting me, any demon, yokai, or murderous human who wanted the scroll would have to deal with him first.

There was just one small problem.

He, too, was after the Dragon's prayer. Whether he had been sent to retrieve it like the demons, or had come of his own volition, the reason didn't matter. I could feel the narrow, lacquered case hidden in the furoshiki tied around my shoulder, and my heart pounded. If he discovered I had the scroll, I would be just as dead as the monsters dissolving in the breeze. I was going to have to be very careful, and choose my actions wisely, or my would-be protector would turn on me.

Briefly, I had the sobering thought that Master Isao would not have approved of this sham, of me lying to this boy to get him to accompany me to the Steel Feather temple. Denga would have certainly seen it as more fox trickery and deception. But I wasn't a warrior; I couldn't chop things to pieces with a sword, and all I knew of the outside world was what the monks had taught me. My temple was gone, my family had been slaughtered by demons before my eyes and I had been given a near impossible task. Not to mention, there was the notion that I had been left at the Silent Winds temple for this very moment. To somehow protect the scroll from everything that wanted it. I wasn't certain what to feel about the whole vision thing, but I knew that if I thought about it now, I would bury myself in a deep hole and never come out again. I couldn't do this alone, and I had no one else to help me. As the old tanuki had said just this evening: I was kitsune, yokai. Not human. This was what I was good at.

I held the stranger's gaze as he thought about my offer, sensing a desperate struggle within him. Finally, he nodded and stepped back from the tree, taking his terrible sword away from my neck. "All right," he said. "If this is the only way to get to the scroll, then I will take you to the capital, and then to the Steel Feather temple. But..." His eyes narrowed, cold and icy, and he raised his sword so that the moonlight reflected down the length of steel. "If you deceive me, or try to run, I will kill you. Understand?"

I nodded, ignoring the stab of fear that accompanied the feeling of relief. Not that I had any intentions of sneaking away, but I had no doubt he wasn't making idle threats. With a sigh, the boy finally sheathed his weapon, and the subtle light coming from the blade vanished, plunging us into darkness.

"The capital is a few weeks away on foot," he stated, calm and businesslike as he stepped back. "My horse fled earlier this evening, so we'll have to walk, at least until I can find a new one. Are you well enough to travel? Do you have what you need?"

"Yes," I replied. Being raised in a temple of ascetic monks, I'd never owned much, and the few possessions I'd had were probably cinders and ashes now. I had my sandals, the clothes on my back, a knife and a piece of a scroll of ultimate, wish-granting power, hidden in my furoshiki. That would have to be enough to get by.

"I don't suppose you have travel papers, do you?" the boy asked.

I blinked. "No. What are travel papers?"

"They're…" He shook his head. "Never mind," he murmured, dismissing the matter. "It can't be helped now. We'll deal with the problem if it arises."

*"Ano,"* I added as the human turned away. "What's your name?"

He hesitated a moment, then replied in a low, empty voice, "Kage Tatsumi."

*Kage*. Kage was the Shadow Clan, a family of secrets and hidden knowledge, according to my studies. It seemed fitting for the dark, cold-eyed boy in front of me. "I'm Yumeko." I tried to smile, though with his back turned he probably wouldn't see it. "Thank you, for taking me to the capital, Tatsumi-san. And, you know, saving me from the demons."

He didn't give any indication that he'd heard. With a quiet "Let's go," he stepped forward and vanished into the shadows like he was part of the night itself. I glanced once more at the sky, at the smoke and embers still rising over the treetops, marking the end of a way of life.

Closing my eyes, I whispered a quick prayer to Jinkei, the Kami of Mercy, and Doroshin, the Kami of Roads, for Godspeed and to guide everyone to their final destination, before I turned and followed Kage Tatsumi into the dark.

# PART 2

# 9

## The Lingering Soul

*B*eing a ghost was an exercise in patience.

When Suki was still very young, her mother would tell her ghost stories in the flickering candlelight of home. At the end of the day, while Mura Akihito was in his shop, slaving over his newest masterpiece, Suki would sit on a stool as her mother swept or cooked, and listen to tales of beautiful women betrayed or abandoned by their lovers, who pined away until their bodies died but their yearning lived on. In these stories, it was always the women who died of broken hearts, Suki noticed. Who took their own lives in grief. Or who were brutally murdered and returned for vengeance. Sometimes, immoral women became something terrible and unnatural. A greedy woman might grow another mouth in the back of her head that consumed all the food it could find. An unfaithful woman might discover that, while she slept, her neck elongated to incredible lengths as her head roamed around freely, licking up lamp oil and attacking small animals. In the most wicked cases, the woman's grief, jealousy or rage would turn her into an oni, a hannya, or even a terrible giant serpent, demons that always met their ends on some great samurai's sword.

Terrible fates, the soul that had once been Suki mused, floating soundlessly down a narrow castle hallway. Certainly, the women who turned into such monsters were grotesque and to be pitied. But right now, she thought she would much rather be a demon.

A few yards ahead of her, Lady Satomi sauntered down the narrow corridor of the abandoned castle, parasol swaying, unaware of the soul trailing behind her. After the terrible night of her death, Suki had attempted to follow the woman, but had lost her in the twisting halls of the castle. Alone, the ghost that had been Suki had drifted aimlessly from room to hallway to courtyard, bewildered and confused. She'd been certain that, before she became a ghost, she had been a maid at the imperial palace. How she'd come to this dark, abandoned castle was a mystery; the last thing she remembered was delivering a coil of rope to a storehouse in the imperial gardens. But this castle was definitely not the emperor's golden Palace of the Sun. Everything felt cold, lifeless, abandoned. Even the demons were gone. After feasting on her body, Yaburama and the smaller demons had departed the castle as well, and with no company but the spiders and rats, time had blurred into a bleak, lonely haze.

But this evening, Lady Satomi had returned, striding through the halls of the abandoned castle as if she did so every night. Stunned, Suki trailed behind her, keeping out of sight while she pondered what to do.

Her first thought, of course, was vengeance. To haunt Satomi relentlessly until she went mad from guilt. But, unlike the ghost stories her mother used to tell, where the spirits could curse and even physically harm their victims, Suki's interactions with the world were limited. She had no body; her insubstantial form passed through everything she touched. If she thought about it, she could manifest as a ghostly version of her old self, but if she lost focus, she would revert to a glowing ball of light. Speaking was difficult and required effort to remember how, and even then, her voice came out faint and breathy. In the stories, some yurei were powerful onryo, grudge spirits whose rage and hate manifested into devastating and sometimes fatal curses, but Suki had no idea how to do that. And even if she did show herself to her murderer, Lady Satomi didn't seem the type to be distressed about the ghost of her former maid.

So she followed her, trailing the woman soundlessly through the empty halls, until Satomi pushed open the front doors and stepped into the courtyard again.

It was full of demons. Suki froze in midair, trembling, before darting behind a dead bush to peer through the branches. Amanjaku skittered over the stones, snarling and waving crude weapons at each other. In the center, the terrible form of Yaburama towered over the mob, casting them in his shadow.

Lady Satomi strode through the mob, ignoring the demons who hissed and cackled at her, face serene as she walked toward the oni. From Suki's perspective, as she hovered behind a chunk of broken wall, Yaburama seemed to be in a bad mood, baring his teeth at any amanjaku who got too close. As Satomi approached, a green amanjaku darted out of her way, and the oni gave it a savage kick that booted it over the wall. Lady Satomi watched as the demon went sailing away, a bemused look on her face, before looking at Yaburama.

"Well, I could say something about your temper, but at least you're on time tonight." The woman sniffed, then gave an amanjaku that had been edging too close to her robes a warning look. "But, sadly, time is waning, and I have much to do. If you would kindly give me the scroll, Yaburama, we can end this unpleasant association, and you can go back to doing…whatever it is you demons do until you're summoned. So…" She held out a slender white hand. "The Dragon scroll, if you would?"

The oni let out a growl. "I don't have it."

"What?" Lady Satomi dropped her arm, eyes narrowing. "Do excuse me, Yaburama, but this *is* the sole reason you were summoned from Jigoku, yes? Why I sent you to that temple of ki-using fanatics, because I thought, surely an oni like Yaburama would have no trouble with a bunch of bald old men. What do you mean you don't have the scroll?"

"The scroll wasn't at the temple, human." The oni glowered down at her. "I killed every monk there, including the master, and tore the temple apart looking for it. There was no scroll."

"And you're certain you killed *everyone*?" Satomi's voice was calm; she could have been asking a maid if she'd looked everywhere for a favorite teacup, not casually discussing the slaughter of an entire temple of monks. "No acolyte snuck out the back and managed to escape? No monk harnessed their ki to a trio of sparrows and flew over the wall?"

"No," growled the oni. "I killed everyone. There were no survivors."

At this, a pair of smaller demons near the oni's feet began

jumping up and down, chattering in raspy, high-pitched voices. Suki couldn't understand what they were saying, but Yaburama spun around, looking murderous, and grabbed for them. One demon yelped in alarm and fled into the crowd, but the other wasn't fast enough and was snatched up in the oni's huge claw. It wailed as the monster lifted it off the ground, waving its arms and babbling, until it was at face level. The oni rumbled at it in a guttural, ominous voice, and the demon squeaked an answer, still squirming helplessly in its grip.

With a growl and a flash of fangs, the oni clenched its fist, crushing the demon inside. Blood shot from its nose and mouth and ran from its ears, before it dissolved into coils of reddish-black smoke that writhed away on the wind.

If Suki could have cringed at the display of violence and blood, she would have, but Lady Satomi only looked amused. "Oh, do let me guess," she said as the oni opened its fist, letting the last of the smoke dissipate. Blood stained his claws and fingertips, but he didn't seem to notice. "In all your murdering and killing and reveling, you let someone slip away through your big stupid fingers. And now they have the scroll."

The oni lowered his arm. "There was…a girl," he rumbled, sounding reluctant and annoyed at the same time. "The amanjaku chased her into the forest, but she managed to escape." He paused, his face darkening even as his eyes narrowed and his voice dropped to a low, terrifying growl. "With the help of the Kage demonslayer."

*The Kage demonslayer?* Suki didn't know that name, but the crowd of small demons went quiet and still, as if the very word terrified them. She wondered what kind of person could scare a horde of maniacal hell-demons, and if it was someone she would ever want to encounter.

"Well," Lady Satomi said, after a moment of brittle silence. Her voice could have frozen the lake in the emperor's garden and sliced all the fish in half with its edge. "This presents a problem, doesn't it? Tell me, Yaburama, if this girl is with the Kage demonslayer, whom I imagine Hanshou also sent after the scroll, how are we going to aquire it without losing an entire village's worth of demons?"

The oni bared its fangs. "I'll take care of him."

"No. You've done quite enough."

The oni snarled, looming over the woman. But Lady Satomi actually turned away from him and gazed at the scattering of crows on the walls and in the dead trees overhead.

"Hear me!" she called, raising one hand, and the feathered creatures stirred, ruffling wings and raising their heads, gazing down with beady eyes. "Find them, my karasu!" Satomi ordered. "The girl and the Kage demonslayer. Be my eyes, seeing where I cannot, and show me what I am dealing with. Go!"

The crows took wing with a cacophony of harsh cries, spiraling into the air and disappearing into the dark. Lady Satomi watched them go, a dark swarm flying into the roiling clouds, before turning back to the heaving, growling oni.

"A temper tantrum is not becoming, Yaburama," she commented, and opened her parasol as drops of rain began to fall. "You had your chance and failed. If the girl and the demonslayer are traveling close to towns, an oni dropping in with a mob of amanjaku is not going to go unnoticed, and I would like to keep the headaches to a minimum until I have the scroll in my hands. There are others I can call upon to take care of this." She pondered a moment, twirling the parasol in her hands. "Kazekira and her disgusting familiars still owe me a favor," she mused. "And they won't draw the eye of every soul in the area. Yes, I think that will work."

She glanced at the oni, and her voice became sweet and crooning. "There now, Yaburama, the problem has been dealt with. You just stay here, like a good dog, until I have need of you again."

For a moment, Suki thought the oni might spring forward and tear the head from Satomi's slim white neck. But then, he let out a snort and stepped back. "Fool mortal. You underestimate the Kage demonslayer. He may look human, but he is a worse monster than I am. Remember this when you need my protection from his sword."

Satomi raised a perfectly arched brow. "I'll keep that in mind."

She turned and strolled away, back toward the castle doors, parasol bobbing behind her. At the steps, however, she paused and looked directly at the place where Suki was hiding, a small smile crossing her lips. Chilled, the soul that had been Suki winked out of sight, becoming invisible. By the time she gathered the courage to peek out again, the woman was gone.

# 10

## The Road to the Capital

*W*e were being followed.

"Tatsumi-san?" Yumeko turned, as I paused in the middle of the trail and turned to stare at the trees behind us. "What are you looking for? Is something there?"

I didn't answer. Around us, large ancient pines grew close together, branches stretching over the path and mottling the trail with shade. Cicadas buzzed, their droning song pulsing through the trees, and a lone hawk soared overhead, its shadow gliding briefly over the trail. The air was cool, smelling of sap and pine needles, and except for the hum of insects, everything was quiet. But I could sense something wasn't right, like a dark spot in the corner of my vision, keeping just out of reach.

It had been three days since the girl and I had fled the mountain, away from the destruction of the Silent Winds temple and the amanjaku in the forest. Not much was said during our travels; the girl had been quiet and withdrawn, and I had no desire to engage her in conversation. It was early summer, the days hot and humid, the skies threatening rain at a moment's notice. We passed villages with thatched huts and terraced fields, where farmers shoved green rice seedlings into calf-deep water. When darkness fell we slept beneath the trees or in abandoned shrines, the nights warm enough for us to be comfortable without blankets, which was fortunate as all my possessions had been lost when my horse fled. Including my travel documents, most of my shinobi gear and my rations for the journey. Thankfully, late summer in Iwagoto meant there were plenty of places to get food in the wild, if you knew where to look. Mushrooms, berries and all manner of sansai—wild plants—were everywhere, and the rivers and streams yielded fish if one knew how to catch them without a line. I'd been trained to live off the land and survive in the wilderness, so we were in no danger of starving, though I was surprised to find the girl knew a fair bit about wild plants, as well. One evening, as I was cleaning the fish I'd caught from the nearby stream, she appeared and dumped an armful of wild persimmons on the ground near the fire. I didn't care much for sweet things, but the ripe orange fruit contrasted with the blandness of the fish and filled our stomachs well that night.

Throughout our travels, I hadn't felt the presence of demons, though Hakaimono had been unusually restless, either sensing invisible eyes on us or reacting to our unexpected companion. I had been alone for so long that having another human constantly present was distracting, for both myself and the sword. I ignored the girl as much as possible, trying not to see the tears that sometimes leaked from her eyes, or hear the faint gasps and sniffles when she was curled up, asleep.

This morning, however, she had greeted me with a smile and a cheerful *Ohayou gozaimasu, Tatsumi-san*, seeming to abandon her dark mood. We'd continued down the road, but this afternoon, I couldn't shake the feeling of being watched. It had continued to plague me, irritating Hakaimono to no end, until I'd finally halted and searched the trees for our unknown stalker. I was giving away the knowledge that I knew something was out there, but at this moment, I would rather face something that I could fight and kill, instead of worrying about a nameless threat I couldn't see.

My gaze stopped as I finally pinpointed the source of my unease. In the limbs of a pine tree that stretched over the road, a small, hunched figure gazed down at us, unblinking.

*Crows again.* I narrowed my eyes, glaring at the bird, which ruffled its feathers but didn't move from the branch. Crows were everywhere in Iwagoto, from one end of the country to the other. Murders of them clustered on rooftops or in tree branches, fighting for space, their guttural caws scolding as you passed beneath. Sometimes they were seen as ill omens, bringers of misfortune, but for the most part, they were a common, everyday sight, and no one gave the squabbling creatures a second glance.

But every once in a while, especially when I was traveling, a single crow would appear, dogging me. Watching me. Killing the bird did nothing; another would appear soon after, as if to taunt my efforts. Or worse, it would stay just out of sight, irritating Hakaimono until it was ready to lash out at anything that moved. At least now I knew the cause of the uneasiness, and would be ready if my unknown stalker decided to attack.

"Tatsumi-san?"

I turned back to find the girl watching me, her head cocked slightly. She hadn't noticed the bird in the tree, and I didn't feel like explaining. Especially since neither of us could do anything about it.

"It's nothing," I told her, continuing down the trail again. "Let's keep moving."

She nodded, falling into step beside me. I could see her in the corner of my vision, dark hair rippling in the breeze, her gaze on the forest around us. Unlike the past two days, when she'd followed silently at my back, staring dully at the ground. The furoshiki cloth was wrapped around her shoulders; she hadn't taken it off once, and every night, made sure it was secured tightly to her person. I imagined it contained the last of her meager belongings, and that perhaps she was afraid I would steal them, though I had no interest in the possessions of a peasant girl.

"*Ne*, Tatsumi-san," she said, looking up from where she had been watching a squirrel on a branch. She did that a lot, I noticed; seemingly fascinated by the smallest things. Like a cat constantly distracted by flitting shadows. "We haven't found anything to eat today. What are we going to do for food?"

"Chochin Machi is a few miles from here," I replied. "We'll resupply when we reach the town."

She nodded again. "It'll be nice to eat real food again," she commented. "Not that I have anything against wild-caught fish and persimmons, but I'm starting to crave a hot rice bowl. And a real bed. Where I don't wake up with spiders in my clothes. Not that I mind the spiders, but I don't want to crush them when I roll about." She cast me a sideways glance. "What about you, Tatsumi-san?"

I shrugged. I had gone days without eating or sleeping, both in the field and in training with my sensei. Sometimes as a punishment, but mainly it was to test my endurance, to see how far I could go before I collapsed. I had been trained to survive on very little; food, sleep and personal comfort were not as important as completing the mission.

The girl let out a long breath and gazed up at the sky, at the sun sinking slowly below the tree line. "Back at the temple, we'd be gathering for the evening meal right now," she continued softly. "We didn't have a lot, but we ate together three times a day. Satoshi had a little vegetable garden in the back—he could grow the biggest daikon radishes you'd ever seen." Her nose wrinkled. "I hated daikon, and we had so much of it. I'd drop pieces through cracks in the temple floor, and then have nightmares of pickled radish monsters hiding under my floorboards, crawling up to force themselves into my mouth as I slept." She paused, her next words even softer. "I would eat a dozen radishes right now, if it meant I could sit down with everybody one more time."

I had no answer for that, so I said nothing. She was quiet, then I felt her gaze on me again. "Do you have any family, Tatsumi?"

"No."

"But…you're a samurai." She cocked her head. "You carry a sword, and you have the mon-crest of house Kage on your back. So, that means you must be part of the Shadow Clan, yes?"

I narrowed my eyes. All the great houses had their own mon-crests that showed their lineage and to which family they belonged but, in my experience, none of the peasant folk cared enough to tell them apart. To them, all samurai were the same.

"How do you know that?" I asked her.

Yumeko blinked. "Master Isao taught me about the different clans and houses," she explained. "He wanted me to know a little of the outside world, in case I ever left the temple. Let's see if I can remember them all." Her brow furrowed. "The Hino, Mizu, Tsuchi and Kaze are the four great families of Fire, Water, Earth and Wind," she recited, "while the Kage, Sora and Tsuki are the minor clans—Shadow, Sky and Moon. Is that correct?"

"You forgot one."

"Oh, right." Yumeko nodded. "The Sun Clan is the imperial family, the Taiyo. But most of them stay in the capital, close to the emperor. They almost never leave their territories unless they're visiting the daimyos of the other clans. Or so Master Isao told me."

I regarded her seriously. "What do you know about the Kage?"

"That they're the smallest of the minor families. Their territory borders the Fire Clan's, and they've lost several battles with the Hino, who have been pushing into their lands over the past decade."

All true. The Fire Clan was the ancient enemy of the Kage; even in times of peace, when the emperor ordered a countrywide truce, the Hino and the Kage were constantly at each other's throats. The Fire Clan was large and influential, and thought that if a clan wasn't strong enough to defend their territory, it should be taken by someone who could. Naturally, the Kage disagreed.

But that was common knowledge. Two clans feuding over territory was as ordinary as rain during the wet season, with borders changing so often that even the magistrates were hard-pressed to keep up. "What else?" I asked softly.

"Well, it's said that the Kage aren't like other clan samurai. That their warriors use darkness and questionable techniques to their advantage when fighting superior forces. That they can melt into shadows or disappear in a cloud of smoke, and that their daimyo is a mysterious lady who is rumored to be immortal."

I relaxed. Those were all common rumors, some of them true, but encouraged by the Shadow Clan to keep our foes guessing and off balance. She hadn't heard anything that the Kage did not approve of, which was good, because the true secrets of the Shadow Clan were not supposed to be known to outsiders; those who discovered too much were usually silenced, quickly and permanently.

Hakaimono approved of this idea, urging me to strike now, to cut her down. *You don't need her*, the demon seemed to whisper in my head. *One quick blow, and it will be over.* There would be no pain. She wouldn't even realize what had happened until she woke up with her ancestors.

I pushed those thoughts away. I had no orders to kill the girl, nor did I believe that she was a threat to the Shadow Clan. Besides, I had promised to accompany her to the Steel Feather temple, and I needed her help to find the scroll. Unless the clan told me otherwise, that was my first and only priority.

The shadows of the forest were growing long. I could still feel the crow's eyes on me, but could no longer see it in the branches around us. As the sun dipped lower in the sky, blips of light began to wink in and out of existence, as fireflies drifted through the wood and floated through the air.

"*Ne*, Tatsumi?" Yumeko asked, holding up a hand so that a firefly perched on her finger, winking green and gold in the twilight. Bringing it close to her face, she watched it curiously, casting her skin in an eerie glow. "The sun is starting to set," she said, unaware as I paused to gaze at her. "Are we very close to Chochin Machi?"

"Yes."

She raised her arm, and the insect spiraled off into the forest. "Why is it called Lantern Town?"

We came out of the trees, and the road sloped gently away down a hill, toward a river and a series of docks on the other side. "See for yourself."

Gazing down the rise, she drew in a slow breath.

Chochin Machi sat on the banks of the Hotaru River, glowing like a torch against the night. It wasn't a large town like Kin Heigen Toshi, the capital city; it boasted a small castle, a handful of inns, shops and restaurants, and a fishing industry that did a fair job of supporting the town. Though that wasn't why Chochin Machi was famous, or why it drew pilgrims and travelers from around Iwagoto.

On nearly every street, every corner and business and shrine, hundreds of red paper lanterns cast their soft glow into the darkness, lighting up the town. They hung from rooftops and tree branches, from doorways and awnings and from the helm of every ship floating on the river. The glow of the town could be seen for miles in every direction, and travelers flocked to it like moths to a flame.

*"Sugoi,"* Yumeko whispered. *Amazing.* Her eyes were round pools of black, and the lights of the town flickered in their depths. "It's beautiful. The monks never told me there was anything like this beyond the temple." She paused, then cocked her head, as if listening for something on the wind. "Are those drums?"

I stifled a groan. Late summer in Iwagoto was festival season, which meant Chochin Machi would be especially crowded tonight. "Stay close," I told the girl. "It's not a big town, but we don't want to be separated."

I turned away and started walking down the rise, hearing her hurry after me. We crossed the arched bridge over the river, where lanterns flickered atop the posts every few feet, and stepped into the ethereal glow of Chochin Machi.

Yumeko's eyes remained wide as we walked down the broad, dusty street that cut through the market district. Unlike many towns that closed their doors when the sun went down, Chochin Machi's shops thrived after dark. Strings of lanterns swung overhead, sometimes blocking out the sky, while individual chochin flickered in the doorways of shops, inns and restaurants, indicating that they were open. Market stalls sold their wares in the streets, everything from food to sandals to miniature paper lanterns, popular souvenirs of Chochin Machi.

As we neared the center of town, the sound of drums, deep and booming, began echoing into the night once more. Trailing the crowd, we came upon a large open square, where a tall wooden platform draped in red and white stood in the center like a beacon. Atop the stage, two bare-chested men with strips of red cloth tied around their foreheads beat a pair of large wooden drums with sticks, sending thunderous notes reverberating through the crowd. Strings of lanterns hung overhead, converging on the platform roof and lighting up the square, while people danced in a circle around the drummers, clapping and stamping their feet to the music.

I bristled, and in my head, Hakaimono stirred, riled by all the noise and movement. I did not like crowds. Too many things could happen; emotions could surge out of control, fights could break out, people could panic. If the gathering here became a riot and Hakaimono took control, this festival would swiftly turn into a bloodbath.

I walked a little faster, hoping to get away from the lights and music and into the darkness where I was comfortable. Preoccupied with watching the crowd, I suddenly realized Yumeko was no longer beside me. Turning, I saw her at the edge of the square, gazing at the circle of dancers, bobbing in place as she did.

With a scowl, I doubled back and moved beside her, leaning close to be heard over the drums. "Yumeko. What are you doing?"

"Tatsumi-san!" She glanced at me, eyes bright, apparently unable to keep her body still. "Dance with me," she implored, gesturing to the singing, stamping mob. "Teach me how."

I recoiled. Dance was not part of my training, being seen as frivolous and impractical by my sensei. I could appreciate the art, and the skill required to play an instrument, but I knew nothing of dancing and had no desire to learn. "No."

"Please, Tatsumi-san?" She took a step back, toward the edge of the circle. The boom of the drums rose into the air, punctuated by the claps of the crowd, and she smiled at me. "Just for a little while. It'll be fun."

*Fun.* I stifled a wince. Fun was a dangerous word among my sensei. *Are we having fun yet, Tatsumi?* Ichiro-san had often crooned, usually when I was struggling with a given task, and right before I was punished for my failure. *Since you're having so much fun, we'll try the same thing tomorrow.* "We don't have time for this," I said.

She wrinkled her nose, then sighed. "Tatsumi-san, have you ever heard the proverb of the kawauso river otter and the Jade Prophet?" she asked. "In this tale," she went on before

I could answer, "there was a kawauso who took nothing seriously, who turned everything into a game and brought joy and frivolity wherever he went. In his wake, people laughed, danced, sang and forgot about their troubles. But one day, the kawauso met the Jade Prophet, who told him, *Life is suffering. Fun is a fleeting waste of time. You must stop these foolish games, and strive to work hard without fail. Only in suffering, dullness and boredom can you find true happiness.* The kawauso took her advice to heart. He stopped all his games, worked himself to death and died a bitter old yokai with no friends, no family and no joy in his life."

"I have never heard that proverb," I said dubiously.

Yumeko grinned. "Of course not. It doesn't exist." And before I could stop her, she took three steps back and melted into the crowd of dancers.

I stared after her, fisting my hands at my side, as the girl joined the rippling throng. Overhead, the drums boomed, the crowd sang and Yumeko danced, swaying her body and clapping her hands to the music. Watching her, I found myself holding my breath, unable to look away. For just a moment, with her dark hair rippling about and her skin glowing under the lantern light, she was mesmerizing.

With a mental shake, I stalked along the edge of the square, keeping an eye on the girl as well as the people around her. *Foolish,* all my instincts told me. *This is foolish. A waste of time.* It had nothing to do with the mission nor did it bring us any closer to our objective. *Do not let her distract you. She is important to the mission, nothing more.*

As I circled after the girl, there was a flutter of something in the corner of my eye, like an enormous moth or bat. My hand shot up, snatching it from the air just before it hit the side of my head. Fragile, papery wings crumpled in my grip. I lowered my arm and opened my fingers to reveal a folded origami crane, the paper pitch-black and without design, lying crushed in the center of my palm.

Apprehension flickered. *A summons? Now?* Warily, I scanned the crowds, searching for hidden threats, for faces that I knew and gazes that lingered too long on me. I spotted nothing out of place, but a ripple of unease crept up my spine—not for me, but for the girl dancing in the crowd.

*What should I do? I can't take her with me. They'll kill her.* I glanced around, wondering if I could slip away and leave Yumeko here, if she'd be in the same place when I returned. But that was risky; I needed the girl to take me to the Steel Feather temple, and Yumeko seemed the type to wander after me if I simply disappeared. If she stumbled upon Shadow Clan business, they would show her no mercy.

Gazing around, I spotted a large square building on the corner of the street, blue curtains over the door welcoming in travelers. A ryokan.

*That will have to do.*

I stalked around the circle, found Yumeko in the sea of dancers and grabbed her by the arm. She jumped, gazing at me with large black eyes, and I felt an odd churning sensation in my stomach.

"Oh, Tatsumi-san." She blinked, then gave me a somewhat wry smile. "Did you change your mind? Were you so moved by the proverb of the kawauso and the Jade Prophet that you decided to give fun a try?"

I glared at her. "That wasn't even a real proverb."

"But it can still teach a valuable lesson. You don't want to become a mean old river otter, do you?"

Setting my jaw, I pulled her to the edge of the square, then nodded to the end of the street. "Do you see the building on the corner?" I asked in a furtive voice. "The one with the largest lantern and the blue curtains over the doorway?"

She gazed over the heads of the crowd. "The ryokan?"

So, she knew what an inn was, at least. Good. "Take these," I said, and dropped a trio of silver tora into her open palm. The coins clinked against each other; three silver disks with the imprint of a snarling tiger in the center. "Go to the inn. Use the money to get us a room for the night. That should cover everything."

She gazed at the money in her hands, then back up at me. "Where are you going?"

"I have…business to take care of. I won't be long."

"Business." Her brow furrowed. "At this time of night?" When I didn't answer, the frown deepened. "Why can't we go together?"

"That is not possible."

"Why not?"

Irritation flared, mingled with a hint of fear. "You ask a lot of questions," I told her in a cold voice. Questions were dangerous. Questions would get her killed faster than anything else. "Perhaps there are things you don't need to know."

She shrank back, then sighed and closed her fingers tightly around the coins. "Just…promise you'll come back," she said quietly. "That you won't disappear into the night and I'll never see you again. Swear to me that you'll come back."

"I have no intention of leaving."

"Do you promise?"

"Yes."

She nodded once and stepped away, but I abruptly reached out and caught her sleeve, making her turn. "I want the same promise," I told her, and a flicker of confusion crossed her face. "That you'll remain at the inn. That you won't try to leave or follow me. Stay in the room until I return, Yumeko. Promise me."

She nodded. "I will."

"Go, then." I released her, and she started across the street toward the ryokan, clutching the handful of coins. I watched until she had ducked through the doorway beneath the curtains, then turned and walked back the way we'd come.

Something rustled in my hand. When I opened my fist, the folded paper crane stirred and unfurled crumpled black wings. With several flaps, the paper creature rose into the air like a dying butterfly and flitted away.

I followed. The crane led me past the square, the drums still pounding out their booming rhythm, to a narrow alley between a teahouse and a textiles shop. The origami creature continued into the corridor, flitting over the ground, but I paused at the entrance and gazed into the dark. Overhead, a single string of chochin stretched away for a good fifty feet, illuminating the wooden walls on either side, before ending at an intersection. Wary of attacks and threats hidden in the shadows, I stepped into the alley.

Directly above me, a lantern flickered once and went out. The next one followed, going dark as its flame was extinguished, as did the next, and the next. One by one, all the chochin on the string down the alley sputtered and went out, plunging the narrow space into complete darkness.

I kept walking. Darkness was no cause for alarm; I was more comfortable in the shadows than the light. I following the dying lanterns until I reached the intersection and stopped, gazing down one road, then the other. They stretched away between buildings, cutting a narrow path behind stores and warehouses, completely empty and dark.

"Hello, Tatsumi."

The soft, high voice echoed behind me. And even though I recognized it, I stifled the urge to spin and draw my sword, forcing myself turn calmly. A figure sat in the back doorway of a storehouse, cloaked in shadow, where nothing had been before. His robes, black and unmarked, billowed around him, and his long hair fell loose down his shoulders and back. His face was painted white, with heavy lines of black around his eyes and down his chin. He wore a single short sword at his waist, but his skills were not of the blade, though they were just as deadly. He was *kami-touched*, what ordinary people would call a majutsushi, or magic user. All the clans had a few unique individuals whose talents reflected their family's element, but the majutsushi were by far the strongest and most powerful. As a Kage shinobi, I could work small Shadow magics—become invisible or create a ghostly twin, the talents of darkness and misdirection. But within Iwagoto, there were majutsushi that could turn the very land against you, call down fire or lightning, or heal a fatal wound in a few heartbeats. The mages of the Kage were not as destructively impressive as the Fire Clan, or miracle workers like the Water Clan; their command of the night and everything in it was subtle, though no less dangerous.

"Jomei-san," I said, and bowed, feeling his gaze follow my every move. "So it's your turn to check up on me, I see."

"That's not a very nice greeting, Tatsumi-san," Jomei said in his high, breathy voice. "If I was the type, I might be offended. You know why we must do this."

"I know."

"Kamigoroshi is not something we take lightly," Jomei went on as if I hadn't spoken. "We of the Shadow Clan know darkness better than most. We dance with it every day, and walk a very thin line between the shadows and the abyss. We know the evil that lurks in the hidden places of Iwagoto, and in the souls of men. And we know, more than any other clan, how easy it is to fall.

"You are the bearer of the Cursed Blade," Jomei went on. "Kamigoroshi, Hakaimono, whatever you wish to call it—that sword has corrupted the souls of better men than you, Kage Tatsumi. We have taught you how to resist its influence, trained you in the ways of the Kage shinobi. And yet, we know the terrible evil you carry, that one day, you might succumb to the darkness." His eyes narrowed. "Which is why we follow you, why these meetings are essential. If there is any hint that you are losing the battle with Hakaimono, we must take care of it immediately, before you lose yourself and the true demon is released."

I bowed my head. He was right, of course. What had come over me? I had never spoken to the majutsushi like that. Perhaps Yumeko's peasant mannerisms were affecting my judgment. "Forgive my outburst, Master Jomei," I said. "It won't happen again."

"Good. Now..." Jomei settled back, lacing his fingers under his chin as he watched me. "Since you seem to have a handle on Kamigoroshi, what of your mission? Did you reach the Silent Winds temple? Were you able to retrieve the scroll?"

"No." I straightened, stifling all emotion. I was a weapon. I felt nothing. "It was gone when I got there."

"Gone?" Jomei's gaze sharpened. "What do you mean gone? Are you saying that the mission was a failure?"

"An army of amanjaku attacked the temple. They were led by an oni." Jomei's brows arched; demons were something the Shadow Clan took very seriously. "The master of the temple sensed them coming," I went on, "and sent the scroll away before they could reach it."

"An oni." The other Kage's voice was grave. "Merciful Kami, who is summoning oni into this realm? Did you kill it?"

"No."

His lips thinned. "Tatsumi-san, I understand that you have been taught to answer only what is asked of you, but I am going to need a little more information than that. Please give me the full report of your mission and all the important details. Leave nothing out."

"As you wish." And I proceeded to tell him what had happened that night, everything from fighting the amanjaku to meeting Yumeko and agreeing to accompany her to Kin Heigen Toshi. I told him of the plan to find Master Jiro at the Hayate shrine, in the hopes that he could show us the way to the Steel Feather temple and the scroll that had eluded me.

"I see," Jomei said when I was done. He steepled two fingers together and tapped them against his lips. "The Steel Feather temple has been lost to legend," he murmured. "There are tales that it is protected by supernatural guardians, but no one knows where it is for certain, if it even exists." His gaze flicked to me again, hard and appraising. "Are you certain that accompanying the girl is the only way you can reach this Master Jiro?"

"I know the name of the shrine," I replied. "I could find it on my own. But the priest would have no cause to reveal what he knows to me. The girl was part of the Silent Winds temple, part of the order that protected the scroll. He will talk to her. And if she can show me the way to my objective, I would do better to follow."

Jomei sighed. "Very well." He nodded. "Continue to travel with her for now. If this Master Jiro knows the location of the Steel Feather temple and the scroll, you must find it at all costs. But be careful. The girl must not discover anything she has not already heard about the Shadow Clan. As soon as you are in possession of the scroll, return to Lady Hanshou."

I bowed. "I understand."

"I must inform Hanshou-sama of this," Jomei murmured. "Demons would have no use for the scroll. Someone is sending them." He rose gracefully, robes falling around him, and gave me a faint smile. "We'll be watching you, Tatsumi-san. Don't disappoint us."

I bowed once more, and when I rose, Jomei was gone.

The lanterns flickered, then sputtered to life one by one, illuminating the empty alley. I retraced my steps to the main road and made my way back to the inn where I had sent Yumeko.

I ducked beneath the curtain over the door then straightened and gazed around the entrance. A raised wooden floor sat a few steps away, with a couple benches placed along the walls to accommodate travelers. Across the room, a staircase ascended to the top floor where I assumed the guest accommodations were located. A woman, probably the hostess, hurried toward me, smiling and then dropping into a bow at the edge of the raised floor.

"Welcome, sir," she announced. "Please, come in. Will you be needing a room for the night?"

"Yes," I said. "But there was a girl here earlier. In a red

kimono with a white sash. She should have gotten us a room."

"Oh?" The hostess frowned slightly, glancing at the door. "She was your companion, was she? Well, she's not here anymore."

I narrowed my eyes. "What happened? Where is she?"

"There *was* a girl like that here," the hostess continued, sounding nervous now. "Just a few minutes ago, in fact. A cute little thing in a red kimono. But then, a wind blew in out of nowhere. It was so strong it nearly knocked me down. And when I looked up, the girl was gone."

# 11

## Weasels on the Wind

*I*t began with a strange wind.

I'd meant to get a room, I really had. And food. And maybe a bath. But especially food. I was starving, and the idea of sitting in a clean room eating a hot meal, instead of in the wilderness chewing on wild plants, sounded wonderful. Even though I was extremely curious about where Tatsumi was running off to, following him, especially when I had the Dragon's scroll hidden in my furoshiki, seemed like a bad idea.

Besides, he'd promised me he would return. I had to trust he would keep his word and come back.

But then, as I stepped over the threshold, a vicious blast of wind tossed my hair and caused me to stumble forward. The wind swirled through the doorway, ripping at the curtains and extinguishing the lanterns inside and out, plunging the room into shadow.

As I straightened, a lock of my hair suddenly fell to the floor, sliced clean through, as if by a very sharp blade.

My eyes widened, and a flutter of alarm went through me. I looked up to see a pair of beady red eyes watching me from atop one of the lanterns on the ceiling. They were attached to a furry brown creature with a pointed muzzle, small rounded ears, and a long, sinewy body.

*A weasel?* I frowned. An ordinary-looking weasel, except…

My mouth fell open. Except for the long, sickle-shaped blades growing right out of its forelegs. Curved and deadly looking, they extended behind the creature's elbows and glimmered in the darkness of the room. *Not a normal weasel at all*, I realized. A creature that possessed magic or other supernatural powers. A yokai.

Like me.

The weasel thing hissed, baring sharp yellow fangs, leaped off the statue and disappeared.

Another wind sliced through the ryokan, flapping the curtains, making me wince and stumble back. As I regained my balance, I felt a stinging sensation against my cheek and put a hand to my face.

My fingers came away smeared with blood.

Heart pounding, I looked through the doorway. The weasel thing was perched on the roof of a wooden vendor stall across the street, still watching me with eyes like embers in the shadows. I dropped my hand from the shallow cut across my cheek.

*It wants me to follow it.*

The other people in the room hadn't noticed the intruder.

They were still straightening up, recovering from being nearly knocked down, twice, by the mysterious wind. If I didn't leave, the weasel thing might keep coming back and slashing at others with those wickedly curved blades. Besides, I was curious, intrigued by the presence of another yokai, and a full-blooded one at that. It might be common to see them in the woods or mountains, but they tended to avoid large towns and places with lots of people. If the weasel yokai had shown himself to me here, it was for a reason.

Wiping my cheek with the back of my sleeve, I left the inn and hurried back into the streets of Chochin Machi.

The yokai flowed with the wind, flitting from place to place, invisible when it was on the move, reappearing when it was stationary. I followed it down the main street, watching as it flew from rooftop to rooftop, making the lanterns sway wildly in its wake. People stumbled as it passed overhead, holding on to their robes and parasols as the wind gusted by.

"What strange weather," someone muttered as I passed. "I wasn't aware that Chochin Machi was so windy."

I followed the creature down a narrow alley, watching the lanterns overhead dance and bounce until it turned a corner and we came to a dead end. With a blast of wind, the weasel thing twisted into the air and vanished. I waited, but neither the wind nor the yokai reappeared; the air was still and silent, and the passage was empty.

I frowned. *So that weasel thing just wanted to trick me. And now I'm lost.* I gazed around, wondering if I could retrace my steps back to the ryokan. Except I had no idea where I was. *Denga-san would find this hilarious.*

A soft chuckle came from behind me, low and mocking. "Well, hello, little fox. Wandering lonely back alleys all by yourself?"

I spun. A woman stood atop a roof, framed by the light of the moon. She was tall and slender, wearing an elegant kimono decorated with swirling white clouds against a sky blue background. Her hair was long, unbound and rippled like strands of ink in the wind. Billowy sleeves draped her arms, hanging nearly to her ankles, as she regarded me with pale, icy blue eyes.

"Um…hello," I greeted warily. "Is this your alley?" The woman didn't move, and I took a cautious step back. If she realized I was kitsune, she probably wouldn't take kindly to a strange yokai in her territory. "I'm just a little lost, so if you could just point me in the right direction…"

The woman's full lips curled as she looked me up and down. "Vermin," she remarked, making me frown. "A filthy and revolting vermin. Just like my kamaitachi." She raised her arm, and the weasel thing appeared on it with a blast of wind that whipped at my hair and clothes. "But at least they're full-blooded yokai, and somewhat useful. You're just a pathetic little half fox, aren't you?"

I laced back my ears. "Well that's not very nice," I said, feeling kitsune-bi spring to my fingertips. "We've only just met. Besides, foxes are *not* vermin—I think you're mistaking me for a rat or cockroach." I took a few cautious steps back. "But I seem to have caught you on a bad night, so I'll be leaving now—"

"Oh, you're not going anywhere, vermin."

She swept her arm out, and a blast of wind ripped at my clothes, making me stumble. At the same time, I felt a blinding pain in my leg, the feeling of being cut with a knife, though I saw nothing strike me. It happened so fast,

I didn't even have time to yelp before my leg gave out and I collapsed to the ground.

Gasping, I looked up to see a second weasel appear on the woman's other shoulder, beady eyes in its black-masked face glaring down at me. The edge of the sickle growing from its foreleg was smeared with blood.

"My name is Mistress Kazekira," the woman said, as both weasels glared at me from her slender shoulders. "I am one of the kami-touched, what the common folk call a wind witch, and the kamaitachi are my familiars. So don't think you can just run away, little vermin." She stroked one kamaitachi's head, but there was no affection in the gesture, only possession, and the weasel yokai cringed away from her touch. The wind witch didn't seem to notice or care. "And I see you are as simpleminded as you are common," she went on, wiping her hands together as if they were dirty. "I didn't lure you out here to chat. I brought you here to kill you."

Ice twisted my stomach. "Why?" I struggled to my feet, feeling my leg throb and pulse like it was on fire, and nearly collapsed again. My foxfire had sputtered out; I raised an arm and called it to life again, a blue-white globe flaring in my hand. It wouldn't hurt them, but maybe they didn't know that. "I haven't done anything to you, or your weasels. Why are you doing this?"

The wind witch laughed heartily, her hair writhing madly around her. "Oh, little vermin," she chuckled, raising her arm. The two kamaitachi crouched on her shoulders, blades gleaming as they targeted me. "If you cannot figure that out, then you really are too stupid to keep living."

"So loud," sighed a new, unfamiliar voice behind me. "At

least you could have the courtesy to kill her quickly. Some of us are trying to sleep, after all."

Startled, the wind witch lowered her arm, and I turned toward the voice. A body sat on one of the barrels close to the wall, cloaked in the shadows cast from the roof. Raising its head, it stood and walked into the light.

My heartbeat fluttered, whether in awe or fear, I couldn't tell. A man stood before me, tall and slender, the moonlight casting a silvery halo around him. His billowing robes were a spotless white, trimmed in red and black, without patterns, markings or a family crest to identify him. His hair was very fine, even longer than the wind witch's, and a bright, stunning silver, the color of a polished blade. An enormously long, curved sword was strapped to his back, the sheath dwarfing a katana's by several inches, the hilt doubled in length. Lazy, heavy-lidded eyes, like molten gold, met my gaze, then slid past me to the witch standing overhead.

"You're making an awful racket," the stranger said in that low, vaguely wry voice, as if he found this situation amusing. "It's fortunate humans are all deaf, or they would hear you for miles. Does it really take such elaboration to kill one little half fox in an empty alley?"

"Seigetsu-sama," whispered the witch. Her face had gone pale, the wind dying to a murmur as she stared at him. "What are you doing here? Do you know this vermin?"

"The half-breed?" The stranger's lips twisted in a smirk. "No, I was just in the area, and decided to take a nap. By all means, continue." He waved at me in an offhand manner and started walking away.

My heart sank. I had thought the stranger was going to help me. He looked powerful, with his golden eyes and giant sword; even the wind witch seemed afraid of him. Kazekira smiled triumphantly and raised her arm, her clothes and hair beginning to snap in the wind once more.

"Although…" The stranger stopped, rubbing his chin, and glanced up at the witch again. "They say kamaitachi move so quickly, the naked eye cannot comprehend them. I've always wondered if that was true."

Reaching back, he drew his weapon over his head, lacquered case and all. Holding the sheath in his left hand, he slid one foot back until he was in some sort of stance, his empty hand hovering a few inches from the hilt of the giant sword.

"Let's play a game," the stranger said, a vicious smile crossing his face as he stared at the witch. "You send your familiars to kill this half-breed, and I try to cut them from the air before they can reach her. If the kamaitachi are as fast as the stories claim, they should be in no danger. If not, well…" He lifted one lean shoulder in a shrug. "You can always find more, right?"

The wind witch stiffened. On her shoulders, the two kamaitachi cowered, looking reluctant. My heart pounded as the silence stretched out. The beautiful stranger didn't move, his hand steady and motionless over the hilt of his sword, ready to draw steel in the blink of an eye.

Finally, Kazekira raised her chin and sniffed. "Much as I would like to play your game, Seigetsu-sama," she said in a lofty voice, "I don't think I can convince my cowardly vermin weasels to cooperate, so you'll have to excuse us." With a sneer, she glanced in my direction. "Consider yourself lucky, half-breed. You get to live tonight. But Seigetsu-sama won't always be around to protect you. My kamaitachi and I will see you soon."

A strong wind gusted through the shrine, stirring dust

and making the lanterns sway. The wind witch rose into the air, robes billowing around her, and drifted away over the rooftops. In seconds, she had disappeared.

As the wind died down, I looked at the stranger, watching as he straightened and slipped the weapon over his shoulders again. Seigetsu-*sama*, the witch had called him, a suffix reserved for those of the highest station. Did that mean he was a lord, perhaps the daimyo of one of the Great Clans? I wouldn't have thought that I would meet someone so important in the back alleys of Chochin Machi, but I didn't know much about the outside world. Perhaps he was taking an evening stroll around town…without the company of his samurai and bodyguards. It seemed unlikely, but, whatever his reasons, I did know that his timing was impeccable.

*"Ano..."* I stammered as the stranger glanced up, those lazy golden eyes pinning me in place. For a moment, I felt almost naked beneath them, all my secrets laid bare. Shaking myself, I offered a smile. "Thank you."

One corner of his mouth quirked. "You're welcome," he stated simply. "And consider yourself lucky. I don't make a habit of saving oblivious half foxes from angry kamaitachi, but tonight I thought I would make an exception." He regarded me with cool amusement. "You know why Kazekira was after you, yes?"

How did he know about the scroll? Come to think of it, how did Kazekira? I swallowed hard, feeling the narrow case hidden in my furoshiki. "I really have no idea."

One silver brow arched. "You're going to have to lie better than that if you want to survive, half-breed," he told me. "There are many out there searching desperately for the scroll, who will do anything to acquire it." I tensed, and he chuckled, shaking his head. "You can relax. I have no interest in the Dragon's wish, or you. But I will offer this bit of advice—don't tell the demonslayer about Kazekira."

My ears pricked. He knew about Tatsumi, as well? Who *was* he? "Why?"

His eyes, golden and mesmerizing, bore into mine. "Because, little fox, powerful kami-touched witches don't randomly attack ordinary peasant girls without reason, especially in a town or city. The demonslayer knows this. If you tell him you were assaulted by a wind witch with kamaitachi familiars, he's going to want to know why she was after you. And what will you tell him then?"

"Oh." I bit my lip. "Good point."

Shaking his head, the stranger started to walk away but paused again, watching me from the corner of his eye. "You will likely see Kazekira again," he warned. "If you do, and the demonslayer somehow gets himself into trouble, remember this." He raised a hand, the last three fingers held up, long and elegant. "Kamaitachi always come in threes. Their loyalty to each other is unbreakable, and if one is threatened, the others will do whatever it takes to save their brother or sister. Remember that, and ask yourself why Kazekira has only two familiars. Sayonara."

Before I could reply, he strode down the alleyway and vanished into the darkness.

Walking was painful. Gritting my teeth, I pushed myself along the wall of the alley, feeling the wound throb and pulse with every motion. Gingerly, I pulled up the hem of my robe, expecting to see a mess of blood smeared across my skin and dripping to the ground. I found the gash easily enough, a thin straight cut right above my knee. But, though it looked fairly deep, it wasn't bleeding.

As I limped toward the main street, there was a blur of shadow, and the bright edge of a sword suddenly blocked my path. Freezing, I looked up into Tatsumi's cold, unamused face.

I shrank from him as he pressed forward, his terrible blade casting his face in a faint glow as it hovered between us. Hitting the wall, I winced as the movement sent a flare of pain through my leg, making me gasp. *"Ite,"* I whimpered. *Ouch.*

Instantly, the blade at my throat lowered a few inches, and Tatsumi frowned at me. "You're injured," he stated, his cold fury thawing a bit. "What happened?"

"I…um… I was attacked," I stammered. Remembering what Seigetsu had said, I thought quickly. "I was going to get us a room at the inn, but then there was this strange wind and…something hit me. I ran, and it chased me here."

"Where is it now?"

"It was invisible," I went on, making his eyes narrow. "Or it was too fast. I didn't see anything when I was cut. But I did look up once and there was this…this weasel thing with knives growing from its legs, perched on the corner of a roof."

"Kamaitachi? Here?" Tatsumi took a step back and scanned the alley, his gaze sweeping the rooftops. His sword flared, almost in excitement, but the shadows surrounding us were empty.

"Kama…itachi?" I repeated, as if this was the first time I'd heard it. "What are they?"

"Sickle weasels," Tatsumi answered, not taking his eyes from our surroundings. "A type of yokai that travel on the wind. The stories say that there are always three of them, and that they have a particular way of defending their territory—one knocks you down, the second cuts you, and the third applies medicine to the wound so you don't bleed to death. This all happens near-simultaneously, so the intruder doesn't know he's been injured until later when the wound starts to bleed." He tore his gaze from the rooftops and glanced at me, appraising. "In reality, kamaitachi produce a type of secretion and coat their claws with it, so when they strike you, the gash doesn't bleed right away. But they're usually found farther north—I've never heard of one attacking someone in a city. Are you sure that's what you saw?"

"A weasel with giant knives growing out of its legs? I am very certain." I was glad that he seemed to believe me. I didn't dare tell him about Kazekira. Better that this was a strange yet random yokai attack, and I the clueless, hapless visitor who was in the wrong place at the wrong time. "They weren't very nice weasels," I grumbled, wincing as my leg throbbed again. "Are kamaitachi always this cranky, or was I just unlucky tonight?"

Tatsumi sighed, sheathing his sword. "Can you walk?" he inquired, not looking at the leg where the kamaitachi had slashed me. I nodded and pushed myself off the wall again. Pain flared, and my leg nearly buckled, but I clenched my jaw and limped after Tatsumi.

On alert for yokai and sudden winds, I followed him back to the ryokan. Tatsumi walked slowly, setting a pace that I could easily keep up with, though his hand did not stray far from his weapon. I scanned the rooftops, shadows and crowds of Chochin Machi for a figure with long hair floating on the wind, but if Kazekira and her sickle weasels were close, they were staying out of sight.

Back at the ryokan, we left our regular shoes at the entrance as was custom and found our room. Curious to see what the inside of a ryokan looked like, I stepped eagerly through the frame, but found a normal room on the other side of the door. It was elegant in its simplicity, with warm tan walls, thick tatami mats and a small alcove with a single ayame-iris in a vase. There were no beds, as it was too early for the futons to be pulled out of the closet, so a low table sat on the floor in the center of the room. A tray with a teapot and cups had been placed on the table, steam curling gently from the spout.

Tatsumi shut the door, removed the straw sandals the inn had provided for interior use and placed them by the door. I followed his example, and he nodded to one of the pillows at the table. "Sit down," he ordered, without any explanation of why or what he was going to do. I did as he instructed, gingerly lowering myself onto the blue pillow, clenching my jaw as my leg throbbed with the movement.

Tatsumi knelt at the end of the table, reached under his obi and drew out a packet of colored paper that could fit in the palm of my hand. He placed it on the table and opened it carefully, revealing small amount of what looked like green dust. As I watched, fascinated, he poured hot liquid from the teapot into a cup, then carefully trickled a few drops onto the powder.

"What…is that?" I asked.

Ignoring me, Tatsumi mixed the green dust with the water until it became a paste. Picking up the entire square, he held it gently in his palm and looked up. Glittering violet eyes met mine, and my stomach turned over.

"Where did the kamaitachi cut you?"

I hesitated, feeling my heart beat faster under my robes. He was so close. The scroll was safely tucked away in the furoshiki over my shoulder, but would he see it? Would he get close enough to feel it?

Tatsumi didn't move, eyes flat and expression blank as he waited. I paused a moment longer, then carefully pulled up the hem of my robe, showing the long, straight gash on my thigh. It was red and angry-looking, and it throbbed like a dozen hornet stings, but it still wasn't bleeding. And somehow, seeing it clearly made it hurt all the more.

Tatsumi didn't blink. In one smooth motion, he scooped up the green paste in two fingers, reached down and smeared it firmly onto the cut.

*"Ite!"* I yelped, jerking my leg back, startled by both the sudden, dizzying pain of my wound, and the casual treatment from the human in front of me. He gave me a puzzled look, as if he didn't understand my reaction.

"It's a healing salve," he explained. "It will numb the injury and keep it from becoming infected." He reached for my leg again, and I flinched away, making him frown. "Do you not want aid? We have to take care of the wound now or it will start to bleed soon. Let me see it."

"It hurts," I gritted out, pulling back my hem to expose the gash again. "I don't know if you've ever been cut by a sickle weasel, Tatsumi, but this is my first time, and it hurts quite a lot. Please, be more gentle."

"Gentle." He gave me another puzzled look, as if the concept was completely foreign to him.

"Yes. Kind? Tender? Not making it feel like my leg is going to fall off?" He still looked baffled, and I frowned. "Haven't you had injuries treated before?"

"Of course. But the intent was always to treat the wounds as quickly and efficiently as possible. Showing pain is a weakness—it exposes you and lets your enemies know you are vulnerable."

"Oh." I was starting to understand my cold, dangerous travel companion a little better. "We were raised very differently, I think."

He tilted his head, regarding me with appraising violet eyes. "You weren't punished for showing weakness while injured?"

"No. Denga-san once said that I didn't need to be punished when I injured myself doing something stupid, because the injury was all I needed to learn not to do it again."

Tatsumi frowned. "I don't understand."

"Well, I learned that you really shouldn't climb onto the temple roof at midnight during a rainstorm. And that if you're going to pop out of a closet to scare a martial arts master, be ready to duck. And if you have to flee an angry bear in the forest by climbing a tree, you should first check that there aren't any hornets' nests hiding under the branches."

Tatsumi only stared at me, looking faintly bewildered. I sighed. "Master Isao taught kindness and patience in all things, especially when one was injured," I went on. "He said that caring for the spirit was just as important as caring for the body." Looking into Tatsumi's blank, emotionless face, I had a sudden, heartbreaking insight. "No one has ever showed you any kindness before, have they?"

"Your wound is bleeding," Tatsumi stated, making me start and glance down at my leg, where a trickle of red was starting to crawl down my skin. Before it could drip to the floor, Tatsumi swiftly pressed a cloth to the cut, making me grit my teeth, and all conversation stopped as he cleaned and bandaged the gash. He might have been a little less rough, but he was *not* gentle.

Thankfully, food arrived soon after: bowls of rice, trays of pickled cabbage and a deep black pot that, when the top was removed, revealed a steaming array of vegetables, meat and bubbling broth that made my stomach leap in excitement. Tatsumi called it a nabe—a hot pot—and I gorged myself until I couldn't eat another mushroom. But the night's danger wasn't yet over. When the meal was finished and the tray removed, my face stared back at me from the table's lacquered surface: yellow eyes and pointed ears reflected in the dark wood. Fortunately at that moment, Tatsumi had been watching the maid depart, and didn't see the flash of kitsune in the room with him. I retreated to a corner, claiming my wound was throbbing, and stayed far away from the table and its treacherous shiny surface.

Not long after, the maid arrived to pull the futons from the closet and lay them out on the floor, and I crawled beneath the blankets as Tatsumi put out the light. After secretly making sure the lacquered case was safe and secured in my furoshiki, I lay in the darkness for a long time, thinking about kamaitachi, wind witches and various demons who wanted the scroll.

And Tatsumi. Kage Tatsumi, the demonslayer of the Shadow Clan. A boy who didn't know the first thing about kindness, compassion or mercy. Who was ruthless, dangerous and would kill anyone—human, demon or yokai—that got in our way. Who didn't realize that the exact thing he wanted, the entire reason for his mission, was sitting not ten feet from him. If he ever discovered I had the scroll…

I shivered and clutched the wrap a little tighter to my chest, feeling the hard length of the scroll case within. I knew I should be afraid of him; there was no doubt that he would kill me if he found out I'd been lying to him. Not only about the scroll, but about my true nature, as well. Even if I was only half yokai, I doubted the demonslayer of the Shadow Clan would take kindly to a kitsune who had been pretending to be human this whole time.

Tatsumi was dangerous, I understood that. But, at the same time, I couldn't help but feel…sorry for him. He didn't know how to laugh, or smile, or have any fun. He didn't know the pleasures of the simple things—laughing, dancing, finding beauty in the world. It seemed like a very boring existence. The brief bout of dancing tonight had certainly lifted my spirits, and I knew Master Isao and the others wouldn't want me to be miserable. I wondered if I could show Tatsumi that there was more to life. Then maybe he wouldn't be so cold and scary. It certainly wouldn't hurt for him to smile a little. I would just have to be careful about it.

Tatsumi, I noticed, did not lie down on the futon but chose to sit in the corner, facing the door, with his sword propped on one leg. And when I awoke early the next morning, he was still there.

# 12

## The Demon Bear of Suimin Mori

The next morning, the fabricated magic of Chochin Machi had faded with the night.

Yumeko and I left at dawn, departing the ryokan before the sun rose over the distant hills. In the gray pre-morning light, the streets were nearly deserted, the floating red lanterns dark and lifeless. The shops, too, were closed and dark; I had slipped out of the inn the night before to buy supplies for the journey, refilling my rice pouch and purchasing enough nonperishable food to last several days. My supply of coin was dwindling, however, especially with the unexpected stop at the inn. If I'd been alone, I wouldn't have bothered with the ryokan. Yumeko was proving to be an unexpected drain on both my time and my supplies.

*Then kill her.*

Instinctively, I cut off my emotions and shut my mind to

the sword, giving it nothing to latch on to. The bloodlust faded and the faint hostility toward Yumeko disappeared, leaving me frozen inside.

Yumeko yawned, covering her mouth as she trailed beside me, barely favoring her leg. The healing salve, a secret mix of numbing agents created by the best poison-makers in Iwagoto, was doing its work. "The town certainly looks different now," she remarked, gazing around the empty street. "I guess it only comes to life after dark. Shame we have to leave so soon—I would've liked to see more of it. Without being harassed by marauding sickle weasels, of course." She glanced at me with a smile. "What do sickle weasels like, Tatsumi-san?"

"What?"

"Well, if we run into any more sickle weasels, I was thinking we could give them something to make them not attack us." She cocked her head at me. "You know a lot about demons and yokai. What do they like? Do they like fried tofu? I'm very fond of fried tofu."

"I don't know what they like."

She sighed. "Maybe I'll try tossing them a rice ball."

*No one has ever showed you any kindness before, have they?*

I shook myself as her words from last night echoed in my head, haunting me. Kindness? Kindness was a vulnerability, a luxury given those who did not hunt demons. To be kind, you had to drop your guard, something I could not afford, especially with Hakaimono poised to take advantage of the smallest distraction. My various sensei—the men and women who trained me—knew that. I was a weapon to the clan, nothing more. Kindness had no place in my life.

As we left Chochin Machi and continued our journey

toward the capital, I spotted a single crow perched on a lantern string over the street. I wondered if my mysterious observer and the attack on Yumeko were related, and if they were, I wondered when and where the person behind them would try again.

I'd be ready if they did.

By the time the sun had fully risen, we had left Chochin Machi far behind and were following the Hotaru River as it wound north toward the capital. After several miles, the flat fields and grassy farmland became hillier, and the path diverged from the riverbanks, heading into the mountains.

As we approached the forest, Yumeko suddenly stopped, her attention drawn to an old wooden signpost staked into the ground.

"Entering Kiba-sama's forest," she read slowly, as the sign was cracked and faded, the words nearly worn away. "Tread softly. Beware of Kiba-sama." Blinking, she looked at me. "Oh, he sounds very dangerous. Who is Kiba-sama? Do you know, Tatsumi?"

I did. My training required me to know the stories and legends of all demons, yokai and spirits that existed throughout the land. "Kiba-sama," I explained, "is the name the locals gave to an onikuma, a great demon bear that makes his home in this forest. The stories say Kiba-sama stands taller than two men, and that he is so large, he can pick up horses with one paw and carry them back to his lair to devour."

Her eyes widened, and she glanced at the edge of the trees. "How exciting. But he doesn't seem very pleasant. What if we run into him?"

"It's unlikely that we will. No one has seen Kiba-sama in a long time, close to twenty years. But we should walk softly." I gazed at the sign again. "The tales claim that, deep in these woods, there is a cave where animals never venture and birds never sing in the surrounding trees. Kiba-sama sleeps there still, and has been slumbering for the past two decades. So when you walk through his forest, tread softly, lest you wake the great demon bear of Suimin Mori, who will be ravenous after twenty years of hibernation."

"Ah." Yumeko looked at the forest again and nodded. "Tread softly. I can do that. The leaves won't even know they're being stepped on."

The trees closed around us as we entered the woods, large pines and redwoods whose branches shut out the sky, making the forest floor dim and cool. We followed the trail over moss-covered rocks and fallen trees, between the trunks of ancient giants, and through patches of forest where the sunlight never touched the ground. The woods were unnaturally still; as the legend promised, no birds sang in the trees, no insects droned, no deer or small animals moved through the undergrowth. An ominous taint hung in the air, a subtle aura of fear that was enough to silence the whole forest.

We came to a ravine, a gap in the earth that dropped sharply away to a nearly dry riverbed, far below. A bridge made of rope and wooden planks spanned the gulf, swaying gently in the open air. A tiny roadside shrine to Doroshin, the Kami of roads and travel, sat next to one of the bridge posts, the base littered with offerings of coin and withered flowers. As Yumeko walked to the edge of the cliff and peered down, I placed a copper kaeru at the base of the shrine, then closed my eyes and put my hands together, offering a quick prayer to Doroshin for safe travels. I wasn't certain that the gods would hear the prayer of a lowly assassin, especially one whose hands were stained with blood and filth, but it was always better to be cautious. Better that the Kami ignored you than risk their wrath and bad fortune.

Opening my eyes, I was surprised to see Yumeko standing beside me, hands pressed together and eyes closed. Lowering her arms, she stepped back and turned to me with a smile.

"I used to pray to Doroshin every night," she explained, with a quick glance at the shrine. "I always dreamed of traveling, of leaving the temple and seeing what's out there, even though it was frightening. I would ask Doroshin to show me a way." She sighed, her gaze traveling to the bridge and what lay beyond.

Her eyes darkened, a shadow falling over her face, but she blinked and shook herself, and returned to normal. "This is not how I wanted it to happen," she murmured, "but I'm here, on the open road, like I asked. I figured I would at least thank him, just in case." Looking at me again, she tilted her head, regarding me curiously. "I didn't think you would be the type to pray, Tatsumi-san."

"The Kami see everyone," I replied simply. "I'm not exempt from their notice, and I carry a sword named Godslayer. Whenever possible, I try not to offend them."

We started across the bridge. The weathered planks creaked under our weight, rocking back and forth as we walked over empty space. Below us, a steady wind howled through the ravine, making the bridge sway in the breeze, but the ropes were thick and strong, and in no danger of snapping.

However, when we were halfway across the chasm, a sudden gust of wind caused the planks to buck wildly. I dropped my weight, bending my knees to keep my balance, as Yumeko yelped and grabbed the railings tightly.

As the wind died down and the bridge stopped moving, high-pitched laughter echoed over the ravine, and I jerked my gaze to the cliff.

A woman stood on the other side of the bridge, blocking our path. She was tall and slender, with long black hair, and she wore wooden geta clogs and a blue-and-white kimono that did little to hide her body. Ice-blue eyes glittered coldly as she watched us from the edge of the ravine.

I sank into a crouch, my hand dropping to the hilt of my sword, as Kamigoroshi flared with excitement. The woman smiled.

"The fearsome Kage demonslayer," she called, still smiling. "Bearer of the infamous Kamigoroshi. Your reputations precede you both. Allow me to introduce myself." She gave a shallow, mocking bow. "My name is Mistress Kazekira, wind witch of the Howling Mountains, and I have been waiting for you."

A wind witch. So, the kamaitachi were probably her familiars. That meant the attack on Yumeko wasn't a random occurrence, but a threat or a warning aimed at me.

I took a step toward the witch, tightening my fingers around the hilt of my blade. "If you know who I am, you know what will happen if you fight me here," I warned. "Leave this place, before I cut a path right through you."

The witch laughed. "Well, that's not very polite, Kage-san," she said, her voice echoing over the chasm. "Threatening a person you just met, and a woman at that. How unforgivably rude. Didn't your people teach you any manners?"

Wind began swirling around the witch, causing her sleeves to flap and her hair to stream behind her. Yumeko gasped, grabbing the ropes for balance, as the bridge swayed dangerously from side to side. I kept my feet, adjusting my weight to balance on the rocking planks, as the bridge shuddered and bounced like a ship at sea.

The wind witch rose into the air, robes flapping wildly in the gale, and grinned down at us. "No, I would be a fool to pick a fight with the Kage demonslayer. I can't stand the sight of blood. But I'm afraid I can't let you go any farther." Raising an arm, she snapped her fingers, and the wind around her surged even faster. "Kamaitachi, heed my words! Cut the ropes, and let us see if they can fly."

"Yumeko," I snapped, turning to the girl, "run! Get off the bridge."

With a shriek of wind, the ropes holding up our side of the bridge snapped. The wooden planks bucked in the gale, making Yumeko scream, before we plummeted downward.

I had just enough time to spin around and lunge for the girl, grabbing her around the waist as the bridge started to fall. I snatched one of the ropes with the other hand and tightened my grip as we swung back toward the cliff with the rest of the bridge. Yumeko gasped, clinging to my jacket, as I looked up to see the gully wall coming right at us.

"Hang on," I growled, and twisted my body around so the girl would be protected. We struck the ravine wall, thankfully in a patch of bushes instead of rocks, the bridge bouncing and clattering beside us. The jolt drove the air from my lungs and nearly ripped my arm from the socket, and I fought to keep my grip on both the girl and the rope.

Clenching my jaw, I looked up toward the edge of the ravine, about thirty feet overhead, and shifted my weight so I could plant a foot between the bridge planks. The tension on my arm eased, and I glanced down at the girl.

"Yumeko," I gritted out, and she looked at me with huge

black eyes. One hand clung to my haori, the other clutched the furoshiki across her chest. "We're going to have to climb to the top. Can you grab the rope?"

She nodded, a determined look crossing her face. Reaching over my head, she grabbed the line, but before she could start pulling herself up, a high-pitched chuckle rang overhead and a gust of wind shook the planks.

The wind witch floated to the edge of the ravine, peering down at us. "Well, isn't this a terrible predicament," she mocked. "Kage-san, if you let go of the girl, you could probably get yourself out of this little dilemma. Of course, she'd fall straight to her death, but that wouldn't bother you, would it? Not the infamous demonslayer." She chuckled again, as a large brown weasel materialized on her shoulder, watching us with beady red eyes. "In fact, I'll make you a deal, Kage-san. Give me the scroll, and I'll take my kamaitachi and leave."

Pressed against me, Yumeko went rigid, and my own heartbeat picked up, making me frown. The witch was after the scroll. Perhaps she was the one who had sent the demons to the temple. "I don't have it," I told her.

"Oh, well, you're no fun at all, Kage-san," the wind witch said, crossing her arms. "How disappointing. I suppose we'll have to do this the hard way, then. Say hello to Kiba-sama for me."

The last of the ropes parted. Yumeko gave a yelp and buried her face in my jacket as the bridge plummeted down the gully wall, taking us with it. I rolled, tucking my chin and hunching my shoulders, trying to absorb most of the impact with my body. For a few seconds, the world spun dizzyingly around me, then it finally stopped.

I pushed myself upright and looked around. We had come

to a halt at the bottom of the ravine, the shattered remains of the bridge curled around us in the brush. I ached, both from slamming into the cliff and from the slide down the gully wall, but nothing was broken, and the bruises would heal. The girl, lying beside me with her eyes closed, was far more troubling. If she was dead, I would have to find the way to the Steel Feather temple on my own.

"Yumeko." I pushed dark strands of hair from her face and saw a thin line of blood running down her temple. A cold knot twisted my stomach, and I shook her arm. "Hey. Get up."

She groaned and cracked open an eye. "Are we dead?"

An odd sense of relief filled me, dissolving the chill in my gut. "No," I muttered, struggling to my feet. "But the wind witch is close. We need to..."

I trailed off, suddenly realizing what lay on the other side of the gorge.

"Tatsumi?" Yumeko climbed to her feet behind me. "Do you see her? Where—"

I reached back and gripped her arm while pressing a finger to my lips. She fell silent, staring at me and then following my gaze until she saw what I was looking at.

On the other side of the riverbed, about forty yards away, the gaping mouth of a cave opened up into darkness. Bones were scattered about the entrance, white and gleaming, and a strange dark miasma coiled and writhed from the entrance.

Yumeko gasped, then clapped a hand over her mouth, as if remembering. *Tread softly. Beware of Kiba-sama.*

A ringing laugh and a blast of wind announced the arrival of the wind witch. She hovered overhead, hair and clothes whipping around her, "Oh, no no no, Kage-san," she called in a shrill voice. "Where do you think you're going? I didn't come all this way to watch you sneak off like a frightened rodent." She gazed at the cave, smiled and took a deep breath. "Oh, Kiiiiiiiiiiiba-sama!" she bellowed, making me wince. Her voice echoed through the gully, bouncing off the walls, and the miasma in front of the cave started to churn. "You've been asleep far too long! Wake up, wake up! I've brought some friends for you to play with!"

A deep, rumbling growl echoed from the cave, making Yumeko wince. "That's right, Kiba-sama!" called the witch. "Come on out! You must be famished after such a long sleep! Look who I've brought to visit!"

There was a coughing roar, and heavy footsteps made the ground tremble. I turned in resignation, even as Hakaimono gave a snarl of excited glee, and a gigantic furry shape filled the mouth of the cave and let out a bellow that shook the ravine walls.

"Kiba-sama," Yumeko breathed, as the monstrous creature turned to eye us with ravenous hunger. The demon bear of Suimin Mori was twice as large as its ordinary brethren, with massive shoulders and clawed forepaws that crushed stone beneath them. Arrows and spear hafts jutted from its hide, snapped and broken, and its eyes blazed with red fire as it reared onto its hind legs, towering over us.

"Yumeko," I said, not taking my eyes from my huge opponent. "Stay back. Find a place to hide and don't move until its safe."

"You're not going to fight that giant thing, are you?"

"I'll be fine." I dropped my hand to the hilt of my sword, feeling excitement and bloodlust pulse through me. "This is what I do."

I drew Kamigoroshi and felt the demon's power surge up, howling as the sword was bared to the light. As Yumeko scrambled back, Kiba-sama charged with a roar, covering the space between us in two giant strides. It lunged, and I dove out of the way, feeling the massive forepaw smash into the stones and crush the earth beneath it. Kiba-sama whirled, surprisingly quick for its bulk, and swatted at me again. I dodged the lethal claws and lashed out with my sword. The blade cut deep into the monster's shaggy hide, but barely left a scratch as I leaped away. Hakaimono snarled in frustration.

*Dammit, its fur is too thick. I'll have to get closer to land a killing blow.*

With a bellow, Kiba-sama reared onto his hind legs, towering over me. I dove aside as the monster came crashing down, trying to crush me under a few tons of muscle, bone and flesh. Rolling to my feet, I palmed the single kunai I was able to keep on my person and hurled it at the demon bear. The throwing knife flew straight at Kiba-sama's forehead but bounced off its thick skull, doing little but annoying it.

The bear charged again with a roar, and I tensed to spring away. But as it drew close, a blast of wind howled through the ravine, and something hit me from behind, slashing a line of fire across my back. I staggered and barely dodged aside as Kiba-sama plowed into the gully wall, crushing stone and vegetation and leaving a massive hole.

The wind witch's laughter rang out overhead. "That was almost it for you, Kage-san," she mocked, as I spared her a split-second glance. Several yards away, Kiba-sama backed slowly out of the wall, shaking his head and shedding rocks and dust. The wind witch laughed again. "Ignore my kamaitachi, and they'll slice you to pieces. Ignore Kiba-sama, and he'll devour you in a heartbeat. I wonder how you're going to—*ite!*"

A fist-sized rock flew through the air and struck the side of her head. Clapping a hand to her temple, the wind witch glared at the other side of the ravine, where Yumeko stood with a stone in one slender hand.

"You talk too much," the girl said angrily as the witch spun toward her. "And your voice is very shrill. Kamaitachi!" she cried as the woman stiffened in outrage. "Listen to me! I know this isn't what you want. I know you've been manipulated, that she's made you her familiars against your will. Help us, and I'll do my best to set you free."

"Silence, vermin." The witch gestured sharply, and a whirlwind shrieked through the gully, lifting Yumeko up and slamming her into the wall. The girl cried out as she collided with the ravine, tumbled to the ground and collapsed limply against the stones.

*Yumeko.* I clenched a fist, knowing I couldn't go to her now, as the monstrous bear stood between us. The wind witch sniffed in disdain, turning away from the girl's limp body. "Do not presume you understand our situation," she said. "The kamaitachi are *mine*, and will remain so, regardless of what you think."

Kiba-sama charged again, swiping a huge claw at my head as it tried cornering me against the ravine. I leaped aside and ran along the gully wall to escape the demon bear. But my legs were moving strangely now, an odd weakness spreading through them, and a tremor went through my body as I landed. Jaws gaping, Kiba-sama whirled and lunged. I slashed at the blocky muzzle, making it recoil with a howl, blood streaming from its nose.

"Oh-hohoho, you are certainly putting up a fight, Kage-san." The wind witch laughed. "By the way, if you're feeling a bit strange, don't worry. That's just the poison on the kamaitachis' claws, starting to paralyze you. You should be completely incapacitated in a few minutes. Tell Kiba-sama thank you for being such a lovely distraction for my kamaitachi. They never would have gotten close otherwise."

*Poison. Dammit.* I could feel the numbness in my legs, making it hard to move, and my fingers were starting to tingle. Kiba-sama stalked toward me, blood and ribbons of drool dripping from its muzzle, eyes burning with madness. Hakaimono raged at me, fighting the barriers of my consciousness, demanding entry.

*Let me in*, a furious howl echoed at the back of my mind. *You're going to die otherwise. Open your mind now!*

"No," I muttered through clenched teeth, and raised my sword. "Not yet."

With another earsplitting roar, Kiba-sama bore down on me once more. This time, I didn't leap away, but scrambled backward, dodging claws and the snapping teeth, lashing back when I could. The wind witch's laughter echoed, and a gust of wind sliced across my leg, making me stagger. I fell backward, and Kiba-sama immediately lunged, huge jaws gaping, to bite me in half.

*Now, Hakaimono!*

Purple fire erupted along the edge of the blade, illuminating the symbols carved into the steel. They flared a brilliant white in the eyes of the bear, who flinched back with a snort of alarm. Power filled me, burning away the weakness of my frail human body; with a snarl, I leaped at Kiba-sama, vaulting off a thick foreleg to land between his shoulders. Spears and arrow shafts jutted out of his fur as I raised the sword high, then plunged it through the back of his neck.

Kiba-sama bellowed and reared onto his hind legs, thrashing and shaking his head in an effort to throw me off. I grabbed the end of a spear jutting from his hide and sank the sword in deeper, as the demon bear roared and bucked. I caught a split-second sight of the girl, still crumpled on the ground, just before Kiba-sama spun and lurched blindly in her direction.

*You will not touch her!* With a final shove, the point of Kamigoroshi exploded out the front of the bear's throat. Kiba-sama gave a strangled bellow and toppled forward, hitting the ground with a crash that echoed through the ravine. His huge body twitched several times, claws raking deep gouges in the earth, before the great demon bear of Suimin Mori gave a final shudder and was still.

I yanked Kamigoroshi free and rose, feeling the sword's savage glee as it reveled in the fight, the violence and the spilled blood. Power and adrenaline coursed through my veins but, as always, I felt the phantom claws of Hakaimono digging into my mind, trying to gain entrance, to force its way into my soul. I shut my mind to the demon once more, forcing it out of my consciousness and back into the darkness where it belonged.

As I dropped from the huge carcass, my legs gave out, as if the muscles in them had been cut through. I staggered, the blade falling from my numb fingers, and collapsed beside Kiba-sama, as slow, mocking clapping echoed through the ravine.

"Bravo, Kage-san, bravo." The wind witch floated into my sight, grinning down at me. I lay on my back, panting, my hand just a finger's width from Kamigoroshi. "That was a truly impressive battle. I understand now why the demons fear you."

*Dammit, I can't move.* I tried pushing myself to my elbows, to roll over and grab my sword, but my body felt like it was made of stone, and my limbs moved only a few inches. The wind witch drifted closer, pulling a short blade from her sleeves as her feet touched the ground.

"Don't take this personally, Kage-san," she told me, and raised the blade in a slender hand, the point angled straight toward my heart. I tried once more to move, opening my mind to Hakaimono, but my thoughts were sluggish, the demon's presence a dim flicker in my consciousness. "But I'll need to kill you quickly, before the poison wears off. Any last words?"

"Who…sent you?" I gritted out.

"Ah, I'm afraid you don't get to know that, Kage-san," the wind witch said, shaking her head. "I can't go betraying my client. What *would* that do to my reputation? And even if I told you, it wouldn't help you now, because I'm about to send your soul to Meido. Or Jigoku, depending on how the gods feel about you. Well," she continued, and raised the blade even higher. "I suppose we should get on with it. Sayonara, demonslayer—"

A blur of red and white crossed my vision, and Yumeko slammed into the woman from the side, tackling her around the waist. Both tumbled to the ground with a shriek of outrage from the witch. From the corner of my eyes, I could see flashes of movement, flailing robes and beating arms as the two women scrabbled at each other.

"Get off me, you disgusting vermin!" With a blast of wind, Yumeko was hurled away, hitting the ground with a gasp several yards from us. The witch rose, furiously brushing off her sleeves, her expression curled into one of hate. "How dare you touch me, you filthy creature," she snarled.

"You will pay for this outrage! You will die screaming for mercy as my familiars slice you into tiny pieces, starting at your ankles and leaving your head for last! Kamaitachi!" she cried, pointing to the girl. "Kill her! Carve her up slowly. Make her suffer the Death of a Thousand Cuts!"

I held my breath, waiting for the shriek of wind, for Yumeko's screams of pain as she was sliced open by the sickle weasels. But the gully was still; not a single breath of air stirred the leaves around us, and the wind witch scowled in confusion.

"Kamaitachi!" she called again, "you useless, lazy things. Didn't you hear me?"

"Oh, they heard you." Yumeko pushed herself upright, one hand curled around her stomach, the other clutching something at her side. "But it seems that the only reason they became your familiars was because of this."

She raised her arm, and a small ivory netsuke, a piece of jewelry designed to fasten the cord of a travel pouch to the obi, dangled from her clenched fingers. This one was carved in the shape of a weasel, curled up as if asleep. It glittered in the sunlight, and the wind witch went pale at the sight of it.

"Someone told me that kamaitachi always come in groups of threes," Yumeko went on, breathing hard. "And they're very protective of each other. You trapped one to force the others to become your familiars, threatening to kill their sibling if they didn't do what you wanted. Didn't you?"

"You little thief!" The wind witch floated toward her, though her skin was ashen now, her eyes wide with fear. "Return that to me this instant. Give it back, and I will let you live."

Yumeko shook her head, a grim smile playing across her lips. "No one should be forced into compliance, not even yokai," she said. "I'm returning their sibling, so they can make their own choices."

"No!" shrieked the witch, as Yumeko drew back her arm. "Stop! You don't know what you're doing!"

Yumeko hurled the netsuke into the air. It sailed up in a graceful arc, flashing as it caught the sun until, with a blast of wind and a streak of darkness across the sky, the piece of jewelry shattered. For a split second, I saw a kamaitachi hovering in the air, looking dazed, before it shook itself and vanished into a whirlwind.

The poison in my body was finally wearing off. I pushed myself to my knees and grabbed my sword, as the witch let out a wail and turned on the girl.

"You meddlesome fool," she spat, and raised her arm, causing the wind to whip around her once more. I staggered upright, but my legs shook, and I nearly fell again. "You cost me my kamaitachi, but I don't need those vermin to kill you. I'll slice you to pieces my—aagh!"

She dropped her arm with a grimace, clutching her wrist, where her billowy sleeve had been cut in two. I looked up as three small furry shapes appeared in front of Yumeko, curved blades glinting in the sun as they faced the witch. Their eyes gleamed an angry red, their muzzles pulled back to reveal sharp yellow teeth, and the witch shrank away at the sight of them.

"No," she said, as with a swirl of wind, the yokai disappeared. "Get away from me! Stay back!"

With a deafening shriek, a gale descended on her, tossing her hair and yanking wildly at her clothes. The wind witch screamed as her robe was torn apart, scattering fabric into the air, and hundreds of cuts opened up on her body. Yumeko winced and turned away, closing her eyes, as the witch continued to scream and the wind continued to gust around her.

Finally, the whirlwind sputtered and died, the breeze fading to a faint whisper. The wind witch, or what was left of her, swayed in place for a moment, eyes wide and unseeing, then collapsed to the rocky ground.

I observed her for a moment, making certain she was truly dead, before looking at Yumeko again. The girl sat against the gully wall, a trio of kamaitachi at her feet, sitting on their haunches with their blades folded back, watching her with solemn red eyes. I tensed, my hand dropping to my sword, but the yokai didn't appear threatening any longer.

Yumeko smiled, pushing herself upright and deliberately not looking at the body of the wind witch, lying crumpled in the dirt. "You're free now," she said softly, and the kamaitachi cocked their heads, as if really listening. "You don't owe me anything. I'm glad I could help."

As one, the yokai lowered their heads and bowed. Then, with excited yips and snarls, they spiraled into the air, wind and leaves swirling around them, and were gone.

# 13

## Song of the Kodama

It took us the rest of the afternoon to get out of the ravine.

"Tatsumi, stop," I said, after we'd walked several yards from Kiba-sama's cave, leaving the demon bear and the body of the wind witch where they had fallen. He paused and looked back at me with cold purple eyes, having said nothing since the fight with the witch and the bear. I ignored the tingle of fear and gestured to his torn haori, where a dark stain was beginning to spread below his shoulders. "You're bleeding."

My voice shook a little. There was a faint ringing in my ears, and I felt like I could lose my breakfast if I thought too hard about certain things. The encounter with the wind witch, the kamaitachi and the great demon bear felt surreal, as if it had happened to someone else. I remembered the struggle in flashes: the terror of falling down the ravine, the ground trembling as Kiba-sama emerged from the cave, the helplessness of watching Tatsumi fend off the bear *and* the kamaitachi. The rage as the witch directed her familiars to attack the demonslayer while he was distracted. I'd snatched a rock from the stream, intending to give the witch something else to think about, and suddenly remembered a voice from the night before, his final words before he disappeared.

*Kamaitachi always come in threes. Their loyalty to each other is unbreakable. Remember that, and ask yourself why Kazekira has only* two *familiars.*

Because they didn't *want* to help her, I'd realized. The weasel yokai were her familiars because she was forcing them to obey. Because she held hostage the one thing that could give them pause.

The third kamaitachi.

At least, I'd hoped that was the case. I couldn't be absolutely certain. It had been a gamble, but I'd had to help somehow, both to free the sickle weasels and to save Tatsumi, who would have died trying to fight both the witch and the demon bear. Calling out to her familiars was the only thing I'd thought of. When the witch had slammed me in the wall and I'd lain there, aching and trying not to pass out, a tiny voice, soft and raspy, had whispered in my ear.

*Our brother. She keeps him in her obi. Save him and free us all.*

I'd seen a streak of brown fur vanish into the air as I raised my head. I'd also seen the wind witch standing over Tatsumi with a knife angled toward his heart, and terror had flooded my veins. There had been no time for tricks, no time for fox magic, kitsune-bi, or illusions. My only thought had been to save Tatsumi.

It was pure luck that, in the struggle with the witch on

the ground, my hand had closed over something small and hard beneath her obi. And that I had been able to grab it just as she'd hurled me away. What had happened afterward… my stomach churned with the memory. I wasn't sorry for what I'd done; she would have killed us both if she could, and the kamaitachi were now free. But it didn't change the fact that the wind witch was dead, torn apart by her own familiars, and I was the one who had caused it.

I tried putting it from my mind as we walked along the riverbank, seeking a spot where we could climb out of the ravine. As the adrenaline wore off, various aches and bruises all over my body began to make themselves known. I also noticed the tear in Tatsumi's black haori, and the darker stain spreading over his back.

"Tatsumi," I said again, and hurried to catch up. "Wait. You're hurt. We should take care of that before we go any farther."

For a moment, I didn't think he would stop; his face was blank, that icy mask remaining over his features. But then he nodded once and walked toward the tiny stream cutting through the gully floor. Reaching into his jacket, he knelt and carefully pulled out a square of paper, revealing a few pinches of green powder inside.

I watched as he added several drops of water and mixed it into a familiar paste. Then he paused, gazing down at the salve as if just coming to a realization.

"Yumeko." His voice was hesitant, almost inaudible. I stepped forward to hear better, leaning close, and he exhaled. "I can't…reach the wound on my own. Would you be able to…?"

It took only a second to realize what he was saying. "O-Oh," I stammered. "Of course." Gingerly, I took the salve from him, ignoring the way his muscles tensed as my fingers brushed his. "Do you have bandages as well?"

He handed me a roll of thin white cloth, then turned and unceremoniously pulled his arms through his loose shirt and jacket and shrugged out of them so that they fell around his waist. Thankfully, he was facing away from me, so he didn't see my face heat like a teapot left on the brazier too long. The monks at the temple would often train or meditate bare-chested, so I was used to seeing male upper bodies, but they'd all been so familiar I'd never given any of them a second thought. Kage Tatsumi was a different story. The late afternoon sun slid over the warrior's broad shoulders and back, revealing taut skin and lean, hard muscle.

And scars. Dozens of them, crisscrossing his shoulders and raked across his back. Some were almost faded away, some were deeper and much more vivid. I reached out and barely stopped myself from tracing a trio of scars slashed vertically down his right shoulder blade. A moment later, I shivered when I realized what they were.

*Those are...claw marks.*

I shook myself and pulled back my arm. The gash from the kamaitachi was a thin, straight slice from the top of his shoulder blade to the bottom of his ribs. Blood had already seeped from the cut and down his skin, staining the edges of his shirt.

After dunking a square of cloth in the tiny stream, I hesitated with a quiet breath, then began dabbing the blood from around the wound. Tatsumi slumped forward with his hands on his knees and his head bowed. He didn't make a sound or twitch a muscle, even when I moved from the blood to the gash itself, wiping it clean before smearing the green salve into the wound as gently as I could. His muscles were tight, like steel bands under my fingertips, as if he expected me to jab something into the cut at any moment. Or, perhaps he was just bracing himself for the pain. I remembered what he'd said to me at the ryokan, his confusion when I'd protested his harsh treatment of my own wound. When he'd asked if I had never been punished for showing weakness.

When the wound was treated, I wrapped bandages around his chest and shoulder, wincing as I tied them off. "All right," I said, drawing back. "I think that will do."

*"Arigatou,"* he murmured after a moment's hesitation, as if still waiting for the worst to come. I watched him pull up his shirt and haori and shrug into them without so much as a grimace, and wondered again at the scars across his back and shoulders. The witch had called him the Kage demonslayer. Why did he hunt and kill such dangerous creatures?

"Tatsumi," I ventured, knowing the dangers of prodding this edgy, dangerous human but unable to help myself. "Have you…fought a lot of demons?"

"Yes."

"Is it for vengeance?" I thought of the oni, casually massacring a temple of monks, leaving death and destruction in its wake, and my blood boiled. "Do you hunt them for revenge? Did a demon kill your family?"

"No."

"Then, why…?"

"Yumeko." His voice wasn't harsh or angry or threatening, but the bleakness in it caused a shiver to creep up my spine. He turned so that he faced me on his knees, purple eyes intense.

After placing his sword on his left side, he fisted both hands on his thighs and bowed his head, as I knelt there in silent amazement.

"Forgive me." His voice was solemn, completely serious, as if he were addressing a daimyo, not a lowly peasant girl. "You saved my life, but I cannot answer your questions. I have been sworn to secrecy by my clan, and they would punish us both if I disobeyed their orders. Please choose another way that I might repay my debt."

"Tatsumi-san..." Guilt flickered; I certainly hadn't been expecting that. "I...you don't owe me anything," I said, though he remained motionless with his gaze on the ground. "I was trying to save us both, after all."

"The witch would have killed me." Tatsumi's voice was flat; he still hadn't moved or raised his head. "The code of the Shadow Clan demands compensation. A life for a life. I'm in your debt until I can repay you."

I nodded. "All right," I said in a quiet voice, as the seriousness of the declaration dawned on me. Master Isao had taught me about the ways of the samurai, how their code was everything to them, their entire way of life. To casually dismiss or ignore a debt was a huge insult to their honor, an unforgivable crime that could end either in the death of the offender, or with the disgraced warrior taking his own life. "Then I'll hold you to that promise, Tatsumi," I said, "until you can save me in return."

He lowered his head in a silent bow, and we continued through the gully without speaking.

Later that evening, after we'd finally gotten out of the ravine, it began to rain. I grimaced, setting my jaw as sheets of water soaked us through the branches, drenching my hair and seeping past my clothes. Tatsumi walked on, seemingly uncaring of the cold and wet. I found myself wishing for my conical hat and mino, a rain cloak made of tightly woven straw, which I'd had to leave behind at the temple.

The rain continued, sometimes slowing to a cold drizzle but never letting up completely. As the light began to fade, we took shelter beneath an old, arched stone bridge. A pair of oak trees grew close to the bridge, and several gnarled roots snaked along the ground beneath the arch. Perched on a root, I watched as Tatsumi dug a hole, filled it with branches and somehow lit a small fire. It crackled cheerfully and drove away some of the chill, and I groaned as the warmth hit my skin and began thawing my clammy fingers.

"Here," Tatsumi said quietly, and dropped a single rice ball into my hands. Murmuring my thanks, I watched him walk to the other side of the campfire and sit down to stare into the flames.

There was a shimmer in the darkness, and the hairs on the back of my neck rose. Looking up, I saw a tiny, pale green figure, no larger than my thumb, watching me from atop a root a few feet away. It wore a round mushroom cap on its head, and its eyes were like black pits under the brim.

Tatsumi saw what I was looking at, and his hand went to his sword. "Tatsumi, no," I warned, holding out a hand. "It's a kodama, a tree kami. It won't hurt us." He relaxed, dropping his hand from the hilt, and I offered the kodama a smile.

"Hello," I greeted softly, as the tiny kami tilted its head, watching me. "Please excuse us, we're just passing through. We're not disturbing your tree, I hope?"

The kodama didn't blink. It watched me a moment more, then padded forward and hopped onto a stone, staring at me with pupilless black eyes. A faint sound rose into the air, like the rustle of leaves stirred by the wind. I nodded.

"I understand. We will stay to the path, and we'll be careful not to tread on any new plants or trees. You have my promise."

"You can speak to the kami." Tatsumi's tone didn't question, though it sounded faintly surprised. "How?"

"The monks taught me," I replied. Not the whole truth of course; I'd been able to see the spirit world—kami, yokai, yurei and the rest of the unnatural—for as long I could remember. One of the perks—or curses—of being half kitsune. Though the monks did teach me the differences between the myriad spirits in Iwagoto. There were the nine greater Kami, the named deities who were worshipped throughout Iwagoto: Jinkei, God of Mercy, Doroshin, God of Roads, and so on. The lesser kami were minor gods, spirits of nature and the elements; they existed everywhere, in the earth, the sky and all places in between. No one knew how many kami existed in the world; when people spoke of them as a whole, it was common to say "the eight million gods," and leave it at that.

But besides the kami, many other strange, magical creatures roamed the land. Yokai were creatures of the supernatural; sometimes called monsters or bakemono, they could change their forms or had some amount of magic power, tanuki, kamaitachi and, of course, kitsune being prime examples. Yurei described the many restless ghosts that wandered the mortal realm, zashiki warashi, onryo, ubume and more. There were even some monstrous plants that preyed on humans and a handful of creatures that didn't fit into any category, so the list of gods, ghosts and monsters was endless. But, even though some yokai were dangerous and some yurei had malicious intent, all were residents of Ningen-kai, the mortal realm, and were to be respected.

Unlike the demons—the amanjaku, and terrible oni like Yaburama. They hailed from Jigoku, the realm of evil and corruption, and did not belong in the mortal world at all.

"Master Isao and the others revered the kami," I went on. "They strove to exist in harmony with all forms of life. The most spiritual among them could see and even speak to the kami on occasion. I sort of had the talent for it, I suppose."

"Is that why the kamaitachi listened to you?"

"Well…not really. I listened to *them*."

The kodama was joined by a friend. Then three more appeared between tree roots, and another materialized near the edge of the fire. I looked up to see dozens of the tiny kami perched on rocks and branches, watching us through the rain. A sound rose into the air, like hundreds of dry leaves fluttering at the same time.

Tatsumi, observing the growing number of kodama around us, didn't move, but his posture remained tense. I could sense he was trying very hard not to go for his sword. "What do they want?" he asked.

"Um…" I closed my eyes briefly, trying to focus on just one voice. Kodama were difficult to understand at the best of times. "Slow down," I said, holding up a hand. "Please, one at a time. I can't hear if everyone talks all at once—it's like trying to pick a drop out of a waterfall."

The sound of whispering branches stopped. The kodama on the rock stepped forward, chattering in a soft voice that sounded like a leaf skipping around the ground.

"They want to know if you are the bearer of Kamigoroshi," I said. "And, if you were the one who slew Kiba-sama today."

Tatsumi blinked, then glanced at the now dozens of kodama, watching us from the trees.

"I had no choice." His voice was calm, neither boastful nor repentant. "I would have avoided that fight if I could. But Kiba-sama would have killed us both."

The kodama broke into chatter again, like thousands of leaves being rustled by the wind. Which was strange, as there was no wind. Finally, the noise died down, and a trio of kodama approached the fire. The kami in the center carried a single leaf like a flag, the stem held upright, the edges bobbing as it walked. Though their faces were tiny and indistinct, I felt this was a very solemn affair. The tree spirits marched up to Tatsumi and bowed, and then the kodama in the center stepped forward, raising the leaf over its head, toward the demonslayer.

"What is this?" he asked warily.

"A gift," I said in amazement, listening as the kodama chatter went on. "It seems that, long ago, Kiba-sama lost himself to his hunger and greed," I translated, as their voices flowed over me, a faint tickle in my ears. "And it corrupted him until he was no longer a bear, but something unnatural and tainted. Even while he slept, the miasma of dread he produced could be felt by all living things. The birds never sang in Kiba-sama's wood, the animals were constantly afraid and in hiding, and the humans rarely ventured into the forest. Fear was suffocating the land, but now that you've put him to rest, it can flourish again.

"That leaf signifies that you are a friend of the forest," I continued, as Tatsumi reached down, carefully took the leaf by the stem and held it up to his face. It glowed faintly in the darkness, pulsing with a soft green light. "If you are ever in need of the kamis' help, whisper your request out loud and release it into the wind. It will carry your message to any nearby kodama, who will aid you in whatever way they can."

His eyes darkened, and he shook his head. "I can't accept this," he murmured, lowering his arm. The kodama voices rustled overhead, echoing my own question.

"Why?"

"I kill demons. It's what I do. I didn't slay the bear out of mercy, or kindness, or anything but survival. If Kiba-sama hadn't attacked us, I would have been content to leave him there."

"Nonetheless," I said after a moment of listening to the voices of the kodama. "They want you to have it. You did the forest a service today, and the kami always repay their debts." When he still hesitated, I added, even though the kodama didn't say it, "You really shouldn't refuse a gift from the kami, Tatsumi-san. They might always repay a debt, but they never forget an insult."

He nodded gravely; that at least made sense to him. *"Arigatou gozimasu,"* he told the nearest kodama, lowering his head in a bow. "I'm not worthy of such a gift, but I will accept it."

The tiny kami returned the bow, straightened and then floated away, like a leaf picked up and carried by the wind. The rest of the kodama vanished, fading into trees, until it was just me and Tatsumi once more.

He stared at the glowing leaf, watching it flicker in the darkness, before it vanished into the pouch beneath his obi. But his brows were drawn into a slight frown, and I cocked my head at him. "Is something wrong, Tatsumi-san?"

He shook his head. "No. But…the leaf should have gone to you," he said, finally meeting my gaze. "You were the one who spoke to the kamaitachi. You figured out how to free them so they would turn on the witch. If you hadn't done that, we would've both died."

"The reward wasn't for slaying the witch," I returned gently. "It was for putting Kiba-sama out of his misery and returning the forest to its natural state. The kodama don't care about individual human lives as much as they want the forest to be healthy. You were the one who killed the demon, thus their favor goes to you."

Tatsumi frowned. "I've killed dozens of demons and yokai," he murmured. "Perhaps a few kami, as well. Until today… I didn't know that yokai could be talked to or reasoned with."

"Not all yokai are evil," I said quietly, surprised to feel a tiny flicker of hurt. "They're part of the natural order, just like the kami. Sometimes, you don't know what they want until you talk to them."

He didn't say anything to that for several heartbeats, staring into the fire as if lost in thought. I tossed a few twigs into the flames and watched the fire consume them, and wondered what would've happened had the wind witch exposed me. Would Tatsumi be sitting here with me now? Would the fact that I'd saved his life have any impact on the revelation that I was kitsune? Or would he take his terrible glowing sword and try to cut off my head?

*I've killed dozens of demons and yokai*, he'd just told me. Did that mean he had killed kitsune, too? According to the monks, my full-blooded kin were tricksters and opportunists, but there were a few cases in which they were truly dangerous. Had Tatsumi's clan ever sent him to kill a fox, and if they had, did *he* think all kitsune were wild, treacherous creatures that should be put down?

"There is something you should know about me," Tatsumi

said, startling me from my thoughts. I looked up to find him still brooding into the flames, his expression thoughtful. "Something that you should decide for yourself, before we go any farther."

I straightened, surprised that he was volunteering information. In all our travels, Tatsumi had shied away from any questions about himself, his family, or his clan. After his tortured confession earlier today, I'd promised myself I wouldn't press him further, that his secrets were his own. After all, I had my fair share of secrets, too.

"You can tell me," I said. "It won't scare me off, I promise. Well, unless you're really a yurei who has been masquerading as a human all this time. Oh, but if that was the case, you wouldn't know you were a ghost, would you?"

He continued to watch the fire. I sensed he was still struggling with himself, debating whether or not to say anything, before he bowed his head with a sigh.

"There is…a rather large price on my head," Tatsumi admitted at last. "Not from the magistrates or clans or any human organization. From the demons, and yokai. From the spirit world. They want me dead. Or, technically, they want the bearer of Kamigoroshi dead."

"Why?"

"Because Kamigoroshi was created to kill demons," Tatsumi answered. "That's the entire purpose of its existence. And not just demons—it also works on yokai, spirits, even kami. Creatures that can't be slain with a normal blade."

"Oh," I said. I'd known Kamigoroshi wasn't a normal sword, but I hadn't known the entire demon and spirit world was aware of it and its bearer. "So, you're saying that if a ghost came right through the wall and tried to grab you, you could kill it?"

"Yes."

"What about fireball yokai? They have no bodies. Can Kamigoroshi kill them, too?"

"I've killed several."

"Oni?"

"Yes, Yumeko." Tatsumi nodded. "Even an oni, if it doesn't kill me first. But that's not the point I wanted to make. Within the blade…is the trapped spirit of a demon. Its name is Hakaimono, and it is old, powerful and very angry. Whoever wields Kamigoroshi is constantly in danger of having their soul possessed."

I drew in a slow breath, trying to process what he'd told me. He carried a demon in his blade; that was why just looking at the sword could make my skin crawl. "What happens if your soul is possessed?" I asked in a small voice. Tatsumi gave me a cold stare.

"What do you think?"

Now it was I who gazed into the fire, watching it snap and curl. For a moment, I found it sadly ironic; this was the most I'd ever heard him talk, and it was about something I could really do without hearing. "Why are you telling me this now?"

"You saved my life," Tatsumi said. "I want you to understand what staying with me really means." He held the sheathed blade up to the light. "Kamigoroshi is a cursed sword, Yumeko. Its bearer is also cursed. Demons and yokai will constantly seek me out to destroy me, which means they'll try to kill you, too. And I… I am not someone you should ever trust. In fact, it would be better if I'd never made that promise."

I looked up quickly. "What are you trying to say, Tatsumi?"

He paused. My heart thumped in my chest, and my stomach knotted as I watched him. The firelight danced in his eyes and flickered over his face, and his expression looked strangely torn. "Being around me will always be dangerous," he finally said. "I will do my best to protect you, as I promised, but enemies of all sorts will come after us. Some might be very powerful. All will try to kill me. And there is the constant danger of Hakaimono. I want you to be fully prepared for what that means."

"Tatsumi-san." I hesitated, knowing I had to choose my words carefully. To not give him any indication that I had the Dragon's prayer. The thing the demons, witches and yokai were really after. "I have to find Master Jiro," I told him. "I *must* reach the Steel Feather temple, to let them know what happened to Master Isao and the others. I have a duty of my own, but more than that…it was Master Isao's last request. I promised him I would find the temple and warn them all. I just hope the demons don't find the Steel Feather temple before me."

His shoulders slumped; the concept of duty was all too familiar for a warrior. And Tatsumi, as cold and hardened and dangerous as he was, didn't seem the type to abandon a vow. "I made a promise, too," I said. "I'm going to the temple, Tatsumi-san, with or without you. You're welcome to follow along. I would welcome the company, and I'm not afraid. But you don't have to be so gloomy about it."

He blinked and looked up at me. "Gloomy?"

Apparently, no one had accused him of being gloomy before, either. "I don't think I've ever seen you smile," I told him. "Master Isao would say you look like a monkey who accidentally dropped its last persimmon into a pond." That statement brought out a bemused frown, and I smiled. "I trust you, Tatsumi. I think you're too strong to let a demon possess you. And if you're worried about monsters or yokai coming after us, don't be. I'm not completely helpless. I certainly surprised the wind witch today."

"You did." The ghost of a smile crossed his face. "Did your Master Isao often compare people to monkeys?"

"Not usually. Mostly it was just me."

He actually chuckled, and it sent a flutter through my insides. Though he sobered almost immediately. "All right," he said. "Then, we continue together. For as long as I can protect you. Until I've paid my debt."

The kodama watched over us all night.

# 14

## Beware of Stray Dogs

*"T*atsumi, listen," Yumeko said the next morning. "You can hear the birds again."

I glanced at her. She was walking beside me down the trail with her head tilted upward, gazing into the branches. Overhead, the sun slanted through the leaves, mottling the forest floor, and several small, feathered creatures flitted back and forth above us, chirping. I hadn't noticed until she pointed it out, but the woods did seem a little brighter today, less oppressive. I guess my slaying Kiba-sama had helped the forest, just as the kodama had said.

My gaze lingered on Yumeko. A smile graced her lips as she followed the movements of the birds, the sun gleaming off her black hair and sliding over her skin. This morning, she had left a small portion of rice at the base of one of the oak trees, a gift for the kodama. Though in the bright sunlight, it was hard to imagine that the night before, it had been filled with kami.

I shook myself. Last night had been surreal in many ways. I still couldn't believe I'd revealed so much, both about myself and the sword. The Kage would not be pleased that I'd told her of Hakaimono, but if we were to travel together, at least now she was forewarned. She had certainly surprised me yesterday, both in saving my life and speaking to the kami on my behalf. I'd never thought I'd be indebted to a peasant girl with no warrior training, but there was certainly more to her than I'd first thought. I was…somewhat relieved that the truth about Kamigoroshi hadn't frightened her away.

Deep inside, I could feel Hakaimono's cold amusement. *Yes*, it seemed to whisper. *Keep her around. Tell her there is nothing to fear, that you will be able to protect her. It will make the moment you strike her down all the sweeter.*

Chilled, I severed the connection and felt the demon fade away, though the echo of its laughter rippled through me, accenting my mistake. I'd spoken of demons and yokai and the things that wanted me dead, but in truth, the greatest danger to Yumeko was standing right beside her.

After a few hours, we left the forest and followed the river once more as it wound lazily through a valley, heading north toward the capital. By my estimations, we were perhaps a day or two from the border, which was going to be a problem. I'd lost my travel papers when my horse had fled the amanjaku, and there was no way to acquire more, legally or not. No one cared about the peasant class, so Yumeko would be fine, but an unauthorized samurai wandering through another clan's territory was cause for alarm. Without proper documents, if we went through the checkpoint between territories, I would likely be detained for an indefinite amount of time while they decided what to do with me. Since that option was out of the question, I was going to have to find a way around, as sneaking through the checkpoint with Yumeko would be too risky.

A flutter of blue caught my eye, coming from a way station standing alone at the edge of the trail. The small wooden establishments were fairly common on the roads between towns, places where travelers could stop and purchase a hot meal or even a bed before continuing to their destination. Blue curtains were draped across the entrance and a miniature tanuki statue holding a sake jug perched in the window, welcoming customers.

Yumeko stopped in the middle of the road, inhaling deeply. "What is this place?" she wondered. "It smells wonderful."

"Just a rest stop," I told her. "You can buy a meal here, if you have the coin. We're probably a few miles from a town…" I trailed off as she gave me a wide-eyed, hopeful look, and sighed. "I take it you're hungry again."

"I gave my rice to the kodama this morning," she replied, looking plaintive. "All I've had to eat today is a plum."

Digging into my money pouch, I silently handed her a few copper kaeru, and she smiled at me before hurrying to the rest stop window. She returned with two bowls of steaming soba noodles, and we took our food around the side of the building to eat. Low wooden benches lined the wall, spaced a few feet apart, but not all of them were empty.

A lone traveler slouched on a bench a few seats down, a sake bottle on the wooden surface and a cup in his hand. He was perhaps a few years older than me, wearing a tattered vest and trousers, and his dark, reddish brown hair was tied back while still managing to look unkempt. A single short blade was shoved through his obi, and a large onyx-wood bow lay on the bench beside him. He caught my gaze and smirked, lifting the sake cup in a mocking salute, before tipping the contents into his mouth.

I ignored him, having seen his kind many times before. A ronin, one of the masterless samurai that, through shame, dishonor, or the death of their lord, had been stripped of all wealth and titles and wandered the country in disgrace. A few found new lords to serve under, but many took whatever jobs they could, offering themselves as bodyguards or hired muscle, while others turned to banditry and murder. They were considered uncouth and uncivilized, having abandoned the code of Bushido and everything they once stood for, and the samurai despised them. Because they were a constant reminder of what could happen to any of them, at any time.

I perched on the edge of the seat as Yumeko sat down beside me, already engrossed in her food. I deliberately did not look in the ronin's direction, though I could feel his gaze on us as he took another swig of sake, drinking straight from the bottle this time. In my travels, I had encountered two main types of troublemakers—the type who took offense to being noticed, and the type who took offense to being ignored. Of course, there were also the ones who were just looking for trouble, and they were impossible to avoid. I hoped this ronin wasn't that type.

"Oi," came a mocking voice from the other end of the benches, dashing my hopes. The ronin was watching Yumeko, a wide smirk on his face. "I saw that look. Don't you know it's rude to stare, little lady?"

Yumeko blinked and looked up from her bowl, a mouthful of soba dangling from her lips. She swallowed quickly. "I'm sorry, I wasn't staring at you," she said. "Unless you're talking about the noodles. And I'm pretty certain the noodles don't care."

"Ignore him," I told her quietly, concentrating on my own food. "He's trying to bait you into conversation."

"I heard that," the ronin stated, sitting upright on the bench. "And *that* was very rude. If I were still a samurai, I might have to demand satisfaction from your quiet friend there." He rose, and I wished I still had the kunai throwing knives hidden in my bracers. Still, if he made any threatening moves, he would be dead before he knew what was happening.

Hakaimono stirred, sensing trouble, and I shoved the demon's presence down.

Slinging the bow over his shoulders, the ronin sauntered forward, that defiant smirk still creasing his face. "Luckily for you," he went on, "I'm a filthy ronin dog with no honor left to his name. Don't want to risk soiling your own by having a civil conversation with me, right?"

Yumeko cocked her head, puzzled and unafraid. "What's a ronin?"

The other's brows rose. Clearly, that was not what he'd expected. "Uh, well. They're… You really don't know what a ronin is?"

Yumeko shook her head. "I lived in a temple all my life," she explained. "I don't know much about the outside world, but I'm sorry if I offended you. If you would, please tell me what a ronin is, so that I won't insult anyone else in the future."

For a moment, the ronin just stared at her. Finally, he chuckled and shook his head. "Apologies, my lady," he stated, and gave an overexaggerated, mocking bow. "As I said before, I'm a ronin. We're dirty, uncouth barbarians who have forgotten our manners along with our honor, so you'll have to forgive me if I'm a bit rusty on the social graces." He seemed proud of that fact as he straightened again, smiling. "Let's see if I can remember how to be polite. My name is Hino Okame. And whom do I have the honor of conversing with this fine afternoon?"

"Yumeko," the girl replied. "And I'm no lady, just a peasant from the mountains. So, I'm a bit rusty on social graces, too."

"Oh?" Without pretense, the ronin sat beside her, making me drop my hand to my sword hilt. Neither the ronin nor Yumeko seemed to notice. "So, you're from the mountains, eh? What are you doing out here?"

"Traveling. Tatsumi and I are on our way to the capital."

"Ever been to the city before?"

"No." Yumeko shook her head. "Never. The outside world so far is…strange. But exciting." She smiled and looked down the road, where it stretched away toward the distant mountains. "I'm learning so much. I can't wait to see what's around the next bend."

"Huh." The ronin snorted. "Well, I'm afraid you'll be disappointed in time, Yumeko-san. The world is full of bandits, murderers, liars and thieves. You can't trust anyone. Especially ronin. Ever seen wild dogs before?" His grin crept back, defiant. "If they think you have food, they'll follow you for a while, but try to pet them and they'll go right for your throat."

I wasn't certain that Yumeko, with her sheltered upbringing, would get what the ronin was implying, but she lowered her bowl and looked the stranger in the eye. "And yet," she said, "I've heard stories of wild dogs who would defend a stranger on the road to their last breath, simply because that person threw a crumb instead of a rock."

The ronin smirked. "You have a strange way of thinking, Yumeko-san," he said, shaking his head. "I bet your brooding friend there doesn't think the same." His gaze slid over to me, narrowing. I saw him take in my clothes and my sword, and a gleam of recognition ran through his eyes. "You're a bit far from home, aren't you, Kage?" he asked, his voice suspicious. "What are you doing way out here in Earth Clan territory?"

"Minding my own affairs."

"Oho, mysterious." The ronin snickered and turned back to Yumeko. "You'll want to be careful around any members of the Shadow Clan, lady Yumeko. It's said that a Kage never lies, but they never tell you the whole truth, either."

"That sounds very difficult, Okame-san. How can you lie and tell the truth at the same time?"

"Trust me, they manage it."

I put down my bowl and stood, facing the ronin, who watched warily from the other side of the girl. "I think it's time for you to leave," I said quietly.

"Yep, looks like I've overstayed my welcome." The ronin chuckled and rose from the bench. "Took longer than I thought it would, though." He swung his bow to his shoulder and raised a hand to the girl. "Sayonara, Yumeko-san. Maybe I'll see you on the road sometime."

"Okame-san," Yumeko said, and held up her hand, where something glittered between her fingers. "Here."

Puzzled, the ronin held out his hand, and she dropped a single copper kaeru into his palm. Frowning, the ronin glanced from the coin in his hand to the girl. "What's this?" he asked.

Yumeko smiled and picked up her bowl. "A crumb."

The ronin shook his head. "You're a strange girl," he muttered, though the coin vanished almost before he'd finished the sentence. "But hell, I won't argue with free coin. Good luck on your travels, wherever you're headed. You're going to need it."

With one last smirk at me, he turned and sauntered off. I watched until the solitary figure had vanished around a bend in the road before I sat down again.

"That was my money you just gave away so freely."

She offered an apologetic grimace. "*Gomen*, Tatsumi. I'll pay you back as soon as I can, I promise."

That seemed unlikely, so I shrugged, resigned to never seeing that kaeru again. "It's fine," I said, retrieving my bowl. "I just hope you're not planning free handouts to every ronin we meet from here to the Steel Feather temple."

"No." She shook her head. "I didn't even think about it. It just...seemed like the right thing to do." She pushed back her hair, looking thoughtful. "Master Isao had a saying. He told me that the tiniest pebble, when dropped into a pond, will leave ripples that will grow and spread in ways we cannot comprehend." She paused, then smiled to herself, shaking her head. "Of course, sometimes that worked against me whenever I played a very small prank on Denga or Nitoru. The consequences would get bigger and bigger, things would spiral out of control, a troop of monkeys would end up in the prayer hall, and then I'd be polishing the veranda for the next month." Her face crinkled in a half grin, half grimace, before she sobered again. "Now that he's gone," she murmured, "I want to remember everything he taught me. Out here, I feel like I can easily lose sight of what's important. I don't want to forget the things that will keep me…grounded."

It sounded as if she was about to say something else, but I didn't press it. We finished our bowls in silence, then headed back to the road. As we began walking again, I noticed the crow, perched on the roof of the rest stop, watching us as we left.

"Why don't you like ronin, Tatsumi?"

I gave Yumeko a puzzled look. Past the way station, the land had opened up into rolling hills with scattered farms and thatched houses between them. Rice terraces set into hillsides dotted the landscape, and specks of people milled between them, working the fields that were the backbone of the whole country. It was very quiet on the road Yumeko and I walked, until the unexpected question came out of nowhere.

She cocked her head at me. "The ronin. Okame-san," she clarified. "He didn't seem so bad, no different than anyone else, except he kept calling himself a dog. Why would he do that? Is it because he chases rabbits? Or has fleas?"

"Ronin have no masters," I told her. "And no honor. They're disgraced, so they wander the land doing whatever they can to survive."

"I have no master," Yumeko said. "Not anymore. Does that mean I'm disgraced, too?"

"No. You're a peasant."

"Peasants are different than ronin?"

"Peasants have no honor to begin with," I said. "No one expects them to behave above their station. Ronin were once samurai and lost their status."

"But, they're still the same, aren't they?" Yumeko's voice

was confused. "They just lost their master and their title. That shouldn't change who they are inside."

"Sometimes it does."

"How?"

"The code is a samurai's whole life," I replied. "Honor defines them. Duty to their master, their family and their clan is everything. Once they lose that, they are nothing, worthless. And everyone sees them as such."

"You keep saying 'them,'" Yumeko pointed out. "But, you're samurai, too, aren't you, Tatsumi?"

I didn't say anything to that, and thankfully, she didn't press the question.

As the sun was beginning to set, we left the valley and entered another forest, which grew thicker as we continued. Bushes, logs and gnarled roots spilled onto the narrow road, forcing us to step over or around them. Cedar, pine and camphor loomed overhead, crowding out the sky, and the air was heavy and quiet.

As we climbed a flight of mossy stone steps, flanked on both sides by huge shaggy trunks, Yumeko paused.

"Something is wrong," she muttered, gazing warily into the trees. "It's too still. The birds have all stopped—"

I jerked back, as an arrow streaked from the trees and struck the trunk behind me.

Raucous laughter echoed around us. Figures emerged from between the trunks, moving to block the steps from above and below—a half dozen rough-looking men with bows and wide, eager smiles. A large man with a bald head and a nose like a spoiled fig appeared at the top of the steps. He carried a large wooden club over one meaty shoulder, and grinned down at us with yellow, uneven teeth.

"Kage-san," he greeted, as two smaller men came to

flank him, pointing arrows in our direction. His voice was slow and gravelly. "How good of you to finally arrive."

Bloodlust surged through me, Hakaimono waking to eager life, surrounded by so many enemies. The urge to draw the sword was nearly overwhelming; I forced my hand away from the blade and stared at the bandit leader, forcing myself to speak calmly. "Do I know you?"

"Naw." The big man stumbled a bit, as if drunk, and gestured to someone behind us. "But Okame told us all about you, friend. I feel like we're practically family."

"Okame?" Yumeko sounded stunned as she glanced over her shoulder and saw the ronin we'd encountered earlier standing at the bottom of the steps, an arrow nocked to his bow. His face was dark, and he didn't meet her gaze. "What are you doing?"

"He was scouting the road for targets," I told Yumeko, observing our situation. Two archers at the top of the steps, and three men behind us, including the traitorous ronin. "As soon as he left us, he went back to tell his friends we were coming."

Yumeko continued to stare at the ronin, her voice soft. "Is that true, Okame-san?"

A heartbeat of silence, then the ronin raised his head with a defiant smirk. "Never trust filthy ronin dogs, Yumeko-chan." He grinned, and the men around him snickered. "They have no honor left to their name. Next time, better to let the impatient samurai cut off my head and leave it in the sun to rot."

The big man chortled. "Well said, dog. And we all know what happens next." He swung his club into his palm with a meaty *thwap* and grinned at me. "Samurai, give us everything you have and we'll let you live. If not, we'll kill you and take it anyway. Oh, and leave the woman. She can keep me company tonight."

"What?" Behind us, the ronin took a step forward, scowling up at his leader. "That wasn't the plan, Noboru!" he called up the steps. "You told me we were going to take the money and let them go."

"Changed my mind." The big man ran a fat tongue along his teeth. "That was before I saw what a pretty little servant was with him. I haven't had a woman in a long time."

"That's because they can smell you coming a mile away." The other ronin's voice was disgusted now. "I didn't sign on for this. I might be a filthy ronin dog, but I'm not a rutting pig."

The bandit leader scowled. "Last I checked," he drawled, "I was the leader of this operation, and you were the mangy nobody we let join out of pity. You don't like how we do things, Okame, you can leave. But the woman stays. Boys…" He glanced around at his men, then pointed at me. "Kill the samurai. Bring me the girl."

# 15

## The Consequences of Crumbs

*M*y stomach dropped as several bows were aimed at Tatsumi. The warrior crouched, hand hovering over his sword hilt, waiting for them. My heart raced, and I felt the surge of fox magic spread to my fingers, making me clench my fists. For a split second, everything held its breath, and the silence drew out like a taut bowstring.

"Ah, the hell with this."

Abruptly, Okame spun, plunged an arrow into the throat of the bandit beside him, jerked it out then strung it to his bow as the man dropped with a startled gurgle. Raising the weapon, he loosed the string, and one archer at the top of the steps who had been taking aim at Tatsumi toppled backward, an arrow jutting from his middle.

"Okame!" bellowed the bandit leader. "You filthy traitor! How dare you turn on us?"

"Hey, I'm an honorless ronin dog, remember?" Okame called back, grinning savagely as he sent an arrow toward his former leader. Noboru swiftly raised his club, and the dart struck the wooden head. "That's what we do!"

"Kill him!" Noboru roared at the remaining archer, and started down the steps. "Both of them!"

Tatsumi's sword hissed free, as the warrior leaped up the steps to confront the huge bandit striding toward us. Fear shot through me as Noboru swung his club in two hands, sweeping it through the air at Tatsumi's head. The warrior ducked, and the bandit struck the trunk of a tree with a loud crack, leaving a massive dent in the wood. Kamigoroshi flashed, cutting across Noboru's bulging stomach, and the bandit howled in pain and rage.

A curse behind me caught my attention. Near the bottom of the steps, Okame was on his back, bow raised and desperately blocking the other bandit's sword as it hacked and stabbed at him. Tatsumi was busy with the bandit leader, and there was no one else around who could help. If I didn't aid the ronin, he could die.

I drew my tanto and stared at the knife for a moment, hands shaking. I had never used it against a person, but I couldn't employ fox magic or kitsune-bi now. Striding down the steps, I raised the knife and slashed at the bandit attacking Okame, cutting his arm. He jerked back with a yelp, glaring at me, giving Okame enough time to sit up, draw the sword at his belt and stab him through the chest.

"*Arigatou*, Yumeko-san," Okame gasped, scrambling upright. There was a gash across his cheek, and a puncture wound seeping blood over his vest, but he was still grinning as he shook his head at me. "That was one hell of a crumb—aagh!"

He jerked upright, grimacing, as an arrow streaked from the top of the steps and hit him in the back. I caught him as he fell forward, and staggered under his weight. He clutched at my robes, loosening the furoshiki, and something dropped from the wrapping cloth. The shiny lacquered scroll case hit the top of the steps with a faint clink, then rolled steadily toward the edge of the staircase.

My heart turned to ice. Swiftly, I stepped on the case, halting it before it could drop off the edge. In my arms, the ronin was a heavy, gasping weight, as we both teetered edge of the stairs.

"Okame-san," I gritted out, gazing desperately at the ronin while trying to keep us both upright and the scroll from rolling down the steps. "All you all right? Can you stand?"

He raised his head with a shudder. *"Kuso,"* he swore, staggering back a pace. "Dammit, I guess I should've known better…than to turn my back."

Whirling, he raised his bow and fired at the top of the steps. The last archer, who had been taking aim at Tatsumi, jerked as an arrow hit him in the throat, and toppled backward into the brush. At the same time, I bent and grabbed the scroll from the edge of the staircase, then stuffed it in my robes as I bounced back up. *Safe! I think. Let's hope Tatsumi was too busy to see that.*

A thunderous crash came from the center of the stairs as Noboru pitched forward, hit the ground and rolled the rest of the way to the bottom. His blank, beady eyes peered up at us as his head flopped to the side, a line of crimson splitting his face nearly in two. I shivered and looked away, as Okame let out a soft curse.

"Yep…" He sighed, staggering back a pace. "That was… incredibly stupid, Okame."

He collapsed to the stones.

I looked around for Tatsumi. Near the top of the steps, the demonslayer calmly flicked blood from his sword and turned to me, crimson streaked across his face and forearms. His eyes glowed purple in the fading light. I tensed, wondering if he would say anything about the scroll or what had happened with the ronin, but he only sheathed his weapon and turned away. "We're done here," he said quietly. "Let's go, before it gets too dark."

I turned back toward Okame, crumpled at the bottom of the stairs, and my stomach twisted. "Tatsumi, wait," I called. He paused, and I nodded at the ronin's still, bloody form. "What about Okame?"

He blinked and tilted his head. "What about him?"

"We can't leave him here. He's injured."

"He tried to kill us," Tatsumi said, his voice flat. "He led us into an ambush. Those bandits would have shown us no mercy."

"He helped us, in the end," I argued. "He's not like the others. I don't think we should leave him here to die." Tatsumi didn't move, and I frowned at him. "Fine. You go on ahead. I'll catch up when I can."

I walked back to the fallen ronin, then knelt at his side to examine the arrow. It jutted out below his left shoulder blade, the shaft sitting in the center of a dark circle of blood, spreading slowly across his vest.

"If you're going to yank that out, just do it quick," came a tight voice. I blinked and looked down to see that the ronin's eyes were open, gazing back at me. "Grab it as close to the head as you can, and give it a good hard tug."

"Won't it hurt?"

"Nah, I get shot like this all the time. Sometimes I shoot *myself* with arrows just so I can rip them out again."

"Really?" I gaped at him. "How is that even possible? Is it some sort of exercise? Do you also try to dodge the arrows or catch them as they come in?"

"I'm being sarcastic, Yumeko-san." Okame gave a pained smile. "Of course it's going to hurt. But it's got to come out sometime. I can't walk to town with an arrow sticking out of me. Just yank it out and leave me here. I'll be fine."

Gazing at the length of wood jutting from the ronin's back, I hesitated, gathering my courage for the deed. Taking a deep breath, I started to reach for the shaft, when a shadow fell over us. I glanced up just in time to see Tatsumi reach down, grab the arrow and yank it out in one swift motion.

*"Aagh!"* yelped the ronin, jerking against the stones. *"Kuso! Ow!"* Panting, he glared back at us. "Dammit, Kage, if you're going to kill me, just cut off my head and be done with it. You don't have to torture me with false hope."

Tatsumi tossed the bloody arrow to the ground. "If I was going to kill you, you'd already be dead," he stated flatly. "Where's your hideout?"

"Our hideout? Why?" Okame struggled painfully to a sitting position, clenching his jaw. "This is all of the gang. There's no one left for you to slaughter."

"Because I don't want to carry your bleeding carcass to town once you collapse from blood loss." Tatsumi crossed his arms, gazing up the steps. "Because Yumeko refuses to leave you in the road to die. If your hideout is close, better to go there. I assume you have basic necessities like water and bandages."

"Water, yes. Bandages…eh, I'm sure I can find something."

I blinked up at the warrior, surprised. "You're staying?"

Cold violet eyes regarded me without expression. "I promised I would, didn't I? I said I would escort you to the capital, and I have yet to repay my debt. So…" He reached down and, in one smooth motion, grabbed the ronin, hauled him to his feet and slung his arm around his shoulders. The ronin yelped and swore, then made a comment about being better off dead. Tatsumi ignored him. "Come on. Let's get this over with."

# 16

## Yokai in the Moonlight

*Master Ichiro would beat you senseless if he saw you now.*

I ignored the thought, concentrating on keeping myself and the bleeding ronin upright as we walked through the forest, eventually coming upon the hideout in a stand of trees. The bandits had taken shelter in an abandoned woodsman's cottage not far from where they'd staged their ambush. The cottage itself was ancient and run-down; the veranda was sagging, the railings rotted away, and the thatch roof was full of holes. Inside it was even worse, the floor covered with thin mattresses and strewn with dirty bowls, loose chopsticks, dice, blankets and empty sake bottles. It smelled of sweat, urine and too many unwashed humans in the same room at once. I dropped the ronin on one of the dirty mattresses, then retreated outside to the veranda, leaving Yumeko to bind his wounds.

Leaning against a rotten post, I gazed up at the sky, watching the sun set behind the trees, as grim thoughts swirled around my head.

*What are you doing, Tatsumi? You should have killed him. Now another has become involved, and if the clan finds out they might order you to kill him anyway.*

Which, under normal circumstances, wouldn't bother me. The death of a single ronin, disgraced and alone, meant nothing, to anyone. Except, perhaps, Yumeko. For reasons I couldn't comprehend, she had taken a liking to the dishonored bandit. That, or she was incapable of minding her own affairs. If the clan ordered me to kill him, I would obey, as I had always done. But it might frighten or enrage the girl into leaving, and I couldn't afford that, either.

I sighed. Everything was getting complicated. First Yumeko, now this ronin. *This is why the clan warned you about attachments. You are a weapon; attachments will only slow you down and make you question your objective. Remember, your loyalty is to the Kage, nothing else.*

A yelp came from inside the cottage, followed by Yumeko's hasty apology. I shook my head. It didn't matter. The ronin was a momentary distraction. Once we were done here, we could get back on the road to the capital and then the Steel Feather temple. I just had to endure until then.

There was a flutter of wings, and a large black crow alighted on the railing a few yards away. Lowering its head, it pecked curiously at the rotting wood, then regarded me with dark, beady eyes. We stared at each other, unmoving in the evening shadows. I thought I could sense a presence behind the crow's unblinking stare, another pair of eyes watching me from the unknown.

Palming my single kunai, I hurled it at the railing. It

struck the wood beneath the crow with a *thunk*, and the bird took to the air with a startled, indignant caw. I watched it flap away over the rooftop, then I rose and walked to the railing to pull the knife from the wood.

"Tatsumi."

Yumeko came onto the veranda, the weathered boards creaking softly under her weight, and I slipped the kunai back into my sleeve. "The wound has been cleaned and taken care of," she told me. "We can go, but Okame says the nearest town is a half day's walk from here. We might as well spend the night and leave tomorrow morning."

I stifled another sigh, seeing the pale outline of the moon through the branches of a tree. "If that's what you want."

She cocked her head, as if she had been expecting me to argue. "And you won't try to kill Okame-san?" she asked.

"No."

"Or leave in the middle of the night?"

"No."

"Or tie him to a tree and hang sweet potatoes from his ears until the squirrels crawl all over him?"

"...no."

"Oh, that's a relief. Though the last one would have been slightly amusing. Denga threatened me with that, once. I didn't think he was serious, but I could never be sure with Denga-san."

"Oi, Kage." The ronin poked his head through the doorframe, smirking at me, and held up a small white bottle. "Care for a drink?" he asked, not seeming hindered by his wounds at all. "We lifted a couple barrels from a cart a few days ago, and I hate to let good sake go to waste. Come on, I'll pour for you." He grinned in a rather wolfish fashion, slightly pointed canines glinting in the darkness. "To show my appreciation that you didn't cut off my head and leave it in the sun to rot."

I looked away. "I'll pass." Drinking sake, shochu and other alcoholic beverages was generally frowned upon by my instructors. My senses had to remain sharp and ready, not dulled by drunkenness.

"All right." The ronin shrugged. "Your loss, but it's unlucky to drink sake alone. Come on, then, Yumeko-chan. Guess we'll have to drink the rest of it ourselves."

"I've never had sake before," Yumeko said, sounding eager as their footsteps retreated into the hut. "The monks used to serve it for special occasions, but they always kept it away from me. Denga said that he'd sooner set his room on fire himself than let me get a taste for it."

"Oho, a sake virgin." The ronin's voice was gleeful. "Well, you don't know what you've been missing, Yumeko-chan. And those monks of yours sound terribly dull. Never let you have sake, what a crime. We'll have to remedy that right away."

I put a hand over my eyes, suddenly regretting that I'd promised not to kill the ronin. Protecting the girl was becoming more and more difficult; not that I cared what she did, but she was beautiful and naive and, by his own admission, the ronin had no honor left to his name. A vision abruptly came to mind: the two of them, together, alone and drunk on sake.

Setting my jaw, I pushed myself off the railing to walk back into the hut.

There was a shimmer in the corner of my eye, and a small white ball rolled toward me down the veranda.

I didn't step back, though my hand dropped to the hilt of my sword. We weren't alone. Perhaps the hut was home to a yurei or other restless ghost, though how the bandits had stayed here for so long without encountering the spirit,

I wasn't sure. The ball rolled silently across the wooden boards until it veered away and dropped off the edge. Bouncing once, it continued to glide across the yard until it hit the edge of the woodpile.

A child stepped from behind the logs, picked up the ball and smiled at me. A boy of five or six, wearing a black robe with sleeves that were too big, wooden geta clogs and a tattered straw hat. His head was shaved, only a tuft of dark hair clinging to his forehead, and beneath that, a single enormous eye, dominating the top half of his face, stared at me across the yard.

Hakaimono stirred. Not a child. Not even human. A yokai, but one that wasn't particularly threatening. I sensed the demon's disappointment; if the yokai wasn't menacing, there was no reason to fight. But at the same time, I couldn't ignore a strange yokai that had appeared out of nowhere. Especially when, sitting on a stump at the edge of the woodpile, it was obviously waiting for me.

"*K-konbanwa*, Kage-san," the yokai greeted, and bowed as I approached. That single bright eye continued to watch me from beneath the brim of his hat. "Isn't it a nice evening?"

"Who are you?"

The one-eyed boy cringed at my flat tone. Leaning back, he reached into his robe and drew out a small lacquered box. Pulling off the lid revealed a white, squarish lump of tofu resting inside, and he held the box to me in both claws. "A gift," he announced with another bow. "Or a peace offering. To show I mean no harm. I am an insignificant nothing, an unimportant speck, not worth the great Kage demonslayer's time. So please do not have Kamigoroshi cut off my head."

Hakaimono scoffed in wordless disgust; apparently it did not believe this yokai to be worth killing. "If you truly mean no harm, you have nothing to fear from me," I told the creature, ignoring the offered tofu. "But you waited until I was alone to show yourself, so I assume you're here for a reason. What do you want?"

"Kage-san is truly merciful." The yokai sat up, and a fat red tongue slithered between his lips, curled around the tofu and slurped it into his mouth. Wiping his mouth on his sleeve, he regarded me with that single huge eye that didn't hold an ounce of childlike innocence.

"My master sent me here with a message for the great Kage demonslayer," the yokai stated. "He knows what it is you seek, and he warns that Kage-san should be careful, for there are others searching for it, as well. Thieves, mystics and daimyo alike—many have heard the legend of the Dragon's prayer and are scouring the land for the pieces of the scroll."

The Dragon's prayer? Was that what Lady Hanshou had sent me for? I knew the scroll had to be important; if the daimyo of the Shadow Clan had sent me to retrieve it, then she was expecting trouble of the supernatural variety. Running into a horde of amanjaku near the temple had confirmed that suspicion, but that didn't tell me anything about the scroll itself. *Dragon's prayer*, I thought. An ancient relic of immense power? A priceless scripture lost to the ages? I wondered what it really was, and why someone had sent a horde of lesser demons—and according to Yumeko, an oni, the most powerful of Jigoku's terrors—to acquire it.

Though it wasn't my place to wonder. My mission was to retrieve the scroll, no matter what it was, no matter who was searching for it.

"Heed my master's warning, Kage-san," the yokai went on, becoming somber. "Most mortals searching for the Dragon's prayer don't know enough to pose a threat. They have heard a bit of the legend, perhaps enough to try to gather the pieces of the scroll, but their knowledge is incomplete. They flail blindly in the dark, ignorant and unaware. But there is one that even the Kage demonslayer should be wary of. Someone that rivals even the power of Kamigoroshi." He cast a glance at my sword, as if afraid to offend it, before lowering his voice to a near whisper. "Long ago, there was a being that was a curse upon the pages of Iwagoto's history. His name inspires fear and loathing, even now. The one responsible for such hate has been called many things throughout the ages, but most remember him as Genno, the Master of Demons."

I straightened, and Hakaimono perked as well; both of us recognized that name. The Master of Demons was a well-known, if terrifying, figure from the country's darkest era. Four hundred years ago, in the midst of the worst civil war the land had ever known, a sorcerer named Genno raised an army of demons and undead to assault the capital and overthrow the emperor. Because the land was so fractured, his strategy nearly worked. The emperor was killed, and the imperial city was on the verge of collapse, when the clans finally put aside their squabbles and united against the greater threat. Many lives were lost, and the country was nearly torn asunder, but the combined strength of the clans was enough to finally turn the tide. In the final battle, Genno was slain, the hordes of undead crumbled and the demons fled, scattering to the winds. But that was not the end of the story. Not content with simply killing the Master of Demons, the new emperor had him beheaded, his body cremated and his head sealed deep within a sacred tomb, so that he would never again rise to threaten the land.

That was the theory, anyway.

I faced the yokai and frowned, making him shrink back.

"The Master of Demons was killed over four hundred years ago," I said slowly, making certain I understood what the one-eyed creature was implying. "I take it he's returned, somehow?"

The yokai bobbed his head. "That is what my master believes," he said. "The wind witch that attacked you earlier was one of his servants. Uh, Genno-sama's, not my master's. My master would not bother with one such as she." His eye scrunched up, as if he were disgusted by the thought, before he shook his head. "But Genno has many demons, yokai and even humans that do his bidding, and now that he is looking for the scroll, he'll try to eliminate any competition. That means you, demonslayer. And any who are close to you."

I thought of Yumeko, her bright gaze and cheerful smile, the light going out of her eyes as a demon ripped her apart. Strangely, it bothered me in a way I'd never felt before. "Why are you telling me this?" I asked the yokai. "If the scroll is so powerful, why doesn't your master want it as well?"

"I don't question the master's orders," the one-eyed creature said, going a bit pale at the very thought. "My only purpose is to serve him in whatever way I can. He told me to warn the Kage demonslayer that the Master of Demons is searching for the Dragon's prayer, and that he plans to kill you. So, I have. And now my job is done." He blinked his enormous eye and gave me a nervous look. "Uh… I can go now, yes? You won't try to kill me once I try to leave?"

The demon in my head gave me a push to do just that, cut the pathetic creature down when its back was turned, a fitting end to such weakness. I stifled the urge and jerked my head toward the tree line. "Go," I told the yokai, who immediately leaped off the woodpile, without turning his back on me, I noticed. "But tell your master this—don't get in my way. If he threatens me or those who travel with me, I'll kill him. That is my only warning. If we meet on the road as enemies, I won't hesitate to cut him down."

The yokai's eye widened until it resembled a tiny moon, and he nodded. "O-of course, Kage-san," he stammered, bobbing as he backed away. "I'll be sure to deliver your message." He stole a glance toward the trees, and I was suddenly certain that this "master" was close, and that he had heard the entire conversation. "Well then," the yokai finished, preparing to dart into the woods. "H-have a good night, Kage-san. Hopefully we will not meet again."

He darted away, a streak of pale skin in the moonlight, and vanished into the shadows of the forest. I sensed Hakaimono's vague disgust that I hadn't severed his spine and ignored it, scanning the darkness beyond the trees. Something was out there. The mysterious master who'd made certain to warn me that Genno the sorcerer had returned to Ningen-kai hadn't done so out of any sense of altruism. Whoever he was, he was another player in this game I often found myself in. Lady Hanshou, the emperor, the clan daimyos—they were the generals, the major players, the ones with perfect knowledge, and we were the pieces on the board. I was a single pawn in a shogi match, being moved by unseen forces, going where I was directed without any knowledge as to why. That was how it had always been.

And now, it seemed another general had stepped up to the table. Genno, the Master of Demons, had returned, and would likely be seeking revenge. Lady Hanshou would want to know about this, as would the rest of the daimyos, and even the emperor himself, but my first duty was to my own clan. As soon as I secured the scroll, I would return and tell her what I had learned, or perhaps pass the information along to Jomei or another servant of the Shadow Clan if they popped up to check on me. Until then, I would continue my mission, and worry about demons when they came.

I turned and walked back to the hut, feeling eyes on me the entire way.

When I peered through the doorframe, the ronin was sitting alone in the center of the room, surrounded by debris and empty bottles. Yumeko lay on a blanket in the corner, clutching a straw pillow, an overturned sake cup lying forgotten beside her. The ronin saw where I was looking and sighed, shaking his head.

"Half a bottle and she was nodding off into her cup," he said, a rueful grin stretching his mouth. "Pity, really. I was hoping she might be a handsy drunk. Guess I'll be drinking alone tonight, unless you'd like to join me, Kage-san."

"No." Taking Kamigoroshi from my belt, I sat in the doorway and leaned against the frame, positioning my body so that it stretched across the entrance. If yokai were still out there and wanted to get into the hut, they would have to get past me, at least.

"Making me pour my own sake. How crass." The ronin sniffed, poured himself a cup and then took a swig directly from the bottle. "Good thing dogs like me aren't expected to have manners or any kind of social graces. So, Kage-san..." He picked up the sake cup with his other hand and eyed me over the rim with a shrewd black gaze. "What's the story with you and Yumeko? You're part of the Shadow Clan, and you're not a ronin, so why are you following a peasant girl all the way to the capital? She's not a servant, I can tell that much. No clan member would let a servant girl boss them around like that." He tipped the contents of the cup into his mouth and swallowed, then grinned at me. "Or maybe, she's really a princess dressed as a peasant to avoid detection, and you're her bodyguard. That would explain a few things. How she can order you around, how you concede to everything she says, even helping a random bandit on the road." He paused, and when I didn't answer, the grin grew wider. "You know, if you don't say anything, Kage-san, I'm only going to assume the worst."

I leaned my head against the doorframe, letting his babble slide over me like water, vanishing like mist as it passed. "Your assumptions mean nothing to me," I said, making him snort. "Presume what you like."

"Oh? Then I suppose you wouldn't mind if I have a little fun with the peasant girl." The ronin put down the bottle and cast a hungry look in the corner, eyes gleaming. "She has a nice body under those rags, and I'd bet my last gold ryu that she's unspoiled. You weren't going to do anything with her, right, Kage-san? She is just a peasant, after all—"

He stopped, his gaze falling to my sword, where I had curled my fingers around the hilt. My body had gone very still, ready to explode into movement, and there was a new emotion boiling just below the surface, one I hadn't felt before. Similar to Hakaimono's violence and bloodlust, but different. It took me a moment to place it, because the feeling in my chest wasn't the demon's emotion; for the first time in a years, it was my own.

Anger.

"Ah." The ronin smirked and picked up the sake bottle. "That's what I thought. Relax, Kage-san. I'm not in the habit of sleeping with random peasant girls, especially if they have a killer bodyguard nearby who is all too willing to cut off my head." He poured the last of the contents into the sake cup, and frowned when only a trickle came out.

"*Kuso.* That's unfortunate, I'm not nearly drunk enough. Well, only one thing to do." He tossed back the last of the liquor, then picked up the bottle and rose, swaying a bit as he stood up. "Noboru, you bastard, I know you had a secret stash hidden somewhere." He started to stagger away, but paused and glanced at me, that wolfish grin crossing his face again.

"You know," he announced, "if you're heading to the capital, I think I'll come with you for a bit. The roads around here are dangerous—bandits and all sorts of lowlifes assaulting honest travelers. I'll travel with you, make it a little less perilous. You can be the bodyguard, I'll be the guard dog. Safety in numbers and all that, right?" He chuckled, fully realizing the irony, and glanced at the corner where the girl still slept, dead to the world. "You don't think Yumeko will mind, do you? No matter. I'll ask her tomorrow when she wakes up. Now..." He turned and staggered toward the back of the hut, toward a separate room. "Where's that sake, Noboru?" he muttered. "Don't think you can keep it from me, I can sniff out liquor wherever it's hiding."

I listened to the sounds of rummaging and the occasional grunt or profanity. After a few minutes, there was an exclamation of triumph, and then nothing could be heard but the soft clinking of bottles. Eventually, even those stopped, and a guttural snore came from the corner room. I drew Kamigoroshi into my lap and waited for sunrise, planning to wake Yumeko the moment the light touched the horizon. With any luck, by the time the ronin roused from his sake-induced hangover, we would be long gone.

Because if he did follow us, I might have to break my promise to Yumeko and kill him.

# 17

## Hospitality

"*Mabushii,*" I muttered, shielding my face as blinding beams of light cut through the pine branches and stabbed me between the eyes. *So bright.* "Why is the sun so bright today? And if someone could please tell the birds to stop singing so loud, I would appreciate it."

Tatsumi, walking a few paces ahead, did not seem at all affected by the mysterious increase in light or noise this morning. He didn't say anything, but I could sense he was secretly amused. "I can hear you laughing, Tatsumi," I warned, scowling at him. "Does my misery entertain you?" He didn't answer, and I groaned, rubbing my eyes to ease the pounding behind them. "I've never been sick a day in my life," I muttered. "I don't understand why I'm ill now."

"You've yet to build up a tolerance for alcohol." Tatsumi cast a glance at me over his shoulder. "Sake can be very strong for the uninitiated. Unfortunately, this is one of the side effects."

"This is *normal*?" I thought back to the previous night, what I could remember of it. The strange, strong drink Okame kept pouring into my cup had burned as it went down, then seemed to light a pleasant warmth in my stomach. I remembered feeling drowsy and strangely lightheaded, and then I couldn't recall anything after that. "It's like a troop of monkeys are screaming and throwing pinecones against the back of my eyes," I groaned. "Why do people even drink sake if they feel like this in the morning? Do you think Okame-san feels the same? I can't remember half of what we were talking about…"

A chill ran up my spine. I couldn't remember anything of what was said last night. What else had I forgotten? Or done? What if I had revealed something I shouldn't have, like what I truly was? If I'd slipped up, if Tatsumi found out that I was kitsune…

I shivered in the bright sunlight. I had to be more careful. The demonslayer might tolerate a human girl leading him to the Dragon's prayer, but definitely not a yokai. If he discovered I had tricked him, I could definitely see Kamigoroshi slicing down to take my head.

"Yumeko?"

I glanced up to see Tatsumi still watching me over his shoulder. His face, though not exactly sympathetic, wore a puzzled frown. "Are you all right?" he asked. "Do we need to stop to rest?"

I shook my head, smiling at how genuinely concerned he sounded. "No, Tatsumi-san, I'm fine. I'm just—"

"Oiiiiiiiii!"

The faint shout came from the road behind us. I turned

and saw a dark, blurry shape hurrying forward, one arm upraised. As it got close, it resolved itself into Okame, huffing and puffing as he jogged toward us.

"Finally…found you," he panted, bracing his hands on his knees. Gasping, he looked up at me with a wry grin. "Thought you could get rid of me, eh? Didn't Kage-san tell you I was coming with you to the capital?"

I glanced at Tatsumi, who wasn't looking at either of us, his gaze on the distant mountains. "No," I said, frowning. "He didn't mention that."

"Well, lucky for you, I'm a light sleeper." Okame straightened, adjusting the yumi bow on his back. "And that I'd already decided to help you out. Because I happen to know you're going the wrong way."

I blinked. "We are?"

"We're not," Tatsumi countered. "This road leads to the imperial highway, and from there, straight to the capital itself. We are on the right path."

"Yes, if you want to go completely around the mountains," Okame said, jerking his head at the mist-shrouded peaks, still cloaked in shadow. "Which will take days of travel, at least. I know this territory and, more specifically, I know the trails and hidden paths through the mountains." His thumb rose, pointed back at himself. "If you follow me, I can get you to the capital much faster than if you keep to the main roads. *And* we won't have to bother with the imperial checkpoint at the border."

I couldn't be sure, but I thought Tatsumi perked up at that. Well, maybe *perked up* was the wrong phrase, but he did seem to take notice. "It *would* be nice to reach the capital sooner," I mused.

"And just think, Kage-san," Okame added. "The sooner

we get to Kin Heigen Toshi, the sooner you can get rid of me. Win-win situation, right?"

Tatsumi regarded us in stony silence, then shrugged and turned away. "It doesn't matter," he said with his back to us. "As long as we reach the capital. And you don't get us lost."

"Good!" Okame exclaimed, rubbing his hands together. "Just follow me, then. We'll be in Sun lands before you know it."

"Huh," Okame mused later that afternoon. "I was sure there was supposed to be a path here."

We were deep in the mountains now, having left the main road a few hours ago to hike into the wilderness. Okame had quickly found a game trail, and we'd followed him through a dim forest of pine and cedar, over a thick carpet of green moss that covered stones, roots and fallen logs. He was, I noted, very graceful despite his self-proclaimed boorishness, moving easily through the woods and brush like he was part of the forest itself. Tatsumi trailed silently at my back, making no sound at all and prompting me to glance over my shoulder every so often, just to make sure he was still there.

But when the trail abruptly ended at a small mountain stream, Okame stopped and crossed his arms, gazing down at it like he expected a new path to appear.

"Well, that's strange," he muttered, gazing up and down the stream. "I don't remember this being here."

"You're lost," Tatsumi stated, his voice cold enough to make the creek ice over.

"I am not lost," Okame protested, glaring back at him. "I'm…momentarily confused that there's a stream here, but that is a temporary setback. I know exactly where we are."

He scratched the back of his neck, frowning in thought. Across the stream, a small spotted deer stepped daintily from behind a tree and stared at us, twitching large ears. "We must've missed the side trail," Okame mused, "but if we head north, we should find it. So..." He gazed around the forest, and the deer bounded into the undergrowth. "If that's the position of the sun, and the shadows are going in that direction..."

"Um." I pointed a finger upstream. "North is that way, Okame-san."

"Right." Okame grinned back at me. "Back on track, Yumeko-chan. We'll be in Kin Heigen Toshi in no time."

Several hours later, with the sun beginning to set behind the distant peaks and the fireflies starting to wink through the branches, Okame stopped and leaned against a moss-covered boulder, shaking his head.

"Okay," he said cheerfully, and raised both hands in a hopeless gesture. "*Now* we're lost."

Tatsumi's sword rasped free with a chilling screech. Okame instantly sprang off the boulder and darted behind it as I spun, putting myself between the ronin and the demonslayer.

"Tatsumi, no." I held up my hands as his cold violet gaze slid past me, flat and murderous. "Killing him won't help anything."

"It will rectify the mistake I made earlier," Tatsumi said, his eyes narrowed to purple slits.

"But it won't help anything now," I insisted. His gaze shifted to me, and my heart pounded under that lethal killer's stare. Kamigoroshi glowed faintly in the shadows, throwing off a sickly luminance that pulsed like a heartbeat. Nothing like the ghastly purple flames I'd seen the night I met Tatsumi, but disquieting all the same. Just being this close to the unsheathed Kamigoroshi made my skin crawl, but I stood my ground. "Tatsumi-san, it's done. We're lost. Let's just try to find the way back and get to the capital without bloodshed."

"And the fact that he's pointing an arrow at your back means nothing to you?"

"I'm not aiming at her," came Okame's voice behind the rock. "I'm pointing it at the guy with the scary glowing sword. If she would take one step to the right, I'd appreciate it."

A cold smile curled one side of Tatsumi's mouth. "You think you're fast enough to shoot me down, ronin?"

"Well, if the other choice is stand here and smile while you cut me in half, I'll take my chances," Okame shot back. I spared a split-second glance at the ronin and saw a dangerous smirk stretching his own mouth, his eyes hard and defiant. "I'm no noble. I'm not offering you my head because I made a mistake. You want it, you'll have to take it the old-fashioned way."

"No one is taking anyone's head," I argued. "That would just be messy and disgusting. Let's just try to find the way out of the mountains. It'll be dark soon, and..." I paused, pricking my ears forward, though that went unseen by the two humans. Down the slope, in a small bowl between the mountains, I could see a few faint, glimmering lights. "Wait a minute. I think I there's a village down there."

The two humans straightened and turned to peer into the valley, as well. "Oh, *there* it is," Okame said, sounding satisfied. "I knew it was around here somewhere." He ignored Tatsumi's dark glare and loosened the bow, sticking the arrow back in his quiver. "Well, what are we waiting for?"

We started down the slope, but it was steep and treacherous, the stones covered in slick moss, forcing you to watch where you put your feet. It was slow going, but I had played this game with the monkeys in the forest, and skipped from rock to rock, landing as lightly as I could before continuing on. Okame slipped once, skinning his hands on a boulder and letting loose an impressive string of profanity. Tatsumi, of course, was as graceful as a deer, stepping calmly from boulder to boulder, making it look like he did this every day.

By the time we reached the edge of the valley, the sun had set behind the mountain peaks and the shadows had grown long. We crossed a bridge over a tiny stream, and followed a winding dirt path toward a cluster of thatched huts scattered in the distance. The air in the valley was thick and humid; cicadas buzzed in the trees and fireflies blinked over the rice paddies, their lights reflected in the dark, muddy water. Tiny rice seedlings had been planted in neat rows through each of the terraced fields, and would soon grow into a waving sea of green. Along the banks of the slow-moving river, I could see nets hanging in the sun to dry, and tiny fishing boats docked along the shore. The sunlight glimmered off the water, and the entire valley had a lazy, isolated feel to it, like it had been forgotten by the rest of the world.

Past the rice fields, the winding trail intersected with a larger, wider road cutting straight through the village. A sign had been erected at the crossroads, handmade and hand painted, kanji scrawled down the board in stark black ink. *You have arrived in Yamatori*, the signpost announced. *Travelers always welcome.*

"Well, that's friendly," Okame said. "It's a good sign, at least. Some of these little hamlets have a very unfavorable attitude toward visitors. They don't like travelers, they don't like samurai and they especially don't like ronin."

"Why?" I wondered.

"Because ronin tend to take what they want," Tatsumi answered flatly. "And the farmers can't do anything about it."

"Hey, samurai aren't any better," Okame returned, glaring at him. "You think they all follow that code of Bushido nonsense?" He sneered. "I've seen samurai take another man's wife and kill the husband for daring to protest. I've seen one cut off a kid's head for startling his horse. I might be a dirty ronin dog, but at least I don't use the code as an excuse to do whatever the hell I want."

"Whatever I want?" Tatsumi's voice was soft, and he shook his head, almost in pity. "One who has no honor," he stated, "will never understand the actions of those who do."

"Says the man with the creepy glowing sword."

"That has nothing to do with anything."

"Right, because scary glowing swords are always used for the purest intent."

"There are more?" I blinked. "I've only ever seen one scary glowing sword, Okame-san," I said. "Are they very common?"

Okame sighed. "I'm going to have to teach you about sarcasm, Yumeko-chan. But not right now, because we're being stared at."

I glanced toward the village. Several men and women had gathered in the road, most of them farmers according to their simple tunics and suntanned skin, and were peering at us intently.

Okame smirked. "Well, they all know we're here," he said, and began walking toward the crowd. "Guess we should go say hello."

The villagers continued to watch us as we drew close. Most of them smiled and nodded or bowed as we passed, averting their eyes and never looking us in the face. I saw a few men whispering to each other, their faces excited but tense. One white-haired woman, sitting in the doorway of her hut, beamed toothlessly as we went by, her eyes nearly sinking into the folds of her face. A little girl in a yellow kimono bounced in place and waved to Tatsumi, who was trailing a few paces behind me and Okame. He ignored her, but that didn't deter her enthusiasm. Everyone here seemed excited to see us.

And yet…

"Welcome, travelers!"

A man approached us, smiling. His bald forehead was shiny with sweat, dark strands along the sides of his head pulled into a topknot. His clothes were a little nicer than the rest of the farmers': a blue-and-gray jacket over black hakama trousers. He walked forward and sank into a bow that bent him forward at the waist. "Welcome to Yamatori, honored guests," he greeted as he rose. "I am Manzo, the headman of this village. Will you be staying long, or are you just passing through?"

"Just passing through," I answered, and he looked at me in surprise, obviously expecting Okame or Tatsumi to answer the question. "We'll be on our way soon. We don't mean to trouble you—"

"But if you could spare a room and some beds for the night, we would certainly appreciate it," the ronin added, stepping up beside me. He gave the headman a disarming grin and reached into his obi. "I can pay you for the inconvenience."

"Pay? Oh, no no no!" The man shook his head vigorously, holding up a hand. "I will not hear of it. You are honored guests in Yamatori. There is no inconvenience. Please, come."

"Well, they're certainly a friendly lot," Okame mused as we followed the headman down the road toward the center of the village. People smiled and nodded as we went by, peeking at us from doorways and between buildings. He waved at a young boy, watching us from behind his hut, and the child darted back behind the wall. "Makes you wonder what happened, to make them so accommodating of samurai?"

"I don't like it," Tatsumi said in a low voice. "Something seems…off."

"You mean people being nice to you? Yeah, I can see how that would be unnerving."

The headman led us up a small rise to a larger house at the top. This one had a thatched roof like the others, but a veranda circled the front, and wings stretched to either side, unlike the single-room huts the farmers lived in. As we followed the headman, I spotted an old monk in black robes sitting under a tree beside the path, a metal staff resting on his shoulder. He smiled and nodded as we passed, and I paused to offer a quick bow before hurrying after the others. Okame gave me a strange look as I caught up, but didn't say anything.

We walked through a bamboo gate and into a small garden, in which a mossy lantern sat beside a tiny pond under the boughs of a pine tree. Remembering the pond in the Silent Winds temple, I peered into the water, expecting to see a few carp or fat goldfish swim up to me, mouths gaping. Sadly, the pond was empty, the water holding only a few rotting leaves, making me frown in disappointment. But my reflection stared back, a girl with furry ears and eyes glowing yellow in the fading light, and my stomach dropped.

"Kitsune," the headman said, and my heart gave a violent lurch. Stomach roiling, I turned to face the human, who gave a nervous smile. "We've had terrible trouble with foxes lately," the headman explained, gesturing at the pond. "Always getting into everything. My poor fish had no chance."

"Oh," I breathed. I quickly stepped away from the edge, hoping no one else had seen the brief flash of a kitsune in the pond. "I'm sorry to hear that."

*Stupid mistake, Yumeko. Be more careful. This is no time to be playing with fish.*

The headman slid open the front door, which was heavy and wooden, I noticed, not made of rice paper on a frame. "Asami!" he called, as we left our sandals below the lip of the wooden floor before following him into the house. "We have guests! Set three more places for dinner."

"You really don't have to do this," I told the headman, as a middle-aged woman in a dark blue kimono appeared in the door and, with a gasp, hurried off again. "We have our own supplies." I remembered the tiny farming community at the base of the mountains near the Silent Winds temple. Sometimes a farmer would show up at the gates of the temple to ask that someone pray over his fields or drive the spirits of evil fortune from his house or family member. The monks had obliged, and accepted only meager forms of payment in return; a sack of barley, or a few skinny carrots. The people there barely scraped by, Master Isao told me. Farming was a difficult life; many villages often went hungry, as over half their rice crop went to the Earth Clan daimyo for taxes each year. I didn't want to take food away from these people if I could help it.

But the headman wouldn't hear of it, stating yet again that we were honored guests in Yamatori, and it would be unforgivable to treat us as less. So we sat cross-legged on thick tatami mats with lacquered trays in front of us, as the headman's wife and daughters brought us dish after dish of food. Much of it was simple, hearty fare: pickled cabbage, cooked river eels in miso, dried plums and seemingly unlimited bowls of pure rice, without a kernel of millet to bolster it. According to the headman, some of the farmers made their own sake, which Okame took great pleasure in sampling; Tatsumi and I stuck to tea. But no matter how often I emptied my rice bowl, another would appear, almost by magic. I couldn't keep up with the amount of food, even as Okame gorged himself on everything. Tatsumi ate very little, saying nothing except to politely turn down the offer of more. If it wasn't for the fact that the headman was eating the same dishes as us, I doubted he would have touched any of his food.

Finally, when I couldn't eat another kernel, the headman rose from his table, smiling and clasping his hands together. "You must be tired after such a long journey," he said, glancing out one of the windows, where a bloated yellow moon was beginning to peek over the treetops. "If you will follow me, I will show you where you can sleep tonight."

I dragged myself upright, feeling my stomach press against my ribs, and stifled a yawn. "You are very generous," I said, earning another strange look from the headman, as if he were again puzzled that I was the one speaking for the group, and not the quiet, black-clad samurai behind me. "But we wouldn't want to intrude upon your lovely home."

"It is no trouble, my…lady," the headman said. "We have a guesthouse out back that we keep for this very purpose. It is quiet and isolated from the rest of the village. You won't be disturbed, I assure you." He gave me a shaky smile, as his two daughters hovered outside the door looking in, wide-eyed and…fearful? "Please, follow me."

We left the house via the back door, but on the other side of the bamboo fence, a small crowd had gathered. As we stepped through, a young woman came forward, smiling and holding a bundle of white daikon radishes. With a bow, she thrust the vegetables into my hands and stepped back before I could say anything.

"Um…thank you." The words were barely out of my mouth when another villager approached and handed me an entire head of cabbage. Yet a third placed a trio of cucumbers atop the growing pile of vegetables; I grabbed them before they could roll off into the dirt. Both women bowed and quickly backed away, ignoring my protests.

I glanced at Okame, and found him beset by villagers, as well. A white-bearded man put a sake gourd around his neck, grinning, while an old woman, possibly his wife, thrust a reed basket of dried fish into his hands. The headman did nothing to stop or discourage this, and more food was added to the pile with smiles and bows, like they were genuinely happy to be giving away their livelihoods.

Tatsumi, I noticed, remained unmolested, probably because you could almost see the hostile aura around him, the *do not touch me* look in his cold purple eyes. However, when a tiny girl in a ragged kimono tottered up and lifted a slightly squashed persimmon to him, he accepted the gift with a solemn bow of his head, before the girl's mother snatched her away with hasty apologies.

By the time we got past the crowd, Okame and I were laden with food, and I was barely able to see past my own offerings. I hoped this guesthouse wasn't far. We followed the headman down a narrow dirt road, passing more fields and storehouses for the rice, heavy wooden buildings sitting on stilts to keep them out of the wet. Around the village, the mountains loomed into the air, black silhouettes against a sky dusted with stars. A nightbird called, a mournful cry in the darkness, crickets sang from the long grass and fireflies winked like a miniature galaxy over the fields. It should have felt peaceful out here.

So why did I feel so…exposed?

I glanced over my shoulder and saw that the villagers had disappeared.

Except for one.

The monk was back, standing like a statue at the side of the road. His black robes blended into the darkness, but his staff and wide-brimmed hat glimmered in the faint light of the moon. Beneath the hat, his face was hidden in shadow, but I could sense he was watching us, and me in particular.

I turned back, and nearly ran into Okame, as both he and the headman had stopped in the middle of the road. With a hasty *"Gomen"* I veered away and nearly crashed into Tatsumi, who smoothly stepped aside to avoid the collision and even caught the cucumber that tumbled free of the rest.

"As I was saying." The headman gave me a mildly annoyed look and pointed a thick finger down the path. "You can see the guesthouse from here. Just keep following the road."

I peered over cabbage leaves and could just make out a squat, isolated house sitting at the edge of the fields. It looked like every other village house we'd seen, with wooden walls and a pointed thatched roof. Soft orange light spilled through the window bars and the open doorway, and

I could see the flicker of a fire pit through the frame. The road curved past the hut and continued down a slope until it disappeared from view.

"Everything has been prepared for you," the headman continued, speaking to Okame and ignoring me. "The fire has been lit, and fresh bedding has been laid out. There is a stream behind the house if you need water, and a cooking pot over the fire pit, should you get hungry in the middle of the night."

I didn't see how that was possible; I didn't even want to think about food until tomorrow morning. But Okame thanked the headman, who gave a somewhat brittle smile and bowed low.

"You honor us with your presence," he said, still staring at the ground. "I hope you have enjoyed your stay in Yamatori. *Oyasuminasai.*"

"Good night," I repeated, and the headman hurried away, striding back toward the village at a near jog. As his silhouette got smaller and smaller, I noticed that the monk who had been standing beside the path was no longer there.

# 18

## Curses and Gaki

Something was wrong with this village.

I felt it, Hakaimono felt it and I was fairly certain Yumeko felt it as well, though the ronin seemed oblivious. It wasn't just the air of excitement and fear that hovered around the village like a dense mist. Or the way the villagers were almost frantic to give away their food, despite the fact that it wasn't uncommon for farmers to starve during the winter months and rice was more precious than gold to them. Suspicious behavior, though it wasn't unreasonable for the village to overcompensate for our needs, especially if they had been treated poorly by wandering samurai in the past. Our food hadn't been poisoned at least; part of my training involved intimate knowledge of the various toxins and what they tasted like, and the meal had been clean.

But there were other, smaller indicators that made my

instincts bristle. The fences around the rice paddies, the bamboo tops sharpened to lethal points. The houses with the heavily fortified doors. The fact that there were no animals of any kind in the village; no dogs, cats or chickens. Yamatori had a secret. I just didn't know if it was one we should be concerned about.

The guesthouse was empty, and the embers glowing in the fire pit threw long shadows over the bare wooden walls. Yumeko stepped through the doorway, then knelt and dropped the bundle of food in a corner with a sigh. The ronin followed her example, only he kept the jug of sake, taking a pull before tucking it into his jacket.

"I don't know about you two, but I like this place," he announced, flopping down before the fire pit. "I haven't eaten this well in weeks, and there's plenty more where that came from." He patted his stomach with a lazy smile. "We'll be gorging like princes all the way to the capital."

"Baka," I said quietly. *Idiot.* "This village is hiding something. They weren't feeding us to be kind. We were put here for a purpose."

Yumeko looked relieved. "You felt it, too," she said, and I nodded. "It's the strangest thing," she went on, gazing back toward the village. "I got the impression that they wanted us gone, but at the same time, they were desperate for us to stay. Everyone was trying so hard to make us feel welcome even though they were terrified." She paused, then glanced back at me, her eyes troubled. "You don't think they brought us out here to rob or kill us in our sleep, do you? That would be terribly dishonest."

On the floor, the ronin snorted, lying on his side and resting his head on a hand. "Farmers are a cowardly lot," he said, as if speaking from personal experience. "The only time they'd attempt to cut our throats *would* be while we slept, but from what I saw, they're too scared even for that." He yawned, scratching his neck, and glanced out the door. "But we should probably post a watch tonight, just in case."

I went to the door, intending to slide it shut, only to discover there was no door on the tracks. Frowning, I glared out toward the village, noticing that the road snaked around the hut and continued down the slope at the back. Not liking the idea that more of the village could be behind us, I stepped outside and followed the path around the hut, until I came to the edge of the rise and could see what lay at the bottom.

A field of gravestones, surrounded by a simple bamboo fence, sprawled in haphazard rows in the grass at the bottom of the hill. Crudely hewn headstones jutted out of the dirt, interspersed with stone lanterns and bibbed statues of Jinkei, the Kami of Mercy and the Lost. Many of the structures, from the markers to the lanterns to the statues themselves, were covered in moss, their faces worn by erosion and time. But there were several headstones, particularly the ones closest to the hut, that looked much newer.

Yumeko appeared beside me, also gazing down into the cemetery. Strange that I could feel her presence, another body close to mine, and not want to step away and put distance between us. "Well," the girl stated after a moment. "That's...interesting. Is it common to put your honored guests a stone's throw from your graveyard?"

"Not usually," I muttered.

Yumeko continued to observe the field of stones. "Do you think there could be yurei?" she asked. She didn't sound terribly concerned about this, as if the idea of meeting a ghost was more curious than frightening. I was less intrigued. Most yurei were harmless, content to haunt the place they had died, mournful and tragic, but not dangerous. There were others, however—onryo and goryo being the most feared—who had died with hatred or jealousy in their hearts, and would return to wreak vengeance upon those had wronged them. Sometimes their grudges would last for years, centuries, as the curse affected not only the people who betrayed them, but their descendants, as well.

"It depends," I told Yumeko, not wanting to explain all this.

"On what?"

"If they were buried appropriately. If they received the proper funeral rites so they could pass on. If they died with no strong emotions or unfinished business that would cause them to linger in the mortal realm." I gazed over the cemetery, "So…yes, it's entirely possible we will see yurei tonight."

"At least there's a monk in town," Yumeko said. "He would've performed the proper burial rights, wouldn't he?"

I frowned slightly and glanced at her. "What monk?"

"The monk," Yumeko repeated, gesturing back toward the village. "He was at the headman's house when we first arrived, and then again on the path here. You didn't see him?"

"No." Not that I doubted her statement. Like the kodama and the kamaitachi, it seemed Yumeko was adept at seeing the spirit world. Better than me, it appeared. I knew how to spot demons and yokai, but that was usually due to Kamigoroshi's influence, Hakaimono's insatiable bloodlust rearing up, alerting me when they were close. Because the demon didn't care much about yurei, I was less sensitive to the presence of ghosts unless they were very powerful or meant me harm.

"There *was* a monk," Yumeko insisted. "He wore black robes, a straw hat and he carried a staff with metal rings that chimed as he walked." She paused a moment, looking thoughtful, then asked, "Oh, do you think *he* could be a yurei who haunts this village, and that's why everyone is acting so strange?"

"Maybe." Ghosts were harder to figure out than demons. Usually they were problems for a priest or onmyoji to take care of, to exorcise or placate the spirit into moving on. The clan never sent me after yurei; no one was certain what happened to the creatures that Kamigoroshi slew: if they were banished to be reborn, or erased from existence entirely. The thought that a human soul could be snuffed out without passing on, to simply cease to exist, was a horrifying and blasphemous idea that even the Kage would not risk. I could kill demons and yokai in waves, but I was forbidden from slaying a ghost unless it was a matter of life or death.

Yumeko sighed. "I don't think I'll be getting much sleep tonight."

We turned and walked back into the hut, loud snores greeting us as we stepped through the doorframe. The ronin had already fallen asleep on the rough planks by the fire, the jug of sake clasped loosely in one hand. Yumeko shook her head, stepped over his body and moved to one of the straw mattresses in the corner. I settled in the doorway, pulling my sword sheath from my belt and laying it across my lap. I could feel Yumeko's eyes on me as she curled up on the mattress and drew a threadbare quilt over her head.

"Tatsumi-san?" she asked after a few minutes of listening to the ronin snore. Near the fire, the body on the floor coughed and shifted to his back, falling silent for the moment.

"Hn," I grunted.

"I'm…glad you're here." Her eyes, dark and luminous, watched me from under the blanket. "I know the road is dangerous, but I feel safer knowing you're close. I would never be able to sleep in a haunted village by myself. So, thank you…for staying."

For some reason, that made my stomach contract a little, and I had no idea why. "We both made a promise," I reminded her. "You would guide me to the Steel Feather temple, and I would protect you on the way. I'm here for the scroll, nothing else."

"I know." Her voice was very soft in the darkness of the room. "But I'm still happy that you chose to stay. I…" A yawn interrupted her, and she covered it with a hand. "I might even be able to fall asleep tonight. Because I know you're there." She wrinkled her nose as a snore came from the slumbering ronin near the fire pit. "If baka-Okame doesn't keep me awake, that is. Good night, Tatsumi-san."

I didn't answer. After a while, her breaths became slow and deep as she drifted into unconsciousness.

For a moment, unseen by condemning human eyes, I gave in to my fascination and let myself look at her. Her pale skin seemed to glow in the moonlight slanting through the latticed windows, her hair an inky curtain across her back and shoulders. She breathed calmly, her face unguarded in sleep, as it was when she was awake. A jet-black strand of hair came loose to fall into her eyes, and I was filled with an incomprehensible urge to brush it back.

Disgust set in, and I turned away, clenching a fist on my leg. Why was I finding myself so distracted lately? I knew my mission—retrieve the scroll at any cost, and return to Lady Hanshou. But here I was, with this girl and now an uncouth ronin, having promised not to leave.

For just a moment, I wavered. For a heartbeat, my guard was down, and disgust flared into a burning, instant rage. I was suddenly filled with the overwhelming desire to leap up and slay my useless companions, to strike them down while they slept and watch their blood gush over the floor and sizzle in the fire pit.

Soundlessly, I rose and stepped into the room, my hand on the hilt of my sword. My shadow fell over the girl, slumbering peacefully on her mattress. It would be easy, I thought, gazing down at the back of her neck, so exposed and vulnerable in the moonlight. Neither of them would realize they were dead until they woke up as yurei, or in the next land, and then I would be free to seek the scroll on my own. I didn't need the girl to find what I was looking for, nor did I need to keep my promises. I was the Kage demonslayer and the Shadow Clan's best shinobi. Honor and human lives meant nothing to me.

My hand tightened on the hilt of the blade, and I began drawing it from its sheath.

*No, Hakaimono! Enough!*

Wrenching control from the demon, I shoved Kamigoroshi back in its sheath and lurched away from the sleeping girl. Staggering outside, I pressed a palm to my face, breathing hard as I struggled to clear the rage and bloodlust from my mind. Hakaimono fought me, unwilling to give up, fury and violence still singing through my veins. Closing my eyes, I recalled the mantra my sensei taught me, chanting it like a sutra in my head.

*Be nothing. You are not a person; you are a weapon. A weapon does not feel. A weapon has no emotions to hinder or slow it down. Feel nothing. Regret nothing. You are but a shadow, empty and soulless. You are nothing.*

"I am nothing," I whispered, and sensed Hakaimono's presence fading from my mind. "I am a weapon in the hands of the Kage. I will not betray them or fail my mission."

When I opened my eyes, I was fully in control. The anger, confusion and doubt had been purged from my body, leaving me with a cold realization. I could not afford to lower my guard, to allow anything, or any*one*, to distract me. Hakaimono had relinquished the fight for now, but this had been a chilling reminder of what was at stake. I'd stopped myself in time, but if the sword had tasted blood, I might have slaughtered the entire village before the demon was satisfied, starting with the very girl I was supposed to protect.

*Yumeko.* I narrowed my eyes. Yumeko was a distraction: intriguing, confusing and dangerous. I didn't know why she affected me so much, but it couldn't go on. Hakaimono had been biding its time, luring me into a false sense of security, before attempting to seize control. It had almost worked. I could not let that happen again.

A soft chime cut through the silence.

I looked up. A monk stood in the road that snaked past the house, his form hazy and blurred in the moonlight. He wore black robes, a wide-brimmed straw hat and carried a staff with four metal rings dangling from the top. Exactly as Yumeko had said. Without taking his eyes from me, he raised his staff, pointing it down the path…and disappeared.

Wary, but knowing omens from the dead could not be ignored, I crept around the house, peering down the slope into the graveyard.

It was no longer empty.

The entire cemetery glowed with a strange, sickly green light that illuminated the dozens of bodies shambling between graves. They were naked, emaciated creatures, with sticklike limbs and bloated, distended bellies. Vaguely human, they walked hunched over or crawled through the dirt like animals, their gaping mouths showing rows of jagged, broken teeth.

*Gaki.*

I crouched in the shadows of the hut, realizing my mistake. This village *was* haunted, but not by a single yurei. Gaki were the spirits of greedy or wicked humans who had died and returned cursed with eternal hunger. No matter how much they ate, they were always starving, and nothing could satisfy them. They were creatures to be pitied, and a single gaki wasn't normally considered dangerous, but if no food could be found, they were known to turn violent, seeking anything, living or dead, to quell their agonizing hunger.

Watching the gaki shuffle between gravestones, a cold fury began creeping through my veins at the realization, fed by Hakaimono. The villagers had known about this. Now I understood the fear and anticipation. We weren't "honored guests" as the headman would have us believe: we were sacrifices to the gaki.

Carefully, I drew back, and suddenly realized I was not alone. The monk stood beside me, also gazing down at the roaming gaki, his face hidden in the shadows of his hat. Before I could do anything, he raised his staff, the metal rings glimmering in the darkness, and brought it down with a thump in the dirt. The rings chimed, a metallic jangle that echoed like a gong in the silence, and as one, the gaki whirled, their hollow, burning eyes fixed on me.

I leaped away as, with howls and piercing shrieks, the gaki rushed forward, scuttling over the bamboo fence and swarming up the rise. Darting into the hut, I ignored the snoring ronin and hurried to Yumeko, grabbing her by an arm.

"Yumeko!" She blinked as I hauled her upright, her eyes wide with astonishment as I set her on her feet. "Get up!"

"Tatsumi? What are you—"

A shriek interrupted her, as a twisted, lanky form appeared in the open doorway. Mouth gaping the gaki screamed and lunged at us, curved nails grasping like bird talons. Yumeko gasped, and I leaped between them, Kamigoroshi flashing from its sheath. The blade sliced through the gaki's bony chest, and the tortured spirit wailed as it shivered into tendrils of black-green mist and writhed away.

"Get the ronin on his feet!" I called, as more gaki appeared through the frame, eyes blazing with madness and hunger. Planting myself in the doorway, I met them with my sword drawn, blocking the way in. Hakaimono, its rage forgotten, flared with excitement at the prospect of killing, bathing the mob in purple light.

Howling, the gaki lunged, teeth bared, claws snatching at me. I cut them down as they surged forward, slicing through limbs and heads alike, splitting sticklike bodies in two. The gaki showed no fear or self-preservation as they came forward, throwing themselves on my blade with mindless fury, their consuming hunger driving them mad. Even if I cut off a limb, the owner would still press forward, raking with the other, or trying to bite me if both were gone. They dissolved into ethereal mist as they were destroyed, but there were always more, a seemingly endless horde crowding the tiny entrance of the hut. A talon got through my defenses and ripped a gash across my neck, and the smell of blood seemed to drive the mob into an even greater frenzy.

Something buzzed by my ear, inches from the side of my face, and an arrow thumped into a gaki's forehead, sending it writhing into mist. As I slashed through another, a second arrow flashed between my arms, and a gaki howled as it disappeared. Through the chaos and fury of battle, I vaguely realized that the ronin either had perfect aim and timing to shoot through a doorway with me still in front of it, or he was getting insanely lucky.

"What are these things?" I heard Yumeko cry, somewhere behind me. "What do they want?"

"Gaki!" the ronin called back, as another arrow buzzed along my ribs and hit one in its bloated stomach. "Hungry ghosts! You can't reason with them. Poor bastards are starving and will try to eat anything, including us."

Another talon got through and latched on to my sleeve, ripping through cloth and taking a bit of skin along with it. Hakaimono snarled in rage and surged up, urging me to let it go, to release its power and slaughter the pathetic crowd before us. I ignored it, pushing the demon's influence down, not trusting myself or the blade right now.

Something larger than an arrow flew past my head and hit a gaki in the face. It staggered back as a large daikon radish dropped to the ground in front of it. With a snarl, the gaki ignored the vegetable and flew at me again, and Hakaimono hissed with pleasure as the sword cut through the skinny neck. The head fell, bounced once beside the radish, and dissolved into mist.

Several more food offerings sailed past my shoulders and swinging arms, into the crowd of gaki, who ignored or even batted them away. "I don't think they're interested in regular food," Yumeko observed, as I gritted my teeth and wished my companions would stop hurling things past my head. "I think they just want to eat *us*."

There was a loud rustle above me, and Yumeko let out a yelp. "Okame, they're coming in through the roof!"

"Dammit!" There was a hiss of a bowstring, a thump and a screech above me as a gaki met its end. "More incoming," the ronin shouted, as the sound of thatch tearing echoed overhead, and bits of straw began drifting around me. "Hey, Kage, how's the mob looking on your end?"

I sliced down two gaki that had rushed forward, catching a split-second glance of the numbers beyond. "About a dozen left," I panted, jerking back to avoid gaki claws tearing open my face. "Just keep them off me for a few more seconds. And protect Yumeko."

More hisses and shrieks rang out behind me, but I couldn't turn from the mob at the door. I heard scuttling feet, the ronin swearing and then a cry from Yumeko that sent a chill through my stomach. Beheading the last gaki, I whirled, ready to rush to her defense, hoping I wouldn't see her lifeless body on the floor, a pair of monsters ripping it to pieces.

The ronin lay sprawled on his back near the firepit, his bow held in front of him as if to ward something away. Yumeko stood beside him with her tanto outstretched, the remnants of green mist coiling around her as it vanished on the breeze. Her sleeve was torn, ripped by grasping claws, but there didn't seem to be any blood.

"Is that…the last of them?" she panted, looking at me.

I nodded once and sheathed Kamigoroshi, feeling a strange flicker of emotion in my chest. Seeing her alive and unharmed…was this relief I felt?

"Tatsumi." Yumeko stepped forward, her eyes gazing worriedly at the side of my neck where the gaki had clawed it. I could feel blood from the torn flesh beginning to seep into my collar. My arm, too, was starting to drip blood on the wooden planks. "Before we do anything, we should take care of those. Do you have any medicine left?"

She took another step toward me, and I remembered her touch, cool and soft, sliding over my skin. So unlike the healers of the Shadow Clan; they took care of my wounds with quick and brutal efficiency, sparing me no discomfort. As with everything in my life, I had come to see the pain that came from their ministrations as normal. As Ichiro-sensei often said: pain was a good thing; it meant I was still alive. But with Yumeko…that had been the first time in recent memory that another person had touched me…without hurting me.

I stiffened and drew away from her. *No distractions*, I reminded myself. *No emotion, no weaknesses.* If I let myself fall under this girl's spell, craving a touch that wasn't painful, Hakaimono would latch on to that flaw and turn me into a demon.

"Don't," I warned in a cold voice, and she halted, blinking in confusion. "Don't come near me," I told her, backing away. "I don't need your help. I'll take care of it myself."

Her brow furrowed, puzzlement and something else going through her eyes. Ignoring that look, and the vague squeezing sensation in my chest, I brushed past her, toward the full water bucket in the corner of the hut. I had my mission, and I would not falter. Nothing mattered except retrieving the scroll and returning to Lady Hanshou. A weapon did not question the demands of its owners, or the purpose for which it was created. A weapon existed only to obey…and to kill.

"Oi," the ronin demanded as I walked away, pointing to his face and the shallow cuts across his skin. "What about me? This isn't Kabuki makeup, you know."

"Why would I think it's Kabuki makeup, Okame-san?"

He sighed. "Never mind."

I watched Yumeko take a cloth from her obi and walk over to the ronin, then crouched down to look at his face. "What about the gaki?" she asked, dabbing at his cheek. "Do you think there could be more out there?"

"I sure hope not. *Ite.*" He flinched back from her administrations, making her frown. "Damn hungry ghosts. Well, come morning, I know several farmers who are going to die screaming for mercy."

Yumeko lowered the cloth, her eyes going wide. "Why?"

"Yumeko-chan." The ronin shook his head in exasperation. "This was a setup if I've ever seen one. That headman knew about the gaki, hell, the whole village did. We were *bait*—they might as well have tied a bell around our necks. I know it, and Kage-san knows it, right, samurai?"

"They were expecting us to die," I agreed, pressing salve to my own wound. "That's why they were so eager to have us spend the night. So the gaki would eat us and leave the village alone."

"Yep." The ronin gave a grim nod. "Only, now I'm very much alive and a lot angry." He took the cloth from Yumeko, then stood and sauntered over to my corner, gazing down at me. "So, Kage-san," he began, "I think a bit of retribution is in order. What say we go kick down the headman's door, stick his head on a pike for the gaki and burn this whole cursed place to the ground?"

# 19

## Talking to Yurei

*He's not serious.* I stared at the ronin, who stood over Tatsumi expectantly. Though Okame wore a grim smile, his eyes were flat and dangerous, promising reprisal.

He was entirely serious.

"Okame-san, you can't," I protested. "They're not even armed. We can't slaughter these people in their homes."

"*You* might not be able to." Okame's evil smile grew wider, showing those slightly pointed canines. "I, however, don't take kindly to being fed to gaki, especially by treacherous, lying farmers. At the very least, I think the headman's house should be razed, and his head stuck on a post at the edge of town, as a warning to other travelers. What d'ya say, Kage?"

Tatsumi wound a cloth strip around his wounded arm and used his teeth to tug it tight. "No."

"No?" The ronin gaped at him, even as I slumped in relief. "Why the hell not? Aren't you a samurai? These peasants just tried to kill us."

"My mission is not to burn down villages." Tatsumi didn't look up. "It would be a waste of time. Stay and take your vengeance if you wish, it doesn't matter to me. Yumeko and I will be leaving this place at dawn."

The ronin gave a disgusted snort. "Suit yourself," he muttered. "I suppose that's poetic justice though—let these peasants get eaten by their own hungry ghosts. I bet in a few years there won't be a village left at all, just a graveyard full of gaki."

"But why are there so many gaki around?" I wondered. "Where do they come from? Do they just pop out of the ground, starving and cranky?"

"Gaki are the souls of humans who were greedy in life, whose selfishness caused great harm," Tatsumi said. "They are being punished for their greed, and will continue to be eternally hungry, until they have suffered enough to move on."

"But the villagers here were the complete opposite of greedy," I argued. "You saw them. They were almost frantic to give things away."

Okame shrugged. "Maybe they're hoping not to come back as gaki when they're inevitably eaten. There's probably a bad joke in there somewhere, but I'm too tired to figure it out."

I shook my head. "Something is wrong here," I murmured, walking to the door to stare down the path. "There's more to this village and the gaki than we're seeing. And I bet that monk has something to do with it."

"Monk?" I heard the frown in Okame's voice. "What monk?"

"The yurei who…never mind. We should talk to the headman," I said, turning back. Okame looked incredulous, but it was Tatsumi's gaze I sought, meeting his eyes. "I'm thinking he can tell us what's going on. We already survived the attack—they're not going to expect us to go marching back through the village, not when we were supposed to be eaten by gaki. I bet he'll explain everything now." Tatsumi didn't answer, and I frowned at him. "Don't you want to know what's going on, Tatsumi? Aren't you even a little curious?"

"No."

"Well, I am."

"I am, too," Okame announced, to my surprise. "Now that you mention it, I sure would like to have a chat with our friendly headman and ask why he's feeding travelers to the resident gaki. In fact, I think we should go right now." He strode to the doorway and peered out, dark eyes searching. "I don't see any hungry ghosts wandering around," he muttered. "And if we do run into more, we know they can be killed, or banished or whatever." He looked back, a challenging smirk crossing his face. "To the headman's house, then. You coming or not, Kage-san?"

Tatsumi continued to say nothing, his expression blank as he watched us. Finally, he rose gracefully to his feet, slid Kamigoroshi through his belt and glided across the floor. I felt a strange tingle in the pit of my stomach, my heartbeat quickening as he drew close.

"Let's do this quickly."

The villagers watched us as we marched down the path toward the headman's house. No one had slept tonight, it appeared. Not a soul was in the open, but I saw them peering through the slats in their windows, eyes wide with amazement and fear. Clearly, they hadn't expected us to survive the gaki attack, and they were wisely staying out of reach. No one challenged us as we strolled through the village, past the headman's front gate and up the steps to his house. Only now I did I notice that his door was made of heavy, reinforced wood, and that several long gashes had been raked across the surface.

Unsurprisingly, it was barred from the inside. Okame rattled it a couple times before stepping back with a dark smile. "Kage-san?" He glanced at Tatsumi and gestured to the door. "Would you like to do the honors?"

Tatsumi's sword flashed from its sheath, slicing through the thick wood like it was made of rice paper. Stepping forward, Okame raised one finger and tapped the surface, and the doors swung back with a groan.

Warily, we stepped into the house. The entryway was empty, but a faint light came from farther inside, flickering over the walls and floors. Sliding open a panel, we saw the headman kneeling in the center of the floor, a lit brazier casting his features in a red glow.

As soon as the door opened, he fell forward, prostrating himself to the floor, pressing his face into the wood.

"Mercy!" His muffled voice floated up from the floor, shaking and terrified. "Have mercy, my lords. Kill me if you must, but spare the village. They don't deserve your wrath."

"They don't?" Okame crossed his arms. "So, you're telling me that they *didn't* try to feed us to the gaki? That they were completely ignorant of what was happening tonight?" He snorted in obvious disbelief. "Well, don't I feel foolish, thinking this whole village was setting us up to get eaten."

I frowned at him. "But I thought they *were* setting us up to be eaten. That's why they were…oh. Sarcasm again. I see."

"Please." The headman didn't lift his face from the boards. "Have mercy. We were desperate. You've seen what we face. You don't know what it's like, living with those creatures. We don't know what else to do."

"They're not unkillable." This from Tatsumi, his voice hard and unimpressed. "If your people would take a stand to destroy them, you wouldn't have so many gaki wandering around."

"We've tried! We've tried killing them, burning them, cutting off their limbs, trapping them underground. No matter what we do, no matter how many we kill, they always come back." The headman clenched his fists on the floor in distress. "It's part of the curse! The curse that damned monk placed on us, and now we're doomed to be haunted by gaki for the rest of our days and beyond."

Ah. Now things started to make sense. "What curse?" I asked, stepping forward. "We've seen the monk. Is he the one responsible for the gaki?"

"You've seen him? Merciful Jinkei, will he never be satisfied?" The headman shuddered violently and sat up, closing his eyes. "I suppose there is no point in hiding it anymore," he whispered. "Please, sit down, and I will tell you our village's greatest secret, and greatest shame."

Okame and I edged forward and knelt on the tatami mats. Tatsumi chose to remain standing, hovering in the doorway, though the headman didn't seem to notice him.

"This village," he began, "has always been prosperous. The stories said that when my great-great-grandfather was headman, he made a bargain with Ojinari, the Kami of the

Harvest, that as long as they took care of the land, it would always be fertile. Even after the rice tax at the end of the season, after the daimyo took his share of the harvest, the village always had enough to eat. The fields never withered, never dried out. The streams and lakes always yielded fish, and the gardens, small as they were, always produced a plentiful bounty. We were never rich, but we never went hungry. In this, we knew we were lucky, far more fortunate than other villages that faced starvation every winter, and we thanked the kami for blessing the land.

"However, as the decades passed, the villagers began to fear that others might discover their wealth of food, and try to take it from them. We are a small village, isolated from the rest of the world—if word got out, ronin or bandits might descend upon us in waves and take all our food for themselves. The village would never have peace again.

"Such was our thinking, flawed as it was. Even though we continued to have bountiful harvests, we began hoarding our food, hiding it away like squirrels burying their nuts. The few travelers that stumbled upon the village were told that we were but poor farmers who could barely feed ourselves, and were sent away with nothing.

"And then, one night in the coldest of the winter's months, a monk passed through the village. He went from house to house, asking for a bowl of rice, a single potato, anything that we could spare. The village turned him away—my great-grandfather ordered everyone to bar their doors and ignore the monk until he left.

"For three days, he stayed around the village, sitting in the snow with nothing but his hat and robes to keep him warm. He would offer to pray for loved ones, to say a blessing over the fields, in exchange for a bite of food. He was ignored. No one gave him anything. They pretended not to hear him, not to see that he was starving, though he never uttered a word of complaint.

"Three days later, they found him sitting outside the headman's door, frozen stiff. He clutched a strip of paper in one stiff hand, written in blood from his own fingers, cursing our greed.

"Three months after he was buried in the cemetery outside town, a young famer's daughter fell on a kama sickle and died. She, too, was buried in the graveyard with the rest of the dead. But that night, she returned, starving and violent. She broke into her former home and tore her family to pieces. The next month, the family returned as well, wretched and wandering, seeking warm flesh to consume, and more lives were lost to their terrible hunger.

"So began the cycle," the headman finished, his eyes dark and haunted. "Every month, on the final three nights, one for each day we left the monk to starve, the hungry ghosts rise from their graves to wander the village. They are not interested in normal food—offerings of rice, vegetables, or sake are ignored. They hunger only for living flesh, consuming those who were once kin. The gaki you saw tonight—those are our dead loved ones, our families, all who perished after that monk drew his last breath outside this door. He is an onryo, a grudge spirit, and his curse continues to punish us for the greed of our ancestors."

"Why don't you just leave?" Okame asked when the headman was finished. "Seems like an easy solution. Pack up and go find a new village, leave the graveyard and your hungry ghost problems behind."

"It's not that simple." The headman shook his head. "Some have tried to flee the village, of course. But the curse follows them. Gaki stalk their footsteps, the ghosts of their families trailing them wherever they go, appearing every night instead of the last three. The ones who try to flee either return to the village in terror, or they die and return as hungry ghosts themselves." The headman looked out the door with bleak, dead eyes. "There is no escape. We are trapped here, and the curse will continue until there is no one left, until the gaki are all that remain of us."

"Huh." Abruptly, Okame rose to his feet. "Well, I *was* thinking about killing you for throwing us to the gaki, but on second thought, it seems your lives are pretty awful as is." He glanced at me and smirked. "So, what say we get out of here before the curse latches on to us?"

"*Can* we?" Tatsumi wondered, his eyes grim. "Will we be stalked by gaki ourselves if we try to leave?"

"No," the headman said dully. "Your ancestors did not anger the monk. The curse will not follow you. You can leave and not look back. I would not blame you, of course. This is our punishment, no one else's."

"Has anyone tried talking to him?" I asked, and those dead eyes shifted to me. "The monk? His ghost is still hanging around."

"The monk." A shadow of real terror crossed the man's face. "We've occasionally seen glimpses of him around the village," he said. "But he disappears before we can speak to him. We think it's more an effect of the curse, an echo of the monk, not the ghost himself." He shivered. "The onryo… we've seen him in the cemetery sometimes, a glowing spirit in white, walking among the graves. But none of us dare venture close—the gaki would tear us to pieces."

"And he only appears when the gaki come out?" I asked.

"Yes. It is as if he wishes to see our misery and terror,

to make certain we are suffering." The headman sighed. "I cannot blame his anger, our ancestors did him a great wrong. But it pains me, knowing I am destined to become a wretched thing that preys on my own family. I cannot even take my own life if I am simply to rise as one of them."

"Yumeko," Tatsumi said in a warning voice from the hallway, as if realizing what I was thinking. I pretended not to hear him and rose, turning to face my companions.

"We have to help them."

"What?" Okame gave me a look of disbelief. "March through a cemetery crawling with gaki to talk to a ghost? In case you didn't notice, I was almost *eaten* a few minutes ago. I could really go the rest of my life without having to experience the real thing."

I ignored the ronin, locking eyes with Tatsumi, who was leaning against the doorframe with his arms crossed. "We have to do this, Tatsumi-san. After hearing their story, how can we walk away now? These people have suffered enough—they aren't the targets of his wrath any longer. If we could just talk to the monk, maybe we could convince him to lift the curse."

"Yumeko." Tatsumi's gaze was hard, and he shook his head. "Grudge spirits can't be reasoned with," he said in a grave voice. "Their anger has consumed them, and their vengeance can never be satisfied. If the monk is truly an onryo, you won't have any hope of placating it, and it could very well turn its wrath on you."

Fear prickled my stomach. "I'm…willing to take that chance," I said. "It won't take long. I just need someone to keep the gaki away while I talk to the monk. This is the last night of the month," I reminded him, as his eyes narrowed. "It will be the only time we can talk to him. When dawn comes, he'll disappear with the gaki and we'll lose our chance to lift the curse."

Tatsumi held my gaze a moment longer, then let out a breath. "You're going to talk to him with or without me, aren't you?" he murmured.

I nodded. "I might not be able to wield a sword or shoot an arrow," I told him, "but I can talk to ghosts and kami. I want to help, and this is something I can do."

He sighed again and glanced out the door. "We don't have much time," he said, making my heart leap in my chest. "When dawn comes, spirits tend to fade when the first light breaks over the horizon. If we're going to speak to the monk, we should do it now."

Okame groaned. "Hold on," he growled as we turned toward the door. After pulling the sake gourd from his obi, he yanked off the top and tipped the container upside down into his open mouth, emptying it fully. He wiped his lips, then tossed the bottle at the headman and turned back to us with a grin. "Okay, *now* I'm ready."

The village was silent as we walked back outside. Overhead, the moon blazed down, outlining the houses in silver and casting hazy light over the distant rice paddies. I didn't glimpse any gaki wandering about, but as we drew closer to the graveyard, I could see the faint green light coming from the bottom of the rise.

We sidled around the wall of the guesthouse, then peered down the slope.

The gaki were back. Or a few of them were, anyway. Certainly not in the numbers that had swarmed us earlier, but more than I was expecting, considering Tatsumi had wiped them all out. And we had been inside the hut when they attacked, which had allowed the demonslayer to deal with them one at a time. Out in the open, fending off a huge mob would be much more difficult.

"And you want us to go down there." Okame sighed and made a face as he stared at the figures lurching about. "Ugh, this isn't going to be fun, but lead the way."

"Wait." Tatsumi held out his arm, stopping us. "We may not have to fight."

I glanced at him. He hesitated, as if struggling with himself, then exhaled. "If we march down there in plain sight, the gaki will be on us in a heartbeat. However, I might be able to perform a technique that will render us unseen, for a short while."

"Huh." Okame crossed his arms. "So, you *are* kami-touched, after all. I thought so. Though the creepy glowing sword was a huge hint." He spared a glance at the black-clad samurai behind us and dramatically lowered his voice as he leaned in. "There are stories," he told me, "that if a Kage child is born kami-touched, it is taken away and raised to become a shinobi."

I frowned. "What are shinobi?"

"Shadow warriors. Secret assassins that strike from the darkness, cutting your throat from behind or in your sleep." Okame snorted. "Every clan employs them—don't let all that talk of honor on the battlefield fool you otherwise. But there are stories that the Kage shinobi have the ability to pass through walls, to become shadows themselves…or to turn invisible."

"There are also stories," Tatsumi said in a soft, lethal voice, "that those who speak of these shinobi vanish, and are never seen again."

"Good thing I don't believe wild tales, then."

A faint chime shivered into the air from the direction of the graveyard.

We turned, peering down the rise. A ghostly figure in white was walking through the cemetery, straw hat and staff bobbing as he moved between headstones, passing shambling gaki, who paid him no attention. He moved slowly, purposefully, trailing fading tendrils of mist that curled into the air, before he himself walked behind a large cedar trunk and disappeared.

"There he goes," I whispered, and glanced at the dark warrior behind Okame. "Tatsumi, you said you could get us down there, without having to fight?"

He drew back a step, his gaze solemn as he peered down the rise. "Yes, but there are a few conditions. The spell only works if we ourselves remain silent and unnoticed. Anything louder than a whisper will cause the illusion to break, as will any sudden movement. Looking directly into a gaki's eyes or drawing its attention will also dissolve the spell. So be quiet, keep your head down and stay close to me. Can you do that?"

"What about me?" Okame demanded. Tatsumi gave him a cold look.

"The more people that go down there, the harder it will be to maintain the spell. I'm already stretching the limit of what I can do with one other—two would be setting us up for failure. It would be better for us all if you stayed here."

"Trying to get rid of me, Kage-san? I'm wounded. It would be such a waste if I was eaten by a gaki."

Tatsumi narrowed his eyes. "Your swordsmanship is lacking," he said bluntly. "You would be no use to us among the gaki should they see through the spell. Trying to protect Yumeko with your blade would be futile, and would put you both in harm's way."

Okame sniffed. "You don't have to insult me, Kage-san. I don't have the right to demand satisfaction anymore, but I *can* be offended. In fact, I think I am."

"You're a better shot with your bow," Tatsumi continued, as if the other hadn't said anything. "If the spell fails and the gaki attack, it would be prudent for you to be farther away, covering our escape. You can kill the gaki before they get to us, and I won't have to worry about protecting you and Yumeko, should the worst happen."

"I…suppose you have a good point. Much as it pains me to admit it." Okame crossed his arms with a sigh. "Fine. I don't like the idea, but I know as much about magic as I do flower arranging. I'll stay back here, put an arrow through the skull of any gaki that gets too close. Yumeko-chan…" He nodded at me, smiling. "Good luck. Don't get eaten—you were just starting to make my life interesting."

"You be careful, too," I told him, and turned to the samurai. "All right, Tatsumi. I'm ready. What do I have to do?"

He hesitated once more, then held out a hand, palm turned up. "We have to stay connected," he told me, and, for some strange reason, my stomach fluttered like a swarm of moths were set loose within. "The spell will cover both of us, but it isn't meant to be used on a group. If we get separated, the gaki will be able to see you, so don't let go, no matter what."

I nodded, took a quiet breath and placed my hand in his. His palm was rough with calluses, but the fingers curling over mine were long and slender, almost elegant. My heartbeat quickened, and the moths in my belly swirled even more frantically before settling into an agitated fluttering.

Tatsumi had gone perfectly still, staring at our clasped

hands, as if fighting his instincts to pull away. I peeked at his face and saw a flicker of emotion in those purple eyes, a hint of uncertainty and the barest shadow of fear. But only for a moment; then his expression shut down, that icy mask dropping into place. Bringing two fingers to his face with his other hand, he half closed his eyes and murmured a chant using words I didn't understand.

A whisper of power went through the air, centered on Tatsumi. It swirled around us, cold and caressing, seeming to muffle sound and make the shadows around us even darker. Somewhere off to the side, Okame uttered a breathless curse. I suddenly felt very strange, as if my body wasn't quite solid, and the moonlight blazing down overhead was passing right through me.

Tatsumi opened his eyes. The glimmering violet orbs peered down at me, but I could not see my reflection within. "Let's go," he whispered. "Remember, stay close, keep your eyes off the gaki and don't let go of my hand. Are you ready?"

I nodded, tightening my fingers around his. He turned, and together, we walked down the narrow winding path into the cemetery.

Several ancient trees grew among the gravestones, towering cedar and looming pine. As soon as we reached the edge of the cemetery, Tatsumi broke away from the path and slipped into the shadows thrown by the giants. Gaki shambled among the gravestones; I kept my head down but saw them in my peripheral vision, their naked, bloated bodies shining grotesquely in the moonlight. My heart pounded, but as Tatsumi had predicted, they paid us no more attention than the falling leaves, though a few passed frighteningly close. Once, Tatsumi pulled me roughly against a tree, pressing us both into the bark as a gaki lurched around the trunk, barely missing him. For a few heartbeats, it stood just a few feet away, raspy breaths hissing into the air, scanning the area as if it could sense *something* was close. I closed my fingers around my tanto and squeezed my eyes shut, not daring to move or even breathe. My heart pounded, and I pressed myself as far from Tatsumi as I could, hoping he wouldn't feel the lacquered case tucked into my furoshiki. If he found the Dragon's scroll now, a graveyard full of hungry ghosts would be the least of my concerns.

Finally, the gaki's footsteps staggered away, and I felt Tatsumi relax. "Move," he whispered to me, and we did, slipping away from the trunk and weaving our way past the gravestones.

As we ducked between two pine trees, something glinted in the corner of my eye, causing me to halt and grab Tatsumi's sleeve.

"Tatsumi-san," I whispered. "I think I see the monk. Over there."

He followed my pointing finger. At the farthest end of the graveyard, a lone headstone stood in the shadow of three enormous cedars. A beam of moonlight slanted through the tree branches, illuminating the headstone and gleaming off a staff with metal rings at the top.

"The monk's grave," I whispered, as with a ghostly shimmer, a section of moonlight detached from the headstone and stepped into view. The yurei monk, in his straw hat and still holding his metal rod, met my gaze over the stones and raised an ethereal eyebrow.

"He sees us," Tatsumi growled.

A piercing shriek made my blood run cold, and a gaki hurled itself over a headstone, jaws gaping like a rabid wolf. Tatsumi spun, Kamigoroshi clearing its sheath in an instant to strike the spindly body from the air. But his hand came free of my grip, and I felt the tearing of magic as the spell dissolved, like a stone hurled through a spiderweb. All through the cemetery, gaki were turning to look at us, eyes blazing bright with hunger, their hisses and shrieks rising into the air.

Tatsumi stepped forward, the cold purple light of Kamigoroshi washing over the stones, matching the chilling look in his eyes. "Go," he told me, swinging the blade in front of him. "Talk to the monk. I'll keep them off you for as long as I can."

I looked up at the approaching gaki, torn between running toward the monk and pulling out my tanto to stand with Tatsumi. Fox magic flared, making my hands tingle, and I wondered if a ball of kitsune-bi to the face would slow the gaki down, even as it exposed my true nature.

As the first gaki drew close, something streaked through the air behind it, striking it in the back. With a shriek, it pitched forward, the shaft of an arrow protruding from its neck, and dissolved into green mist. Another jerked and went careening over a headstone, and a third crumpled to the dirt in a tangle of flailing limbs, before writhing into nothingness.

"Okame," I breathed, sparing a quick glance at the top of the hill. I could just make out a lean figure silhouetted on the roof of the shack, just as another gaki screamed and tumbled into the weeds. Tatsumi waited patiently as the first wave drew close, his blade held loose at his side.

"Yumeko." His voice was eerily calm, though I heard a ripple of something terrifying underneath, a barely restrained bloodlust that sent shivers up my spine. "Go."

I went.

I darted between headstones and wove between the aisles of rock, searching for that ghostly shimmer of white. It waited for me in the shadow of the trees, standing patiently beside its grave, a bemused expression on its pale, glowing face. I dodged around a headstone to avoid a gaki and winced as its claws raked four white gashes into the rock. It scuttled around the grave, jaws gaping as it reached for me, when an arrow hissed through the air and struck the back of its neck. It dissolved with a chilling wail, and I hurried on.

Gasping, I stumbled past the last of the gravestones, darted around a tree, and was abruptly standing before a transparent figure in white.

"Well." The monk's voice was a shiver of an icy wind, the echo of a long-forgotten emotion. His face blurred in and out of reality, like a pebble dropped into the reflection of a pond. "This night has been full of surprises. Hello, little fox. What brings you to my lonely corner of the village?"

I drew in a breath, not surprised that he knew what I really was. He didn't sound like an onryo, the terrible grudge spirit that Tatsumi had spoken of. His voice was calm, pleasant even, and maybe a little sad.

"*Konbanwa*, yurei-san," I began, as a shriek rang out behind me in a flash of purple light. Tatsumi was keeping the gaki busy, as he'd promised. "Oh," I went on anxiously, "is it proper to call you yurei-san? I haven't spoken to any ghosts before this."

His hazy features lowered into a frown, but he seemed more puzzled than angry. I hurried on in case he took offense. "Please, master monk," I implored, clasping my hands together in a bow, "the people here have suffered greatly at the hands of their own loved ones. I've come to ask if you would lift the curse. You were dealt a terrible wrong all those years ago, but none of these people were responsible for your death. And it must be terribly boring, drifting around as a ghost. Surely your desire for vengeance has been satisfied by now."

"Ah, little fox." The ghost of the monk bowed his head. "I wish I could. It was never my intention to place such a powerful curse upon this village. I was…angry…back then. Though time for me blurs and runs together. I do not know how long it has been since I cursed this village's greed and died with retribution on my lips. I wish only to move on, to complete my journey to Meido, or wherever my soul is destined."

With chilling screams, several more gaki met their ends on Tatsumi's sword. But ominous green lights were beginning to rise from several graves, slowly taking form as more hungry ghosts began to materialize. I felt the hair on the back of my neck stand up, but the yurei didn't seem to notice.

"Unfortunately, the curse keeps me tied to this world," the monk continued. "I cannot pass on until it is lifted, and I cannot seem to lift it myself. Or perhaps I can, but I've forgotten how." His shoulders slumped, one ghostly hand lifting to his face. "I'm tired," he whispered. "So tired of lingering, of being stuck in this tiny village, surrounded by the monsters I brought into this world. I watch the villagers constantly, hoping one of them will gain the courage to try to lift the curse, but they are too fearful to even approach the graveyard. Not that I blame them." He glanced at the sky, where a faint pink glow could be seen over the treetops. "Dawn is almost here," he said. "The gaki will vanish for another month, and I will continue to haunt this place."

Despair flickered. "Can't you do anything?" I asked.

The ghost shook his head and gave me a sad, resigned look. "You were brave to come here, kitsune," he said, drawing back. "But you are not from this village, and you cannot lift the curse. If the curse can be lifted at all—"

*"Omachi kudasai!"*

The shout echoed behind me, high-pitched and frantic. I spun, and saw a figure running full tilt through the cemetery, arms out and hands clutching something in front of him.

"Please wait!" he cried again, as I blinked in surprise. *The headman? What's he doing here?* "Please," the headman called, his voice drawing the attention of every gaki in the cemetery. "Master monk, please hear me out!"

The gaki snarled and bounded after him. Leaping atop a headstone, a gaki tensed to pounce, but an arrow slammed into its back and it tumbled off the stone with a howl. As the headman passed Tatsumi, one of the hungry ghosts turned and lunged at him, claws grasping. Tatsumi's blade hissed down, severing the gaki in two, but its nails still tore a bloody gash across the man's neck. He staggered, nearly falling, but regained his footing and came on.

I stepped back as the headman reached us, instantly falling to his face on the ground. "Forgive us, master monk!" he cried, holding up the thing he'd been carrying: a full bowl of rice. "We were wrong, to let you suffer so. We will never again let any traveler starve as you did. Please…" He held the bowl even higher, even as he stayed prostrate in the dirt. "Accept this as a token of our regret. Or, if your vengeance requires it, I will offer my own life for the rest of the village. Turn me into a gaki, drag me to Jigoku, it matters not. Whatever you need to do to pass on and leave us in peace."

Heart in my throat, I looked at the monk. He gazed down

at the headman with a stunned expression. Behind us, the gaki shrieked and howled as they flung themselves at Tatsumi, and the hiss of arrows continued as Okame picked them off one by one, but both the headman and the monk seemed to have forgotten all about them.

Then, the monk smiled, and a single silver tear ran from his eye, writhing into mist as soon as it hit the ground. "That was all I wanted," he whispered. "One bowl of rice. A single offering of kindness. But even in the face of cruelty, I should not have let my anger consume me so. This has become my punishment, as well." His expression became peaceful, and he bowed his head. "I think we have all suffered enough."

The cries of the gaki faded. I looked around the cemetery to see that the hungry ghosts were standing motionless, looking lost. Even those that had been fighting Tatsumi stopped moving, their arms dropping to their sides and their faces lax. As I watched, they shimmered, becoming transparent as they started to fade. A glowing ball of blue-white light rose from each of their bodies, filling the air until the entire cemetery glowed with ethereal luminance. Left behind, the shells of the gaki disappeared, writhing into mist that disappeared on the breeze.

*"Arigatou."* I looked back at the monk as he whispered the words. He was fading, too, his ghostly form becoming fainter and fainter as he smiled at me. "Thank you," he whispered again. "You could not lift the curse on your own, but your courage illuminated the way for those who could. May the Kami bless you, and may you never lose that fire that burns within your soul."

"Safe travels to you, master monk," I said. "May your journey to the other side be swift and clear, and may Jinkei light your way so that you will never stumble."

He bowed to me, and a moment later, became a glowing sphere of light that floated into the air, joining the rest. For a moment, they hovered overhead, almost too bright to look at. Then, as one, they scattered, flying to every corner of the heavens, becoming smaller and smaller until they turned into distant stars and were lost from sight.

# Part 3

# 20

## Blood Magic

Lady Satomi was back.

And, from what Suki could see, she was not happy.

"Useless minions," she muttered, standing in the center of a small, horrifying room. A single candle flickered on a low table, and a cracked, full-length mirror stood in the corner, reflecting the room's grisly state. The walls were streaked with old blood, the floor stained with dark, unidentifiable patches. Lady Satomi stood there, stunning in blue robes patterned with cranes and dragonflies, her hair perfectly styled and held in place with ivory combs. She looked supremely out of place in the center of the gruesomeness, except for what she held in her hand. The head of a large crow lay cradled in her palm, dripping blood between her fingers to spatter the edges of her robes. The body of the bird lay in the center of the table, a small knife resting beside it in a pool of blood. Suki could barely look at the still twitching corpse, having had to leave the room when the actual deed was performed. Though being able to go through walls made that easier, at least. Lady Satomi's eyes were closed, a frown stretching her full lips, as if she was watching something she found distressing. Finally, she let out a huff and opened her eyes.

"Two kamaitachi, one wind witch and a giant demon bear," she grumbled, tossing the severed head to the table, where it landed beside its cooling body. "And Kazekira still couldn't manage to kill them and take the scroll piece. Sliced to bits by her own familiars, how disgraceful." She shook her head, plucked a cloth from the mirror and wiped the blood from her hands. "I suppose that is what I get for relying on outside help. If you want something done right..."

Picking up the knife, she regarded her reflection in the surface. As Suki watched, mystified, the woman lowered the blade to the inside of her arm, then cut a short, straight gash along her skin. Blood welled and bubbled from the cut, and Satomi began chanting in a low, hypnotic voice.

Suki felt the whisper of some terrible power go through the air, and trembled in an effort not to flee the room. On Satomi's raised arm, the line of blood swelled, congealed and became solid. Dozens of legs wriggled, and the long, segmented body of a centipede emerged from the blood and began crawling up her arm.

Satomi smiled. Reaching down, she plucked the monstrous insect from her skin and held it between two fingernails as it writhed and coiled in her grasp. "Go," she whispered to it. "Find the demonslayer and the fox. Kill them both, feast on their insides and return to me with the scroll. I will be waiting."

She tossed the centipede to the floor, where it landed with an audible thump. As soon as it hit the ground, it scuttled across the room on hooked yellow legs, squeezed through a crack in the boards and vanished.

Lowering her arm, ignoring the blood that dripped to the floor, Satomi nodded in satisfaction. "Well, that should take care of it," she murmured to herself. "The demonslayer has become quite troublesome, but once he is dead, this piece of the scroll will be mine." She sighed, as if wearied by the amount of work still left to do. "Now, I must write an invitation to the palace, and find someone halfway competant to deliver it to the Hayate shrine. That useless new girl should be able to manage that, at least."

She glanced down at herself, as if realizing for the first time she and her magnificent robes were covered in blood that stained the silk and was still running down her arm. "Such a messy business," she sighed. "And trying enough without being spied upon. Are you getting a good look, little spirit, or whoever is haunting this castle? I can feel you watching me, you know. You're not terribly subtle."

Suki jolted back, flaring into existence, and Satomi turned to her with a smile.

"There you are. Well, well, still hanging around, Suki-chan?" the woman mocked, as Suki floated there, stunned. Satomi chuckled, shaking her head. "Poor lost lingering soul. Too weak and frightened to even come back as a grudge spirit. How very pathetic. But you are of no importance to me anymore."

Suki clenched her ghostly fists, wishing she could do something, anything. Even pick up the dead crow's head and hurl it at the evil woman. Satomi chuckled again, then bent to grab the bloody cloth from the table. "If you wish to haunt me, little soul," the woman crooned as she wiped her arm clean, "you go right ahead. But if you become annoying, or if you get in my way, I know a few blood priestesses and onmyoji who would be happy to bind your spirit to a wall scroll. Or the mirror. Or perhaps stuff you into a monkey." Her lips curled even further, showing teeth as she stepped forward. "Would you like to be a monkey, Suki-chan? Personally, I think it would be an improvement, don't you? Catch!"

She hurled the bloody cloth at Suki's face. Instinctively, Suki jerked back, throwing up her arms to shield herself. The rag passed right through her arms and face and struck the wall behind her, and Suki felt her body shiver like mist in response. With a soundless cry, the distraught ghost turned and fled, vanishing through the walls of the castle, hearing Satomi's cruel laughter follow her as she did.

# 21

## The Legend of Oni no Mikoto

"*I* think we've crossed the border, Kage-san," the ronin announced, shading his eyes as he gazed down the hill with Yumeko. "I'm pretty certain we're in Taiyo lands now. The capital shouldn't be far."

Standing in the shade of a ginkgo tree, I gazed down at the sweeping vista before us and concluded that he was right. These were definitely the lands of the Sun Clan. We had crossed into the territory of the Taiyo. While not as martially powerful as the Fire Clan, or as numerously large as the Earth Clan, the Taiyo were perhaps the most influential of all the Great Clans, for they made up the imperial family. They ruled the capital city of Kin Heigen Toshi, and as far back as history could remember, the emperor or empress had always been part of the Sun Clan.

The silvery glint of a river, snaking through the valley

toward the distant peaks, caught my eye. "There's the Hotaru Kawa," I said. "If we follow it north, it will lead to the capital."

"Yep. And we got here without having to pass through the border checkpoint, which would've been a pain in the ass." The ronin grinned back at me. "See, it all worked out, Kage-san. A dog always finds its way."

I didn't answer. The ronin had kept his word and had led us through the mountains, but he was also responsible for getting us lost in the first place. Still, I could admit he had proven useful in the gaki village; his skill as a warrior had certainly helped in the last battle, even if it wasn't with a sword. And we *had* avoided the checkpoint, though I would need to be careful of any imperial magistrates or guards who might demand to see my travel papers. At best, depending on the circumstances, I would have to pay a hefty fine for traveling through another clan's territory without proper documentation. At worst, I would be imprisoned and executed, my clan shamed and dishonor brought to my family. Yumeko would be fine; no one paid attention to peasant girls, and ronin were rarely given a second glance. But I was a Kage samurai, or at least I looked the part, and samurai were treated with caution in territories not their own. Especially if that samurai was part of the Shadow Clan.

"It's been a while since I've been to the capital," the ronin stated, his gaze following the river through the valley. "It'll be nice to relax, get a halfway decent meal, and then maybe I can convince you to have some fun for a change, Kage-san." He gave me that defiant grin. "I take it you've never played cho-han before?"

Cho-han was a dice game popular in all of Iwagoto's gambling dens, which were rough, seedy places frequented by bandits, ronin, gang members and crime lords. My missions for the Shadow Clan sometimes took me into the darkest of these underworlds, chasing down demons hiding among killers, but reputable samurai rarely ventured into such places, and those that did never admitted to it.

"No," I said.

"No, you've never played it, or no, I can't convince you to try?"

"Take your pick."

"Ah, well. Your loss, samurai." The ronin shook his head and glanced at Yumeko, sitting peacefully under the ginkgo tree. "Maybe Yumeko-chan would be willing to try her hand at it. She can talk to the kami, right? Could she ask Tamafuku, the God of Luck, to bless my dice for a round or two?"

He was baiting me, and I knew he was baiting me, but anger flickered all the same. I knew what kind of humans filled those gambling halls: predators with hungry eyes and bloodthirsty smiles. The thought of Yumeko surrounded by a circle of human wolves, their ravenous eyes watching her every move, filled me with a cold fury I did not understand.

"Tamafuku?" Sitting in the grass, Yumeko cocked her head, and the cricket that had been perched on her elbow sprang away into the grass. "Well, I could try," she said. "I've never spoken to any of the Great Kami before, just the minor ones. Do you know where we can find Tamafuku so I could talk to him?"

"Well, there is a giant statue of him just inside the gambling hall," the ronin said.

"Oh? Does he live inside the statue then? Do you think it gets up and moves around when no one is looking? There was a teapot in the Silent Winds temple that did that sometimes, until the day Nitoru kicked it across the room."

"Never mind." The ronin sighed. "Forget I said anything."

With a yawn, the girl rose, stretching both arms over her head. "At least we're almost to the capital," she mused, gazing down the valley. "What *I'm* hoping for is an inn with good food and soft futons. It will be nice to sleep on a bed for a change and not out in the open. Or in a leaky hut. Or in a cave with a very uncomfortable stone floor." Her dark gaze slid to me, the smile growing wider. "Unlike certain samurai who will remain nameless, most of us cannot fall asleep wherever we want."

I masked a frown, confused. I could never sleep as she did, stretched out and prone, easy prey for someone to cut off my head or tear me apart. Sleep for me came in snatches, in an upright position with my back to the wall and Kamigoroshi in my lap, ready to be drawn in a blink. Comfort had nothing to do with it.

The ronin pulled his sake jug around to his front. "We're still a few days out from the capital, if I had to guess," he remarked, pulling the top off the gourd. "But there should be a couple towns between here and Kin Heigen Toshi. I think Yashigi is just up the river." He lifted the jug toward his lips, but then gave a yelp and yanked it away from his face. *"Kuso!"*

My hand dropped to my sword, and Yumeko blinked at him in shock. "What's wrong, Okame-san?"

"There's…a…*frog*...in my sake!" the ronin sputtered, sounding outraged and horrified. He tilted the gourd upside down, shook it twice, and a tiny green creature tumbled into the grass with the rest of the liquid.

Yumeko burst out laughing. Her voice was like tiny birds, and sent a strange prickle over my skin. "Oh, don't be upset, Okame-san," she said, as the ronin stared mournfully at the empty jug, as if hoping it would refill. "Frogs are good luck, after all. You must be blessed by the kami."

"Not from where I'm standing. Unless they've decided to bless me with soberness, which they can keep to themselves, thank you very much."

I glanced at the place the frog had fallen, but could no longer see it in the grass. Only a bright green juniper leaf skipping across the ground, being blown by the wind. The ronin gave a heavy sigh and hung the gourd around his neck. "Well, shall we get going?" he muttered. "I'm going to need a lot more sake if I'm going to keep traveling with the pair of you."

We reached Yashigi just as the sun was going down, casting long shadows over the valley and turning the river the color of blood. The long wooden bridge over the Hotaru Kawa teemed with people entering and leaving town; merchants with carts, ronin, peasants, a few mounted samurai, all mingled together, hooves, wheels and sandaled feet thumping and groaning as they crossed.

"So many people," Yumeko murmured, gazing around with wide eyes. "Even more than Chochin Machi. I've never seen so many people in one place."

Beside her, the ronin chuckled. "This is nothing, Yumeko-chan," he told her. "Just wait till you see the capital."

An imperial magistrate, flanked by two mounted guards, clopped down the center of the bridge on horseback, parting the crowds before them like waves. Discreetly, I moved to the side of the road, keeping my gaze averted and blending into the passersby. The magistrate and his guards passed without pause and continued across the bridge, though I did notice the ronin eyeing me with suspicion when they were out of sight.

Across the bridge, a wide main road cut through the center of town, branching into dozens of side streets. Rows of wooden buildings with blue-tiled overhangs lined the sidewalks, rectangular cloth signs fluttering in the breeze. Despite the fading light, people still milled about the streets: women in kimonos, samurai sauntering through the crowds, merchants standing outside their businesses, enticing customers to enter. A tofu seller jogged past us, two large wooden buckets balanced from a pole on his shoulder. A trio of boys clustered around a stall selling cooked eel, watching as the vendor pulled live eels out of a barrel, drove a nail through their gills to fillet them and placed the skewers on the grill.

As they'd been in Chochin Machi, Yumeko's eyes were wide, her gaze never still, as she took everything in. As we moved down the sidewalks, the ronin was all too happy to point things out and to offer an explanation on whatever questions she had. I said nothing as we wove through the foot traffic, keeping a firm hand on Kamigoroshi and scanning the crowds for danger. The girl and the ronin remained oblivious, but I had felt eyes on us the moment we crossed the bridge. There was no doubt in my mind; we were being watched.

"Man, I'm starving," the ronin stated, pausing at the entrance of a restaurant, blue curtains hanging over the door. A fat tanuki statue wearing a straw hat and clutching a sake bottle stood beside the entrance, beckoning travelers inside. "What do you think, Yumeko-chan?"

Yumeko blinked at the statue and crossed her arms. "I don't think this is a proper representation," she stated in a serious voice. "I've never known any tanuki to have that big a scrotum."

The ronin made a spitting noise and turned away, coughing and beating his chest. "He means food, Yumeko," I explained, as the ronin gasped and waved his hand at us in agreement, leaning against the wall. "This is a restaurant, if you want to get something to eat."

"Oh," Yumeko said, and frowned. "Well, of course. I'm fairly hungry myself. Though I still think the statue is all wrong." She sniffed and passed it by, wrinkling her nose. "How would one even walk with those dragging along the ground? I would think they'd get horribly chafed."

I managed not to wince as I followed her through the door, but just barely.

"Welcome, sir, welcome!" the host greeted as we came into the room. Though I brought up the rear, he looked only at me, ignoring the ronin and Yumeko entirely. "Will you be dining with us tonight?"

"Three of us," I told him, earning a brief, puzzled look as he glanced at my companions. It wasn't every day a samurai sat down to eat with a ronin and a peasant girl. Under my flat stare, however, he quickly bowed and ushered us to a low table in the corner. After explaining that our waitress would be right over, he bowed once more and left.

A young woman arrived soon after, and both Yumeko and the ronin enthusiastically placed their orders, while I tried not to think of how this would deplete the last of my coin. After the waitress left, I poured myself a cup of tea and quietly nursed my drink, listening to the murmur of voices around us.

"They say Oni no Mikoto has appeared again," the man at the table behind us muttered.

"The Demon Prince?" said his companion. "Kami preserve us. Where was he seen this time?"

"Omachi, on the bridge outside town. Two ronin were traveling together, and he challenged the stronger of them to a duel." A pause, and then he added in a hushed voice, "The survivor said he'd never seen anyone move so fast."

"That's because Oni no Mikoto isn't a man," said his companion gravely. "Well, this will stir up a hornet's nest, as all the fools who think they're warriors will be off looking for a fight, hoping the Demon Prince finds them worthy enough to challenge. Baka." The man snorted. "Worthy enough to kill, more likely."

The waitress returned, setting a tray before us. It held an assortment of dishes: cooked meat, vegetables and three bowls of rice. "Is there anything else I can get you?" she asked, as the ronin immediately grabbed a chicken strip with his chopsticks and shoved it into his mouth. Politely, she didn't seem to notice.

"I have a question," Yumeko said, as the ronin continued to pick food off the tray. "Who is Oni no Mikoto? Is he really a prince of demons? I have trouble believing there is an oni wandering around the valley, challenging people to duels. Wouldn't people notice that?"

So, she had been listening, too. Somehow, I wasn't surprised. The waitress's eyes widened a bit, and she dropped her voice. "Oni no Mikoto?" she whispered in a dramatic voice, as if this was not the first time she had spoken about him. "He's become our most famous local legend. They say on moonlit nights, a lone swordsman will sometimes appear on the bridges around the area, blocking the way forward. He had the body of an angel and the face of a demon, and will not allow anyone to cross the bridge unless they defeat him in a duel. But he shows himself only to those he finds worthy—the strongest and most skilled warriors in the land. Apparently, his legend has grown beyond the valley, because now we have swordsmen traveling here from all over, hoping to meet Oni no Mikoto on the roads. But in the three years since the Demon Prince first appeared, no one has been able to defeat him.

"So," she finished, as Yumeko listened in rapt fascination, "if you are traveling through the valley, and you happen to meet a single swordsman on a lonely, moonlit bridge, first count yourself both lucky and cursed—you are among the few worthy of Oni no Mikoto's attention. Then turn around and walk away. Oni no Mikoto is not a man. He is a demon with a sword, and he will take your head for a prize as he has done to the countless warriors who came before."

"Ha." The ronin snorted with his mouth full. "If it was me, I'd just shoot him."

The waitress looked affronted. "You cannot just shoot Oni no Mikoto!"

"*Nande*? Why not?"

"Because," the waitress sputtered. "It's…dishonorable!"

"Bah, I'm no samurai. I don't follow that code of honor anymore." The ronin picked up a squid and stuffed the whole thing in his mouth. "Some stranger wants to kill me for trying to cross a bridge, he's getting shot between the eyes."

I reached for my rice bowl but paused, a faint shiver going through my veins. A black paper crane sat on a corner of the tray, almost invisible against the lacquered surface. My heart sank, but I couldn't leave it there. As the waitress sputtered again, I quickly palmed the folded crane and slipped it into my sleeve.

The waitress still seemed at a loss for words. "You cannot… That is… How barbaric." She stepped back, giving the ronin a look of distaste. "Well, you won't even see Oni no Mikoto," she said loftily. "Someone like you isn't worthy of his attention."

"I hope not," was the reply. "I'd lose all respect for this Demon Prince if he showed up to challenge a filthy ronin dog."

"Excuse me." I rose, causing all three to look my way. The ronin frowned, one cheek bulging like a squirrel.

"Where you going, Kage?"

"I must take care of a small matter. I'll return shortly." Without waiting for an answer, I walked away, feeling Yumeko's eyes on my back as I left. The ronin grunted, muttered something about "Toilets," and continued eating as I ducked through the curtained doorway into the streets.

Outside, the sun had set. Many of the shops had closed their doors, though there were a few stubborn businesses that continued to stay open even after dark. I walked to the edge of the main road and felt the paper crane in my sleeve stir. It slipped out and fluttered away down a narrow side street, becoming lost in the darkness. Setting my jaw, I followed.

Jomei was waiting for me in the shadows of a warehouse, his painted face seeming to hover against the black. The paper crane perched on his knee, fanning its wings as if it were truly alive.

"You're late."

I bowed so he wouldn't sense my reluctance. Why was I feeling so hesitant tonight? This meeting was the same as all the others. "Forgive me, Master Jomei. I was held up. There were…complications."

"Yes, I saw that." The mage's voice was faintly amused.

"You've picked up quite the party, Tatsumi-san. Now, not only is there a girl, but an uncouth ronin dog following you about. Would you care to explain why you haven't killed him yet, or at least lost him somewhere along the road?"

"He was part of a bandit gang that ambushed us," I began. "But he ended up turning on them instead. Yumeko…insisted that we help him, after the fight."

"The peasant girl told you not to kill the bandit," Jomei said. "And you listened to her?"

"She's my only lead to Master Jiro and the Steel Feather temple," I replied. "If I'd killed the ronin, it might've frightened her, or angered her. I couldn't take the risk that she would leave."

Jomei pinched the bridge of his nose between thumb and forefinger, briefly closing his eyes. "This girl is becoming more and more problematic," he muttered, and a shiver of unease crept up my spine. If Jomei thought Yumeko was becoming a danger to the clan, or if he believed she was no longer essential to my mission, he would give the order to have her and the ronin killed. He might order me to dispose of them both on an isolated stretch of road outside the city. No one would notice, or care, if a ronin and a peasant girl suddenly disappeared without a trace. Both of them were dangerously naive, far too trusting of the demon beside them. Oni no Mikoto might be a local legend, but a real demon lurked in their midst, hungering for blood, for their very souls. They wouldn't suspect a thing until it appeared and cut them down. If Jomei gave the order to kill both my companions, it would be all too easy to carry it out.

And I…didn't want to do it. The notion shocked me. I'd never questioned orders before, never faltered in what I had to do. If I was told to "cleanse" a hamlet because the villagers were using blood magic to summon demons, I would slaughter every man, woman and child there. If they ordered me to Jigoku to slay O-Hakumon, the ruler of hell himself, I would jump into the abyss without a second thought. My life was not my own. As always, duty to the Shadow Clan was everything.

"Am I to kill her, Master Jomei?" I asked softly. My stomach tightened, and it was suddenly difficult to breathe. If my orders were to kill Yumeko, so be it. I would carry out my duty, as I'd always done. And I would hope that, somehow, her face would not haunt me for the rest of my life.

Jomei sighed. "No," he said, igniting a sudden and unexpected flare of relief. "If she can truly lead you to the scroll, there's no reason to kill her yet. Right now, she is naive and harmless, and the ronin seems a bumbling fool. Continue traveling with them, if you must. As long as they pose no threat to the secrets of the clan."

I bowed my head. "As you wish, Master Jomei."

"When you reach the capital, be sure to check in with Kage Masao in the Shadow Clan district. He'll be expecting you."

"Understood."

"Oh, and here." The shadow mage tossed something at me. I caught it with a clink; a circle of cord strung with copper kaeru and a few silver tora. "Your stipend for the month. Since you seem to have an extra mouth to feed. Make it last."

"Thank you, Master Jomei."

"Go, then." Jomei waved a hand, dismissing me. "Return to your 'companions' before they grow suspicious of where you are. Remember," he added as I bowed once more and turned away, "the clan will be watching them, and you, demonslayer. Do not give us a reason to act."

When I returned to the table in the corner, most of the

food was gone. The plates were picked over, with only bones and scraps remaining. Only my bowl of rice sat untouched on the edge, though the ronin was eyeing it as if contemplating snatching that up, as well.

"Sorry, Tatsumi-san," Yumeko said as I knelt across from her on the cushion. "I tried to keep baka-Okame from eating everything, but he didn't want to share. We can order more, if you like."

"Dogs don't share, Yumeko-chan." The ronin grinned, using a fish bone to pick at his teeth. "We're horrible gluttons like that. Besides, who wolfed down a dozen fried tofu balls all by herself?"

"Because you had already eaten all the fish, and the chicken, and most of the squid. If I didn't claim *something* there would've been nothing left."

"That's not true. I left you the pickled radish."

"I hate pickled radish."

"Well, be faster next time. When it comes to food among thieves, Yumeko-chan, it is every man, woman and dog for themselves."

I ate my rice in silence.

# 22

## The Eyes of a Dead Crow

*Never taunt a hungry fox* was a saying Master Isao had been unusually fond of. I'd always wondered why, until now.

We left Yashigi the next morning and for several miles walked down a meandering dirt road through the fertile valley of the Sun Clan. The mountains remained in the distance as we followed the river past farming communities, temples and shrines, open meadows and dense woodland. The scenery was beautiful, the weather perfect in every way; I was fully enjoying the sights and the feel of the sun on my skin.

The ronin seemed less enthusiastic.

*"Ite,"* he grumbled, rubbing the back of his neck as we stopped in the shade of a bamboo grove. "*Kuso*, my back is sore. That inn must've had the lumpiest futon in the world. It felt like there was a damn pinecone right in the middle of the mattress, but when I pulled it up there was nothing there."

"That's unfortunate, Okame-san," I said. "My futon was so comfortable, it was like I was sleeping on clouds. Maybe it was something you ate?"

He glared at me, suspicion flaring in his dark gaze. "I seem to remember you poking around my corner of the room right before we went to sleep," he said accusingly. "You wouldn't have anything to do with my lumpy mattress, would you, Yumeko-chan?"

"Me? What a wicked thing to imply, Okame-san. I mean, you checked under your futon, right? It's not like I could make a pinecone look like a bit of dust on the floor." I smiled at him sweetly and tossed a pickled plum into my mouth. I was beginning to get the hang of this sarcasm thing. "Perhaps all the boiled squid was giving you a stomachache?"

"Quiet," Tatsumi growled. "Something is watching us."

We fell silent. Around us, the woods were still, beams of sunlight slanting through the bamboo. Cicadas droned, and a breeze rustled the stalks, muffling the sound of approach. I didn't sense anything dangerous, but Tatsumi possessed an almost supernatural premonition for things that wished us harm. If he said something was watching us, I believed him.

"I don't see anything," Okame said, just as I spotted what Tatsumi did. Across the road, a large black crow sat hunched atop a tree branch, feathers bristling like quills, beady eyes unblinking as it stared at us.

Okame, following my gaze, let out a snort. "Oh, how horrifying, a bird is watching us," he gasped, putting a hand on his heart. "Watch yourself, Yumeko-chan, it might poop in your hair."

The crow didn't move. It stared at us with intense, sullen hostility, and I felt a shiver creep up my back. "I don't like the way it's watching us," I said. "It looks...angry."

"Really? Looks like a bird to me," the ronin said. When I didn't answer, he shrugged and unshouldered his longbow. "Here then, I'll fix it."

In one smooth motion, he raised the bow and loosed an arrow at the tree, and the muffled thump of the dart striking home rang out a second later. The crow let out a strangled caw and tumbled from the branch in a flutter of wings and black feathers.

As it fell, a strange sensation rippled through the air, a subtle release of power that raised the hair on my arms. All magic had a certain feel, I'd discovered. Fox magic flickered and pulsed like heatless fire. The monks' ki energy tingled like the air before a storm. Tatsumi's shadow magic was almost invisible, but it was still there if you were very observant; it felt like a cool, dark mist settling over your skin.

This felt like a million spiders, maggots and centipedes were wriggling under my clothes. I shuddered, but as quickly as it had come, the feeling faded as the magic scattered to the wind and was gone.

"There." The ronin shouldered his weapon, seeming oblivious to the strange energy pulse. "Fixed. No more creepy birds. We can go now, right?"

Tatsumi sighed. "You might have made it worse."

Resisting the urge to flail my arms to make sure there were no insects in my sleeves, I walked across the road to where the bird had fallen. Circling the trunk, I saw the arrow tip poking up from the weeds and peered down, expecting to see the corpse of a large black crow.

A chill went through my stomach. There was no body, not technically. The arrow shaft, jutting up from the dirt, pierced the rib cage of a bleached white skeleton, fragile wing bones crumpled in the grass, surrounded by feathers.

The skull lay against a tree root, beak open in a last indignant caw, completely bare of skin. It looked like it had been dead for months, rather than the few seconds it took to cross the road.

I swallowed hard, feeling the two boys come up behind me and peer over my shoulder. Okame let out a low curse, as I stepped closer to Tatsumi, glancing up at his expression. "That's not normal, is it?" I asked in a small voice. "I'm pretty certain that's not normal."

"No," Tatsumi answered, his eyes narrowed to violet slits. "It's blood magic."

A shudder went through me. Blood magic. Master Isao had told me about it, once, as a warning. Unlike normal magic, where it was believed the kami-touched were chosen by the gods themselves, blood magic could be performed by nearly anyone, from the lowliest farmer to the highest-ranking magistrate. As its name suggested, blood fueled its power; the more blood spilled, the stronger the spell. It could raise the dead, manipulate emotions, or summon a demon from the depths of Jigoku. But such power came with a hidden, terrible price. Blood magic was the magic of death and corruption, the magic of Jigoku. The more you used it, the more pieces of your soul you gave away, bit by bit, until you were a husk of something that had once been human. Eventually the practitioner was consumed by the darkness of his own making and became one of Jigoku's own, an oni or other demon, damned to the abyss until the end of time.

"Blood magic." The ronin curled a lip at the pile of feathers and bones at the bottom of the tree. "Well, that's great, now I've killed someone's favorite abomination. There's probably a fuming blood mage out there who's making a wara ningyo in my image right now."

"Unlikely," Tatsumi said. Wara ningyo, straw dolls fashioned in the target's image, were a common item for carrying out curses, but they needed a bit of the victim itself—hair, blood or fingernails—for the ritual to work. Once, when I was younger and angry at being made to repolish the floor in the main hall, I'd used fox magic to make a bit of straw look like a curse doll and hung it outside Denga's quarters. It was hard not to wince at what had come next. That was the one and only time I could remember Master Isao being furious with me.

And then, I had another thought, one that turned everything inside me to ice. "Someone sent this thing," I said, looking at Tatsumi. "To follow us. Because of the scroll." Quickly, I added, "Because they think we have it. Or that we know where it is."

"Wait, what?" The ronin stared at me like my ears had suddenly appeared. "Clearly, I've missed the first half of this story," he said. "Back up a bit. Who's following us? What's this scroll you keep talking about?"

Tatsumi didn't answer, but I saw him stiffen. Clearly, he did not like talking about the scroll, especially in the company of the ronin. I didn't, either. I could feel the scroll case hidden within the furoshiki, my great, terrible secret. But it made sense. Master Isao had warned that many would be searching for the scroll, armies of men, yokai and demons trying to find it. Ruthless mortals who would stop at nothing to acquire its power. And if that was the case, then…

"Whoever is using these dead crows to spy on us," I continued, as the realization slowly unfurled like a roll of parchment, "could be behind the attack on the temple. The one who sent the demons to kill everyone and steal the scroll."

I gazed at Tatsumi, who still hadn't moved or changed expression. "It's possible, isn't it?" I asked. "Demons wouldn't have any use for the scroll. Someone sent them. A blood mage."

"Yes," he admitted at last. "Demons…don't just appear in the mortal realm for no reason," he went on, looking reluctant to explain. "Either a mortal has been consumed by darkness and has turned into one, or they're summoned from Jigoku using blood magic. Oni, especially, are extremely powerful and almost impossible to control for long. It would take a talented blood mage to summon and bind one to do its bidding, even for a short while."

"And now we're talking about oni," said Okame. "Oni, blood mages and demons. Should I start screaming now, or should I wait till you get to the part with the eighty-foot skeleton?" Looking at me, he shook his head. "And here I thought you were a simple and innocent peasant girl, Yumeko-chan. How did you get involved with demons and blood magic?"

"Well…"

"Explain later," Tatsumi said brusquely. "We should keep moving." Scanning the road and the surrounding trees, his eyes narrowed. I followed his gaze and saw another crow perched in the branches of a tree, glaring at us. "The blood mage knows we're onto him. It's not safe to be out in the open. Hurry."

We continued down the road with a bit more urgency. I thought back to the dead crow, to the mysterious blood mage who could be following our movements, and my stomach turned in both fear and anger. Whoever had sent the amanjaku and the terrible Yaburama knew I had the Dragon scroll. They were also responsible for the deaths of Master Isao and everyone in the Silent Winds temple. I was putting Okame and Tatsumi in danger; there was no doubt that the blood mage would try to take the scroll again. But with every attempt, I might learn a little more about this new enemy. Who he was, what he wanted, and most important, where he might be. Vengeance was something Master Isao had always cautioned against, especially since yokai could lose themselves to revenge, obsessing over a grudge until it consumed them. But if I ever came face-to-face with the one who had destroyed my temple, he would come to fear the vengeance of an angry kitsune.

"So, Yumeko-chan." Okame's voice jerked me out of my dark musings. The ronin had dropped alongside me, hands clasped behind his head as we walked together down the path. "Normally, I don't like poking into matters that aren't my business," he began, "but I just heard the words *demon*, *oni* and *blood mage* in the same sentence, and any one of those is enough to keep me awake at night. Also—and stop me if I've missed anything—I just watched a bird disintegrate after I shot it, because someone who can raise dead crows has taken an interest in us, because of a scroll. Did I get all that right?"

"More or less." I frowned a bit. "Although, I think he would do more than just bring crows back to life. That would be a very strange skill to have, unless he really loves crows."

"Right. So, I think I deserve some sort of explanation, and I know better than to ask He of the Scary Glowing Sword." He nodded at Tatsumi several paces ahead. "I'd probably get my head lopped off before I could open my mouth. So, I'd appreciate it if you could tell me what's going on, Yumeko-chan. I've faced gaki, yurei and now undead crows. Am I going to have to fight demons anytime in the future?"

"It's...possible," I said, and briefly explained what had

happened the night the demons had attacked the temple, using the same story I'd told Tatsumi. That Master Isao had sensed a great evil coming, and had sent the scroll away before the demons arrived. I told him about the oni, and the amanjaku, and my promise to Master Isao to warn the other temple of the demons. And that I had to find Master Jiro at the Hayate shrine to discover the location of the Steel Feather temple. When I was finished, Okame gave me a shrewd look, as if something I said didn't quite make sense.

"So, a horde of demons attacks your temple, at the same time Kage-san with the demonslaying sword shows up," he mused. "That sounds very convenient. I assume he wasn't there to admire the leaves."

"I don't think Tatsumi is one for leaf watching, Okame-san."

"Right." Okame sighed. "So, what's so special about this scroll, that the Kage demonslayer and an entire hoard of Jigoku abominations would show up to claim it?"

"I… I don't know," I stammered. "Master Isao never told me why it was important."

Guilt prickled. I felt bad for lying, but it was probably better that the ronin know as little about the scroll as possible. The last thing I needed was someone else who wanted to summon the Dragon. Too many knew about it already.

"Huh." Okame crossed his arms, his expression unusually grim. "So, your Master Isao sent this scroll away, presumably to another temple, and Kage-san just decided to escort you there, hmm?"

"No, not really. I asked him to."

"And he agreed. The antisocial, don't-bother-me-or-I'll-kill-you Shadow Clan samurai agreed to escort a peasant girl across several territories to a mysterious temple hidden somewhere on the other side of the country."

"Um. Yes?"

The ronin shook his head and bent closer, lowering his voice. "You don't see what's going on, do you?" he muttered. "He's not taking you to the temple out of the kindness of his heart. He wants the scroll, Yumeko-chan."

"Of course he does. Everyone wants the scroll, Okame-san." I could feel the lacquered case again, pressed into my skin under the furoshiki and had to force myself not to touch the spot where it was hidden. "But I promised Master Isao that I would warn the Steel Feather temple about the demon attack, and I don't think I could make it there on my own, especially if there's a blood mage after us. You've seen how Tatsumi fights. His sword was created to kill demons. He's my best chance of reaching the temple alive."

"And what happens when you get there, and he demands the scroll from the monks?"

"I'm…still working on that."

He shook his head. "Well, good luck, Yumeko-chan. Personally, I don't know what would be scarier—an oni or an angry Kage demonslayer. I hope you know what you're doing."

I hoped so, as well.

The sun began to set while we were still several miles from the next town. As the shadows grew long and the first stars began to appear, I quickened my pace to walk alongside Tatsumi.

"It's getting late, Tatsumi-san. Shouldn't we be looking for a place to spend the night?"

"Sagimura isn't far," he answered. "If we don't stop, we'll

reach it before the hour of the Boar." He paused a moment, before adding, "I'd rather sleep in a village tonight than out in the open."

I shivered. So, he felt it, too. The sensation of danger, of eyes on us wherever we went. In fact, the closer we drew to Sagimura, the more uneasy I felt. Not only that something was watching us, but that something was coming. Chasing us. Stalking us.

And if *Tatsumi* didn't want to stay out in the open, then whatever was out there was something I did not want to meet.

The moon was a full silver disk overhead when the road took us over a bridge that spanned the Hotaru River. On the other side, over the distant rice paddies, I could just catch the glimmers of light that came from Sagimura. There was just one problem.

A stranger stood in the center of the bridge, the moonlight blazing down on him, a shining katana held loosely at his side.

# 23

## The Demon on the Bridge

"Oni no Mikoto," Yumeko whispered.

The swordsman waited for us in the center of the bridge, unmoving as a statue. I didn't know what I was expecting of the Demon Prince, but it wasn't the tall, almost elegant figure in front of us. He wore dark blue hakama trousers and sandals, but his chest was bare, lean muscles exposed to the moonlight. Long white hair, not uncommon in Taiyo lands, fell unbound past his waist. A white-and-red oni mask covered his face, its mouth split into a wide, tusk-bearing grin, curved horns spiking up from its forehead. His sword glimmered at his side, curved and lethal.

"Well, shit," Okame muttered. "It really is Oni no Mikoto, or someone doing their damndest to imitate the legend. Good thing I'm not impressed by legends. Or that silly code of honor. Don't worry, Kage-san," he said, grinning back at me. "I'll take care of this."

In one smooth motion, he drew back his string and loosed an arrow at the figure on the bridge. I watched, knowing the ronin was a near perfect shot, wondering if the next thing I saw would be the stranger toppling backward with an arrow jutting from his chest.

Oni no Mikoto didn't move. He didn't dive out of the way, or take a step back. His sword flicked up, a blink of silver in the darkness, and knocked the dart aside. The arrow clattered against the rails before dropping into the river.

*"Sugoi."* This from Yumeko, her voice awed. "That was… very fast."

The ronin blew out a soft breath. "Yeah," he said, sounding half annoyed, half intimidated. "That confirms it, then. We need to find another bridge."

"There is no other bridge." I stared at Oni no Mikoto, impatient. The Demon Prince regarded us in silence, seemingly unconcerned that he had just been shot at. I could sense his contemplation, the weight of his gaze regarding each of us in turn. Then, that long gleaming blade rose and pointed, very deliberately, at me, before lowering to his side again.

Okame snorted. "Looks like you've just been challenged, Kage-san. Better you than me, though I like I said, I don't have to worry about honor and fair fights. I suppose you'll be accepting the duel, then. Wouldn't want to risk dishonor to… I guess everything, really. Yourself, your clan, your children, your livestock, the road you're traveling, the sandals on your feet, the rice balls in your pack—"

"Really? The rice balls, too?" Yumeko frowned at him. "I didn't know you could dishonor your food."

"*Everything* can be dishonored, Yumeko-chan. Just ask

any samurai. Of course, they'd probably cut off your head for asking such a dishonorable question."

"Enough."

Oni no Mikoto spoke. His voice was calm and smooth, and had a cultured edge that caught my attention. Definitely not a vagabond ronin or bandit; he almost sounded like Kage Masao, the well-bred courtier and advisor to Lady Hanshou. "Kage-san," the Demon Prince continued, "if it wasn't clear before, I challenge you to a duel to prove whose skill is superior. If you wish to cross, you must defeat me first. You can, of course, turn around and leave without consequence. I have no interest in cowards."

Kamigoroshi flared, eager and almost gleeful. I ignored the exciting pulsing of the sword and gestured at Yumeko and the ronin, a few paces away. "What of my companions?"

"The girl may cross, if she chooses. The ronin..." I sensed his gaze shift under the mask, his voice taking on the faintest edge. "I would prefer he stayed within my sight, if only to prevent an arrow in my back once he crosses the bridge."

For any samurai, a statement like that would be an unforgivable insult, implying that he would strike from behind like a coward, but the ronin only shrugged.

"Don't worry about me." The ronin put away his bow and settled against the railing. "There's no way I would miss this. I'm only disappointed there's no gambling hall to place bets. I'd walk out of here a rich man."

I could almost feel the disdain coming from the masked stranger across from me. Gambling, especially on another's life, was something criminals, merchants and pit crowds partook in. Not respectable samurai.

"Yumeko," I said, finding the girl hovering close to the railing. "You should leave. Sagimura is on the other side of the bridge—find an inn and wait for us there. We shouldn't be long."

"What? I'm not going anywhere." Yumeko glared at Oni no Mikoto, then turned to me, her eyes conflicted. "This duel," she began. "It's to the death, isn't it?"

I looked at my opponent. There were several kinds of duels. Some used bokken, wooden practice swords, to prove who was stronger without bloodshed. Some duels were to first blood, and though they could be deadly, often ended without fatalities. Among skilled samurai, iaijutsu duels were favored, where two swordsmen stood an arm's length apart with their swords sheathed, and the first to move, draw his blade and cut his opponent was the winner of the match. They, too, could be deadly, but death was not a foregone conclusion.

"Yes," Oni no Mikoto said calmly. "As I am the challenger, I will allow you to choose the type of duel you prefer, be it iaijutsu or something else. But there will be no first blood, no quarter given and no surrender. This will be to the death. Only one of us will cross this bridge tonight, unless you wish to turn around and go back."

"Why?" Yumeko asked. "What do you gain from killing people? Are you really a demon?"

"A demon?" The masked stranger sounded taken aback. He stared at her, then shook his head. "You wouldn't understand," he told her gently. "Those with no passion can never comprehend the drive for perfection. I am no demon. I am merely an artist who, for years, had no canvas to practice upon. I dedicated my life to swordplay, to perfecting the balance between myself and the blade. But dueling with wooden swords, or being forced to stop at first blood—that is like painting a picture with only half the colors. The 'safe' duels I fought hobbled me and told me nothing. The only way to truly test my skills is to fight with no limitations. Only then will I know if I have achieved perfection."

"But...you kill people," Yumeko said. "You lurk on bridges and ambush travelers, just to prove that you're better at swordplay. Why?"

"Lurk?" The stranger sounded amused. "What a distasteful image. Were you a man, I would ask you to back up your insult with steel. Oni no Mikoto does not *lurk.* I challenge, and then I offer a clear choice. Anyone can refuse the duel. There have been several who have recognized a superior opponent and have declined the challenge, at no loss of honor to themselves. I do not wish to fight those who are not worthy. Acknowledging they are outmatched saves me valuable time, which I appreciate. All too often, I find my opponents are boastful and overconfident, and have a much higher opinion of themselves than their skills account for. I hope that is not the case here.

"So, Kage-san." That pale oni mask turned back to me. "I humbly await your answer. Will you, as several have done before you, turn around and leave? Or will you face Oni no Mikoto with honor and cross swords with him tonight?"

"Neither."

I could sense his surprise, even though the demon mask gave nothing away. The ronin was mistaken; ideals of honor and glory meant very little to me. I had no pride to stand on, no loss of face to endure. Despite appearances, I wasn't samurai; I was a Kage shinobi, one who struck from the shadows, who used misdirection and tricks to best my foes. Shinobi were already seen as dishonorable assassins, because true bushi faced their enemies head-on and did not stoop to skulking in the dark. I had my personal honor, and followed the code of the Shadow Clan, but Bushido wasn't as important as completing my mission, at any cost.

If I could have avoided this battle, I would have. But Oni no Mikoto was an obstacle, and it would take too much time to find a path around. "I would rather not fight here," I told him, feeling Hakaimono rise up like a blood-filled typhoon. "But you're in my way, and I have a mission to complete. I'm not going to cross blades with you, I'm going to cut a path right through you to the other side."

"Excellent!" Oni no Mikoto sounded ecstatic. "You honor me with your acceptance. Come then, Kage-san. Let us see whose skills are sharper."

"Yumeko," I said, not taking my eyes from my opponent, "get back. This is my fight, understand? Don't try to interfere."

From the corner of my eye, I saw her take a step toward me. "Don't die," she ordered quietly. "You promised to take me to the Steel Feather temple. It would be very rude to break your promise by getting killed, Tatsumi-san."

"I'm not going to die," I told her. Within, Hakaimono was growing stronger, a surging tide of violence and bloodlust. "Go," I repeated. "Get to safety. This will be over soon."

The ronin pushed himself off the railing. "This should be interesting," he said, and moved away, retreating several yards down the bridge and giving us plenty of room. After a moment, Yumeko followed.

I faced Oni no Mikoto over the center of the river, the moon shining down on us both, lighting the bridge. A cold breeze hissed across the planks from the water, ruffling my clothes and tossing his long hair.

"Does your sword have a name, Kage-san?" Oni no Mikoto asked.

"Why?"

He shrugged. "I'm a scholar of the blade. I have studied the history of Iwagoto's swordsmanship, its finest warriors and weapon smiths, and through the years, the names of a few special blades have appeared time and time again. The emperor's sword, Dawn's Glory. The paired blades of the famed duelist, Mizu Sasaki. If your sword does have a name, I would like very much to hear it. It would be a great honor to cross blades with a weapon from the history scrolls."

"There is no honor in this sword's name."

Oni no Mikoto's head tilted, as if he was seeing me for the first time. "You…are of the Shadow Clan," he said slowly. "There are but two swords of note that originated within the Kage. Sasori, the blade of the Shadow Clan daimyo… and the cursed sword that brought destruction to the land and nearly wiped the Kage from existence."

I felt a smile creep, unbidden across my face, as I heard myself speaking words that weren't entirely my own. "A true oni would know better than to cross blades with Kamigoroshi."

"Then it is true," Oni no Mikoto whispered, sounding faintly in awe. "You possess the Godslayer, the cursed sword of the Kage."

I took a breath, pushing the other presence down and reclaiming my voice. "You can turn back," I told him softly, as Hakaimono snarled at me, annoyed. "Kamigoroshi doesn't care what soul it devours, be it human or demon. There is still time to bow out. You said so yourself—it is no dishonor to acknowledge a superior opponent."

"Kage-san." Oni no Mikoto stepped forward. He was shaking, but it wasn't in fear, I realized, but excitement. "This is the fight I have searched for my whole life. Long

I have waited for a worthy opponent, one who would push me beyond the limit of my skills. How many can say they have dueled a legend? How many can say they have crossed blades with the sword that almost single-handedly destroyed one of the Great Clans? No, Kage-san, I will not relinquish this battle." He raised his own weapon in a two-handed grip, the curved sword glittering between us like a shaft of moonlight. "I am Oni no Mikoto, the undefeated blade of the Taiyo, and it will be an honor to fight you."

I hesitated a moment more, then slowly drew Kamigoroshi. It howled eagerly as it was unsheathed, baleful purple light spilling over the planks.

We faced each other on the bridge, unmoving, the wind tugging at our hair and clothes. I stood motionless, Kamigoroshi loose at my side, while Oni no Mikoto did the same, his blade held upright in two hands. Time seemed to slow, each of us sizing up our opponent, gauging strengths and weaknesses, waiting for that moment we would both explode into battle.

*Not yet*, I thought, as Oni no Mikoto shifted his stance just slightly, drawing one foot behind the other. I tightened my grip on Kamigoroshi, feeling my muscles tense and Hakaimono's impatience flare, eager for blood. *He's going to come in fast. Be ready—*

With a crash and a splintering of boards, a huge serpentine creature burst out from under the bridge, rising fifteen feet into the air between us. Pale light gleamed off a hardened carapace, and dozens of segmented yellow legs skittered over the planks as the creature crawled onto the bridge. A bulbous crimson head swung around to face me, green ichor dripping from two sickle-like mandibles, as the omukade, a giant, man-eating centipede, reared up with a piercing hiss and lunged.

# 24

## The Great Omukade

*M*y stomach seemed to drop to my toes.

A monstrous centipede loomed into the air, towering over Tatsumi and Oni no Mikoto, making them look like insects themselves. Its segmented carapace was jet-black, its head bright crimson, and two lethal mandibles opened like a pair of sickles as it sped toward Tatsumi.

The warrior dodged, springing aside, and brought Kamigoroshi across the centipede's back in a flash of purple light. But the blade screeched off the armor-like chitin, leaving a gaping scar in the carapace but unable to pierce through.

"Kuso!" Okame scrambled backward as the monster spun on Tatsumi, dozens of legs clacking over the planks, and lunged again. Once more, the demonslayer leaped aside, and the pinchers sank into the railing behind him, slicing clean through the wood like it was rice paper. Tatsumi cut at the huge yokai, this time aiming for the bright yellow legs. With a spurt of green ichor, three severed appendages clattered to the bridge, twitching and thrashing about, but the omukade writhed around to follow him, not slowed in the least.

An arrow bounced off the shiny carapace, then another, and a third. "Dammit," Okame growled, firing a fourth arrow at the monster's head. It skidded off the top of its skull, and the centipede didn't even look up. *"Kuso,"* the ronin spat, reaching back for another arrow. "Tough ugly bastard. Every spot is armored. At this rate, it'll eat Kage-san and then come after us."

Oni no Mikoto suddenly appeared, leaping over the centipede's long, writhing body and raising his sword over his head. The omukade, still facing off with Tatsumi, didn't notice the masked swordsman until the Demon Prince sliced down with his blade. Like Kamigoroshi, it screeched off the monster's thick carapace, and the centipede whirled on him with a hiss.

*Every spot is armored.* "Okame," I gasped, turning to the ronin, who was fitting another arrow to his bow. "The eyes! The eyes aren't protected. Aim for the eyes."

"What?" Okame lowered his bow and gaped at me, then the centipede. The huge yokai thrashed about in the center of the bridge, snapping at Tatsumi and Oni no Mikoto as they desperately tried to avoid getting caught between its huge pinchers. Tatsumi lashed out with Kamigoroshi as the centipede's head snaked down, and the monster recoiled, furiously gnashing its jaws.

"Dammit, it's moving around too much," Okame growled, sighting down his bow at the huge yokai. "And its eyeball is the size of a persimmon, so it's really hard to get a shot.

If the bastard would stop moving around, I just need it to be still for a second…"

I swallowed hard. "Keep aiming," I said, stepping forward. "I'll get it to stop."

Walking to the edge of the bridge, I watched the battle raging in the center: Tatsumi and Oni no Mikoto trying to put a dent in the centipede's armor, to little effect. The centipede had lost several more legs, which lay scattered over the planks, twitching weakly, but it didn't seem hampered by the loss of its limbs. Heart pounding, I put a thumb and forefinger into my mouth and did what always annoyed Denga-san.

A long, piercing whistle echoed over the bridge. The omukade froze at the sound and glanced up. For just a moment, its cold, beady gaze met mine, just before an arrow flew overhead and struck the very center of one bulbous black eye.

The yokai wailed. Its huge body thrashed wildly, smashing into posts and railings, snapping beams and splintering wood. Tatsumi and Oni no Mikoto quickly dove aside, but the Demon Prince was struck by a writhing coil that knocked him to the edge of the bridge and sent him over. I saw his lean form plummet toward the river, long pale hair streaming behind him, before he struck the water and vanished below the surface.

And then, I looked back at the bridge, and saw the omukade glaring at me with its one good eye, mandibles trembling with rage.

*Well, that certainly got its attention.*

I turned and ran as the monster charged with a shriek, multiple legs skittering over the bridge. I didn't dare look back, but the furious chitter of snapping centipede jaws told me it was closing rapidly.

*Tree, tree, I need a tree!*

Spotting a twisted pine at the edge of the riverbank, I changed direction and darted toward it, snatching a leaf from the ground as I did. As I neared the tree, I whispered a few words of fox magic and released the leaf just before I ducked behind the trunk. And I hoped none of the others would see the second Yumeko appear, cringing at the base of the pine.

On the other side of the trunk, I held my breath, praying the omukade wouldn't see through the illusion. I needn't have worried, because with a screech that made my ears ring, the centipede crashed headfirst into the trunk. I felt the solid *thunk* of its mandibles slicing through the fake Yumeko, sinking deep into the wood and making the tree rattle.

As the centipede thrashed, trying to dislodge itself, I sprang to the first overhanging branch, pulled myself up and instantly reached for another. Years of climbing the old maple tree in the temple gardens made it easy to shimmy up the trunk, and fear of the monster below made me quick.

I was halfway up the tree when the omukade tore itself loose with a splintering of tree bark. Looking down, I met its flat, soulless gaze as it peered up the pine and gave a hiss of fury. Gnashing its pinchers, it began to climb, dozens of bright yellow legs moving it up the trunk with frightening speed.

I climbed higher, hearing the hissing and scraping of the yokai as it pursued. As the branches became smaller and narrower, the centipede began to slow. But its body was so long, it was able to reach even the tallest limbs without much effort, though the tree itself began to sway and groan under the monster's weight.

Finally, there was nowhere else to run. I had reached the top of the tree, and the centipede was still coming. Pulling my tanto, I climbed as far away as I could, watching the bulbous crimson skull push through the branches below my feet. Mandibles scraping together, it slithered up the trunk toward me. The pine creaked and groaned, and the trunk bent and swayed dangerously, but it held.

As it drew closer, and I could see every detail on its hideous, segmented body, I noticed something. The top half of the huge creature was covered in that shiny black carapace that deflected arrows and sword strikes. But the underside, between the dozens of skittering legs, looked softer, almost fleshy. Certainly not the impenetrable armor of its top half. But how to get beneath it was the question.

Raising my tanto with one hand, I started gathering my magic with the other, hoping that a desperate blast of foxfire to its face would distract or startle it long enough for me to do…something.

"Yumeko!"

The familiar voice rang out below me, and close. I spared a glance down and saw Tatsumi on a lower branch, Kamigoroshi engulfed in purple flames, casting the demonslayer in an eerie light. His eyes seemed to glow crimson as he extended his other hand in my direction.

"Jump," he ordered, making my stomach drop. "Now."

I swallowed. "It's an awfully long ways down, Tatsumi."

"I'll catch you," he replied. "I promise. Hurry!"

Well, between getting eaten by a centipede and falling to my death, I suppose I'd take the latter. As the omukade lunged with a hiss, I gathered myself and leaped away from the trunk, a shriek lodging somewhere in my throat as I plummeted downward. I barely had time to panic when something caught me around the waist, halting my downward plunge. Tatsumi pulled me onto the branch and set me on my feet, still holding Kamigoroshi in his other hand. I was shocked at how strong he was, able to catch a falling body, one-armed, from a narrow, uneven ledge without losing his balance.

As I looked into his face, a shiver raced up my spine. His eyes *were* glowing, a subtle crimson light shining in their depths, looking entirely inhuman.

"Are you hurt?" he asked, and his voice sounded a little different, too. Lower, somehow darker, but strained. As if he was fighting…something.

"The underside isn't protected," I told him, seeing his eyes narrow in confusion. "The carapace—the armor—it doesn't have anything on its belly. You have to strike from beneath."

His eyes widened, and he nodded. Above us, the omukade swung its head and body toward our branch, hissing and gnashing its jaws. Still holding me around the waist, Tatsumi abruptly dropped from the limb, falling to a branch underneath. I bit back a yelp, resisting the urge to clutch at his haori jacket, as he set me on my feet, gazing up at the long body of the omukade, twisting through the limbs overhead. The head peered balefully down at us, hissed and started sliding through the branches in pursuit.

"Can you lure it away?" Tatsumi asked in a low voice. "Get it to chase you?"

I realized what he was getting at, and gave a shaky nod. "I don't think that will be much of a problem," I gasped, as overhead, the omukade snaked through the branches after us, gnashing its jaws.

Tatsumi nodded. "Go," he ordered, and we fled, scurrying down the trunk, dropping to lower branches while trying to outpace the huge yokai slithering through the limbs like a serpent. About halfway down the tree, I noticed that Tatsumi had disappeared, or I could no longer see him through the leaves and branches.

Something buzzed past my face, startling me, just as an arrow clinked off the centipede's hide. Hissing angrily, it halted, glaring around for the sudden attacker, perhaps remembering the arrow it took to the face.

"Okame, wait!" I called, glancing down at the ronin. He stood under the tree with a grim look on his face, bow raised and pointed at the centipede. At my words, he paused and lowered his weapon, but in that moment of distraction, my fingers missed a branch and I fell, dropping several feet. Pulse spiking, I lashed out wildly and felt my palm smack into another limb, halting my fall. I heard Okame's cry of alarm as I dangled, my feet swinging over empty space, and I grabbed desperately for the branch with my other hand.

Something warm dripped onto the back of my knuckles. Gulping, I looked up to see a pair of shiny black pinchers a few feet away, opening wide to snick off my head. At the same time, a blur of darkness streaked overhead, as Tatsumi ran full tilt along a branch and sliced Kamigoroshi through the exposed belly of the omukade.

The omukade screamed, rearing up as it split in two with a spray of green-and-yellow ichor. Its top half, now separated from the rest of its body, slid from the branches of the tree and collapsed to the ground on its back, legs curling frantically as it struggled to right itself.

"The head, Okame!" I shouted over the mad hissing of the huge yokai as it thrashed and writhed, too tough to die even now. "Cut off the head—that should kill it for good!"

Understanding dawned in the ronin's eyes, and he turned to the downed monster. But before he could react, Oni no Mikoto strode up to the struggling yokai, raised his sword and brought it slashing down beneath the monster's still gnashing jaws. The bulbous crimson head rolled back, the spasming legs stilled and the lethal jaws finally stopped moving, as the great yokai admitted defeat at last.

I breathed a sigh of relief, then tried pulling myself up the branch, as my hands were starting to slip and surviving an attack by a great omukade, only to fall from a tree and break my neck, seemed like very bad luck.

The branch shook, and a pair of tabi boots appeared next to my fingers. I looked up to see Tatsumi standing over me, Kamigoroshi held loosely at his side. His expression was chilling, a faint, curious smile gracing his lips, as if this situation amused him and he was contemplating what to do next.

"Tatsumi?" I panted, as he continued to stand there, watching me. "What...what are you doing? Help me."

For a moment, he continued to stand there, regarding me in that way that made my skin crawl. Kamigoroshi flickered and pulsed, and in the eerie light, Tatsumi's eyes glowed red, his pupils slitted like a cat's.

Then one of my hands slipped, and I yelped as I lost my hold on the branch.

Strong fingers closed around my wrist in a grip of steel, lifting me up and pulling me back onto the limb. Gasping, I clutched the black haori in front of me, my heart racing in my ears, as I waited for my arms to stop shaking and my pulse to return to normal.

"Yumeko." Tatsumi's voice was strained again, but sounded normal this time. He had gone very stiff, his arms held rigid at his side, his heartbeat racing under my palm. I suddenly realized we were pressed very close, our chests nearly touching, our faces a few inches apart. The narrow end of the scroll was pressing painfully into my ribs.

*"Gomen!"* Face burning, I released him and stepped away, shifting my weight to balance on the narrow branch. He relaxed but continued to watch me, his expression grim, his eyes back to normal. And even through the embarrassment, I felt a tiny flame of relief. There was no hint of the scary, red-eyed Tatsumi I thought I'd seen a few seconds ago. Maybe it hadn't been real. Maybe, in the eerie light coming from Kamigoroshi, I had imagined it, after all.

*"Oiii!"* called a voice from below. "Yumeko-chan? Kage-san? Are you two all right?"

"*Hai*, Okame!" I called back. "We're fine. We'll be right down."

A few minutes later, we had all gathered at the base of the tree, the massive corpse of the omukade looming above us, both on the ground and still dangling from the branches. I wondered what people passing by would think, if they looked up and saw two-thirds of a giant centipede curled around the limbs of the tree.

"That," Okame said as Tatsumi and I walked up, "was disgusting. Look at that thing! I don't care how ancient and special it was, there is no logical reason bugs should ever get that big."

"It must be ancient," I said, staring at the monstrous

corpse. “But…why did it come after us? It’s like it knew exactly where we were.”

“It matters not.”

The Demon Prince turned to Tatsumi. “The monster is dead,” he announced, as if being attacked by and killing a giant centipede was commonplace. Something he did every evening before tea. “We are victorious, and the night is still young. Now that there are no more interruptions, shall we continue our duel, Kage-san?”

# 25

## Proposal for a Demon Prince

*"Nani?"* Yumeko stared at him. "Now?" She waved an arm at the giant corpse, leaking greenish fluid into the trampled grass. "We barely survived being eaten by a giant centipede. Is this really the time to keep fighting?"

"The duel was issued, and accepted," Oni no Mikoto said in a reasonable voice. "Interruptions aside, honor demands that we continue until a clear victor is determined. Kage-san." He bowed his head at me. "Shall we return to the bridge? I am ready."

I nodded wearily. If this was the only way to cross, then I would have to cut him down. I didn't necessarily want to; he had proven himself in the fight with the omukade and refused to flee when it would have been the wiser choice. And from the glimpses I'd caught of his fighting, he was extremely skilled and fast, perhaps the best swordsman I had seen. He was going to be a deadly opponent, indeed.

But he wasn't going to let me go, and I still had a mission to complete. If he wanted this duel, then I would give him an honorable death.

"Wait." Yumeko stepped forward as we started toward the bridge. "Oni no Mikoto, stop."

"Peasant girl." Oni no Mikoto turned, and his voice, though polite, was chilly. "You travel with Kage-san, so I assume you are either his servant or someone under his protection. But servants do not give orders to samurai. Just a courteous warning, for the next warrior you encounter might take real offense."

Yumeko blinked, but didn't cower or back down. *"Sumimasen,"* she told Oni no Mikoto. "Was I supposed to bow? I was supposed to bow, wasn't I?"

The ronin snickered. "Actually, I think he expected you to prostrate yourself at his feet and grovel. That's usually what happens when peasants encounter samurai."

"I'm sorry," Yumeko continued. "I meant no offense. I grew up in a temple and never had to address samurai before. Um, besides Tatsumi-san, and he doesn't seem to care."

I raised an eyebrow at that, but no one was looking at me.

"I'm not very good at protocol," Yumeko went on. "But I truly do not wish to offend. Should I fling myself on the ground now, Oni-sama?"

"No." Oni no Mikoto sighed. "Just...what is it you want, girl?"

"If Oni-sama would humor me for a moment," Yumeko continued, "and look at the omukade's right eye. What do you see?"

The Demon Prince glanced at the yokai. The omukade's

head lay there, its jaws open in a last, furious snarl, a few of its legs still twitching in death. "An arrow," Oni no Mikoto said, gazing at the ruined eye, where the shaft was easily visible in the moonlight. He paused, putting the pieces together, and drew in a slow breath. "Then..."

He glanced at Okame. "Then, you are the one who shot the monster," he said, as if just coming to the realization. "On the bridge when it first attacked, Kage-san and I could do nothing against it. None of our blows could get through, but..." He looked at the eye again. "Something drew it away. That was you."

The ronin shrugged. "I may have hit the thing," he replied, and nodded at the girl, "but Yumeko-chan got its attention and told me where to shoot. You want to thank someone for not ending up as centipede food, thank her."

"I see." Oni no Mikoto turned to face Yumeko again. "Then, it appears I owe you a debt of gratitude," he said, and though his posture was stiff, his voice remained polite. "That's what you want, isn't it, girl? The boon of a samurai. Very well." He straightened. "I will grant this one favor. Though understand this—I will *not* abandon my duel with Kage-san." His gaze slid to me. "This is a battle I have waited for since I picked up my sword, and I will not miss it. You may ask me anything but that."

"Very well, Oni-sama," Yumeko stated. "If you can't agree not to fight, then grant me this instead. Postpone the duel."

The Demon Prince seemed taken aback. "Postpone?"

"Yes," she confirmed. "I realize this is important to you, but I have an important mission to complete, and Tatsumi has already promised to accompany me until it is done. He is my escort to the capital, and I cannot allow him to die before I finish my task."

"You cannot…allow." Oni no Mikoto blinked at her behind his mask, looking confused, then stunned. Unexpectedly, he sank into a low bow at the waist. "Forgive me, my lady," he said earnestly. "I was unaware of your station. I mistook you for a simple peasant, but if Kage-san is your yojimbo, I have made a grave mistake. I humbly beg your pardon for my error in judgment."

I frowned, vaguely annoyed at the assumption. I was no one's bodyguard. No one save the Kage commanded me. Though I wasn't going to correct the swordsman's conclusion. If he thought Yumeko was a lady and I was her yojimbo, protecting her on the roads, then so be it. It might save us questions later.

"Yes, you should feel ashamed," the ronin broke in, pointing at the girl. "Obviously a simple peasant could not be under the protection of the infamous Kage demonslayer, because peasants cannot have missions or goals or anything meaningful in their lives except serving samurai. Surely she must be a shrine maiden, or wandering onmyoji. That is the only explanation for this travesty, isn't that so, Oni-san?"

Had it been anyone else, the explanation would have made sense. Yumeko had grown up in a temple and spoke about her Master Isao all the time. Monks, shrine maidens and onmyoji held a different position in Iwagoto; they weren't part of the warrior caste and, technically, were considered peasants, but they were respected for their wisdom and enlightenment, and were recognized as teachers, masters of their art or spiritual advisors. Onmyoji, especially, were revered among samurai and peasants alike; they were diviners, exorcists, fortune-tellers and specialists of the spirit world, and they were highly sought after for their talents. Because many onmyoji traveled the land, and because they typically dealt with all manner of ghosts, yokai and restless spirits, my path had crossed with theirs on more than one occasion.

It was unlikely, but not impossible, to think Yumeko could be a traveling onmyoji, and had requested the aid of the Shadow Clan's demonslayer to act as her bodyguard. But I had been traveling with the irreverent ronin long enough to recognize his veiled sarcasm and disdain for the warrior caste and knew he was misleading the other without telling an outright lie.

"But, Okame-san," Yumeko began, "I'm not—"

"Besides," the ronin continued loudly, "is this really the time to keep fighting? You fell into the river, and Kage-san looks spent. If this is truly the duel you've been waiting for your whole life, do you really want to proceed now, when neither of you are at your best?"

"Hmm." The Demon Prince crossed his arms. "You make an excellent point," he admitted, his tone begrudging. "If we fight now, how will I know if it was skill that won the battle, and not blind luck or misfortune? If we are to duel, we must both be prepared and leave nothing to chance. Very well." He gave a decisive nod and turned to Yumeko. "My lady," he said, "please allow me to accompany you and your escorts to the capital and wherever your travels take you afterward."

Startled, I narrowed my eyes, as Yumeko straightened. Apparently she had not expected this, either. "Why?" she asked.

"I know my way around Kin Heigen Toshi," Oni no Mikoto continued. "I have lived there for many years, and my name carries much weight. I would be happy to offer assistance while you are conducting your business in the capital."

"We don't need assistance," I told him. "Thank you, but we can get by on our own."

"Forgive me, Kage-san." Oni no Mikoto sounded amused as he glanced at me. "But we were just attacked by a giant centipede monster. I may not know much about demons, but I have to assume that was not a random assault.

"The life of a demonslayer must be a dangerous one," Oni no Mikoto went on, as unease flickered within me. Here was yet another who knew entirely too much about the Shadow Clan and Kamigoroshi. Another I might have to kill, should the clan order it. "Especially if he is acting as a bodyguard to an onmyoji. The road ahead could be full of peril and evil creatures—protecting both your charge and yourself will prove challenging if demons continue to target you."

He glanced at the tree and the giant centipede still coiled around the branches. "I cannot have you dying before we complete our duel," Oni no Mikoto went on. "That would be a dishonor to us both. Therefore, I will come with you and offer whatever assistance I can. Once your task is complete and Yumeko-san has no further need of your protection, we can continue what we started."

The ronin threw back his head and laughed. "I love the way samurai think," he announced, grinning. "So, you're coming with us, to make sure Kage-san stays alive, so you can kill him later." He snickered and shook his head. "Man, I can't wait to see where this goes."

"I didn't know Oni-sama was so well-known in the capital," Yumeko said, as the Demon Prince politely and deliberately ignored the ronin. "Do people find the mask frightening?"

"Ah. Of course," Oni no Mikoto said. "Forgive my rudeness, I haven't even properly introduced myself." He reached up and pulled the oni mask away, revealing a smooth, beardless face only a few years older than me. Small details instantly stood out: high cheekbones, a slightly pointed chin and the pale, elegant look that marked him as a noble of the court. He had narrow, almost effeminate features, and had underlined his already sharp eyes in black. Not the most makeup I'd seen on a noble, even a male one, but it was impossible to mistake him for anything else.

"I am Taiyo Daisuke," the former Oni no Mikoto announced with a formal bow to Yumeko. "It is a pleasure to meet you, Yumeko-san. Thank you again for the honor of accompanying you on your mission. As a traveling onmyoji, you must see a lot."

"Taiyo," echoed the ronin, sounding incredulous. "You're part of the imperial family?"

"The fourth son of one of the emperor's many cousins," Taiyo Daisuke replied with a rather wry smile. "Thankfully, two of my brothers married well and hold important positions within the court, and the third is an imperial magistrate, so I don't have to worry about meeting my family's expectations."

The ronin smirked. "That's a very unsamurai-like attitude, Taiyo-san. Won't you have to commit seppuku for having such a dishonorable thought?"

"My clan knows I will do whatever is required to uphold the honor of the Taiyo," the former Demon Prince said easily. "At the moment, nothing is required of me. So I am free to pursue my own agendas."

"Which is lurking on bridges and challenging strong warriors to duels," the ronin said.

"Which will now include escorting Lady Yumeko and her companions to the capital," the noble corrected. "Yumeko-san?" He smiled at the girl and gestured to the distant lights over the river. "I would suggest spending the night in Sagimura. The inn there is simple but agreeable, and the staff are very attentive. I have always found it a pleasant stay when I leave the capital to go on my pilgrimages."

"Pilgrimages," the ronin snorted. "Is that what you call them, then?"

No reply from the noble. Even I had to admit, the former Demon Prince had excellent selective hearing. "Shall we go then, Lady Yumeko?" he asked the girl. "If we hurry, we may yet reach the inn before dinner is served."

Yumeko returned his smile and, for just a moment, something inside me bristled. "That sounds wonderful," she said, instantly perking at the mention of food. "Thank you, Taiyo-sama."

"Please, Yumeko-san." The samurai held up a hand. "Taiyo-sama is my father. The four of us just fought and killed a giant centipede together. I believe we've earned the right to call each other by our first names. Just Daisuke, if you would."

"Daisuke-san," Yumeko repeated, still smiling. "Thank you."

"Well." Taiyo Daisuke stepped back, gazing across the river. "I believe this is the very first time someone met Oni no Mikoto on a bridge and crossed to the other side." His gaze fell to the oni mask, still held loosely in one hand, and he smiled a bit sadly. "I suppose I won't need this anymore," he murmured. "Whatever the outcome, whether it ends in victory or defeat, I have a feeling that Oni no Mikoto's next duel will be his final one. So..."

Drawing his arm back, he hurled the mask into the air. It arched up, spinning red and white, before dropping lazily into the river. For a moment, it floated on the surface of the water, a small pale oval against the black. Then, the snarling oni face disappeared as the current pulled it under, and it was lost from view.

# 26

## The Capital

*M*y eyes hurt from staring.

Kin Heigen Toshi, the City of the Golden Plain, could be seen long before we even reached its impressive gates. Built on the juncture where two rivers—the Hotaru and the Kin no Kawa, the River of Gold—met, it spread for miles in every direction. The tightly packed inner city was surrounded by river and protected by steep stone walls, but the urban sprawl had crossed the natural moats and continued to creep across the plains. I had never seen so many buildings in my life; from afar, it looked like a ragged blanket of roofs, walls, bridges and roads had been spread over the entire valley.

Near the very center, rising from a vertical hill and surrounded by sheer stone ramparts, a magnificent castle soared into the air, towering over the city. Though its bottom walls were white and trimmed in dark wood, its roofs and top floors had been covered in what seemed to be pure gold, for they gleamed brilliantly against the cloudless sky, almost too bright to look at.

"Behold, the Palace of the Sun," Daisuke told me, sounding almost as proud as if he'd designed the castle himself. "Home of the emperor, and the heart of Iwagoto."

"I've never seen anything like it," I admitted, shading my eyes against the glare. "Is it really made of gold?"

"Gold leaf, my lady," Daisuke replied. "The walls and roof are gilded with it. Sadly, we've yet to figure out a feasible way to build a castle of pure gold. Though Emperor Taiyo no Ryosei did try, until the peasants revolted."

"It seemed they weren't satisfied with starving to death while their emperor built himself a palace made of gold," Okame added behind us. "Ungrateful wretches."

Daisuke ignored him. He had changed outfits since the night at the bridge and was now wearing a pair of dove-gray hakama trousers and a sky blue haori jacket with silver clouds curled along the hems and billowy sleeves. The crest of the Taiyo, a blazing sun within a circle, was etched onto each shoulder. In the light of day, with his double swords thrust through his obi and his long white hair tied behind him, he looked every inch the noble warrior.

Very unlike Okame, leaning against a tree at our backs, the end of a reed poking from between his lips. Or Tatsumi, standing to the side, a shadow that nearly blended into the shade cast from the branches. I could feel both of them watching us, one cold and alert, one mockingly amused, and wondered if either of them had felt anything close to amazement before.

"When it was built," Daisuke went on, unaware of the intense scrutiny at our backs, "the emperor at the time, Taiyo no Kintaro, demanded a castle that would shine brighter than sun itself, so that everyone would see our family's influence for miles around. Since its construction, it's been burned to ashes no less than four times but has always been restored to its former glory. A Taiyo has ruled from that palace for over seven hundred years."

"It's beautiful," I said, squinting as one of the roof tiles caught the sun and flashed a searing white against my eyelids. "Though, I am curious—does everyone living around the castle go blind on very bright days?"

He chuckled. "You learn not to look directly at it in the summer."

We followed the road, which soon merged onto a wide thoroughfare, with crowds of people traveling to and from the capital. As we crossed the bridge and walked beneath the wide, sweeping gates, my heart beat faster in excitement. Everything here was so grand! So large, and noisy and fast paced. I felt very small as we walked past dozens of shops and market stalls, unable to stop myself from looking at everything.

There was a sharp tug on my sleeve, and Tatsumi pulled me to the side of the road, just as a man jogged by pulling a two-wheeled cart. He shouted something that might've been an apology or a curse and continued down the street without breaking stride.

"*Oi*, was that really necessary?" I called after him, then turned Tatsumi, who raised a brow. *"Gomen,"* I apologized. "I suppose I should pay attention to what's going on around me."

"That is probably prudent."

"Oh, lighten up, Kage-san," Okame broke in, striding up

beside us. "She's never been to the capital—of course she's going to be distracted. So, Yumeko-chan..." He grinned at me. "We have officially arrived in the capital. Is there any place you want to see? Anywhere you'd like to go? I can point out the more interesting spots, if you want to play tourist for a bit. Or, we could always wait until the sun goes down. Kin Heigen Toshi *really* gets interesting after dark."

"Does it? How so?"

"We're not here to sightsee." Tatsumi's voice was flat. "We can't wander the city without a plan—we have a mission to complete. Besides," he said, turning to the ronin, "you said you had business in the capital. Shouldn't you be leaving?"

Okame shrugged. "I have nothing important to do," he said casually, waving it off. "I can be boring and responsible and start looking for a job anytime. It's not like there aren't always merchants that need guards or gambling halls that need bouncers. And it's been so interesting traveling with the two of you, I think I'll hang around a little longer. Why, Kage-san?" His grin turned wolfish, even as Tatsumi's eyes narrowed. "You're not trying to get rid of me, are you?"

"Yumeko-san." Fortunately, Daisuke stepped in before Tatsumi could make good on the *I'm going to kill you* look on his face. "This mission of yours—where must we go to complete it? I've lived in this city my whole life. I know where almost everything is. If you can trust me with your mission, I can probably show you the way."

"I...yes. I need to find the Hayate shrine," I told him, remembering Master Isao's final instructions. "It is urgent that I speak to the high priest there. He has information that will point me in the direction I must go."

"The Hayate shrine," Daisuke repeated slowly, and nodded. "Yes. I know where it's located, but it's clear across the city, in the Wind district. It will take us the rest of the evening to walk there. Kin Heigen Toshi is quite large, after all."

"That's all right," I said. "I need to find it—it's important Tatsumi and I get there as soon as possible. Would you show us the way, Daisuke-san?"

He smiled. "Of course."

Kin Heigen Toshi continued to be amazing as we followed Taiyo-san through the sometimes straight, sometimes winding roads. Buildings rose around us; teahouses and temples, bathhouses and shrines, inns that were elegant in their simplicity and lavish estates of the wealthy and affluent. Shops and merchant stalls lined the streets, selling everything from straw sandals and parasols to exotic spices and trinkets from across the Scorched Sea. Daisuke commented on the places and buildings we passed, pointing out special features, explaining a bit of the history if it was a temple, shrine, or other place of importance. He was indeed quite knowledgeable about his city, and I found myself listening to the noble in rapt fascination. Once, Okame remarked that we could probably take a shortcut through a place called the red light district, and then *he* could tell me all about the area. But before I could ask what he meant, Daisuke turned and gave him such a withering look, that offer was quickly rescinded.

Tatsumi, as usual, stayed farther back, as soundless as a trailing shadow, making no attempt at conversation. As we turned down a narrow street with a canal on one side and a wall on the other, I dropped back to walk alongside him.

He eyed me, not entirely suspicious, but expectant. "Isn't this incredible, Tatsumi?" I murmured, watching a kingfisher dart up from the canal in a streak of bright blue. "I never knew there were places like this in the world."

"Hn."

"Master Isao didn't talk much about the lands outside the temple," I went on. "I think he and the others were afraid the outside world would lure me away. If I'd known there were places like this, just beyond the temple walls, he might've been right."

Tatsumi didn't answer, and I frowned at him. "You're being very quiet, Tatsumi-san."

"I'm always quiet."

"Yes, but you've been even broodier than normal lately," I persisted. "Is something wrong? Did you step on something sharp?"

"We should be concentrating on the mission," he replied, a bit shortly. "Not playing tourist with nobles, or visiting gambling halls and red light districts with ronin. This isn't a pleasure trip."

"I know that." Glancing at the noble, walking a little ahead and talking with Okame, I lowered my voice. "But Daisuke-san is taking us to the Hayate shrine—it would be rude to go off without him."

He looked away. "We don't need them. They'll only get in the way and slow us down. Once we figure out where the temple is, we should leave them behind."

"He's helping us, Tatsumi. Okame helped us, too, in the gaki village. We can't just leave them. Besides, what about your duel with Daisuke-san?"

He eyed me. "Are you saying you want to see one of us die?" he asked in a strangely brittle voice. "Or do you not want me around at all? Perhaps you would prefer the ronin and noble to escort you to the temple."

"Of course not." I frowned at his strange, sudden hostility. "That's not what I'm saying, Tatsumi-san."

"No?" His voice dropped, becoming nearly inaudible. "Maybe it should be."

"Oi, you two," Okame called from up ahead. "Whatever you're whispering about back there, can it wait? Our guide says the shrine is across the road."

I hurried past a pair of boys with fishing rods to join Daisuke and the ronin at the edge of the street. Directly across the road, a red torii gate stood before a stone staircase that went straight up the forested hill.

"This is the entrance to the Hayate shrine," Daisuke said, gazing up the steep staircase, looking undaunted by the thought of climbing it. "Though it is rather late to be calling on the priest," he added, glancing at the sky through the branches. The sun had set a few minutes ago, and the first of the stars were coming out. "Is he expecting you, Yumeko-san?"

"Not that I know of," I replied, feeling Tatsumi stop beside me. "But I need to talk to him soon. Tonight, if I can."

"All right." Okame sighed, giving the staircase a resigned look. "Priest first then, gambling hall later. And maybe some red light district fun afterward. It's going to be a busy night, I hope you two can keep up." He specifically looked at Daisuke as he said this, as if gauging the other's response. The noble, for his part, ignored him and raised a hand toward the steps.

"This is your mission, Yumeko-san. We follow you."

I took a deep breath, relieved and nervous all at once. I was almost there. Just a few more steps until I completed the first part of my mission. Finding Master Jiro, who could tell me where to find the Steel Feather temple. My journey wasn't over; we still had to get to the temple and I had no idea where it was, but I imagined we would have to cross several unfamiliar territories and search the harshest, most unforgiving terrain, all the while being pursued by blood mages and demons. I would still have to keep the scroll safe, from demons *and* my own companions. From a dangerous, single-minded demonslayer who might kill me if he realized I had tricked him, that I'd possessed the scroll all along. This wasn't the end, far from it. This was another beginning, and for a moment, my head spun at what I still had to do.

*One step at a time, little fox.* I remembered Master Isao's voice, his words whenever I faced a mountain of chores or an especially daunting task. *The spider does not spin its web in a heartbeat, nor does the albatross fly across oceans with a few flaps of its wings. Many would consider what they do impossible, and yet, they still complete their tasks without fail, because they simply...start.*

*One step at a time.* I took one step, then another, until I had crossed the road and stood before the torii gate. Beyond the arch was sacred ground, the realm of the kami. I offered a respectful bow to the spirits whose territory I was entering, and started up the steps.

It was a fairly steep, long stairway, and I was careful to keep to one side of the steps, as the center of the path was reserved for the kami. The edge of the staircase was quite worn, rough with age and time, making it important to watch where you put your feet. As I climbed the last step, I spotted a komainu statue, the maned lion-dogs that protected the shrine from evil spirits, atop its plinth flanking the staircase, mouth open in a fearsome snarl. Another stone pedestal sat on the other side of the steps, but this one was empty, as if the second guardian had decided to abandon its post.

Briefly, I wondered what had happened to it; komainu guardians always came in pairs. But the thought was quickly forgotten as I passed beneath a second torii and saw the small but elegant shrine across the tiny courtyard. The haiden, or prayer hall, sitting on a raised platform atop a flight of four stone steps, was the vermillion red of the torii gate. A sacred rope was draped across the entrance, indicating the holiness of the building. Beyond the haiden was the honden, the main building where the kami were housed, and no one but the priest and resident shrine maidens were allowed to enter.

"Looks like no one's here," Okame mused. There were no people near or around the haiden; the courtyard was empty, as was the purification fountain near the entrance. But in a place like this, where the only sound was the wind in the pines and the trickle of water into the fountain, the presence of the kami could be felt everywhere; even the brash, irreverent ronin seemed loath to break the stillness. "Maybe we should check the outbuildings? The priests' quarters should be around somewhere, right?"

Daisuke gazed across the courtyard toward the haiden, a thoughtful frown on his face. "Before we do anything else, we should first pay our respects to the kami," he stated in a solemn voice. "We are guests here, and I have no desire to invite bad fortune into my house by offending them."

"I guess you're right," Okame said. "Though I can usually offend by simply existing. It's a talent, I suppose."

In preparation to speak to the kami, we gathered around the purification fountain, a stone trough with ladles balanced around the edges. Daisuke dipped one of the long wooden ladles in the water and poured some over his left hand, then his right, before swiping a finger over his lips and carefully replacing the ladle. I followed his example, noting that Okame did the same, though his expression was slightly sour as he dumped the extremely cold water over his hands, rinsed his mouth and spit into the bushes. Even Tatsumi followed the ritual, carefully cleansing his hands and touching water to his lips in a very calm, practical manner.

Thus cleansed, we turned and made our way to the haiden at the top of the steps. It was an elegant structure, with a green-tiled roof that curved up at the corners and bright red pillars beneath. A wooden offering box sat before a lattice screen that covered the window into the building. Fascinated, I watched as Daisuke dropped a silver tora into the box, then shook the rope dangling to the side.

A chime rang out from a large bell overhead, and immediately, I felt an awakening all around us, as if dozens of eyes suddenly turned our way. The kami of the shrine were aware of our presence now. I hoped they would not take offense to a presumptuous half kitsune invading their territory.

Seeming unaware of the sudden attention, Daisuke bowed once, and then a second time. Bringing his hands before his face, he clapped twice, slow and deliberate, then closed his eyes in silent prayer. When he was finished, Okame repeated the ritual, tossing a copper kaeru into the offering box, ringing the bell and clapping twice before closing his eyes to pray.

Trying to be patient and wait for my turn, I noticed Tatsumi, still standing at the bottom of the steps. His arms were crossed, and he was gazing at the torii gate across the yard. He looked tense, his jaw set and eyes hard, as if he wasn't comfortable here. I walked down to stand beside him.

"Are you all right, Tatsumi-san? You look a little pale."

"I'm fine."

"Are you going to make a wish to the kami? Maybe pray for our mission to go well?"

He shook his head. "The kami wouldn't listen to someone like me."

"Why?"

"Because calling on the gods requires purity of heart as well as body," Tatsumi replied. His gaze shifted to his open palm, and a shadow went through his eyes. "Even if I cleansed myself a thousand times, my soul is tainted beyond forgiveness. The kami want nothing to do with me."

"Oh." I thought about that a moment; it sounded so sad, to be ignored by the gods. "Tell me, then," I offered.

He blinked and looked at me, seeming confused. I met his gaze and smiled. "Your wish, Tatsumi. If you could pray for anything, right now, what would it be? I'll ask the kami for you."

"Yumeko..." His eyes softened. For a heartbeat, I could see past the cold and shadows and blank mirror gaze, and the vulnerability there made my stomach clench.

"Excuse me."

We turned, and that brief expression of gentleness vanished from Tatsumi's face like the snap of a door being shut. I looked into the courtyard and found we were no longer alone.

A young woman stood a few yards away, a broom held in both hands, watching us with a stern expression on her face. She couldn't have been but a year or two older than me, wearing the traditional red hakama and spotless white haori of a miko—a shrine maiden. Her straight black hair, even longer than mine, was tied behind her with a simple red ribbon, and her dark eyes shone with disapproval as she stepped forward.

"I am sorry," she announced, her gaze flicking to Daisuke and Okame, walking down the steps to join us. "But the shrine is closed for the evening. Business hours end once the sun goes down. If you wish to say a prayer or make a wish to the kami, please come back…tomorrow."

Her voice trailed off for a moment as she stared at me. I felt a twisting in my stomach as our gazes met, and for a moment, I thought she could see me. Really *see* me, what I was. My heart pounded, and I held my breath, wondering if the shrine maiden would shout *kitsune!* and I would be exposed to them all.

"Please excuse us," Daisuke said, coming forward. The miko tore her gaze from me to face the approaching noble, who smiled as he reached the bottom of the steps.

"We didn't mean to intrude," Daisuke continued, as I still waited, frozen, to see what the shrine maiden would do. "We're looking for the head priest here. Would you be able to tell us where he is?"

"Who wishes to know?"

I took a quick breath. "I do," I said, stepping away from Tatsumi. The miko gazed at me calmly, her dark eyes assessing, but she didn't point and scream *demon fox* at me, so I hoped I had been mistaken. "I've come from the Silent Winds temple," I went on, seeing no change in her expression. "I've journeyed far to find this place. Please, it's important I speak with him. Can you tell me where he is?"

She held my gaze a moment longer, then turned away. "Come with me," she ordered simply, and began walking across the courtyard. We all hurried to follow her, as she led us around the shrine to a row of much smaller, simpler buildings. At the steps to the veranda that circled the first structure, she turned, halting us in our tracks, and pointed a finger in my direction.

"You. Follow me. Only you—the rest of your party must wait here." She glanced at the others, as if expecting a protest, and narrowed her eyes. "The head priest is very busy at the moment. I do not wish to disturb him with a large group of visitors stomping through the premises. I will take the girl to speak to Master Jiro—everyone else, please make yourselves comfortable until we return."

"Oh." I turned to look at my companions, wondering what they thought of this. Okame shrugged, and Daisuke gestured at the steps, indicating that I should follow her. I glanced at Tatsumi, and he gave a slight nod. I supposed he didn't think a petite shrine maiden was going to be a threat, or maybe he didn't care one way or another. "All right."

I trailed her up the steps, down a wooden veranda and past several rooms where the murmur of voices could be heard through the shoji. At the end of the veranda, the miko slid open a door and gestured for me to go inside. I did as she asked, stepping into a small, mostly empty room with a tatami mat floor, a low table and a single flower in an alcove. The head priest was nowhere to be seen.

The door closed with a snap. I whirled to see the miko take a strip of white paper from her haori and press it to the doorframe, the kanji for *barrier* written on the surface in clear black ink.

*An ofuda?* I felt a pulse of spiritual energy ripple from the paper strip and spread over the walls. The hairs on my arms rose as a shimmering wall of force surrounded the room, similar to the ki barrier the monks created, but one of pure magic, drawn from the kami and the energy of the world.

The shrine maiden turned, her black eyes hard as they

met mine. "I've put a barrier around this room," she announced. "No spirits, demons or yokai can get in or out, and no one outside will hear us. Your friends, if they even are your friends, won't be coming, *kitsune*."

My ears flattened as I stepped back, feeling fox magic rise to the surface. So, she had seen me, after all. "I just came to speak to Master Jiro," I said, in what I hoped was a calming voice. "I'm not here to cause trouble."

"No?" The miko's gaze narrowed. "Did you think you could just walk in here and I wouldn't know a yokai when I saw one? Even a half yokai. I speak to the kami every day. I see their world as clearly as my own." She gestured past the sealed door. "Those men outside—none of them know what you really are, do they, fox? You're deceiving them all." A hard smile crossed her lips. "You won't find me so easily fooled."

"I came here for help," I insisted. "I'm from the Silent Winds temple. My master sent me to find the head priest of the Hayate shrine."

"Why?"

"Because..." I closed my eyes. I didn't want to fight the miko, but it was clear she didn't trust a word I was saying. She saw only a kitsune, and the reputations of the mischievous foxes preceded me. If I wanted to talk to the priest, I had to get past the shrine maiden.

"Because..." I sighed again and reached into my furoshiki. "I have this."

The shrine maiden's eyes got huge as I pulled out the lacquered scroll case, holding it between us. The blood drained from her face, and she took a step backward, staring at the item in my hand as if it were a live snake. "Merciful Kami," she whispered. "That is... You have a piece of the scroll."

She stood there a moment, then leaned forward with narrowed eyes. "Who else knows of this?" she snapped. "The men outside—are any of them aware that you have the Dragon's prayer?"

I shook my head. "None of them know I possess the scroll," I told her. "Or, this piece of it, anyway." I hesitated a moment, wincing. "Although there is…one, who is searching for it, who was sent to my temple retrieve the scroll."

"The samurai in black," the miko guessed. "The warrior of the Shadow Clan. Who is he?"

"His name is Kage Tatsumi," I told her. "He carries a sword named Kamigoroshi."

She closed her eyes. "The Kage demonslayer," she whispered. "I thought I felt something evil close by. I suppose that makes sense, that Hanshou would send him." Her eyes opened, angry and fearful, glaring at me. "How could you bring that creature into this shrine?" she demanded. "Do you know how dangerous he is, what he could do to the spirits who call this place their home?"

"I needed him," I told her. "He agreed to help—"

"Because he wants the scroll," she interrupted. "That's the only reason *you're* still alive, kitsune, the only reason the demonslayer hasn't killed you. If he finds out you have it…"

"My temple was attacked," I said. "An oni came through, murdered everyone, and tried to take the scroll. I barely escaped." I shivered, remembering the terror of the horde, the monstrous oni crashing into the hall, and the horror that came after. I had to swallow the lump in my throat before continuing. "Before he died, Master Isao sent me here. He said that the head priest would know where to find the Steel Feather temple."

"Which has the second piece of the Dragon's prayer," the

miko finished gravely, and sighed. "Yes, I can see the truth of your words." She took a step back, rubbing her eyes as if they pained her. "Though I don't know why the monks let a yokai run off with something so important. I suppose they were desperate."

I ignored the contempt in her voice, slipping the case back into my furoshiki. "My name is Yumeko," I told her. "Master Isao and the monks raised me. I spent my entire life in that temple. I didn't know the story of the Dragon until recently, but I did promise to take care of the scroll. I have no intention of letting it fall to the demons, or into the hands of evil humans. I've come a long way, fought bandits and gaki and omukade, to talk to the head priest." I pinned back my ears, feeling a tiny bit of desperation and anger rise to the surface. "If I really was pure yokai, I would have dropped the scroll in the river and let it wash out to the sea."

"You're right. I am sorry, kitsune." The shrine maiden straightened, becoming more formal. "I apologize for my bluntness," she offered. "I am known as Reika, and I'm the senior shrine maiden for the Hayate shrine. I am also the only one who knows about the Dragon scroll besides Master Jiro."

"You know the legend, then. About the scroll and the Dragon's wish."

"Yes." Reika nodded. "Master Jiro told me about the scroll, the Dragon's prayer and what will happen if the Dragon is summoned. But there is one thing he would not reveal, and that is the location of the Steel Feather temple." A faint, bitter smile twisted her lips. "I suppose it was for my protection."

"I have to get to the Steel Feather temple," I said. "I promised I would deliver the scroll to the monks there. Will you allow me to speak to Master Jiro?"

"I would," the miko replied, "if I knew where he was."

I blinked. "He's not here?"

Reika shook her head. "Three days ago," she explained, "a courier arrived with a message for Master Jiro, summoning him to the Imperial Palace. He left to attend the meeting, and put me in charge of the shrine until he returned. That was the last I saw of him." Her lips thinned, and she shook her head. "I shouldn't have let him go. He confessed that he had an ominous feeling about the meeting and warned me to be on my guard. I should have insisted he stay here. And now, he's missing and I have no idea what happened."

"Have you been to the palace to look for him?"

She gave me a bemused look. "I've been trying, but you cannot just show up at the imperial palace without an invitation," she exclaimed. "The guards keep turning me away at the gates. They say that no one has seen or heard of Master Jiro." The miko made a frustrated gesture. "But I know he's there. I know he went to speak to a woman named Lady Satomi, and never came back." She gave me a wary look. "And then, a kitsune arrives at the shrine with part of the Dragon scroll, wanting to know the way to the Steel Feather temple. How could I not think the two were related?"

I started to answer, but a shiver suddenly went through the air, causing a chill to race up my spine. Reika turned, eyes widening, as the edge of a blade slashed through the sliding screen door, cutting the ofuda in half. The door panels toppled to the floor with a clatter, revealing Tatsumi's lean, dark silhouette in the frame, Kamigoroshi unsheathed and glowing in the fading light.

# 27

## Summoned by Shadow

Something wasn't right.

I'd watched Yumeko leave with the shrine maiden, feeling Hakaimono's restless stirring in my mind. As soon as we'd passed beneath the torii gate at the stairs, the demon had recoiled. This was sacred ground, sanctified by priests and protected against evil. Demons were not welcome in this place. Even though Hakaimono's presence had been masked within the sword, it was still uncomfortable for me to be here. To make matters worse, Hakaimono held a special, venomous hatred for priests, shrine maidens and spiritual figures of any kind. When the miko had first appeared, I'd had to suppress the instant desire to tear the head from her body.

Still, I sensed no evil from the shrine maiden herself, and when she told the rest of us to wait while she continued on with Yumeko, I was wary, but protesting would not have gotten us any closer to our objective. Especially when there were other ways of listening in on the conversation while not being physically present.

Wandering to the side of the building, I leaned against the railing and crossed my arms, affecting a pose of casual patience. While the ronin sat heavily on the steps and pulled out his sake jug and the noble walked quietly to the edge of a rock garden, I furtively held two fingers to my lips and whispered a few words under my breath.

Around me, everything grew very quiet. Sounds faded, becoming muffled, like the world was suddenly underwater. Closing my eyes, I tilted my head very slightly and angled my focus toward the building behind me.

Voices whispered past my ears, as I sent my consciousness into the rooms, searching for Yumeko's voice. This was a special Shadow Clan technique, used by some of our shinobi to listen to a private conversation in a room, across a yard, or in a crowded restaurant without giving themselves away. Since my missions usually involved death and not information gathering, I rarely used it, as focusing so much of your attention elsewhere left your body vulnerable. But the shrine seemed secure enough; there were no demons here, except the one hidden in my blade. Unless the ronin got bored and decided to bother me, I would be safe to listen in on Yumeko and the shrine maiden.

However, as I pressed farther into the building, hearing what I assumed were more mikos, talking about their daily lives, I suddenly hit a wall. Not a physical one; I could go through wood or stone or rice paper with ease. But a wall of magic, shimmering with energy, prevented me from going any farther.

*A barrier?*

I opened my eyes, and the magic scattered to the winds. The ronin still lounged on the steps, drinking, and the noble seemed to be admiring the well-tended rock garden in the shade of a pine.

Pushing myself off the railing, I turned and walked around the veranda and up the steps, brushing past the ronin, who gave me a puzzled look.

"Oi, where you going, Kage-san? I thought we were supposed to wait here."

Ignoring him, I continued down the hallway, pulling my sword as I did. With a yelp, the ronin scrambled after me, demanding to know what I was doing, but I didn't pause. I'd underestimated the shrine maiden, thinking she wasn't a threat. That wasn't a simple barrier I'd encountered; it was a complex seal, blocking any sound or magic from getting in or out. If she had Yumeko in that room and decided to attack, none of us would be able to hear what was going on.

As I drew closer to the last room, I could feel the magic pushing against me, trying to keep me back. I saw the nearly invisible shimmer blocking the door and narrowed my eyes. Raising Kamigoroshi, I aimed, then brought the sword slicing down across the frame, feeling the blade rip through the barrier and shatter it into a thousand pieces.

The doors fell, clattering to the floor beside me. I stared into the room as Yumeko and the shrine maiden whirled around, their eyes going wide as they spotted me.

"You!" The shrine maiden stepped forward, seeming unafraid, even as Hakaimono snarled with hate and urged me to split her in half like the doors. "Kamigoroshi, you are not welcome here. Get out, and take your human host with you!"

"It seems the head priest isn't here today." I stepped into

the room, and the miko retreated a pace. I glanced past her, making sure the girl was all right, before turning to the shrine maiden. "You deceived us to get Yumeko alone. Did you think your barrier could stop me?"

Scowling, the miko pulled another ofuda from her sleeve and brandished it before her. It read *loyalty* in stark black ink down the paper. "Leave this place, abomination," she ordered again. "If you come a step closer, I will summon the guardian of the shrine to drive you out!"

"Do it," I said, feeling Hakaimono flare with eagerness, "and you will have one less shrine guardian."

"Tatsumi, wait!"

Yumeko stepped between us. "It's all right," she told me, as the noble and the ronin pushed into the room, as well. I could feel their shock as they took in the scene; me with my sword bared, facing a shrine maiden brandishing ofuda. And a slip of a girl between us. "I'm fine, Tatsumi. There's no danger here. Reika-san was just telling me how Master Jiro went missing and that she needs our help to find him."

"What?" the miko exclaimed, obviously just as surprised as the rest of us. Yumeko half turned, looking behind her, as the shrine maiden lowered her arm, frowning.

"That's what you wanted, isn't it, Reika-san?" She cocked her head, as if the solution was perfectly clear. "To find Master Jiro. And we need his help to get to the temple. So, obviously, we should aid each other. Right, everyone?" Yumeko glanced back at the three of us, her gaze plaintive. "Daisuke-san? Okame-san? You'll help, too, right?"

"Of course," the ronin exclaimed immediately. "We're always happy to aid a friend of Yumeko-chan's. Just leave it to us." He paused, scratching the back of his head. "Though it would help if I knew what the hell was going on."

I sighed, lowering my sword. Shrine maidens, ronin, farmers, yurei. Was there anyone Yumeko wouldn't trust as soon as she met them? "You said the head priest has gone missing?" I asked the shrine maiden, who eyed me warily but nodded. "How long ago?"

"Three days," the miko answered, and stepped back with an exasperated look at the doors, lying in the frame. "You might as well come in." She sighed, waving us through. "Sit down, and I'll explain the whole situation."

We stepped carefully over the broken door panels and sat down in front of the low table, with the miko on the other side. And we listened as she told us of the head priest, the mysterious summons to the palace and his meeting with a woman named Lady Satomi.

At thc namc, Taiyo-san straightened, a flash of recognition going through his eyes. Yumeko noticed it, as well.

"Do you know her, Daisuke-san?" Yumeko asked.

"I do." The noble's expression turned faintly sour. "Not personally, but I know who she is. Everyone in the palace does. She's the emperor's favorite concubine. She came to the city less than a year ago and has been growing her influence ever since. There are some who believe the emperor favors her too much, that a simple concubine should not be given such status, but any who speak too loudly against her find themselves dishonored, exiled from the city or worse. And…"

He trailed off. "And?" I asked softly.

He exhaled. "It is nothing. Peasant gossip, nothing an honorable bushi would concern himself with. But there have been…rumors of late, whispers, about Lady Satomi. The servants are all terrified of her, and she never seems to have the same handmaid more than a month or two at a time.

There was a little servant girl… Suki, I believe her name was, who was last assigned to Lady Satomi's quarters. By chance, I ran into her once, when she first came to the palace." He tapped his fingers on his arm, frowning. "I have not seen her since."

Yumeko cocked her head. "What happened to her?"

"I do not know." The noble shook his head. "I do not keep track of Lady Satomi's maidservants, but I believe she has yet another girl working for her. If what you say is true, and the head priest has gone missing, that does indeed appear suspicious. What would Lady Satomi want with Master Jiro?"

"I intend to ask her," the shrine maiden said, "if I can get into the palace."

The noble's jaw tightened. "I would be very careful, were I you," he warned. "Lady Satomi may not be a warrior, but she is the emperor's favorite and a lady of the court. Within the palace, she holds a tremendous amount of sway and power. She will be a dangerous opponent if you attack her head-on. If you do not bring down the wrath of the emperor himself."

"Daisuke-san," Yumeko said, as if just realizing something. "You're a noble of the great imperial family. *You* could get us into the palace, right?"

"I…" Taken aback, the noble stared at her a moment, then nodded. "Yes," he finally admitted. "I could. It would take some planning, but I think I could manage it."

*I could, too*, I thought, unreasonably annoyed with the smile Yumeko gave him. Hakaimono perked up, intrigued by my flash of irritation, and I shoved the demon's presence down.

"However," the noble went on, "there are proper channels we must take. I cannot simply walk you through the gates of the Imperial Palace and demand to see Lady Satomi. Such dishonorable behavior would ruin my family's reputation and make us the laughingstock of the court, and my father might commit seppuku in shame. And if Lady Satomi decides she is being threatened, she could turn the court against you, have you arrested, or even executed. This is not something we can take lightly. One wrong step in the court will be disastrous for us all. But…" He paused, brow furrowed in thought, before nodding. "Yes, of course. That might work. I think I have a way."

"What do you have in mind, Daisuke-san?" Yumeko asked.

"Tomorrow night," the noble went on, "the emperor is holding his annual Moon Viewing party in the palace gardens. It is a very prestigious event, and a great honor to be invited, so all the important nobles and families will be there."

"Including Lady Satomi," the miko guessed.

"Most certainly. My family has already been invited, of course. The trick will be getting the rest of you through the gates. A difficult proposition, but I think I can manage it."

"And you would do this for us?" The shrine maiden stared at the noble, eyes narrowed in suspicion. "Forgive me, Taiyo-san," she said, as he raised a brow at her. "But… you are a noble. Not only that, you are part of the imperial family. Why would you help a shrine maiden, a ronin and a kinsman of the Shadow Clan into the emperor's party?"

"Lady Reika." The noble gave her a solemn look. "I met Suki-san only once," he said. "Normally, I do not notice the comings and goings of the servants in the palace, but this meeting, brief as it was, stood out. I discovered she was the daughter of a craftsman, and had an ear for beautiful music. She was…genuine, something quite rare within the Imperial Palace." His brow creased, a look of weary disgust briefly crossing his face. "The dance of the court never changes. Every year, it is exactly the same—silken words that hide daggers of venom beneath the veneer of decorum and compliments. A smile can be as dangerous as a sword, and the wrong choice of words can mean the difference between great favor and eternal shame. When I met the girl, it was refreshing to speak to someone who did not care about earning favor or keeping up appearances. For Suki and her father's sake, I feel it is my responsibility to discover if the rumors about Lady Satomi are idle peasant gossip, or if they have any truth to them."

"Wow," the ronin interjected. "A noble who actually realized a peasant was a real person. Better be careful, Taiyo-san—next thing you know, you might start courting dogs and having conversations with monkeys." Yumeko frowned at this, looking puzzled, and the ronin hurried on before she could ask a question. "But that still doesn't explain *how* you're going to sneak a ronin, a priestess and…her—" he nodded at Yumeko "—into the Imperial Palace."

"Sneak you into the emperor's party?" The noble seemed genuinely horrified. "What a shameful thought. I may find the courtly events a bit repetitive, Okame-san, but I am not so bored as to consider treason." He sniffed, letting us all know he was offended, before continuing. "However, a distinguished onmyoji and her yojimbo is a different story. Those who practice onmyodo, the ancient art of yin and yang, are highly respected. The emperor himself often calls upon onmyoji for advice in political affairs, to tell his fortune or divine the future of the country. I'm certain he would welcome Yumeko-san and her companions into his presence."

I saw the shrine maiden glance at Yumeko and narrow her eyes; perhaps she could tell that the girl wasn't an onmyoji, or anyone with magical abilities. But she didn't correct the noble's assumption, and neither did Yumeko, though the ronin looked vaguely uneasy at the thought of meeting the emperor.

"So, it's decided," the shrine maiden said. "Tomorrow night, we will attend the emperor's Moon Viewing party, find Lady Satomi and discover what has happened to Master Jiro. Are we all in agreement, that this must be done?"

"Yes," Yumeko said immediately. "And once we find Master Jiro, we can finally go to the Steel Feather temple."

"Sounds like fun," put in the ronin, rubbing his hands together. "I've never been invited to the palace before. I can't wait to see it up close."

"Agreed," said the noble. "Although, if I may..." He glanced at Yumeko, then the ronin. "The emperor's party attracts nobles from across Iwagoto. All are looking to make an impression, to see and be seen. And, for the most part, you will not want to stand out among the crowd. Perhaps a change of attire would be...prudent."

The ronin snorted. "Don't show up looking like filthy peasants, then?"

"If at all possible."

"Miss Reika?"

I turned, ignoring the sudden surge of bloodlust. Hakaimono was angry that the scene with the miko hadn't ended in violence and was now lashing out at everything around it. A pair of shrine maidens, probably the two I'd heard in the rooms next door, appeared on the veranda, peering cautiously into the room.

"Miss Reika," one said again. "So sorry to disturb you, but there are samurai at the entrance that will not leave. They say they are looking for one of their kin."

"Thank you, Minako-san," the shrine maiden said, as a cold lump settled in my gut. "Please inform them that I will be there shortly." As the two miko bowed and hurried off, the priestess gave the rest of us an exasperated look.

"It appears your presence continues to disturb the peacefulness of my shrine," she remarked. "Now I have samurai at the gates, upsetting the kami and scaring the mikos. Which one of you is responsible for this, I wonder?"

"Hey, don't look at me," the ronin said, holding up his hands as the shrine maiden glared at him. "I'm not in the habit of being around samurai, present company excluded. If anyone, it's the noble Taiyo, wanting to know why their golden kinsman is hanging around with such riffraff."

"No," I said softly, and rose, causing them all to glance up. "It's the Kage. They're here for me."

Stepping over the shattered door panels, I walked out of the room. I knew, somehow, that the members of the Shadow Clan had come for me, and I did not want them to know the faces of those I had traveled with. But I hadn't gone very far when light footsteps echoed behind me, and *her* voice floated over the breeze.

"Tatsumi, wait."

I turned. Yumeko had followed me out to the veranda and was now watching me depart, her gaze conflicted. "What about your promise?" she asked quietly. "We still need to find Master Jiro, and you said we would go to the Steel Feather temple together."

"I haven't forgotten." An odd reluctance tugged at me; for some reason, I found myself hesitant to go. "I'll meet you at the palace," I told her. "Don't look for me. When it's time, I'll find you." She still looked hesitant, and I offered a faint smile. "I swear it."

The Kage were indeed at the entrance of the shrine; four samurai in dark hakama and haori, wearing the black-and-purple colors of the Shadow Clan. It wasn't surprising; agents of the Kage were everywhere and had likely taken note of my presence the moment I stepped into the capital. "Kage Tatsumi," one said with a short bow as I approached. "Master Masao wishes to speak to you. If you would please come with us."

I followed my clansmen through the darkening streets of Kin Heigen Toshi, as the sunlight disappeared and lanterns flickered to life. We walked in silence, parting the crowds as we glided through the city. A group of samurai walking the streets was enough to cause most normal civilians to politely cross to the other side, but a group of Shadow Clan samurai warranted even more caution. As the Hino family were infamous for their short tempers, and the Taiyo were known for being as proud as they were beautiful, the Kage had garnered a reputation as being sinister and untrustworthy. A standing we did little to dispute. The Shadow Clan had many secrets; better that the empire expected such behavior of us. It kept them from prying too deeply into our affairs and discovering they had every right to be cautious.

The Shadow district, where the Kage family maintained an estate within the Imperial City, lay on the outskirts west of the palace. As a sanctuary away from home for the smallest of the Great Clans, it was tucked into a corner along the outer wall, far from the bustle of the inner city, out of sight and out of mind. Which suited the Kage perfectly. Like the name suggested, the streets through the Shadow district were narrow and dark, with few lanterns to throw back the gloom. As I made my way down familiar roads and alleys, I could feel eyes on me, invisible, but Hakaimono didn't even stir. Shinobi prowled the rooftops overhead, silent and lethal, keeping watch over everything that happened within Shadow Clan territory. Ironically, their presence made the Kage district one of the safest in Kin Heigen Toshi; no kidnapper, thief or murderer would risk operating in a territory whose warriors knew the darkness better than them.

The Kage estates lay at the end of the Shadow district, over a canal of sluggish black water that was rumored to be haunted by an irritable kappa, a type of man-eating river yokai. With the amount of shinobi in the area and the fact that Hakaimono had never sensed the presence of yokai near the canal, I doubted this rumor was true and thought that it might even have been started by the Kage themselves to keep curious civilians away from the estate.

The Kage estate itself was surrounded by high stone walls and guarded by black-clad samurai, though I knew even more shinobi lurked in hidden nooks and crannies, watching us as we walked through the gates. Once we passed through the tall, iron-banded doors, all but one samurai bowed to me and left, leaving me in the care of a single bushi. I followed him up the steps into the Kage estate, smaller than Hakumei-jo, the home castle of the Shadow Clan, but no less elegant.

And no less confusing. Both structures were designed to be baffling, and those without intimate knowledge of the estate's interiors would soon find themselves hopelessly lost in the labyrinthine corridors of the Shadow Clan palace. Added to this were many hidden rooms, trapdoors, secret tunnels and spaces between walls and floors, where shinobi could ambush intruders and vanish without a trace. Within Hakumei-jo, it was said that there were hidden rooms, tunnels and passages not even the shinobi knew about, and that the only person who possessed all the secrets of the Shadow Clan palaces was the architect who designed them. But she'd left no record of her work behind, no blueprints or journals, and in the end, took her perfect knowledge with her to the grave.

Thankfully, I had been to the Shadow Clan estate a few times before and was familiar with the layout. And, unlike Hakumei Castle, the interior of this palace did not switch around or change appearance several times a year, so I was able to keep my bearings as I followed my guide through the long, twisting corridors of the Kage estate.

However, as we turned a corner, a trio of men melted out of the shadows to block our path. They wore dark robes, and their faces were painted white with black markings across their cheeks and forehead. The majutsushi of the Shadow Clan.

"You are dismissed," the lead figure told the samurai. "Return to your post. We will take the demonslayer from here."

The warrior bowed deeply, turned on a heel and strode away without looking back. The sorcerer waited until the footsteps had faded into the dark before turning jet-black eyes on me.

"Kage Tatsumi," he murmured as the others stepped forward, surrounding me. I kept my face blank, my hands at my side, though my head was filled with images of slicing them in half, drenching the corridors in blood. The robed figure's painted black lips curled in a faint smile, as if he were reading my thoughts. "I can feel your hate from here, demonslayer," he said in a raspy whisper. "You know what's coming, and you desperately want to kill us all, don't you?"

"Hakaimono's desires are not mine, Master Iemon," I replied carefully. "I am fully in control, both of myself and my weapon."

"Are you?" The majutsushi's lips curled higher. "Not according to Master Jomei. You have been seen in the company of a girl, a ronin and now, a samurai. A Taiyo noble, of all people. Did you think we would not notice your abnormal behavior? Have you forgotten the rules?" His stark black gaze narrowed. "What have we told you about dealing with those not of the Shadow Clan? Answer me."

"I am to have little to no dealings with those outside of the Kage," I replied obediently. "I am to avoid contact with people whenever possible. If it is not possible, I am to act as society dictates, until I can remove myself from their presence as quickly as I can."

"And why is that, demonslayer?"

"Because my existence puts them in danger," I quoted. "Because humans inspire emotion, which Hakaimono will use to weaken my defenses."

"And if that happens?"

"I will lose control, and the Kage will be forced to put me down."

Master Iemon nodded. "You know this," he said harshly. "You know you must always work alone. Humans will only tempt you, distract you, and worse, they will bring out the emotions we have spent a lifetime teaching you to suppress. The Kage demonslayer must *never* give in to anger, fear, frustration or grief. Feeling anything only brings Hakaimono closer to the surface, and if you lose control of the sword, that will bring great shame and dishonor to the Kage, as we must clean up the mess you left behind."

"I understand, Master Iemon. But—"

"But?" The majutsushi hissed, "There is no *but*, no excuse. You are nothing, demonslayer. You exist only to serve the Kage. Your personal feelings mean nothing, because you should not have them." He straightened and stepped back, appraising me. "It appears that the Kage demonslayer's resolve is slipping. Perhaps a reevaluation of the subject's mental state is necessary."

Rage filled me, and I fought the urge to draw Kamigoroshi and cut my way free, knowing Iemon was watching my reaction. Reevaluation meant days of mental and physical stress to determine if I could remain in control. It meant being shackled to a pair of stone pillars and beaten with bamboo rods, to see if I would lose myself to the demon. It meant plunging my hand into a bed of hot coals to prove I would follow orders at any cost, or kneeling motionless before a wooden target while fellow shinobi hurled shuriken and kunai past my face.

But, with Iemon and the rest of the majutsushi watching, judging my reaction, there was only one acceptable answer. Bowing low at the waist, I cast my gaze to the floor, feeling Iemon's eyes on the back of my neck. "My life and my body belong to the Shadow Clan," I murmured, as Hakaimono recoiled in angry disgust. "If this is what the Kage requires of me, I will submit."

"No, Tatsumi-kun," came a new voice behind me. "Not this time."

"Masao-san!" Iemon exclaimed, as the courtier sauntered

into the hallway. Clad in a flowing kimono of purple silk, a spray of golden bamboo covering one side, he stood out among the stark black robes of the majutsushi. The pair that had been flanking Iemon backed away, but the lead majutsushi stood firm as Kage Masao's presence filled the corridor like a swan stretching its wings.

"Good evening, Master Iemon," Masao greeted. "Please forgive the interruption, but I'm afraid I must intervene. The demonslayer will come with me."

Iemon's black lips thinned. "The demonslayer is under our watch," the majutsushi argued, as Masao regarded him lazily from behind his white silk fan. "We are responsible for determining if he is a danger to himself and the citizens of Iwagoto."

"Tatsumi-kun is on a very important mission for Lady Hanshou herself." Masao snapped his fan shut and smiled at the glowering majutsushi. "He does not have time to be dragged away and tormented by your cadre of ghouls." Iemon stiffened, but the courtier's smile didn't falter. "Worry not, Iemon-san. If he loses control and eats someone, I will assume full responsibility."

"Very well." The majutsushi stepped back, a sour look on his face. Victory went to the courtier, and I took a quiet breath of relief. "Then we leave him in your *capable* hands, Masao-san. I am certain you will know what to do if Hakaimono makes an appearance." He smirked, his expression saying the exact opposite, as if he was hoping I would lose control and rip the courtier to shreds, but Masao only nodded serenely.

"Oh, you flatter me, Master Iemon." The courtier fluttered his fan again, a faint blush tingeing his cheeks. "I am not worthy of such praise. Besides, with your excellent training and guidance, I am sure to be in no danger. Tatsumi-kun has had the most thorough upbringing, I am certain. And if the boy does lose control, Lady Hanshou would certainly not blame the death of her most trusted advisor on *you*. She is, of course, the kindest and most benevolent of rulers, and her punishments for those who disappoint her are reserved for only the vilest of failures."

Behind his makeup, Iemon went slightly pale. "Yes. Well." He backed away, suddenly eager to be gone. "We will take our leave, then. Good evening, Masao-san."

"And to you, Iemon-san."

As the majutsushi turned and drifted away down the corridor, Masao's pleasant smile turned faintly savage, and he closed his fan. "Keep to your magic and manipulating the kami, Iemon-san," he said in a quiet voice. "Don't attempt to play the game of the court with a master."

Tucking the fan into his obi, he looked at me, and the vicious mask disappeared, as if it had never been. "Tatsumi-kun," he said brightly. "So sorry to keep you waiting. Will you walk with me for a bit?"

We started down the hallway, moving in the opposite direction Iemon and the rest of the majutsushi had gone. I was glad to be rid of Iemon and the three majutsushi, but strangely enough, being in the presence of Kage Masao felt just as unnerving, as if there were live vipers hidden beneath his robes, though I didn't know why.

"I understand that the Silent Winds temple had been destroyed when you got there," Masao commented after a minute or two of walking.

"Yes, Master Masao," I replied. "Amanjaku had killed everyone, and the scroll was already gone. There were reports of an oni, but I didn't see it."

"Demons," Masao mused, sounding grim. "So, Jomei was right. A mortal is summoning them from Jigoku, which means they're likely after the scroll, as well. Lady Hanshou will not be pleased." He sighed and gave me a sideways look. "This girl you've taken up with, who is giving Iemon a heart attack. Who is she?"

"The only survivor from the temple," I told him. "She claims her master told her where he sent the scroll, but not how to get there. That's why we came to the capital—there is someone here who knows where this hidden temple is located. I promised to escort her there once she has the information."

"I see." Masao gave no indication of what he thought of this. "And do you trust this girl?"

"I..." I paused. *Trust no one*, that was Master Ichiro's number one rule. *Believe nothing but what your senses tell you*, he would always warn. *Humans manipulate. Yokai deceive. Everything has ulterior motives, and the second you let your guard down, they will slit your throat from behind.*

I'd heeded his warning, of course. Everything, everyone I met, was looking to kill, harm or manipulate me in some fashion. That assumption had saved my life on more than one occasion, when the sobbing child at the river had lunged at me with bared fangs, and the frightened woman in the alley had attempted to strangle me with her hair.

But Yumeko... It was strange, and possibly dangerous, but I felt...almost comfortable around her. Or, at least, I didn't believe she would try to stab me the moment I let down my guard. Master Ichiro would flay the skin from my back if he discovered I was having such thoughts, but Yumeko was different, genuinely curious and unassuming. She had saved my life, she didn't demand anything of me and she was the first person to ever touch me without inflicting pain.

"I trust she will take me to where the scroll is," I told the courtier. "I trust she will do everything in her power to get there."

"Good." Masao nodded. "Continue to aid her, then. Protect the girl from the demons and blood mages that might try to stop you. Do whatever it takes to ensure your mission is a success. And the moment she leads you to the scroll and you have it in your possession, kill her."

A cold lance went through my stomach, but I nodded once, keeping my voice impassive. "Understood."

"Excellent." Masao smiled cheerfully. "I don't understand why Iemon was so worried. Obviously you will do what you must to finish your mission for Lady Hanshou. So, Tatsumi-kun, what is the next step? Where is this person who knows the location of the scroll?"

"We don't know," I said, earning a puzzled frown from the courtier. "He was supposed to be at the Hayate shrine, but three days ago he was summoned to the Imperial Palace and disappeared."

"Summoned to the palace? By whom?"

"Lady Satomi."

"Oh? The emperor's concubine?" Masao pressed his lips together, looking thoughtful. "There are rumors of her cruelty, but no more than most of the inner court. So, are you part of this little game as well, Lady Satomi? How very… interesting." A sly expression crossed his face, before he shook it off and looked at me again. "A woman of Satomi's station will be difficult to get to," he said. "I assume you are going over the wall, but what then? How do you plan to discover what she knows?"

"There is an event at the palace tomorrow night—" I began, and Masao snapped his fingers together.

"Of course. The emperor's Moon Viewing party, how could I forget?" For a moment, he regarded me with an amused smile on his lips. "A shame you can't attend the normal way, Tatsumi-kun. I can just see the ladies of the court eyeing you like a pack of ravenous wolves."

"I'm not sure I understand, Master Masao."

"I'm sure you don't." Abruptly, Masao turned and pressed the end of his fan beneath my chin, forcing me to look up at him. I went rigid as he peered at me, studying my face. "Ichiro and Iemon have probably never told you," he murmured, "but did you know that you are extremely handsome, Tatsumi-kun? A shame they chose you to be the bearer of that cursed sword. Such wasted potential. Of course, in the court, the right clothes would make the difference, but still." His eyes gleamed as he lowered the fan and stepped back, smiling in a way that caused a flutter of trepidation to go through my stomach. "Well, do your best, demonslayer. And good luck with Lady Satomi. I fear you might find the emperor's court more challenging than you think."

# 28

## The Moon Viewing Party

*I* didn't quite recognize the girl in the reflection.

I knew her face. That was the only thing that was familiar. Everything else—hair, makeup, clothing—seemed foreign and strange.

I stood in the shrine maiden's room, doors and windows firmly shut with strict orders that we not be disturbed, and stared at the kitsune in the small oval mirror above her dresser. The layered red-and-white robe, trimmed in gold and patterned with beautiful designs, was easily the most elegant thing I had ever worn. It was also heavy, nearly covered my toes and was quite cumbersome, especially the wide, billowy sleeves. My hair had been combed, trimmed and hung in a pleated braid down my back, tied with red-and-gold silk ribbons. A tall peaked cap sat atop my head behind my pointed fox ears; I pinned them back in distaste, and the cap toppled off and fell to the floor.

Reika sighed. "You can't do that when you're at the palace," she chided, picking the cap off the tatami mats and placing it on my head again. "If you're going to fool everyone into thinking you're a respected onmyoji, you can't be twitching at every little thing."

"These robes are so heavy," I said, wrinkling my nose. I could feel my tail beneath the fabric, pressed against the backs of my legs, and I shifted uncomfortably. At least the cumbersome fabric concealed the scroll, still hidden in the furoshiki, quite well. "I'm going to be tripping over my own feet every few steps. Can't I just make my normal clothes look like this?"

"Fox magic is nothing but illusion and trickery," the miko returned, the disdain in her voice reminding me of Denga-san. "If you are discovered to be half yokai within the Imperial Palace, not only will you be executed, everyone associated with you will be punished, as well. The ronin, the noble and the Kage demonslayer—all could be killed, because you didn't want to be uncomfortable for a night. Do you really want to risk that?"

I sniffed. "Can I at least get some geta clogs so I don't trip and fall on my face in front of the entire Imperial court?"

She grimaced. "I can raise the hem a couple inches, just give me a minute."

She knelt beside me and began tugging on the fabric, muttering at me to hold still. As I looked in the mirror again, my thoughts wandered. After Tatsumi had departed last night, disappearing into the city with his clansmen, Reika had kindly provided rooms for me and Okame. Daisuke had left as well, returning to his family's estate in the Sun district, though he'd promised to return the next evening to escort us to the palace. This afternoon, Reika had sent a few mikos out to find attire suitable for an onmyoji "of my station," and had firmly suggested that Okame should head to the marketplace for an outfit as well; one that didn't scream "filthy ronin dog." The ronin had scoffed at first, but the shrine maiden insisted she wasn't going to jeopardize our mission because of his stupid pride, and practically chased him out of the shrine, threatening to send the shrine guardian after him if he didn't leave. After the ronin finally heeded her orders, she turned her attention to me.

"What are the names of the last five emperors?" Reika demanded, still kneeling at the hem of my robes. I stifled a groan. All morning, she had lectured me about the ways of the court: their customs, what was socially acceptable and what behaviors would scream "uncouth peasant." The amount of details to remember when simply offering a bow made my head spin, as was the list of topics that were deemed unacceptable for this time of year. When asked a question, it was considered rude to simply say yes or no; better to reply with poem and verse, using as many similies and flowery phrases as possible.

"Um…" I hedged, knowing Reika was expecting an answer. An onmyoji of my station, she'd explained earlier, would certainly know the history of Iwagoto's royal family. "Taiyo no Genjiro, Taiyo no Eiichi, Taiyo no Fujikata, Taiyo no…um… Kintaro?"

"Now you're just guessing," the shrine maiden said. "And you cannot say 'um' or 'ano' in the imperial court. Peasants and commoners stutter. Nobles never do."

With a sigh, I shifted my weight, earning a *tch* of displeasure from the shrine maiden. Abruptly, I missed Tatsumi; though he never said much, his quiet presence could always be felt. I wondered where he was now, what he was doing. I hoped I would see him again, that he would meet us in the palace like he promised. I also hoped I wouldn't put a foot in my mouth at the imperial court and expose us all.

"There," Reika said, and rose, brushing off her knees. "I think you're as ready as you'll ever be." Stepping back, she crossed her arms and regarded me with a critical eye, before nodding once. "Good enough. You look like an onmyoji, on the surface at least. Now, it's almost sundown, and I must prepare myself, as well. Why don't you go and see if the ronin has made it back yet? And please, do not get dirty before we even reach the palace."

Trying not to step on the bottom of my robes, I walked outside.

Okame was leaning against the railing when I stepped onto the veranda, and his brows shot up as he saw me. *"Sugoi,"* he exclaimed quietly, pushing himself off the post. "Yumeko-chan, you look…different. I didn't even recognize you."

I grinned at him. "You as well, Okame." The ronin had shaved, his goatee trim and neat instead of bristling over his chin, and his reddish-brown hair pulled behind him in a tight ponytail. His white hakama and brown haori jacket weren't fancy, but they were new and clean and well fitted. He didn't exactly look like a noble, but he didn't appear to be an aimlessly wandering ronin, either. "You look almost respectable."

"Bite your tongue," he retorted, and looked away, a tinge creeping up his neck. "I can't believe I have to parade around the emperor's palace pretending to be a samurai with a bunch of stuck-up aristocrats."

I cocked my head. "Why do you hate the samurai so much, Okame-san?" I asked. "Tatsumi said that ronin were samurai at one point, before they lost their master. What happened to yours?"

He gave me a crooked smile. "That is a long story for another day, Yumeko-chan. Let's just say there was a time where I fully believed in honor and duty and the code of Bushido. But that was years ago, when I was young, stupid and eager to prove myself."

"What happened?"

"I got slapped with the cruel hand of reality," the ronin said, smirking. "And I realized that the revered code of Bushido is nonsense. There is no honor in the world, especially among samurai. It just took my becoming a ronin to realize it."

I blinked at the underlying bitterness in his voice, wondering what had turned him into the jaded ronin he was now. "You'll have to tell me the story one day."

"I will. But right now, we have bigger concerns. Like making it through the emperor's party without being discovered as charlatans. Just remember," he went on, gently tapping my sleeve, dangling over the veranda, with a finger, "I'm no more a yojimbo than you are an onmyoji. And pretending to be either is a death sentence should anyone find out."

"I know," I said. Reika had explained it, in great detail, this morning. As soon as Okame left, she had dragged me into a room, slammed the door and proceeded to lecture me about being so reckless with my lies. I was lying to Daisuke about being an onmyoji, I was lying to Okame about being a peasant, and I was lying to the Kage demonslayer about being a normal human girl. I had gotten lucky so far, she'd told me, glowering like a small furious cat. Especially when traveling with the infamous Kage demonslayer.

And tonight, she went on, we would be inside the walls of the Imperial Palace, surrounded by nobles, samurai, aristocrats and the emperor himself. Where, if it were discovered we weren't who we claimed to be, it would mean execution for us all. This wasn't one of my kitsune games, Reika had warned. This was quite literally life or death. So I had better start taking it seriously.

I chewed my lip. She was right. I was dragging a lot of people into this crazy, made-up story, and the lies kept stacking on top of each other. Sooner or later, that tower was going to collapse. "Are you sure you want to come with us, Okame-san?" I asked, glancing up at the ronin. "You don't owe me anything, you know. You're free to leave if you want to."

"Are you kidding?" The ronin shot me his wolfish grin, eyes glinting. "Forget obligation, this is the most fun I've had in years. When I was a samurai, I was never important enough to be invited to the emperor's grand parties. It's going to be poetically ironic sauntering in there with a Taiyo, the proudest of the proud, and seeing the looks on their pinched, stuck-up faces."

"But it's dangerous. What happens if we're found out?"

"The danger is what makes it fun, Yumeko-chan," Okame said. "None of the nobles are going to ask if you're really an onmyoji—that would be the height of discourtesy. As long as you don't agree to tell any fortunes, divine the future or exorcise a demon, we should be fine." He shrugged and leaned against the railing, looking carefree. "So I wouldn't worry about it. The court monkeys will all be too busy preening, fawning over the emperor and trying to out-strut each other to pay much attention to us."

"There will be monkeys?" I blinked in shock. "Well, that will make it entertaining, at least. But monkeys are terribly messy, won't they be worried about that?"

"That was quite cruel, Okame-san," said a new voice, and Taiyo Daisuke came around the corner of the building. He wore a magnificent kimono of dark blue silk, with miniature golden suns patterned over the sleeves and down the front, and he held a colorful silk fan in both hands. His long white hair had been pulled behind his head, and glimmered against the dark silk of his robes. "You shouldn't fill Yumeko-san's head with such lies. At least a few of them will be too busy destroying a rival's reputation with gossip, or setting up advantageous marriages, to be doing much fawning."

Glancing up at me, he smiled and lowered his head in a respectful bow. "Lady Yumeko," he said in a solemn voice, "I feel I must apologize again for my boorish behavior the night we met. It is fortunate that the sakura blossoms have already faded and passed away, for surely they would weep at having to compete with your beauty."

"Um…" I wasn't quite sure how to respond to that; no one had ever paid me such a compliment before. Fortunately at that moment, Reika slid open the door and joined us on the veranda, saving me from stammering a reply in a most unnoble-like fashion. The miko still wore the red hakama and white haori of the shrine maidens, but her hair was up and had been decorated with ribbons and tiny bells. Two other miko appeared behind her, similarly dressed, and both of them gaped at the stunning aristocrat, their mouths slightly open. Daisuke, likely used to such reactions, politely ignored them.

"Stop that." Reika swatted one of the miko with a sleeve, making her jump. "Both of you. You look like a pair of gasping carp. Do not embarrass me tonight. Taiyo-san," she continued, turning and bowing to Daisuke, making the golden bells in her hair jingle. "Forgive this inconvenience to your valuable time. I cannot express my gratitude enough."

"Not at all, Reika-san," Daisuke replied. "I'm glad to be of help. And a change in the court scenery will be good for everyone. Shall we go? The sun is setting, and it is a long walk to the palace."

"A moment, please," said the shrine maiden, stopping us. "There is one more who will be coming."

Reaching into her sleeve, she withdrew an ofuda, the white strip of paper used to focus holy magic. The kanji for *loyalty* was written down the surface, the same ofuda she'd brandished at me when we first met. Closing her eyes, the shrine maiden began chanting something under her breath, and the air around her began to stir with power.

"Guardian of the Hayate shrine," I heard her whisper. "Most loyal of protectors, come to me."

The wind around her scattered in all directions, rattling the branches overhead. We waited, holding our breath.

A furry creature trotted around the building and came to a stop at the bottom of the stairs. It was a dog, small and lanky, with triangular ears, reddish-orange fur with a white belly, and a bushy tail curled tightly over its hindquarters. A crimson rope collar hung around its neck, a golden bell dangling from the very center.

*Inu!* I fought the sudden urge to leap back, to sprint down the veranda and duck into one of the rooms, closing the door between us. I'd never liked dogs, and the feeling seemed to be mutual. Once, when I was wandering the grounds outside the temple, a pair of village dogs, lean and ravenous-looking, had spotted me and given chase. None of my tricks had worked on them; they'd ignored the images of roaring bears and fleeing rabbits, as if somehow knowing they weren't real. To escape my pursuers, I'd ended up climbing a tree, where I'd stayed until nightfall, when Denga had come looking for me and chased them off.

"Kit-kitsune?" Okame exclaimed, making me jump and look back at him. The ronin was staring at the dog with a bemused expression on his face. "The guardian of this shrine is a kitsune?"

"It's not a fox," I told him, relieved and just a tiny bit annoyed. "It's a dog. Honestly, Okame, it doesn't look anything like a fox."

"This is Chu," Reika said calmly, making the dog look up at her and wag its tail. "He is the guardian of the Hayate shrine. One half of them, anyway." Her eyes clouded over, a furrow wrinkling her smooth brow. "Ko, the other protector, disappeared the night Master Jiro left. I think she was either summoned by the head priest, or sensed that he was in danger and went to find him, because neither of them has returned."

"He is rather small for his type," Daisuke said, in a voice that was trying to be kind. Okame snorted.

"Small? He's a runt. How the hell is this lint ball the guardian of anything, unless he protects the shrine from sparrows and rats?"

Chu laced back his ears and growled at the ronin, baring a set of sharp white teeth.

Reika sighed. "This is the form that allows him to follow

me into the city," the shrine maiden told the ronin. "In fact, when he is wearing this body, he is hardly noticeable at all. He will even be able to slip past the gates of the Imperial Palace with little to no attention. One of his many talents—people simply don't notice that he is there." A slightly evil smile curled her lips as she gazed at the ronin. "Chu doesn't hold grudges, but were I you, I would think twice about insulting him. His true form is much more…impressive."

Okame raised a skeptical eyebrow, but didn't say anything else. Chu rose gracefully to his feet and trotted away, as if taking the lead, and we followed him across the yard and down the steps of the Hayate shrine. As we passed under the torii gate at the entrance, I noticed that both stone pedestals were empty.

"Oh, Yumeko-san, before I forget…" Daisuke turned to me, smiling, as we stepped onto the streets of the Wind district. "I spoke to one of my uncles about you," he began, "and he was very interested that an onmyoji would be attending the party tonight."

"Oh? That was nice. Your uncle sounds like a very kind man."

"Yes, and he will be quite pleased to see you. You see, a few months ago, there was a terrible scandal surrounding the emperor's last onmyoji—rumors of treason and blood magic, whispers of assassination. It was a horrible mess. In the end the onmyoji and his assistants were executed, but the position of court diviner has yet to be filled. My uncle thinks the emperor will be delighted to have an onmyoji tell his fortune." Daisuke's brilliant smile grew even wider, even as I realized what he was implying, and stifled the urge to pin back my ears in alarm. "If all goes well tonight, Yumeko-san, you might have an audience with the emperor of Iwagoto himself."

Despite my nervousness, it was impossible not to be awed by the splendor of the Imperial Palace. Sitting atop its peak, the golden structure caught the last fading rays of light and glimmered like a miniature sun itself. As we drew closer, I caught glimpses of gilded roof ornaments: golden fish, dragons and phoenixes topped the sweeping corners, silhouetted against the sky and gazing down on us mere mortals, far below.

As we approached the enormous gates, I spotted a pair of samurai near the entrance, dressed in armor and holding their yari spears upright. I worried that they would step forward, angling those spears to block our path. But they didn't move, though the older one did turn his head when Daisuke walked up, a grin curving his mouth below his moustache.

"Oh, Daisuke-sama," he called in a gruff, almost affectionate voice. "When did you get back? How did your pilgrimage to Sagimura go?"

"Very well, Fujio-san," Daisuke answered. "I am glad I took the time to travel. It was…very enlightening."

Behind him, Okame snorted. "I'll bet," he muttered, and was swatted on the arm by Reika. The guard's attention shifted to her and the other three shrine maidens.

"Ah," he said, nodding once. "Entertainers for the emperor's party, I presume. It has been a while since we have had a kagura dance at the palace." His gaze fell on me, taking in my robes, my peaked cap, and his brows lifted. "Is that…an onmyoji, Daisuke-sama? Fortune does seem to favor you, doesn't it? His Highness will be thrilled."

Daisuke only smiled as we passed the guards and stepped

through the gates of the Imperial Palace, but my heart, which had calmed down since we'd left the shrine, started pounding again. Through the gate was an enormous open courtyard with more samurai wandering about. Beyond that, over the tops of the trees and past what seemed like a labyrinth of walls, gates and parapets, the Imperial Palace loomed against the sky like a glittering golden mountain.

Without thinking, I started toward the distant palace, but paused when Daisuke called me back. Turning, I saw him and the others heading away from the castle, toward one of the gates on the far wall of the courtyard.

"We're not going to the palace itself, Yumeko-san," he explained, once he realized where I was walking. "The party is being held in the castle gardens, over there." He gestured to the far wall, where a faint glow could be seen over a large and bushy tree line. "This way, if you would. We're almost there."

I felt a momentary twinge that I wouldn't be seeing the golden palace up close, but it faded as I passed beneath the gate and entered the imperial gardens.

My first thought was that I had stepped into an extremely well-groomed forest. Upon further inspection, I realized even that was wrong. Every tree, every bush, rock, flower and pebble, seemed to have been placed with the utmost care and deliberation. All the bushes were trimmed into symmetrical shapes, all the trees standing straight and tall, their branches at perfect, orderly angles. Not a leaf or petal or scrap of bark lay on the grass or blew across the lawn; even as I watched, a man whom I could only assume was a groundskeeper paused at a chrysanthemum bush and plucked an offending flower from one of the branches before stuffing it into a bag and hurrying on.

It was a beautiful garden, I would admit, stunning and awe-inspiring. And about as lifeless as a sakura painting on a hanging wall scroll. There was no natural growth, none of the joyful chaos of a real forest. The emperor's garden felt like I did at the moment, stuffed into an elegant but uncomfortable robe meant to impress everyone who saw it, wishing I could take it off and move around naturally.

"Beautiful, is it not?" Daisuke murmured, gazing around with a serene smile on his face. "Everything here is designed with such precision. The castle employs a hundred servants and fifty master gardeners to keep everything clean and perfect."

"It is nice," I agreed. "But it would be terribly difficult for anything to live here. The gardeners would have a nervous breakdown if a single rabbit got into the flowers."

The path through the gardens was well lit by strings of chochin lanterns, and we followed the bobbing orange lights until we reached yet another gate where a stern-looking samurai eyed Okame and me before turning to the noble in front.

"Taiyo-sama," he said with a bow. "Please forgive me, but the emperor's party is by invitation only. I know your family is already within, but I don't recognize your companions. I must ask that they show me their invitations, or I cannot allow them to pass."

"I am allowing them," Daisuke said easily. "This is Yumeko-san, a respected onmyoji from the Earth lands, and her yojimbo, Hino Okame. They are here as my guests."

The samurai grunted, looking over Daisuke's shoulder at me, before shifting his gaze to Reika and the two shrine maidens behind us. "And what about them?"

Reika and the others sank into a formal bow. "Please excuse us," the miko said. "We are from the Hayate shrine, here to perform tonight's kagura dance for the emperor."

The guard frowned. "I didn't hear anything about an onmyoji attending," he said stubbornly, glaring at me again. "She's awfully young. I've never heard of her, certainly. How do we know she's experienced enough to see the emperor?" His jaw tightened, and he jerked his chin at me. "Who have you served before, girl? Which lords have you attended?"

"Excuse me," said a voice, saving me a reply. A man came forward, thin and disheveled-looking, his clothes rumpled and his hair standing on end. He wasn't a samurai or a noble; his clothes, though not as tattered and threadbare as some peasants, were quite plain. His robe was dusty, and he smelled of sawdust and wood shavings.

Seeing the newcomer, the samurai immediately stepped forward to block his path, momentarily forgetting about us. "Halt. How did you get in here? State your buisness, now."

The man sniffed and drew himself up. "I'm looking for someone," he said in a reedy yet confident voice. "I have permission to be here. I need to speak to the magistrate now."

Daisuke brushed my arm. "Come," he said softly, as the samurai stated again, in a louder voice, that the area was off-limits. The noble looked troubled, as if wanting to speak to the newcomer, but he continued to usher us away. "We do not need to be present for this, nor do I wish to shame a samurai who was only doing his job. Let us leave him to his duties and slip away quietly."

Reluctantly, I turned from the man, who was now arguing with the guard in a high-pitched voice and waving his twig-like arms. The samurai didn't even glance at us as we slipped through the gate and melted into the shadows beyond. Okame caught my gaze and grinned, but I couldn't quite return it.

Past the guard, we followed a bamboo wall, turned a corner and entered a large open area on the edge of a beautifully scenic lake. A red-and-gold pagoda sat on an island in the center, connected to a bridge that arched gracefully over the water. Shamisen music drifted through the air, played by an older woman kneeling on a rug, who plucked at the strings with practiced ease. Overhead, the individual cords of lanterns were a ceiling of floating lights, casting a bright, hazy glow over the throngs of people milling about. For a moment, I could only stare in awe at the sea of colorful robes, each one brighter and more extravagant than the last. The women wore many layered kimonos, so intricate and heavy-looking that I wondered how they could move. Some of the men wore hakama and jackets with stiff, flared shoulders, but several of them were clad in robes only slightly less elaborate than the women's.

I felt a nudge, as Okame stepped close and nodded across the lawn to where a platform had been set up in front of a folding screen. Seated on a cushion before a lacquered table, surrounded by attractive women and imposing samurai, a handsome man in brilliant yellow-and-white robes sipped from a golden cup.

I swallowed. "Is that…?" I whispered unnecessarily.

"Taiyo no Genjiro the one hundred and forty-third," the ronin murmured in my ear. "The Son of Heaven, and the emperor of Iwagoto."

"Daisuke-san!"

A man came toward us, weaving around individuals and through clumps of nobles as he did. He had white hair and a sharply pointed goatee, and waved to the noble as he approached. "Uncle Morimasa," Daisuke said, and turned to me with a slight bow. "Please excuse me, Yumeko-san. I will be right back."

I nodded, and the noble strode away, smiling at his relative. But he hadn't gone more than a few paces before a pair of noblewomen swept up to him, blocking his path. Daisuke's polite smile never wavered, and he looked wholly interested in what they were saying even as he smoothly edged around them, only to find his path blocked by another. By the looks of the crowds converging on him, it seemed he might be a while.

Moving to the edge of the lawn, I stood beside a perfectly groomed azalea tree and gazed around, wondering which of these elegant, fluttering humans could be Lady Satomi. I also wondered if, somewhere among the sea of robes, Tatsumi was there, hidden by a spell or a disguise. I imagined him in an elegant black kimono, patterned in purple and gold, his violet eyes shining as they met mine through the crowd.

"You're blushing, Yumeko-chan," Okame remarked, grinning as he bent down to stare at my face. "What are *you* thinking about?"

"N-nothing!" I turned away, feeling my cheeks flame, hearing the ronin snicker behind me. "I was just…*ano*… thinking of robes, and how mine is very hot, and how nice it would feel to take it off. And…that didn't come out how I wanted it to at all, stop laughing, Okame-san." I didn't dare turn around to face him. "*Baka*. Be serious. We're supposed to be looking for Lady Satomi…"

And then, one of the women seated closest to the emperor raised her head and looked right at me.

Behind my robes, forgotten and unnoticed by everyone, Chu began to growl. I suddenly felt itchy, like insects were crawling around in my sleeves, scuttling over my skin. The woman held my gaze, a faint smile gracing her full, painted lips. She was very beautiful, standing out among her fellow nobles, her crimson-and-black kimono hanging a bit more loosely in some areas than others. Not blatant or obvious, but suggestive.

Something squirmed through my hair at the base of my skull. Frowning, I reached up and grabbed something long and thin, pulling it from my head.

A red-and-black centipede wriggled between my fingers, coiling back to bite me. I threw it away with a violent jerk, barely managing not to yelp. The insect landed in the grass and was instantly pounced upon by Chu, who snatched it between his jaws and shook it like a rat. Okame, his laughter forgotten, muttered a curse.

Heart pounding, I glanced back at the woman, who was smiling at something the emperor said and not looking at me anymore. But I knew she was responsible for the unwanted visitor, and an icy chill raced up my spine as, quite suddenly, everything came together. *This* was the person responsible for everything. The giant centipede, the undead crows, the demons that destroyed the temple; it was all because of *her*. The unseen hand behind it all. The blood witch in the emperor's court.

I trembled, not knowing if it was from fear or rage, and felt Reika move beside me, also gazing at the red-clad woman. Chu was still growling quietly near my feet, though no one around us seemed to notice the dog. "Well," Reika said softly, "judging from Chu and how white your face has gone, I have a feeling we might have found our Lady Satomi."

I nodded. The woman glanced my way again for just a moment, a smug triumph shining from her eyes, and I clenched my fists. If this was Lady Satomi, I also had the feeling that she wasn't going to make things easy for us.

"Yumeko-san."

Daisuke returned, the taller man at his side, both smiling at me as they approached. I wrenched my gaze from Lady Satomi and turned to face the nobles. "Yumeko-san," Daisuke said again, "this is my uncle, Taiyo Morimasa."

"Hello," I said to the older Taiyo. Then, remembering where I was, bowed low and said, "It is an honor to make your acquaintance."

"The honor is mine, Yumeko-san," Morimasa replied. He looked much like Daisuke, except his hair was in a warrior's bun atop his head, and he had a neatly trimmed goatee. "You honor us with your very presence. We have not had an onmyoji at court for quite some time. Forgive my impudence, but your name is unknown to me. Which master did you serve under? I had heard rumors that the great Tsuki no Seimei was holding a contest to choose a new apprentice."

"I…did not serve a master," I said, groping for a reply. "I just…um…had the talent for it, I suppose. I learned on my own."

"Amazing," the older man said. "And at such a young age. Truly remarkable. Well, that decides it—you must perform for His Highness tonight. It would be a great honor to have such a talented onmyoji take the stage before all the court. What do you say, Yumeko-san? Will you show us your talent?"

I felt trapped, like a rabbit huddled in a corner with

wolves closing in on all sides. Okame and Reika looked just as uncomfortable, though neither were jumping in with excuses. This was not a request. Even I, with my limited knowledge of Iwagoto's society and politics, knew that a chance to serve the emperor was the greatest honor one could receive, and that turning him down was the most unforgivable of insults. Even if my refusal did not result in imprisonment or execution, our quest would end right here. If we wanted to find Master Jiro, I had to keep the farce going.

Though I had no idea what I was going to do.

"Certainly, Taiyo-san," I told Morimasa, making Okame start and stare at me. "It would be an honor."

"Yumeko-chan!" the ronin burst out, then seemed to catch himself. "Er...please excuse me," he told Morimasa with a quick bow. "I'm her yojimbo, so it's my job to worry about her. She can be rather reckless at times. Yumeko-chan," he went on in a low voice, staring at me rather wide-eyed. "Are you *sure* you can do this?" With the undertone of *what the hell are you doing?* "If you mess up in front of the emperor, it affects us all."

"Your yojimbo might have a point," Reika said in a voice of resigned disapproval. "Though for this request, I don't know what else you can do but accept."

"Of course you must accept," Daisuke broke in, looking both puzzled and slightly offended. "Meeting the emperor, performing for him and the entire court—there is no greater honor."

"Exactly," I told the ronin, and forced a smile. "You heard Daisuke-san. When will there ever be another chance to meet the emperor? Don't worry, I know what I'm doing." *I hope.*

Okame looked dubious, but I turned away and faced

Morimasa again. "Please forgive the interruption, Taiyo-san," I told the frowning noble. "As I said before, it will be an honor to perform for His Highness tonight."

"Wonderful!" He beamed. "His Excellence will be delighted. If you would please follow me."

With a last encouraging smile at the concerned ronin and shrine maiden, I stepped forward and followed Morimasa across the yard.

Nobles stared at me, watching with amusement, curiosity and suspicion as I passed. A few sneered or smirked behind their fans, their scorn plain to see. Perhaps they saw through my onmyoji disguise, or perhaps I was not dressed fancily enough. I tried to ignore them and think of what I was going to say to the emperor, though the pounding of my heart and the frantic swirling in my stomach made it hard to concentrate.

"Wait here a moment," Morimasa said, pausing in the shadow of a cluster of trees a distance from the emperor's dais. "When the time is right, I will announce you. As you hear your name, come forward and present yourself to His Highness, but stay at least twenty feet from the edge of the platform. Do you understand?"

"Yes."

He nodded and turned away, walking toward the platform and the men and women clustered around it. I couldn't see Lady Satomi, as she was on the emperor's other side, but thankfully, she couldn't see me, either.

I took a deep breath to calm my nerves, just as a hand clamped over my mouth from behind and yanked me back into the trees.

"It's me," said a low, familiar voice, stopping the surge

of kitsune-bi to my fingertips. "I'm letting you go, so don't alert everyone here by screaming."

"Tatsumi!" I whispered, whirling on him as he released me. "You scared me! Why are you…?"

I blinked and trailed off. For the Tatsumi before me was not the Kage samurai I had traveled with from the Silent Winds temple. He was clad completely in black, except for a ragged crimson scarf that seemed to float behind him in the breeze. Instead of sandals, he wore split-toed boots that stopped just below the knee, bracers on his forearms and a sleeveless, unmarked jacket that was a much tighter fit than his regular haori. A mask covered his mouth and jaw, obstructing half his face, though the eyes above the cloth were the same, a cold, piercing violet.

"What are you doing, Yumeko?" Tatsumi asked, his voice soft but intense. His gaze seemed to burn in the darkness.

"Um…" I glanced around to make sure no one could see us. The air shimmered as I turned my head, and I could suddenly feel the dark, cool touch of Tatsumi's Shadow magic, surrounding us. "Performing for the emperor of Iwagoto?"

"You're *not* an onmyoji." Tatsumi's eyes narrowed. "You have no magic. Talking to the kami is not the same as telling fortunes and divining the future, which is what the emperor will expect. If you're exposed as a charlatan, you'll be executed."

"I know, but what else can I do, Tatsumi?" I whispered. "I can't refuse the emperor."

"I can take you out of here." Tatsumi stepped closer. "Right now. No one will see us—we'll use the same spell we did in the gaki village. When it's safe, I'll come back to look for Master Jiro. We don't need to talk to the Satomi woman. I can get into places most people cannot."

"What about the others?"

"I don't care about the others." Tatsumi's voice was flat. "My mission is to get us to the Steel Feather temple. Nothing else matters. If you are caught and executed, the mission ends here."

His hand rose, the back of his knuckles coming very close to my cheek. I looked into his eyes and saw conflict burning within.

"Tatsumi..."

"You cannot die, Yumeko." His hand didn't move any closer, but he didn't pull back, either, and his voice was very soft. "We both made a promise, to find the Steel Feather temple together. I need you to show me the way. The mission isn't over yet."

"I'll be all right." Carefully I reached up and took his hand. He flinched as our skin touched and then, almost tentatively, his fingers curled around mine. I met his gaze and smiled. "I know what to do, Tatsumi. Trust me."

He held my gaze a moment longer, brow furrowed and eyes shadowed, then nodded once. I backed out of the trees, feeling the delicate strands of magic fray apart as I moved, and turned toward the emperor's platform.

Taiyo Morimasa met my gaze, his eyes widening in relief, as if he had been looking for me and hadn't been able to see me until now. Gesturing impatiently, he waved me forward. Resisting the urge to look back at the trees, I took a deep breath, lifted my chin and walked toward the platform and the emperor of Iwagoto.

# 29

## The Emperor's Fortune

*I* watched the girl walk away, her stride confident, toward the emperor in gold who waited on his platform, surrounded by nobles and samurai. The eyes of the court followed, all gazes on the slight figure in billowing red and white, her long braid swaying behind her. She did not look frightened or even tense, but there was an unfamiliar sensation in the pit of my stomach that compelled me to make her vanish. To drop down, cover us both in darkness and spirit her away. Or, if that wasn't possible, to draw Kamigoroshi and slaughter everyone who was a threat, nobles, samurai and emperor alike, to save the girl striding so boldly toward the person who could order her death.

I could still feel her hand, her soft fingers curled around my palm, and clenched my fist against my leg. Yumeko could not die tonight. Letting her walk away was foolish. I didn't know what she was planning, if she even had a plan, but I'd said I would trust her. A peasant girl with no magic, who had grown up in a temple sheltered from the rest of the world, who was brave and unassuming and clever but ultimately no onmyoji—I was letting her face the most powerful man in Iwagoto with nothing but the assurance that she would be fine. I saw the ronin, the shrine maiden and the noble press forward with the rest of the crowd, forming a semicircle behind the girl, and my chest tightened. For the first time, I wished I could be there, in the crowd, instead of lurking at the edge of the light, hiding in the shadows.

*Great Kami*, I found myself thinking, *watch over her. Tamafuku, God of Luck, if you can lend your aid to one person tonight, let it be her.*

Yumeko stopped her approach about fifteen feet from the emperor's dais, sank to her knees and bowed low with her hands and forehead touching the ground. It was clumsy; her posture wasn't quite rigid enough and her fingers weren't at the right position, but at least she had the general idea of how to behave when facing the ruler of the country. And it appeared to satisfy the emperor, for he smiled and held out a billowing golden sleeve.

"Onmyoji Yumeko," he said in clear, high tones. "Welcome to the Palace of the Sun."

"His Highness honors me," Yumeko replied, sitting up slowly. "I am not worthy to be here, but I will try my best to please."

I sensed disapproval and scorn emanating from the watching crowd, from the nobles and aristocrats in particular. Yumeko's common birth was suddenly painfully clear in the way she spoke, without nuance or the flattering, flowery phrases of the court. I had the sudden image of dropping into their midst and cutting them all into bloody ribbons, and I wasn't quite sure if those were Hakaimono's thoughts, or my own.

"My advisor tells me you learned onmyodo without a master," the emperor went on, and a murmur went through the crowd. "Is that correct? You have truly mastered the ancient knowledge on your own?"

"Yes, Your Highness. That is correct." She did not give any more explanation, though it was clear the court was waiting for it.

"Remarkable," the emperor exclaimed, sitting back. "Truly extraordinary. Of course you must show us your talents, Yumeko-san." He raised both arms, golden sleeves billowing like sails. "I give you permission to tell my fortune," he announced grandly. "What do the ages hold for the greatest empire in the world? Peer into the future and tell the court what you see."

A hush fell over the garden. Yumeko hesitated, then rose slowly, dramatically, to stand tall before the emperor. "The future," she said, her voice echoing over the crowd, "is an ever changing stream. Every choice, every decision we make, sends it down a different path. To glimpse the fortune of another is to see hundreds of possibilities at once. It is never a task to be taken lightly or in haste." She raised her arms, as if drawing on the power of the kami, and a sudden wind caught her hair and robes, billowing them outward. "Let us see what the future holds for you, Your Highness."

The crowd was motionless now, hanging on her every word. The emperor himself leaned forward, hands on his knees, staring at the robed figure before him. For a moment, I forgot this was Yumeko, the peasant girl I'd rescued from the Silent Winds temple. Standing in the center of the yard, arms outstretched and the light shining over her hair and bright crimson robes, she really did look like a revered onmyoji, shimmering with power as she prepared to divine the future of Iwagoto's emperor.

Yumeko brought her hands together, cupping them below her chin, two fingers raised in a familiar gesture. She closed her eyes, and the court seemed to hold its breath. For a moment, the girl was silent. Not a breath of air stirred the yard; all attention was focused on the robed figure standing alone before the emperor.

"Taiyo no Genjiro." Yumeko's voice, quiet as it was, made several nobles jump. "Lord of the Palace of the Sun." She paused, then said, very clearly, "There is an intruder in your garden."

The emperor straightened, as did many of the nobles and samurai. A few bushi started looking around, hands on the hilts of their swords, as murmurs began rippling through the crowd. I crouched low in the shadows, as Hakaimono stirred, whispering that I should strike her down before it was too late.

*Would she really expose me?* Kage Masao's question about trust came back to me, and my blood chilled. *Would you sell me out tonight, Yumeko, to save yourself?*

"It is very close," Yumeko went on, her voice quiet and somber. "Lurking in the shadows. Watching you and your guests as we speak." A few of the women gasped and pressed closer to each other, and one samurai half drew his sword. My hand slipped to Kamigoroshi, fingers hovering over the hilt, as Yumeko continued.

"It is very cunning, this intruder," the girl said. "Silent, unnoticed, it has already left a trail of destruction behind it, and if allowed to roam free, will continue to bring ruin to everything it touches."

"Where?" the emperor gasped, half rising from his seat. "Where is this intruder?"

"It is close," Yumeko repeated, half turning in place. I tensed as the girl spun toward me, but she continued to turn, away from where I crouched in the shadows. "It is..." She paused, raising a hand toward a patch of bushes near the edge of the light. "There."

The whole court turned, staring at the spot she pointed to. For a moment, nothing moved or dared to breathe. The court was frozen in rapt fascination, unable to move or look away. At the base of a sakura tree, a section of bushes rustled loudly, drawing horrified gasps from the closest spectators.

A small brown rabbit hopped from the brush into the open.

An exhalation of breath went through the crowd, though the women closest to the "intruder" let out tiny shrieks before they realized what it was. The rabbit sat up, twitching its ears as it observed the humans, who stared back in confusion and shock.

A shout echoed over the garden. A man in simple clothes, dirt smudging his hands and grass stains on his knees, rushed forward, his eyes going wide as he stared at the creature on the lawn.

*"Usagi!"*

Ignoring the staring nobles, the man—most likely a groundskeeper—lunged at the rabbit, diving forward with hands outstretched. The usagi instantly spun and flashed into the bushes, and the human landed on his stomach in the grass, plunging his hands into the branches. Digging through the leaves, the gardener searched frantically around the bush, before coming to realize he was being watched.

Spinning around, the now pale groundskeeper blinked at the equally stunned court, then pressed his forehead to the grass in the lowest of bows.

"Please forgive!" he cried, but at that moment, the rabbit streaked past him in a tan blur. With a howl, the gardener leaped upright, stick in hand, and chased it to the edge of the trees, where both vanished into the darkness beyond.

Silence fell. Everyone continued to stare into the shadows, as if not knowing what to do. I spared a glance at Yumeko and saw her standing quietly in front of the dais, a small, triumphant smile on her face.

A slow clapping shattered the stillness, making several nobles jump. The emperor rose to his feet, bringing his hands together, a wide smile breaking over his beardless face.

The rest of the court erupted into applause. It swept through the air and swelled above the trees, as the crowd turned as one to face the girl in the center of the garden. Yumeko bowed, humbly accepting their recognition, as the sound of success rose above the trees and scattered to the winds.

# 30

## The Viper in Silk

*I* let the applause wash over me, listened to it rise and swell, and allowed myself a tiny sigh of relief. Who knew that such a small thing, an illusionary rabbit at the right moment, could charm an emperor? Of course, the appearance of the gardener had not been planned, but his reaction had certainly helped convince the court that what they were seeing was real. I hoped the man would be all right, that the appearance of a single rabbit within the emperor's pristine gardens would not get him punished, but it was too late to regret that now.

*Denga, if you could see me now*, I thought, smiling as I met the gazes of Daisuke, Okame and Reika in the crowd. *My good-for-nothing fox trickery just fooled the most powerful person in all of Iwagoto, and his entire court. I've come a long way from making the teapot dance around the room.*

"Brilliant!" As the applause died down, the emperor stepped off his platform, beaming in my direction. "Astonishing. What remarkable talent, Yumeko-san. Would you consider using it in service to the country?" My brows rose, and he smiled, gesturing over the trees toward the palace, glimmering gold against the night sky. "There is an opening in my court for a royal onmyoji. I could certainly use someone with your skills."

*Oops. Well, I suppose there's such a thing as doing* too *well.* I thought quickly, knowing that refusing the emperor, even now, could have terrible repercussions. "His Highness honors me," I said with a low bow. "I am grateful for the offer, but there is a…very important task that I must complete, a vow to fulfill, before I can accept."

"Ah. Of course." The emperor nodded; even he would not dare suggest one break a promise and risk the dishonor that came with it. "Well, when you are finished with your task, consider returning to the palace, Yumkeo-san. You are always welcome within my court."

I bowed. "His Highness is too kind."

"My last onmyoji told me of the coming of the Great Dragon," the emperor went on, making my stomach leap to my throat. "I thought the story was simply an ancient myth, but he was certain he saw the Dragon rising in one of his visions." The emperor frowned. "Sadly, he was discovered to be a practicioner of blood magic and executed, and the words of a blood mage are tainted and cannot be trusted. But it would please me to have another onmyoji in my court, to inform me if the Harbinger is indeed approaching, and what I can do to claim its power for my own."

I felt a crawling sensation under my robes, and looked up into Lady Satomi's dark eyes, glittering with hostility over the emperor's shoulder. Only for a moment, before she turned to the emperor and smiled, all traces of menace vanishing beneath a beautiful porcelain mask.

"My lord," she crooned, gazing at him from beneath long, thick lashes. "The moon is rising. Would you not like to view it from the lake pavilion? The water is very clear tonight—you should be able to see his reflection from above and below."

"Ah, of course. Everyone!" the emperor called, clapping his hands and bringing the court's attention to him. "Lord Moon has begun his journey across the heavens. Let us retire to the edge of the lake, so that we may wish him well. I am eager to hear the fine poems you have composed to honor his journey tonight."

The crowd dispersed, heading in the direction of the lake. Including the emperor, who seemed to forget about me as soon as he stepped away, his yojimbo falling into step around him. Lady Satomi, however, did not leave, but continued to watch me, a faint smile on her face. None of the other nobles, guards or samurai seemed to notice her; all continued to move toward the lake edge, leaving us alone.

"Well." The woman's cruel gaze raked me up and down, spreading the sensation of dirty claw marks across my skin. "That was amusing."

I stifled the sudden wave of panic, feeling the weight of the scroll under my robes, wondering if Satomi could somehow sense it. If she would summon an oni, right here, to crush me like an egg. I shivered, then took a breath to loosen the cold knot in my stomach and looked Satomi in the eye.

"The...the emperor thought so."

"The emperor is a child who is easily impressed with illusion and cheap tricks. He does not know the difference between a charlatan and true power." One corner of a pouty red lip curled up in a smirk. "You will not find me so gullible."

I felt fox magic surge to life and clenched my fists to keep kitsune-bi from springing to my fingertips. "You've been following us," I accused in a whisper. "Those dead birds are yours, aren't they?" She raised an elegant, mocking eyebrow, and I bit back a growl, knowing I couldn't fly at her and force the truth from her pouty red lips. "You've been watching me and Tatsumi ever since we left the forest," I said in a low voice. "Were you the one who sent the demons to the temple?"

"What an awful thing to imply." Lady Satomi touched a hand to her chest, as if appalled. "Certainly you would not expect one of my station to engage in such things. Dead birds? Demons?" One corner of her lip curled, and her voice dropped to a menacing whisper. "Blood magic is punishable by death, little fox. As is lying to the emperor of Iwagoto. Your little performance worked only because I allowed it. This is a court of puppets, and I manipulate all the strings. Who do you think they will believe, if certain things come to light?"

"Satomi-san."

Daisuke's voice echoed behind me, even as I fought to hold my ground, to not step back from this evil woman. Lady Satomi's malicious look vanished, as she smiled at the noble who joined us, switching faces so quickly that she seemed to cast off a mask. Okame and the shrine maiden appeared beside me as well, and a tiny, barely audible growl rippled up from the ground, as Chu took one look at the woman and bared his teeth. Lady Satomi didn't even glance at the dog.

"Good evening, Taiyo-san," she greeted, bowing to

Daisuke, who nodded in return. "Did you see the remarkable performance of our talented onmyoji?" She turned her smile on me, and it looked completely genuine. "I cannot remember the last time I was so amazed. I could hardly believe it was real."

"Lady Yumeko is indeed talented," Daisuke agreed, with a small smile in my direction. "It is an honor to have her here." He turned back to Satomi, and his words became forcibly polite. "Satomi-san, if we could trouble you but for a moment. It will not take long."

"Of course, Taiyo-san," Lady Satomi said. "It is my pleasure. What can I do for the son of the honorable Hironobu-sama?"

Reika stepped forward, her scowl indicating she was not fooled in the slightest. "Master Jiro, of the Hayate shrine," she said without preamble. "Does this name mean anything to you?"

"Hmm? Should it?"

"You called him here," Reika went on, as anger flickered through me, knowing the woman was playing with us. "Three days ago, he received a summons from the palace to come and meet with you. He never made it back to the Hayate shrine. That was the last anyone saw of him."

"Master Jiro," Lady Satomi said thoughtfully, as if trying to remember. "Master Jiro. Oh, yes, I remember now. I called him to the palace for tea, and to answer a few simple qustions I had. Horrible, offensive little man. He was quite rude to me." She smiled faintly at Reika. "Aren't priests supposed to be the pillars of humility and wisdom? I found him terribly wearisome and repulsive, to tell you the truth."

The miko regarded the other woman without expression,

refusing to be goaded. "Where is he?" she asked, her voice remarkably calm. Lady Satomi's lips curled even further.

"Oh, he's safe," she replied, waving her fan in an offhand manner. "He is fairly close by, actually. Though I'm afraid you'll never find him without me. Even your lurking little shinobi watching us from the shadows will not be able to uncover his location."

I drew in a sharp breath, making Satomi turn her smile on me. "Did you think I was unaware that the Kage demon-slayer had infiltrated the palace?" she purred, her voice very low. "Nothing happens in this court without my knowledge. I know he is listening to us right now, and if he strikes me down, you will never find your precious Master Jiro, and he will never complete his mission."

"Then you'll take us to him," Okame said, and she raised a brow in his direction. "Right now."

"Interesting." Lady Satomi gazed at the ronin like she might a particularly obstinate dog. "And what, may I ask, do you think you can do to me? Attack me here, in the emperor's garden?" She chuckled. "With the exception of Taiyo-san, who would certainly face a terrible blow to his family's honor and reputation, the lot of you would be executed before dawn."

"There are other ways," Reika said. "I'm sure the emperor would be very interested to hear—"

"Oh, *do* be careful of what you accuse me, girl." The woman's voice was like silk threads that could slice open your throat. "We wouldn't want *other* secrets to suddenly be revealed." She looked in my direction, the threat in her eyes perfectly clear. "Would we?

"Besides, you didn't let me finish," Lady Satomi went on, her lips pulling down in a pout. "You see, I *could* refuse, and watch the lot of you strut and threaten like tiny male sparrows. But as amusing as that would be, I know I will be hounded for the rest of the night. If not by you, then by the Kage demonslayer, who I am sure is listening to this conversation. I do not wish to draw the ire of the Shadow Clan's immortal daimyo, nor do I wish to watch my back every time I stroll down the halls of the palace. That would grow very tiresome." She sighed. "So, yes, I will take you to your priest. I have no further use for the old fool, anyway. In fact, you'd be doing me a favor, taking him off my hands." She raised an elegant white hand, indicating the sweeping landscape. "You wouldn't mind a quick stroll across the garden, would you? It is quite lovely in the moonlight."

Daisuke narrowed his eyes, and glanced to where the emperor and his guests had gathered at the edge of the lake. "The emperor's concubine is not permitted to venture off alone, late at night," he said in a voice of chilly politeness. "Especially with a group of strangers. There will be speculation, rumors at the very least. Will you not need an escort, Lady Satomi?"

"You are adorable," Lady Satomi purred. "Such a good boy, to be concerned about staining my honor." She tittered, making Reika's scowl darken. "Worry not, Taiyo-san. The emperor and his guests will not miss me. They will not notice I am gone. Even if they do, tonight's sake is especially strong—they will forget all about it tomorrow.

"So," she continued, drawing back. "Shall we go? I assume you are eager to see if the priest is all right. Follow me, my precious ducklings. I will show you where he is."

Warily, we followed the woman around the edge of the lake, away from the emperor and the rest of the court, heading deeper into the garden. As the shadows closed around us, I found myself scanning the bushes, searching for movement, for a ripple of darkness that didn't quite belong. I wondered if Tatsumi was trailing us, keeping an eye on his prey as we moved through the trees, farther from the crowds and anything familiar.

I also wondered if, deep in the garden, out of sight of any guards or witnesses, she would try to kill us with blood magic. It seemed unlikely; there were four of us, six if you counted Tatsumi and Chu. The odds appeared stacked against her, but I didn't know how blood magic worked, or how strong a sorceress she was. Perhaps she could summon flocks of dead crows or raise skeletons from the ground. It seemed a good idea to be cautious.

Near a corner of the outer wall, we came to what I assumed was an old storehouse, a tall, square-based building with a peaked roof and a single door in the front. It was similar to the storehouses I'd seen in farming villages, except those were smaller and stood on stilts to protect crops from rain and vermin. An aura of menace hung over the building like a shroud, and my stomach curled in dread.

"A storehouse?" Reika gazed at the structure, then glared at the woman walking calmly toward the door. "You've been keeping Master Jiro locked up in a *storehouse*?"

"What a crude accusation. I am highly offended." Lady Satomi didn't break stride as she reached the entrance. She pushed back the door, and turned back to us. Framed in the doorway, her crimson robes standing out against the black, she gave us a cruel smile. "Your Master Jiro is not here," she stated, "but the path to reach him is within. Follow if you dare, little ducklings. Into the dark we go."

She took a step back through the doorway and vanished into the shadows.

"Hurry," Reika said, stepping forward. "We mustn't lose her."

"Wait."

Surprisingly, it was Okame's voice that cut through the night, stopping her. The ronin stared at the storehouse with crossed arms and narrowed eyes. "I might not know a lot about blood witches and court politics," he said, "but I know a trap when I see one."

Reika whirled on him. "We cannot stop now," she said. "I will not let that woman get away with this. Stay here if you are afraid—I will find Master Jiro with or without your help."

"I didn't say I was afraid," Okame snapped in return. "Of course we're going in. I just don't think we should walk merrily into an ambush, if that storehouse is filled with demons, monsters or giant centipedes wanting to eat our faces."

"It's not," said a new voice overhead.

We looked up. A figure in black crouched on the roof of the storehouse, silhouetted against the moon, a crimson scarf rippling behind him. My heart leaped, Chu flattened his ears with a growl and Okame snorted.

"There you are," the ronin said, as Tatsumi landed gracefully in front of the storehouse. Chu's growls grew louder, but the shrine maiden spoke a quiet word, and he stopped. "Finally decided to show up, eh, Kage-san?" Okame continued. "I won't even point out the previous shinobi comment I made a few days ago that resulted in a threat to my life. I'll just stand here, being quietly vindicated."

"Kage-san," Daisuke said, staring at Tatsumi. "You are… shinobi?"

"He's the Kage demonslayer," Reika broke in, her voice flat. "Of course he is. How are you even surprised by this?

Regardless…" She turned to Tatsumi. "Kage-san, you said there are no demons or other creatures lurking within the storehouse, is that true? Kage-san?"

Through this whole exchange, Tatsumi hadn't said anything, his gaze solely on me. At Reika's question, however, he blinked and glanced at the shrine maiden, the cold mask of the demonslayer dropping into place as he turned.

"I didn't sense any," he replied. "There are no demons, but…" His gaze flickered to the open doorway, eyes narrowing to violet slits. "There is something. Not living, but… powerful. It reeks of blood magic and death. Whatever is in there, it's nothing of this realm."

With a metallic shiver, Daisuke drew his sword, the razor-sharp blade catching the moonlight as it was unsheathed. "Then we will face it with honor."

"I was afraid you would say that." Okame snorted and pulled his bow over his head. "Into the jaws of death once more. As long as it's not a giant centipede."

"That doesn't seem very likely," I told him as we started forward. "I don't think a giant centipede could fit through the door. Unless she summoned one from inside the storehouse, but then how would it move around?"

Tatsumi moved to my side. "Stay close, Yumeko," he said softly. "If this is the blood mage that has been following us, we'll be her first targets."

I nodded. With Reika leading, an ofuda held before her and Chu at her feet, we walked across the grass and slipped into the darkness of the storehouse.

# 31

## THE MIRROR OF NO REFLECTION

*The blood witch is close.*

I could feel the pulse of dark power in the air as we stepped through the frame, and I tightened my hold on Hakaimono. The demon fought me, knowing something was close, wanting to feel blood and flesh sliding over its blade. Bloodlust surged through my veins, filling me with the urge to kill, but I was also acutely aware of Yumeko, walking close at my side. I could see her from the corner of my eye, feel her presence in the space around me, and was torn between the almost painful desire to protect the girl and tear the head from her neck.

*Focus*, I told both myself and Hakaimono. *Your objective is getting to the priest.*

The room beyond the door was musty and warm, the air stale. Boxes, sacks and wooden barrels were stacked in rows throughout the chamber, with garden implements stored against the walls and atop the crates. A single lantern hung from a wooden beam, casting a flickering orange light over the floor, but the rest of the storehouse was shrouded in darkness.

"Where's the witch hiding?" the ronin muttered into the silence.

A soft chuckle answered him, creeping out of the shadows. "No need to be rude. I'm right here. This way, little ducklings. Follow the sound of my voice."

Cautiously, we did, easing around the stacks of crates and barrels, inching toward the back wall, where a faint crimson glow began emanating from the far corner.

Lady Satomi waited for us at the end of the last aisle, her features cast in a red glow. It came from a tall, full-length mirror in the corner of the room, the glass reflecting the smiling woman in its depths. A dirty sheet lay crumpled at the base of the mirror, indicating it had been covered a moment ago, and the entire structure seemed to pulse with a subtle malevolence.

Yumeko took one look at the woman in the corner and leaped back, brushing my arm as she darted behind me, making my senses spike. I glanced at her, confused. She had made herself very small against my back, as if she were afraid of the mirror itself. I supposed she, too, could feel the darkness radiating from it, the sense that it was something unnatural.

"What trickery is this, witch?" the shrine maiden said, raising her ofuda like a sword.

"This? It's called a mirror," Satomi replied with exaggerated slowness. "Commonly used to make certain you are presentable to the rest of society. Perhaps you should get one for yourself?"

"That's not what I meant! Where is Master Jiro? You said you would take us to him."

"Did I? I suppose I did. Well, then…" The woman reached up and carefully drew a hairpin, long and pointed with an ivory ball on the end, from her hair. For a moment, she held it before her, the thin metal glimmering in the light, before raising her other hand and jabbing the point into her index finger. Her face remained serene as she drove the needle tip into her skin without flinching.

A drop of blood welled from the puncture wound, swelling like a tick on the end of her finger. As we watched, Lady Satomi calmly raised the injured hand and pressed the spot of blood to the surface of the mirror. As the glass rippled, like a stone dropped into a puddle, the woman smiled.

"Your precious master is through here," she said to the shrine maiden, and lifted her gaze to all of us, the challenge in her voice apparent. "Save him if you can."

And with that, she stepped forward, *into* the mirror, and vanished through the glass.

The ronin let out an emphatic curse. "Wait, *what*? The hell just happened? Everyone saw that, right? You all saw her get sucked into the mirror. What was that?"

"Blood magic," I said grimly, as Yumeko peeked around my arm. The reflection in the mirror was distorted now, the images hazy and twisted. A single spot of red still marred the glass, floating on the surface. "Lady Satomi is a blood mage," I confirmed, as our grotesque reflections gazed back at us, swirling in unrecognizable circles. "A powerful one, if I had to guess. The mirror serves as a gateway to another place entirely. That is not the spell of a novice."

"A gateway?" Yumeko continued to hover at my back. "Where does it lead?"

"It doesn't matter." Again, the shrine maiden stepped forward, her face determined. "If Master Jiro is on the other side, I will find him. No matter what stands in my way."

"Hold on, hold on," the ronin protested. "I'm all for jumping into strange mirrors and all, but what if it dumps us into a pit of demons? Or centipedes?"

With a sharp yip, Chu rushed forward, leaped toward the mirror and vanished through the glass in a streak of orange and white. As the rest of us stared in shock, he reappeared, bounding back through the mirror to give us an impatient look, before leaping through once more.

"Okay," said the ronin with a shrug. "Good enough for me."

I shut my eyes and stepped through the gateway, feeling strands of magic slide over my skin, cold and clinging, like walking through a spiderweb in the dead of winter. When I opened my eyes, I gazed around and felt Kamigoroshi stir to life.

"Oh, Kami." I heard Reika whisper.

The six of us—five humans and a dog—stood beneath an ancient torii gate, the once colorful wood half-rotted and crumbling into ash. Spread before us was the devastated, shattered remains of what had once been a village or town. Houses and buildings lay destroyed, smashed to kindling, walls crumbled and roofs fallen in. For many of the structures, nothing was left but a few blackened sticks and charred ruins. Rubble lay everywhere, the air smelled of death and nothing stirred in the shadows. No signs of life, or people, or anything alive. This place, whatever it had been, was a village of yurei now.

"Where is she?" the shrine maiden muttered, gazing around with narrowed eyes. "Where did the witch slither off to?"

"And where the hell are we?" the ronin echoed, his breath clouding into the air before writhing away on the sharp, chilly breeze. "Also, and this may be cause for some concern—I don't see a mirror lying around. How are we going to get back?"

There was no sign of the blood mage. Or a mirror of any sort. The ruined village lay silent and empty; no glimmer of pale skin or flutter of kimono sleeves could be seen through the devastation. A half-burned banner flapped mournfully from a beam, the only sound in the absolute stillness.

"That's the crest of the Yotaka," the noble said, gazing the rippling, half-burned cloth. "A vassal to the Sora family. Which means...we're in Sky Clan territory?" He shook his head in amazement. "But that can't be right. Sora lands are hundreds of miles from the Imperial City."

That explained the sudden drop in temperature. Sky Clan territory lay on the northern edge of Iwagoto, and claimed the frigid Kori no Hari peaks as their domain. From the distant snowcapped mountains, looming beyond the village, we were probably on the very edge of the Sora family lands.

"Satomi is a blood mage," I reminded them grimly. "She probably has several of these gateways seeded throughout the palace, in case she needs a quick escape, or a location to work her blood magic in peace."

"Oh, that's just great," the ronin snapped. "Quick, let's all follow the blood witch through the mirror of death without knowing what's on the other side. Oh look, an empty, ruined village in the middle of nowhere, I wonder what could be here? Certainly not demons, or gaki, or—"

"Yurei," Yumeko whispered.

"Or ghosts," the ronin agreed. "Right, I'm sure there are no angry ghosts around, either."

"No," the girl said, and pointed down the road. "Look."

We turned. A glowing ball of blue-white luminance floated silently in the middle of the road where nothing had been before. It bobbed once, then glided soundlessly away, trailing a long tail of light behind it, then reappeared, hovering several feet off the ground.

*"Hitodama,"* the shrine maiden whispered. "A human soul lingering on in the world."

"A ghost?" the noble mused.

"Yes and no." The miko's voice was full of pity. "Yurei are the spirits of the deceased. This is someone's soul that, for some reason, is unable to pass on."

"It looks like it wants us to follow it," Yumeko observed, as the light bobbed away, then returned, pulsing softly against the dark.

The ronin blew out a breath. "Well, there's nothing around here," he said. "Let's see where the glowing dead person wants to take us."

Cautiously, we followed the bobbing orb of light, ducking under beams and charred pillars, weaving through the skeletons of watchtowers that had fallen into the road. The village, except for our own footsteps and breathing, remained deathly silent and still. Ahead, the glowing sphere moved at a steady pace, always close enough to see but keeping a good distance between us. Eventually, the village gave way to the edge of a forest, where the sphere drifted through the trees until it paused at the foot of a rise. A flight of stone steps, cracked and covered in roots, ascended through the trees and disappeared over the hill. It waited long enough for us to reach the first step, before it floated up the staircase and vanished.

"Hurry," the shrine maiden said, as she and the dog took the lead. "I can sense Master Jiro is close. We mustn't lose it."

"Come on, Tatsumi-san," Yumeko urged as I hesitated. "We have to keep up."

This was, I mused as we began climbing the stairs, a very strange party I found myself in. I was used to tracking down demons, blood mages and murderous yokai, but it had always been alone. Not in the company of a ronin, a shrine maiden, an aristocrat and a dog. And a peasant girl who haunted my thoughts, whose presence I was constantly aware of.

For a moment, walking through a dark, unknown forest, I wondered if any of the others found this situation as odd as I did before I purged those thoughts from my mind. It didn't matter what they thought, or if they died while pursuing a dangerous blood mage. They were not my responsibility. My objective was to find the priest who could give us the location of the Steel Feather temple and the scroll. Nothing else mattered.

Especially since I had already been ordered to kill one of them when this was over.

The stairs ended at the gates of an ancient castle, peaked roofs soaring toward the full moon. The double doors of the gates were open, creaking in the breeze, and through the opening I could see the courtyard, as vacant and dark as the village below.

"Empty," Yumeko mused as we warily approached the front gates. "I wonder what happened to the castle?"

"And all the people in the village?" the ronin added.

I didn't reply, though I suspected I knew the answer. To summon an oni and a horde of demons from Jigoku required a massive amount of blood and sacrifice, more than the blood mage had in their body.

An entire village's worth.

The hitodama reappeared, floating in the gateway of the castle. "It's waiting for us," the shrine maiden said, stepping forward. "Hurry. Master Jiro is there."

"A frontal assault is inadvisable," I said quietly, making the shrine maiden pause. She scowled at me, and I nodded to the gate. "If this is the blood witch's lair, I doubt she'll be alone. And she's expecting us. If you go in now, you could be attacked by demons or worse."

"What are you suggesting, demonslayer?"

"I'll go. This is what I'm trained for. I'll find the priest and return before the castle defenses suspect me. The rest of you don't need to come." *And I won't need to worry about keeping Yumeko safe.*

"So, we're supposed to wait here and trust Master Jiro's life to you?" the shrine maiden demanded. "No offense, Kage-san. I know you are an expert killer, but the bearer of Kamigoroshi does not inspire much faith in anything else. I will not entrust Master Jiro's safety to one who is here only for the information he possesses. I'm afraid I must insist on coming with you."

"Sadly, I think I'll have to agree," the ronin added, grinning. "And I never really learned how to 'stay' on command. You know what they say—can't teach an old dog new tricks."

"The blood witch will try to stop you," the noble broke in, gazing solemnly at me. "She could summon demons and abominations and all sorts of horrors. And you still owe me a duel, Kage-san. Forgive me, but I cannot allow you to die just yet."

I looked at Yumeko, whose lip curled up at the corner. "I'm coming, too," she said calmly. "We've traveled all this way. You don't have to face her alone."

*Alone is better*, I thought. *Alone means I don't put people in danger.*

A chill went through me. Why was I having these thoughts? The safety of others was not something I'd ever considered before. Perhaps Master Iemon had been right; I was slipping, my concern for others a dangerous indication that I was losing control of my emotions. When this was over, I would submit myself to the majutsushi's "re-evaluation," and hope that could destroy any lingering attachments. It was unpleasant, and I might not survive, but it was necessary.

Yumeko was still watching me, dark eyes shining with worry. I didn't deserve that concern, but I didn't tell her this. What I said was, "Do what you will," before heading toward the gate and the castle beyond.

The blood witch was nowhere to be seen as we passed through the large wooden doors and stepped into the courtyard. Rubble was scattered everywhere; broken stones, overturned barrels, a few smashed carts, all strewn through the yard. I saw several suits of armor among the stones, and the glint of bleached bone that confirmed what had happened to the samurai here. Broken spears jutted from the ground, arrows were embedded in posts and beams, and katanas lay rusting where they had fallen, glimmering faintly in the moonlight.

"Looks like a battle was fought here," the noble mused.

"Or a massacre," the ronin added, prodding the top half of

a suit of armor with his bow. A rib cage dislodged, fell out of it, and he grimaced. "I hope I'm horribly, horribly wrong, but this poor bastard looks like he was ripped in half."

Hakaimono's presence, which had been building with excitement and bloodlust as soon as we stepped through the gate, went perfectly still. A chill raced up my spine, and I froze, gazing around the courtyard.

*Up*, something whispered in my head. *Look up.*

I looked up. To the peaked roof of the castle, silhouetted against the moon.

Something dark and massive rose from the castle roof, standing against the moonlight, an enormous shadow with thick shoulders and black horns curling into the air. Even from this distance, I could see its eyes, burning like embers in the night, and the mane of black hair falling down its back. It swung an iron-studded tetsubo to its shoulders, and a slow grin broke across its face as our gazes met. It dropped to a crouch and leaped off the roof into the air.

"Oni!" I yelled, drawing my sword, as the huge creature landed in the courtyard with a boom that shook the ground and shattered the stones beneath it. Dust and chips of rock flew outward and everyone fell back as the oni straightened, towering a good fifteen feet overhead, to smile down at us.

"The Kage demonslayer," the demon rumbled, its burning crimson eyes locked on me. "I've been waiting for you."

Movement rippled around us, as dozens of smaller demons appeared on the walls and formed from the shadows. The amanjaku snarled and cackled, waving crude weapons, red eyes seeming to float around us like crimson fireflies. Some of them wore pieces of stolen samurai armor—a helmet or shoulder pad that was far too big—or brandished the wakizashis of the fallen in a blasphemous parody of honor.

The shrine maiden's dog gave a sharp yap and bounded forward, leaping over rubble toward the towering demon in the center of the courtyard.

"Chu!" cried the miko, as the demon casually swung its club at the fleeing animal. The tetsubo smashed to the ground, crushing stone and leaving a large hole behind but somehow missing the dog, which fled across the stones, darted up the steps of the castle and vanished through the open doors.

"Chu, wait!" The shrine maiden started after him, then paused, as if remembering the giant demon blocking her way. The oni snorted, swinging its weapon to its shoulder again.

"Pathetic beast. Barely enough for a mouthful. But I am not interested in dogs." Its burning gaze swung to me again, sending a flare of savage excitement through my veins. "Come, then, demonslayer," it growled. "It is your blood I want, your entrails I wish to smear over the ground. Fight me alone or with these puny mortals, it matters not. I will crush you all into pulp and scatter your bones for the amanjaku to squabble over."

"Go," I told the rest of them, forcing myself to speak calmly, to not release the gleeful laughter bubbling in my throat. "Follow the dog, find Master Jiro. I'll take care of the oni."

"What? Like hell you will." The ronin came forward, his bow already strung, his mouth curled in a defiant smirk as he gazed at the demons around us. "I see a lot more monsters than the big ugly bastard in the center there. I can at least keep the minions off your back while you cut off its head."

"Indeed," added the noble, sweeping his sword in front of him. "You are not allowed to die tonight, Kage Tatsumi.

Lady Yumeko," he added, keeping his gaze on the giant creature before us. "Do not worry about Kage-san. I will not permit him to fall. On my honor, I will fight as if his life were my own."

The oni chuckled. "Good," it rumbled, and took a step forward. Stones cracked under its weight, and the air around it shimmered with heat. "Good! Come then, humans. I have been bored for days. At least try to make a fight of this."

"Tatsumi," Yumeko whispered, and for a moment, the intensity in her voice calmed the rage within, piercing the bloodlust and vicious glee. "That's the oni who destroyed the temple and killed everyone there. Please be careful. But if you can…tear him apart for me."

The oni laughed, the savage sound booming into the air, stirring the amanjaku into a shrieking, cackling frenzy. "Yes, demonslayer," it mocked, as Hakaimono rose up with a howl of its own, turning my vision black and red. "Take me apart, if you can."

I bared my teeth in a savage grin. "So eager to die, Yaburama?" I heard myself say, and for the briefest of moments, caught a flicker of shock in the demon's eyes. "You always were a conniving bastard, even in Jigoku. I'll be happy to send you back."

The oni's face contorted with rage, and it lunged at me with a roar, swinging its club in a vicious arc. I snarled back with the fury of a hundred demons and leaped out to meet him.

# 32

## Fox Magic Unleashed

*I* shuddered as Tatsumi gave a snarl unlike anything I'd heard before and sprang to meet the oni, whose giant tetsubo was sweeping down to crush him to the earth. At the last second, he twisted aside, the iron club missing him by centimeters and crashing into the stones. As he darted in, Kamigoroshi flashed purple in the darkness, cutting into the demon's arm and releasing a spray of blood. It sizzled as it touched the ground, smoke writhing into the air from the puddles, and the oni howled.

With ringing shrieks and cries, the amanjaku surged forward, swarming into the courtyard, as Daisuke and Okame raised their weapons. The ronin's bowstring hummed, releasing arrow after arrow, and demons screamed as they died. Daisuke took several steps forward, putting himself between us and the horde. For a moment he went perfectly still, only his pale hair rippling in the wind. Then, as the first amanjaku reached him, he exploded into motion, his sword a blur as it sliced through demons, so quickly he was moving on to the next foe before the amanjaku realized it was dead.

"Yumeko!" Reika snapped, jerking my attention away from the battle. "This way, before it's too late. We have to find Master Jiro!"

A bark rang across the courtyard, Chu peering at us from the doorway, looking impatient. Reika sprinted forward, kicking away an amanjaku as she leaped over a rubble pile, making the demon yelp in pain. With one final look at the three humans, surrounded by amanjaku in the shadow of the massive oni, I followed.

Demons chased us, leaping from the walls and crawling from beneath the verandas, scuttling toward us in a red, blue and green swarm. I dodged a pale blue demon, avoiding the spear it thrust at me, and leaped over a second as it swiped a kama sickle at my legs. Fox magic rose up, but before I could think about throwing kitsune-bi around, Reika shouted "Light" and flung an ofuda at the group of demons in front of us. The paper exploded in a blinding flash that caused the mob to shriek and cringe back, covering their faces. We scrambled between them, leaped up the steps onto the veranda and ducked through the entryway of the castle.

"Close the doors!" Reika cried, spinning and putting her shoulder to one of the heavy wooden barricades, Chu barking and dancing around her feet. I rammed my palms into the second, pushing as hard as I could, and the doors gave a reluctant groan as they swung shut. Reika shoved a cracked board through the handles, just as a blow rattled the outside, followed by the angry voices of the amanjaku.

"There," she panted, backing away. "That should hold them for now." I dared a quick glance around, seeing a dark hall with wooden pillars marching down the center, though everything in it—shoji screens, fusuma panels, shelves and bits of pottery—was smashed to bits and covered in filth.

"Something has been very messy," I pointed out. "I suppose demons aren't very good housekeepers. Do you think there could be more?"

"Inside the castle? Merciful Jinkei, I hope not." Reika dusted off her hands. "The real question is, where is Master Jiro? This is a huge castle. How are we going to find him?"

With a glow of light, the hitodama floated through one of the walls, swirled around us and drifted away down a narrow corridor. I nodded.

"Follow the light," I said, but at that moment, an amanjaku carrying a large bone appeared at the other end of the chamber. Spotting us, he pointed the bone in our direction and let out a high-pitched yowl that reverberated through the halls of the castle.

I pinned back my ears, as answering shrieks and hisses began echoing out of the darkness. "I suppose that answers one question."

"Go!" the miko cried, as Chu darted after the hitodama and the sound of scrabbling claws rang out around us. We fled, following the bobbing light down long corridors, through empty rooms with shredded wall panels and overturned furniture, hearing the snarls of the demons as they closed in.

As we rounded a corner and burst through yet another door, we found ourselves in a large, spacious chamber of polished wood and high ceilings. Torn, filthy tatami mats covered the wooden floors, and the walls were lined with weapon racks. Empty now, but I could guess this might have been a sparring or training area once.

Unfortunately, we could run no farther. Across the room, a large amanjaku wearing a samurai helmet grinned at us triumphantly, as demons poured into the chamber through a hole in the wall, hissing and cackling as they spread across the floor. Turning around, we saw that the way we'd come was blocked, too. Demons surrounded us, grinning madly as they crept forward, pointing blades, spears and claws in our direction.

Heart pounding, I drew my tanto, as Reika pressed close and Chu backed up, growling and showing his teeth at the approaching demons. They laughed and snickered, crimson eyes bright with bloodlust, knowing we were trapped.

"What now?" I whispered, suddenly remembering the first time I'd run into a horde of demons. Tatsumi wouldn't be coming this time; we were on our own.

Reika pulled out an ofuda and gave me an impatient look. "What do you mean 'what now'?" she snapped. "The demonslayer isn't here, *kitsune*!"

*Oh.*

I felt the grin cross my face before I could help myself. No Tatsumi. No demonslayer, or unwitting humans who thought I was something I wasn't.

"Chu!" Reika called, drawing back the ofuda, which started to glow. "Guardian form now!"

She hurled the slip of paper into the air, where it flew toward the dog and burst into a ray of light. The small orange dog threw back his head and howled, and as he did, swelled to ten times his previous size. His fur changed color, turning a brilliant red, and a golden mane fell around his neck. Now he was the size of an ox, with massive shoulders, a curly flowing tail and a thick, blocky head that was a cross between a dog and a lion. A komainu, I realized in awe, the living incarnation of the statues that sat next to the shrine's torii gate. Chu, or the guardian spirit he had become, let out a booming roar that shook the timbers and sent several demons flying with one swat of his enormous paw.

Shrieking, the amanjaku swarmed the room, their attention riveted on the majestic beast in the center of the floor. Taking one step back, I felt the familiar rush of fox magic rise to my fingers, and this time, did nothing to stifle it. As the horde closest to me rushed forward, I raised my arms, blue fire dancing at my fingertips, and sent a wave of kitsune-bi into their faces.

The amanjaku screamed, cringing back from the supernatural flames, covering their eyes as the column of foxfire roared through the chamber, casting everything in a blue-white glow. The fire wouldn't burn, nothing was in danger of incineration, but in the seconds of pandemonium that followed I grabbed a handful of reeds from the floor and hurled it into the air, sending fox magic after it.

As the reeds fluttered down, a few dozen Yumekos and Reikas filled the room with small pops of smoke, eliciting yelps of alarm from the shocked amanjaku. As the replicas scattered, and the amanjaku began stabbing at them in a panic, I snatched up a pebble and threw it at the helmeted demon, where a second Chu materialized in front of him with a roar. As the demon howled and fell backward, slashing wildly with his blade, his helmet came off, rolling across the planks, and stopped in front of a pillar.

Darting around the edges of the chaos, I peered through the bedlam for the real Chu and Reika, hoping they were all right. The shrine maiden stood in the center of the room, purifying ofuda in each hand, hurling them at passing demons. Where they touched, there was a burst of power, and the amanjaku writhed away into smoke as they were exorcised. Chu rampaged around her, swatting the demons that got too close with huge clawed forepaws or crushing them in his teeth. For now, both looked like they were doing fine. The hitodama hovered overhead, casting the room in hazy light, waiting for us.

I sprinted to where the helmet lay forgotten next to the pillar, snatched it up and put it on my head. Fox magic flared, and in a puff of white smoke, my appearance changed. Gazing down at myself, I no longer saw the elegant white robes of the onmyoji; I saw a squat, ugly body with festering red skin, tattered rags and hooked claws. I chuckled, and it sounded evil and raspy in my ears.

A green amanjaku rushed up to me, snarling and chattering, making frantic gestures back toward the room. I couldn't understand a word it was saying, if it was even using words, but it clearly thought I was the commander of the horde of amanjaku, which was unfortunate for it. I stabbed the demon in the chest with my tanto and it blinked at me in shock, before writhing into tendrils of smoke and vanishing into nothing.

*Well, that's useful.*

Bounding back into the chaos, I began slicing unwitting demons into smoke clouds while they were distracted by the dozen or so replicas still dancing about the room. Fortunately, amanjaku didn't appear to be terribly smart, and would chase illusions of me around the room with maniacal persistence, hacking at them until they popped with a puff of white smoke and a single reed, drifting to the ground. When this happened, the amanjaku seemed to think it a victory, for they would jump up and down, pumping their fists in the air, before hurling themselves at the next replica. Slipping through the confusion, I stabbed one demon after the other, sending them back to Jigoku.

An angry shout made me pause. I looked up, just in time to dodge the wakizashi of the amanjaku commander whose helmet I'd stolen. The demon hissed and ranted at me, baring his fangs and swinging his blade in short, furious arcs. I dodged and parried with my shorter dagger, backpedaling across the room until I hit one of the pillars, then instantly ducked as the amanjaku swung his sword at my head. The blade hit the beam, lodging in the wood for a split second, and I snatched a leaf from the floor as I rolled away. The amanjaku commander yanked his sword from the post, spun around and came face-to-face with two more of himself. One wearing a helmet, and one not.

For a moment, he squinted in confusion, trying to decide which was which. Then with a howl, he lunged at me, the demon with a helmet, sinking his blade deep into my chest.

Or so he thought. The amanjaku wailed, clutching at the sword, before it exploded in a puff of white smoke, the helmet falling to the ground with a clank. The amanjaku commander barely had time to blink in shock before I lunged through the smoke and stabbed him in the heart.

As the demon snarled and twisted into fading wisps of darkness, I became aware of the silence in the room. Feeling hostile eyes on my back, I spun around to find myself in the shadow of a growling Chu, his lips pulled back from his enormous fangs, tensing to lunge.

"Chu, wait! It's me." I shook off the illusion in a puff of smoke, noting how very large the dog spirit was up close. As the mist dispersed, I yanked the leaf from my head and held it in front of his nose. "Not a demon," I told him, as his nostrils twitched. "Just a kitsune. One who has thought nothing but nice things about you since you appeared in tiny dog form. See?"

The komainu looked wholly unimpressed; with a snort, he turned and padded back to Reika, standing alone in the center of the room. An ofuda was held between the shrine maiden's two fingers, meant for me, I realized. Of the amanjaku, nothing remained but a few bits of stolen weapons and armor. The replicas were gone as well, pieces of straw blowing limply across the floor.

I took a deep breath and let it out in a puff. "Well, that was…exciting," I remarked, as Reika lowered her arms, the ofuda vanishing somewhere into her robes. Chu shook himself, and shrank down to a normal dog again. I was trembling, not with fear, but with the thrill of using so much fox magic all at once. Never in my sixteen years had I been allowed to unleash my full power, to really see what my magic could do. It was exciting and heady and a little bit frightening, knowing what I was capable of. Was this the power Master Isao warned me about? What the others were afraid of?

*Kitsune magic is the power of illusion. You might think it useful only for mischief, but seeing something that isn't there, or making people believe you are someone else entirely, can be a dangerous, terrifying force. Use it carefully, lest you become an instrument of chaos.*

"Your ears are showing," Reika remarked in a flat voice, bringing me out of my thoughts with a start. "I can normally see a faint outline, but they're fully exposed now. Probably a side effect of using so much of your power."

I swallowed, resisting the impulse to reach up and touch

them. "Do you think they'll go away eventually?" I asked, knowing that, if my ears were visible, my tail probably was, as well. That would be a definite problem if Tatsumi or any of the others saw them. "What will we do if they don't fade before we leave the castle?"

"Worry about it when we get there," the shrine maiden answered. "We have to keep going." She looked at the hitodama, who still hovered near the ceiling, glowing faintly. "If you are truly here to help us," she said, as the glowing orb trembled, "then lead on. And let us hope that there are no more 'surprises' ahead."

The hitodama hesitated a moment. Then it floated from the ceiling, circled the room once and flowed out another door.

No more demons ambushed us on our way through the ruined castle; either they had fled or we had killed them all. The light wove unerringly down narrow hallways, through more empty, destroyed rooms, and finally led us to the top of a wooden staircase that led down into the dark.

"He's close," Reika murmured, as Chu glanced up at her and wagged his tail. "I can feel his presence now. Hurry."

After descending the flight of stone steps, we came into a large room. Torches stood in the corners, flickering with ominous red flames, and cells with thick wooden bars lined the walls, but all were empty.

In the center of the room, a man in a tattered, once-white robe sat cross-legged on the hard stone floor, hands cupped in his lap as if in meditation. His head was bowed, his shoulders hunched and he didn't move when Reika called his name. Manacles encircled his wrists, rusty black chains that shackled him to the stone floor. A small white dog, nearly identical to Chu, lay motionless beside him.

Both were encased in a flickering, nearly invisible dome of power, a barrier much like the one I had seen the night the Silent Winds temple was attacked. But this one was much more menacing, radiating evil and corruption, making my skin crawl the closer we got.

"Blood magic," the shrine maiden whispered, sounding furious and horrified. She pulled out another ofuda and raised it before her, paused a moment while the paper flared with energy, then hurled it at the barrier. It flew through the air and struck the dome flat, the word for *purify* written across its surface, before the barrier flickered once, twice and then shattered like wasps swarming from a hive.

"Master Jiro!" Reika and I hurried forward. As we drew close, I saw that the black chains around the priest had vanished, melting into a line of dark reddish sludge across the floor.

"Master Jiro," Reika said again, kneeling before him, while Chu whined and shoved his nose against the crumpled form of the white dog. "Master, can you hear me? Are you all right?"

A shuddering, wheezy breath came from the hunched form, and his shoulders trembled as he raised his head. His face was gaunt, his cheeks sallow and his eyes were sunken pits in his face, looking distinctly skeletal. He blinked at Reika, brow furrowed, as if unsure he was seeing correctly.

"R-Reika-chan?" he whispered. "Are you…really here?"

"Yes, Master Jiro," the shrine maiden returned softly. "I'm here. When you didn't come back, I knew something was wrong. We're here to rescue you. Can you stand?"

"I…don't know." The priest tried to straighten, then slumped back with a groan. "I'm weak," he whispered. "That woman…used blood magic to keep me here. She asked me questions, and when I didn't give her what she wanted, she started draining my life force. Ko's, too." He glanced at the still motionless white dog beside him. Chu had given up trying to nose it to its feet and now sat there whining and looking miserable. "I tried to make her go home," the priest muttered, "but she wouldn't leave me. The demons…they would have tormented me even more…had she not been here."

Watching the white dog, I gasped as her side rose and fell; it was slight, but it was there. "She's alive," I told the priest, stepping around Reika. "She not gone yet. We can still save you both."

He peered at me, wan confusion crossing his face. "Kit-kitsune?" he murmured, and shook his head. "I… I must be hallucinating, after all."

Abruptly, Chu leaped to his feet, wagging his tail, as the white dog suddenly stirred. Raising her head, she peered around in confusion, before she spotted me a few feet away, and her lips immediately curled to show tiny fangs. I took a quick step back, retreating behind Reika, as the dog staggered upright. Still glaring at me, she wobbled shakily over to the priest, whose face lit up as he saw her.

"Come on, Master Jiro," Reika said, putting one of his arms around her shoulders and gently drawing him upright. He staggered and swayed, but finally got his feet under him. "We're leaving this place. Let's hope the others are still alive so we don't have to face that oni again."

"Oni?" the priest gasped, as my stomach twisted. "Yaburama is still here?"

"You know his name?" I asked. The priest turned wide, fearful eyes on me.

"Sadly, I do. Yaburama…is a monster. He is one of the

four great demons of Jigoku, the oni generals of O-Hakumon himself." Master Jiro's face contorted in fear and loathing. "I do not know how that woman, even with her control of blood magic, could have summoned something like Yaburama into this world and not had him turn on her immediately. Even minor demons are difficult to control—an oni like Yaburama would require an extraordinarily powerful blood mage to have any hope of binding him to her will."

"We have to get out there," I told Reika, who nodded. "Tatsumi and the others are fighting the oni now—we have to help them. Master Jiro, you're the head priest, can you do anything that might stop Yaburama?"

"I am sorry, kitsune," Master Jiro said, his eyes genuinely sympathetic. "I am grateful for your assistance, even if I am unsure of your motives, but we cannot stand against an oni of that power. The demon generals are very nearly immortal. If your friends stayed behind to face Yaburama, they are likely already dead."

# 33

## Yaburama's Folly

*T*his was going to be a fight.

I dove aside as the oni's tetsubo swept down, smashing into the earth and sending rocks flying. I rolled to my feet, and instantly had to spring back as the huge club raked across the ground, missing me by a thread and hitting several amanjaku who had swarmed down to ambush me. They flew through the air before exploding into writhing tendrils of smoke as they returned to Jigoku, and the oni grunted.

"Are you just going to bounce around like a cricket, demonslayer?" it challenged, coming at me again, the iron club leaving holes in the rock every time it landed. "Or are you actually going to fight me?"

I bared my teeth. As the tetsubo descended once more, I darted forward, between Yaburama's treelike limbs, and slashed the back of his leg. The oni snarled and spun around, crushing the ground with his club as I leaped back. At the same time, the human noble, cutting his way through several amanjaku, sprinted behind the oni and sliced through the back of his other leg.

Yaburama howled. Whirling, he lashed out with a kick, barely missing the human as he darted past, sending more amanjaku flying. The wounds to his legs didn't appear to slow him down as he leaped into the air, landing between us with a crash that made the ground tremble like an earthquake. I kept my balance, but the noble staggered, falling to one knee, and the oni raised his club to smear him across the stones.

An arrow sped through the air, striking the monster in the forehead, causing him to rear back with a snarl. I spared a quick glance over and saw that the ronin had climbed to the top of the watchtower by the gate. He sent another dart at the grimacing oni, who snorted and raised his arm, letting it hit him in the shoulder.

In that moment of distraction, I whispered a quick incantation and lunged, a shadow Tatsumi appearing to join me. Yaburama saw us coming at the last moment and swung his club—at the wrong one. I dodged beneath his legs, vaulted off a knee and, as I rose toward his face, sliced Kamigoroshi across his neck, cutting open his throat.

Dark, steaming blood sprayed from the opening beneath the oni's chin. Instinctively, I threw up my arm to shield my face, but it still burned through my clothes, searing like liquid fire as it reached my skin. Hitting the ground, I staggered back, clenching my jaw against the pain, waiting for the oni to fall.

*Almost too easy.*

Yaburama started to laugh.

His voice rang out over the courtyard, deep and mocking. "Is that it?" The oni sneered, yanking the arrow from his face, not seeming to notice the second in his arm. "Is that the best you humans can do? Do you think you can defeat one of the demon generals of Jigoku so easily?" He laughed again, shaking his horned head, then turned and picked up a chunk of wall taller than a man, hefting it in one claw. Eyes glowing, he smiled down at us. "Let me show you how very mistaken you are."

The noble and I tensed, ready to leap aside, but Yaburama straightened, drew his arm back and hurled the boulder across the yard. It spun end over end and smashed into the base of the watchtower, snapping the legs and causing the structure to collapse with a roar and a cloud of dust.

"Okame-san!" cried the noble, as the oni bellowed in triumph, raising his club in the air, and the amanjaku cackled.

As the watchtower remains settled over the likely dead ronin, Yaburama turned, eyes glowing as he glared down at us. "This bores me," he growled. "I grow weary of fighting insignificant humans. Amanjaku!" he roared, raising his head. "Kill the human noble! Flay him, eat him, wear his skin for a coat, I care not! But get him out of my way. I wish to fight the demonslayer in peace."

The minor demons shrieked with excitement and lunged forward, surrounding the noble like ants swarming a grasshopper. The closest demons perished instantly as the former Oni no Mikoto cut them down, his blade moving so fast it was nearly a blur. But there were dozens of amanjaku, a seemingly endless horde, and their numbers began to push him back.

I started forward, intending to thin the swarm a bit, when the oni's huge tetsubo smashed into the ground between us. "Where do you think you're going, demonslayer?" Yaburama rumbled, putting himself between me and the amanjaku swarm. "The fight is here. Or should I remind you?"

He swung the tetsubo at me with savage force. I dodged as the club crashed into the stones and cut at the hand that held the weapon, severing a clawed finger. Yaburama snorted in annoyance and instead of pulling back, raked the weapon across the ground. I managed to leap aside, but the unexpected move set me off balance, and the second sweep caught me in the shoulder. Pain exploded through my body as I was hurled through the air and struck the ground several yards away then rolled to a painful stop. Kamigoroshi was torn from my grasp and went skidding over the stones in the opposite direction.

Dazed, I struggled to rise, but the ground trembled, and a clawed foot landed on my chest, shoving me back to the stones. The air whooshed from my body and my ribs bent and threatened to snap, as the huge oni peered down at me, smiling.

"A disgraceful way to die, demonslayer," Yaburama mused, as I gritted my teeth in an effort not to gasp for air. Inside, something was building—a rising flood of desperation, rage and hate. "Smashed underfoot like a cockroach, nothing but a smear on the bottom of my toe. How embarrassingly shameful." He chuckled and leaned his full weight against my chest; bones snapped in blinding bursts of agony, and I couldn't help the howl of pain that emerged from my throat. "But do not worry," the oni went on as I gasped in agony. "This will be over soon. And once I kill you, I'm going to tear apart your friends, as well. That little human girl looks especially tasty. I'm going to pull off her head, twist her around so that her insides turn to mush and eat her like a peach."

*Yumeko.* Rational thought disappeared. Something deep inside me snapped, and a flood of darkness rushed in with a howl. I felt a brief stab of terror and despair, and then nothing.

"Does it hurt, demonslayer?" Yaburama lowered his arm, bringing the end of the tetsubo very close to my face. "I'll make you a deal. Beg for mercy, and I'll crush your skull instead of stomping on you like an insect. So, what do you say to that? Ready to beg?"

"Beg?" I looked up, meeting the oni's gaze, and smiled. "I have a better idea. How about I send you to Jigoku in pieces?"

Yaburama bared his fangs. "You first."

He raised his foot and stomped down hard, and the world disappeared like a snuffed candle.

# 34

## The Destroyer

*I'm free.*

I raised my arms as Yaburama's foot smashed down at my head, catching the disgusting appendage with both hands. I heard the oni's grunt of surprise, felt him press down harder, trying to crush me into the ground. Thinking I was still that weakling mortal.

*You always were a fool, Yaburama.*

Sitting up, I threw him off, shoving him back and rising to my feet. Yaburama stumbled backward several paces before catching himself, gazing down at me in shock.

I grinned, feeling the air on my skin, seeing the world through my own eyes, and not the weak, pathetic eyes of my human host. I breathed deep and let the scent of blood, violence and death fill my lungs, before glancing at the oni towering overhead.

"What's the matter, Yaburama? Expecting someone else?"

He bellowed a laugh, shaking his horned head. "You've finally come," he rumbled, striding forward. "I thought I was going to stomp your host into bean paste before he lost control." He chuckled, narrowing crimson eyes at me. "How long has it been… Hakaimono?"

"Too long. Over four hundred years."

Yaburama snorted, then crouched down to gaze at me at eye level. "You're a bit…smaller than I remembered."

I smirked, seeing my reflection in the oni's crimson gaze. Human-sized, because I shared this pathetic body with my host, and Kage Tatsumi was even smaller than the average human male. At least I still recognized myself; after four hundred years of being a formless voice trapped in a blade, it was good to see a real body again. Onyx skin, white mane, horns, claws, fangs; I'd almost forgotten what I looked like.

But that wasn't important. I was free. I was finally out, and there was a whole country to take my revenge on. So much destruction to cause, lives to take and blood to spill. It was going to be beautiful. Let's see if the fools could drive me back into the sword this time.

But first…

Yaburama was still crouched at eye level, a mocking grin twisting his mouth. I clenched my right hand into a fist, drew it back and punched the oni square in his smirking jaw.

He flew backward, his feet leaving the ground for a moment, before he crashed into the stones with a boom that made the earth shake. I laughed, feeling the power racing through my muscles, my old strength returning to me. Not completely whole yet, but soon.

"Did you forget who you were speaking to, Yaburama?" I called, as the oni struggled upright, looking dazed. Flinging out a hand, I opened my fingers, and Kamigoroshi flew across the stones into my palm. "Did you forget that I commanded the Four Generals? That the strongest demons ever spawned in Jigoku feared me for a reason?"

"Damn you," Yaburama growled, rising to his feet. Blood streamed down his chin from his lips, and he wiped it away with the back of his hand. "Those days are gone, Hakaimono. You've been away for too long. There's a war coming, and a new Master of Demons who will lead the land into chaos and destruction." He raised his tetsubo, baring bloody fangs in a snarl. "Too bad you won't get to see it."

He lunged at me with a roar, swinging the tetsubo in a savage arc. I stepped back from the first blow, ducked under the second and then, as the weapon came straight down at my head, braced myself and threw up my empty hand, catching the end of the club in my palm.

Yaburama's eyes bulged. He strained against the club, trying to drive it down into my skull, but neither I nor the tetsubo moved. I smiled at him from the shadow of the weapon, and curled my claws into the wood.

"I am Hakaimono the Destroyer," I growled up at him. "The strongest demon Jigoku has ever known. And soon, this entire realm will remember why!"

Shoving the tetsubo away, I leaped into the air as Yaburama staggered back, flailing and off balance. As he caught himself, swinging his club once more with an angry snarl, I brought Kamigoroshi flashing down. The blade struck the oni's forearm, shearing through flesh and muscles and bone, continuing out the other side. The tetsubo and part of Yaburama's arm struck the stones with a thud, and Yaburama's snarl turned into a howl of pain.

Hitting the ground, I spun and darted back toward the

reeling oni. Maddened with pain and rage, bloody arm stump dripping steaming puddles over the ground, Yaburama roared and swung at me with his other claw. I ducked, rolled beneath it and sliced his leg as I went by. The oni staggered, swayed like an oak in a storm, then toppled over, his body falling one way while his severed knee remained where it was. He hit the ground on his back and lay there a moment, gasping, blood pumping from the stumps of his limbs and spreading over the stones.

Smiling, I walked casually up to the panting oni and leaped to his chest, pointing the bloody sword in his face. "Well, this was fun," I said calmly. "Nothing like a good old-fashioned massacre to get the blood pumping. Tatsumi never had it in him for savagery. Oh, I'm sorry, you were saying something, weren't you? Something about letting me rot in that cursed blade for another four centuries?"

"Damn you, Hakaimono," Yaburama rasped. "You've been stuck in Kamigoroshi for too long. You don't know what's been happening the past few centuries."

Smiling, I raised the sword over my head. "I'm sure I'll figure it out."

Yaburama snarled and tried to rise. I brought Kamigoroshi down in a flash of steel, slicing through the burly neck, being sure to sever it from his body this time. The oni's head toppled backward and rolled several feet before coming to a stop, his jaw clenched in rage.

Throwing back my head, I filled my lungs and let out a roar of triumph, hearing my voice boom into the air and echo over the castle peaks. Free! There was so much to do; so many lives to take, so much destruction and fear and chaos and death to wreak upon this pathetic realm. I was back, and this world would pay dearly for the centuries I was sealed away.

A gasp came from the castle entrance, and I smiled.

Turning on Yaburama's chest, I spotted the girl at the top of the stairs, the shrine maiden, a pair of dogs and an old human priest behind her.

# 35

## The Demon of the Blade

"Jinkei preserve us." I heard Reika whisper behind me, in a voice that sent a chill racing up my back.

I couldn't answer, staring at the center of the courtyard, at the figure outlined in moonlight. At the jet-black skin and wild mane of white hair, at the horns, fangs and claws. At the demon that still had Tatsumi's face. Tatsumi, or the thing he had become, turned atop the smoking corpse of the headless Yaburama, Kamigoroshi blazing in his hand, the blade shining red with blood. The oni's head lay several feet from the body, also letting off coils of smoke as it disappeared, vanishing back to Jigoku. I should have been happy to see Yaburama dead; the oni that had destroyed the Silent Winds temple and killed everyone there was lying headless in the center of the courtyard. I should have felt vindication, or at least some form of relief.

But right then, gazing at the figure standing atop the corpse, all I felt was terror. Because the oni that had replaced Yaburama, who smiled at me from Tatsumi's body, was a hundred times more frightening.

"Ah, there you are, Yumeko-chan." I jumped at the voice, at the sound of my name coming from the demon's mouth. "I was wondering when you'd show up."

He leaped into the air, so high it almost looked like he was flying, before descending toward us. Chu snarled and erupted into his real form, muscles tensing to lunge at the oni, but Master Jiro's voice cracked into the air.

"Chu, no! He's far too powerful. Everyone, stay close."

As Tatsumi landed at the edge of the steps with a crash, the priest pulled out a tattered ofuda, the kanji for *protection from evil* written down the slip. Holding it in two fingers, he brought it to his face and closed his eyes as the demon grinned and began sauntering up the steps, leaving a trail of blood spatters behind him.

A domed barrier flickered to life, glimmering a faint, almost invisible blue-white in the darkness, encompassing me, Reika, Master Jiro and the two dogs. Chu had quickly shrunk back to his smaller form, but it was still a tight fit. I could see Master Jiro trembling as he concentrated, beads of sweat forming on his brow, as the terrifying form of Tatsumi climbed the steps and stood a few feet away, smiling at us through the barrier.

"Oh, now you didn't need to do that," he said, in a voice that was a deeper, chilling version of Tatsumi's. "I just wanted to have a few words with Yumeko-chan, here." His cold red eyes met mine through the wall of magic, and he chuckled. "So, you're nothing but a shifty fox masquerading as a human," he mused. "A weak little half-breed—no wonder I couldn't sense what you really were. How deceitful. What other lies have you told Tatsumi, I wonder?"

I trembled, but forced myself to meet the monster's terrible gaze. "Where is he?"

"Tatsumi? Oh, he's still in here, somewhere." The demon tapped his head with a curved black claw. "I imagine he can see and hear everything that's going on, just like I could. He's not strong enough to force me out once I've taken over, though. No human has been." His smirk widened as he regarded me, "I did want to thank you personally, little fox," he said. "After all, it's because of you that I'm here."

A cold chill went through my stomach. "What do you mean?" I whispered.

"Well, normally, I can't get through Tatsumi's wall—he keeps himself and his emotions tightly guarded, and doesn't give me any footholds into his mind. But with you around, he's been slipping more and more each day. You distract him, make him feel things. Make him question who he is and what he wants. And that's all the invitation I needed. His last thought tonight, before finally losing himself, was of you."

I sank to my knees on the stones, horror and anguish weighing me down as surely as the heavy robes. *No*, I thought in despair. *Tatsumi. You can't be gone...because of me.*

The demon crouched down, balanced on the balls of his feet, so that we were face-to-face. "If it makes you feel better," he said in a mock whisper, "he can hear every word we say, but he can't do anything about it. And, I must tell you, after being trapped in his mind for so long, his pain and despair is a beautiful sensation. Oh, and do you want to know something else?" He bent close, lowering his voice even further. "He was actually starting to trust you, little fox," he whispered. "Tatsumi never trusted anyone in his life—his clan punished any attachments or weaknesses." His hand rose, pointed a curved black claw at my forehead. "But he was starting to trust *you*, a kitsune who lied to him, who has been deceiving him from the very beginning. And now, he sees exactly what you are and how you betrayed him."

I shut my eyes as my throat threatened to close up. "Let him go," I whispered, feeling the oni's cruel, amused gaze through the barrier.

"Sorry?" The oni's voice was mocking. "What was that?"

Opening my eyes, I looked up, meeting the demon's crimson stare. "Release him," I said, and my voice didn't tremble this time. "Return to the sword, or you'll see exactly what a kitsune can do."

The demon laughed. He rose, towering over me, his fangs shining a terrible crescent moon grin as he stepped back. "You're entertaining, little fox," he told me. "Which is why I'm going to let you live awhile longer. Don't worry though—I'll kill you and everyone you care about soon enough. When you're not expecting it, someone close to you is going to die. The ronin, the noble, the priest, the shrine maiden and the two puppies. I'm going to kill you all, and Tatsumi will be forced to watch as I rip the limbs from your body one by one. This is his punishment, too, for keeping me trapped in his stubborn head all this time." His eyes glittered, and for a moment I saw unbridled rage and loathing deep in their depths, making my blood chill. "So fear not. When we meet again, I promise I'll make your death slow and painful."

Leaning forward, he deliberately stretched out a hand and placed it on the barrier, which snapped and sputtered, flickering erratically at his touch. Smoke rose from his clawed fingers, coiling into the air, but it didn't seem to bother him. Smiling, Demon Tatsumi bent close, dropping his voice to a rough whisper. "If you think you can stop me, Yumeko-chan, I encourage you to try your best. The game has just begun."

Stepping back, he crouched and then leaped into the air, soaring onto the roof of the castle. Another leap took him even higher, a black shadow drawing farther and farther away. For a moment, he paused on the highest tower, a horned figure silhouetted against the moon, his wild mane billowing behind him, before he dropped to the other side of the castle and was gone.

After a few minutes of searching, we found our missing companions. The ronin lay buried under the collapsed watchtower, pinned by beams but struggling weakly to free himself. Miraculously, despite a large purple bruise on his forehead and several gashes across his arms and legs, he didn't seem seriously hurt.

"You have the luck of the kami themselves," Reika muttered, sounding reluctantly impressed as she wrapped strips of cloth around his many cuts. "That, or your head is harder than a cannonball."

"Ha, my hard head is infamous," Okame said proudly, tapping his knuckles against his skull. "Nothing gets through this, all right."

"I'm not sure you should be boasting about that."

Taiyo Daisuke was another matter. After scouring the battlefield, Chu finally led us to an isolated corner of the courtyard. The noble knelt on the stones in a pool of blood, his head down and his chin resting on his chest. He was surrounded by broken weapons and pieces of armor, and still clutched his sword tightly in one hand.

A ghostly figure stood beside him, a girl in simple robes, her hair tied behind her. Raising her hand, she touched the side of his face, a wistful smile crossing her lips, before she shivered into nothingness. A glowing white sphere, the light that had led us to Master Jiro, rose from where she had been, and drifted away over the wall.

"Daisuke-san." I sniffed as Chu approached the fallen noble, ears pricked in hopeful anticipation. "Can you hear me? Are you still alive?"

The body of the samurai didn't move. I swallowed the tightness in my throat, and was about to turn back to find the others, when Chu whined and shoved his nose under the noble's empty hand.

Shakily, it rose, as if attached to a string, to pat the dog between the ears. I gasped, and the samurai lifted his head, squinting against the dark.

"Yu…meko-san," he murmured, as I released a shaky breath. "You're all right. Did you find… Master Jiro?"

I nodded mutely, and he relaxed. *"Yokatta,"* he whispered, an expression of relief. "But…what about the demon? Where…is Kage-san?"

The weight in my chest got bigger. "Gone," I said quietly. "Yaburama is dead, but Tatsumi…isn't here anymore."

"Then… I failed." The noble bowed his head. "I couldn't protect him."

"No," I told him, and the noble looked up sharply. "He's not dead, Daisuke-san. Yaburama couldn't beat him. That's not what we have to worry about now. Tatsumi is…"

*A demon. One even worse than Yaburama. And it's my fault.*

"Forgive me, Yumeko-san," Daisuke said, still squinting up at me. "I have either taken a blow to the head, or am hallucinating from blood loss but, are those…forgive my rudeness…ears?"

"Yes, she's kitsune," came an exasperated female voice, and Reika walked around to my side, a bandaged ronin close behind her. "She's been kitsune the entire time you've known her, both of you. This is nothing new, and right now, we have larger issues to worry about. Taiyo-san…" She gazed at Daisuke, her face softening a bit in sympathy. "We'll need to dress your wounds. Can you stand?"

Daisuke, still staring at my ears, nodded painfully, then winced. "Give me but a moment."

Abruptly, Okame stepped forward, lifted the noble's arm around his shoulders and pulled him upright. Daisuke clenched his jaw, gritting his teeth in pain, and the ronin braced himself until the noble had gotten his feet.

"Okame-san," he muttered when he had gotten his balance, still leaning against the ronin. "I am…pleased to see you unharmed. Forgive my weakness. I am ashamed that I could not help you or Tatsumi-san."

The ronin snorted. "I didn't see much after that bastard oni collapsed the tower," he replied, "but it looks to me that you cut down the entire hoard of ankle-biters on your own. I don't know how you managed it, but that doesn't sound like a weakling to me."

The noble gave a faint smile. *"Arigatou gozaimasu."*

Okame sighed, glancing up at me and the shrine maiden. "So," he said with forced cheerfulness, "Yumeko-chan is a kitsune, the priest is saved, and apparently Kage-san went insane, carved the oni into little pieces and took off. Big night. Anything I'm missing?"

"Lady Satomi," Reika said. "Let's not forget her. We still

have no idea where she is, or what she's doing. Certainly, she lured us here to kill us, but now that we found Master Jiro, she will likely strike again. We need to find a way out of here, quickly."

"Agreed," said a new voice, Master Jiro's, as he stepped over rubble piles and bits of armor. Ko was at his side, and the head priest looked grave as he joined us. "There is no time. We must…"

His legs trembled, and he nearly fell, causing Reika to grab his arm. I snatched a wooden bucket from the dirt and placed it upside down in front of him, and the priest lowered himself onto it with a groan. For a moment, he sat there, breathing hard, then lifted his head.

"Time is now against us," Master Jiro panted, gazing around at us all, though his gaze lingered on me. "Kitsune…" He paused. "Yumeko-san…do you have the Dragon scroll?"

I nodded, feeling numb inside and out. "Yes, Master Jiro."

His eyes narrowed. "You must take it to the Steel Feather temple. The monks there will protect it. Nothing else matters but getting the scroll to the temple, do you understand? The Dragon cannot be summoned into this world again. Reika-chan," he continued, making the shrine maiden straighten, "we will go with her. Protect her on the journey. We must not let the scroll fall into the hands of evil like Lady Satomi."

"Yes, Master Jiro." The shrine maiden bowed. "I understand."

"Hey, don't forget about us," the ronin broke in. "I've come this far, fought demons and blood mages, and just got my ass kicked by an oni. I feel I've earned the right to continue with Yumeko-chan, at least until we get to this Steel Bird temple or wherever she's going."

"Indeed." Daisuke's voice was tight with pain, but resolved. "I, too, will accompany Yumeko-san. To make up for my failure in protecting Kage-san, my blade will be at her side until my debt is paid. This I swear."

"I will take the scroll to the temple," I told the priest. "I've already promised to do so. But..." My throat tightened, and I took a deep breath to open it. "Tatsumi," I whispered. "Can we save him? Can the demon be driven out?"

Master Jiro bowed his head. "To answer that question," he began, "you must know who you are dealing with, and the bloody history that is tied to it." He glanced at Daisuke, still leaning against the ronin, and his mouth thinned. "Taiyo-san's wounds must be addressed," he stated. "And Lady Satomi could still be about, not to mention Hakaimono. We must flee. But when we are safe, I will tell you the story of the Shadow Clan, the Dragon's prayer, a woman named Lady Hanshou, and the cursed sword named Kamigoroshi that is tied to them all."

# EPILOGUE

*I*n the golden palace of the emperor, all was quiet. The Moon Viewing party had gone splendidly, and everyone had returned to their rooms with a sense of satisfaction. Or, at least, in the pleasant haze of alcohol. The emperor, especially, slept soundly on his futon in a sake-induced torpor, his sleep free of dreams and the nightmares that had plagued him of late.

In the lavishly furnished apartments of the royal wing, in a bedroom cloaked in shadow, a full-length mirror shimmered, and the smiling form of Lady Satomi stepped through the glass. Brushing imaginary dirt from her robes, she sauntered to her writing desk, sat down on the stool and lit the candle. She then pulled open the bottom drawer and removed an object wrapped in silk cloth, placed it on the desktop and removed the covering.

The naked skull stared at her, empty eye sockets dark and unseeing. As Satomi waited, they flickered to life, lit with a baleful purple glow that threw eerie shadows over the rice paper walls. Satomi lowered her head in a bow.

"Everything is going to plan, master," she said in a low murmur. "Yaburama should have killed the boy by now and taken the scroll. The priest will tell the survivors where the Steel Feather temple is located, and we will simply follow them until they reach it. Then the second piece will be yours, as well."

The flames in the skull's eye sockets pulsed, and a raspy whisper emerged between its grinning yellow teeth. "I fear you may have underestimated the Kage demonslayer, Lady Satomi," it breathed. "Yaburama is one of Jigoku's strongest oni, which is why I summoned him for you. But Hakaimono is a true monster. If he makes an appearance, if Yaburama cannot kill the boy quickly enough, then you might have another problem on your hands."

"You needn't worry, master." Satomi smiled. "Everything is under control. Soon, you will have the last two pieces of the Dragon's prayer, we will summon the beast and you will rule this country as you were meant to."

"And you will not turn on me, as you did everyone before you?"

"Of course not, master!" Satomi put her hand to her chest, sounding horrified. "I am your loyal servant. Everything I do, I do for your glorious return."

The light in the skull's eyes faded, becoming faint pinpricks against the black. "Be sure that you remember who your master is, Lady Satomi," the voice rasped, growing fainter with the light. "You are a talented blood witch, but as replaceable as any mortal, and I have an army of yokai and demons who will answer my call. Do not disappoint me. I will await word of your success."

Satomi gave a smile and a small bow, and when she raised her head, the light in the skull's eyes had gone out, and she was alone.

As the glow faded and darkness returned, Satomi's smile faded, replaced with trembling anger.

"You think you are so clever, master," she whispered to the skull. "But only a mortal soul can summon the Dragon, and your army of demons cannot call the Harbinger for you. When the time comes to speak the wish, it will not be for your glorious return, I can promise you that."

Smiling again, she rose from the desk, turned around, and came face-to-face with her maid.

"You?" An annoyed frown instantly darkened her face. She tried to remember the name of this newest girl, and failed. "I didn't call for you. What are you doing here, you worthless thing?"

The girl's eyes lifted to meet her own, flashing gold in the darkness, right before she shoved the blade of a sword through Lady Satomi's chest.

Satomi's mouth gaped. Stunned, she gazed down at the shining length of steel in her breast, at the blood beginning to well around the edges. A thread of crimson ran from her lips, trickling down her neck, and she raised her eyes to her maid's face.

The corner of the girl's mouth pulled into a smirk. There was a soundless explosion of white smoke, and when it cleared, a man stood before her, his blade still sunk into her middle. He was beautiful; his long hair the brightest silver, like polished metal, his eyes a lazy gold.

"Good night, Lady Satomi," the beautiful stranger said,

his voice low and cool. "I believe you've done enough for one era."

"You..." Satomi gasped, finally recognizing him. "You're—"

He pulled out the sword and beheaded her in one smooth, blinding motion. Blood spattered the wall and the cluster of folded cranes on the desk, and Satomi's head struck the floor with a muffled thump. Her last expression, as the skull rolled slowly across the boards, was one of shock.

Standing in the slain woman's bedroom, feeling the cold eyes of the skull on his back, the stranger smiled.

"I'm afraid I can't allow the boy to die just yet," he murmured, as the blood from Satomi's corpse spread across the floor, seeping into the cracks. "And the little half fox is... interesting. I wonder if she'll be strong enough to bring the demonslayer back?" He chuckled to himself in amusement. "Hakaimono might yet meet his match in this game. I suppose we'll have to wait, and see what she does."

"Master?"

Seigetsu glanced down as a small yokai, a child-sized figure with a single, enormous eye in the center of his face, crept into the room. Gazing down at the headless corpse, it wrinkled its nose, then looked up at him.

"The guards are coming closer, master. We should flee while we can."

"Go, then," Seigetsu told it. "Do not wait for me. I will join you when I am done."

The small yokai bowed low and scuttled off, vanishing out the door, and Seigetsu was alone.

His gaze moved to one corner of the room, to the full-length mirror and the ghostly figure of a girl, hovering before it. One silver brow arched, and his lips curled in a slow smile.

“Satomi is dead,” he told the ghost, who watched him with large pale eyes. “If you are lingering here for vengeance, you can move on. My task is done.” He flicked blood from his blade, sheathed it and turned away. “Whoever you were,” he said, walking to the door, “I hope you find peace. Sayonara.” His lean form swept through the doorframe, onto the outside veranda, and disappeared from view.

The ghost of Suki shimmered, becoming a ball of softly glowing light. For a moment, it hesitated, floating over the floor and the shocked, bloody head of Lady Satomi, casting her features in a pale glow. Then it rose into the air and flew quickly out the door, following the beautiful man down the veranda, and both vanished into the night.

* * * * *

*Thank you for reading book 1 of the*
*Shadow of the Fox trilogy!*
*Look for book 2,*
Soul of the Sword.
*Only from Julie Kagawa*
*and HQ Young Adult!*

# GLOSSARY

amanjaku: minor demons of Jigoku

arigatou: thank you

ayame: iris

baba: an honorific used for a female elder

baka/bakamono: fool, idiot

chan: an honorific mainly used for females or children

chochin: hanging paper lantern

daikon: radish

daimyo: feudal lord

Doroshin: Kami, the God of Roads

furoshiki: a cloth used to tie one's possessions for ease of transport

gaki: hungry ghosts

geta: wooden clogs

gomen: an apology, sorry

hai: an expression of acknowledgment, yes

hakama: pleated trousers

hannya: a type of demon, usually female

haori: kimono jacket

hitodama: the human soul

inu: dog

ite: ow, ouch

Jigoku: the Realm of Evil, hell

Jinkei: Kami, the God of Mercy

jorogumo: a type of spider yokai

kaeru: copper frog, currency of Iwagoto

kago: palanquin

kama: sickle

kamaitachi: yokai, sickle weasel

kami: minor gods

Kami: greater gods, the nine named deities of Iwagoto

kami-touched: those born with magic powers

karasu: crow

katana: sword

kawauso: river otter

kitsune: fox

kitsune-bi: foxfire

kodama: kami, a tree spirit

konbanwa: good evening

kunai: throwing knife

kuso: a common swear word

mabushii: an expression meaning "so bright," like the glare of the sun

majutsushi: mage, magic user

Meido: the Realm of Waiting, where the soul travels before it is reborn

miko: a shrine maiden

mino: raincoat made of woven straw

mon: family emblem or crest

nande: an expression meaning "why"

nani: an expression meaning "what?"

netsuke: a carved piece of jewelry, used to fasten the cord of a travel pouch to the obi

nezumi: yokai, rat

Ningen-kai: the mortal realm

nogitsune: an evil wild fox

obi: sash

ofuda: paper talisman possessing magical abilities

ohayou gozaimasu: good morning

Ojinari: Kami, God of the Harvest

omachi kudasai: please wait

omukade: a giant centipede

onikuma: a demon bear

oni: ogre-like demons of Jigoku

onmyoji: practitioners of onmyodo

onmyodo: an occult magic focusing primarily on divination and fortune telling

onryo: yurei, a type of vengeful ghost that causes terrible curses and misfortune to those who wrong it

oyasuminasai: good night

ryokan: an inn

ryu: gold dragon, currency of Iwagoto

sake: alcoholic drink made of fermented rice

sama: an honorific used when addressing one of the highest station

san: a formal honorific often used between equals

sansai: edible wild plant

sensei: teacher

seppuku: ritual suicide

shinobi: ninja

shogi: a tactical game akin to chess

shuriken: throwing star

sumimasen: I'm sorry, excuse me

tabi: split-toe socks or boots

Tamafuku: Kami, the God of Luck

tanto: short knife

tanuki: yokai, small animal resembling a raccoon, indigenous to Iwagoto

tatami: woven bamboo mats

tetsubo: large two-handed club

tora: silver tiger, currency of Iwagoto

ubume: yurei, a type of ghost who died in childbirth

usagi: rabbit

wakizashi: shorter paired blade to the katana

yamabushi: mountain priest

yojimbo: bodyguard

yokai: a creature with supernatural powers

yurei: a ghost

zashiki warashi: yurei, a type of ghost that brings good fortune to the house it haunts